Principia Martindale

Principia Martindale

A COMEDY IN THREE ACTS

BY *Edward Swift*

HARPER & ROW, PUBLISHERS, New York
Cambridge, Philadelphia, San Francisco
London, Mexico City
1817 *São Paulo, Sydney*

Grateful acknowledgment is made for permission to reprint lyrics from "It Took a Miracle" by John Peterson, copyright 1948, renewed 1976 by John W. Peterson; assigned to Singspiration, division of The Zonderhaven Corporation, all rights reserved, used by permission.

FIRST EDITION

Designer: Sidney Feinberg

Library of Congress Cataloging in Publication Data

Swift, Edward, 1943–
   Principia Martindale: a comedy in three acts.
   I. Title.
PS3569.W483P7   1983   813'.54   82–48150
ISBN 0–06–015110–2

83 84 85 86 87 10 9 8 7 6 5 4 3 2 1

To:

Minda Lynn
Suzanne Seay
    and
Linda Slater-McGilvray

Nena Boyd
Jane Van Sickle
    and
Judy Hensley

In memory of Lottie Moon,
our baptism and the life therein

The author wishes to thank Sister Louise Owens for permission to quote her song, "The Holy Ghost Will Set Your Feet A-Dancing," and Singspiration, a division of Zonderhaven Corporation, for permission to quote "It Took a Miracle."

Principia Martindale

 **1973**

Donald Applebee was easily recognized on any downtown street in Fort Worth, Texas. He was a round, red-faced man in his mid-fifties, tall, sandy-haired—he wore it long and flowing—and talkative. He usually dressed in faded Levi's, rubber sandals, even in the winter, and just about always carried a blue-plaid book satchel filled with Crayolas and coloring books. There was hardly a person who lived or worked downtown who had not seen him and avoided him. From a distance he almost looked like an overgrown child, and most of the people who had tried to get close to him had ended up saying that he was exactly that: a child at heart.

After he left Judson and went to live in Fort Worth, Applebee took a job in a pawnshop but spent most of his time in the Water Gardens, a concrete park of spillways and pools commissioned by the Amon Carter Foundation, designed by Philip Johnson and located on the south side of downtown. It was the only place where the traffic couldn't be heard and where the sound of the rushing water sometimes washed Principia Martindale right out of his head. He would usually take something with him to the Water Gardens, something to help occupy his mind: a deck of cards, a paperback Western or a coloring book. He was hopelessly addicted to coloring books, had been all his life. He said that coloring was the best medicine in the world to help you forget your problems, if not solve them.

During warm weather he would amble down to the gardens, sit on the edge of one of the shallow pools, soak his feet awhile and try to relax. Sometimes he would read, or play solitaire, but most of the time he would color, or just sit there with his box of Crayolas between his knees and attempt to put the colors back in their original order, but that never worked out very well because he could never decide where to start. Indecisiveness always troubled him, and when he was troubled he would strike up a conversation with someone sitting near him, and before long he would be talking about Principia Martindale all over again.

There were people he knew who avoided him and people he didn't know who also avoided him because he was always doing something to ease his mind: coloring, sharpening his Crayolas on the legs of his jeans or talking to himself or just anyone who would listen. No matter how he started a conversation he would always end up on the same topic: Principia. She was never very far out of his thoughts, even when he thought she was, even when he found himself wanting her to be.

Down at the Water Gardens, he would talk to first one person and then the next, but only Johnnie Chapman would stay and hear him through. "Johnnie ain't never got up and left nobody yet," she told him when they first met. "So you can just go on talking; Johnnie Chapman, she'll still be here when you get done."

Johnnie was as black as anybody could be. Applebee called her the blackest black woman alive, and Johnnie called herself the only purebred Nigger in Fort Worth. She figured that she was somewhere between sixty and seventy-five years old, but couldn't be sure because no one in her family had ever kept records of any kind. She had been the eleventh of sixteen children, but her mother couldn't remember when Johnnie had been born; or where she had been born, and her father's face had long since faded from her mother's memory.

"That's just the way things are sometimes," Johnnie always said. "Better not have your mind cluttered up with so many details. I know everything about myself, and I know nothing about myself all and at the same time. It's the best way to be nowdays."

Johnnie worked a shoeshine stand in the Greyhound bus terminal, and when she wasn't bent over somebody's feet she was searching for coins left in the pay telephones and disinfecting the receivers with rubbing alcohol. She wore the same maroon dress to work in almost every day and was never seen in public without her head tied up with a rag. She had plenty of rags, little ones for shoeshining, and big ones for her head. When they got dirty she'd take them to the Water Gardens and wash them out. That's what she was doing when Applebee first saw her. He said that she had the kind of look in her eyes that made him think she was studying something way off in the distance. That, he said, was why he had first started talking to her and why he had never stopped. He said he could tell her just about anything and she'd understand.

"When my mother died," he once told her, "my father thought he could resurrect her in three days." It was mid-June, late in the day. Applebee had his feet in the water and Johnnie was about to join him. "He had her body brought home," he continued, "and on the second day he called the neighbors together. They sat up all night singing and carrying on like you've never seen, and just before dawn they moved her body out into the front yard so the first rays of light could find her. When the light fell on her face my father was sure she would sit up and walk among us. He had already made a list of questions he wanted to ask her about life on the other side."

"People don't resurrect no more," said Johnnie. "Not like they used to, so he must have been mighty disappointed after going to all the trouble. Must have been something bad wrong with his thinking too, that's all I can say." She placed shopping bags filled with scraps of material on either side of her, used them for armrests and let her tired feet down into the water.

"Up until then," Applebee continued, "he always seemed so practical. Even his religious side had a practical side that my mother didn't have, but when she died he fell apart, said he couldn't live without her, and that's when I realized just how much he loved the woman, or thought he did. Why? I can't tell you because she wasn't exactly what you would call lovable. She was hard and unemotional, if you wanna know the truth, except when it came to her religion, and then she let everything out at once, all the praise and love and admiration that she thought Jesus deserved. After she died I wondered if my father had ever been jealous of Jesus. I know I would have been. If I had loved her the way he had.

"I should have learned something from all that," he said, lifting his feet out of the water and rubbing them together. The dirt wouldn't come off, so he put them back in to soak. "I should have learned that the human heart holds no logic known to man, and from time to time the ole heart goes off like a sirene and won't give nobody no peace. When it goes off like that there ain't no turning it off, and it won't stop until it's done."

"It won't stop," said Johnnie, "until you figure out why you let it go off without knowing what you were doing. There is most certainly a logic to the human heart—it just ain't always as obvious as you'd like it to be." She took a cleaning rag and wiped off her feet, then put them back in the water again. "Maybe there ain't no way of learning about things like this," she said. "Maybe there ain't no way of protecting yourself from somebody else, but from where I sit it seems to me like when you first laid eyes on that Martindale woman you lost all control of a heart that were not too very strong to begin with but somehow managed to stay in shape up until then. You just let it go off and leave you like some ole ambu-lance that ain't never stopped. Bet you said you didn't want it to happen either, but you let it happen anyway; just about always does work that way."

She gathered her skirt up between her knees and stood in the water in front of Applebee. "There's something I've been meaning to do for you just as long as I've been knowing you," she said. "You has the dirtiest, fattest and ugliest-looking feets I ever looked at. Somebody as big and fat as you are around the middle just can't bend over as far as it takes to wash your toes, so I'm gonna wash 'em for you. Feel real good."

While she scrubbed Applebee's feet, he started talking about Principia again.

"To a lot of people she was nothing but a Bible-beating Baptist crusader," he told her. "They thought that she was just another fanatic and there was nothing else to her, but I never believed that; not for a minute. I was one of the first to believe in her, and it wasn't just because she got under my skin when I first saw her either. It was the way she got under there and stayed under there all these years. It was the way some part of her she didn't know much about just reached out and wouldn't let go of me, or some part of me that I couldn't control just reached out and wouldn't let go of her. I guess it was just meant to be that way."

"Parts of people don't just leap up all by theirselves and grab

holt of parts of other people," said Johnnie, running a wet rag
between his toes. "I ain't trying to say it's preordained either, me,
I don't believe that way, but if there's some part of you deep
down inside that needs to be touched, and you meet somebody
who you think can touch it just right, then that part's gonna feel
like it's leaping right out of you and you're gonna feel like you
ain't helping it leap, but you are. Some part of you you don't have
much to do with is doing it all, and you're too busy to even know
it. We're all the same, even down to my own children. Raised six
of the prettiest-looking girls Fort Worth ever looked at and
watched the boys lose their hearts one by one. One of 'em even
jumped off a roof when he couldn't have his pick, but didn't hurt
him none. Some part of him didn't want to kill hisself so it was a
real real low roof he got up on and then jumped off feet first, but
thought he jumped off head first. Goes to show you that a body
just don't know his feet from his head sometimes. So what happens gets blamed on the ole heart when it ain't the heart working
at all; it's something way back in the back of your slimy ole brain
that's causing you all the upset."

Then she scooped up some water in her hands and let it trickle
over his feet. "Just play like all your worries is getting cleaned up
right here and now," she said. "Try not to let yourself think about
anything else either."

"Yesterday afternoon when you weren't here," he continued,
not stopping to realize what she had said, "I saw somebody and I
thought it was Principia. I knew it couldn't be so I looked away
and then looked again, and there wasn't anybody there, but off in
the distance there was some kid with a purple flag—purple was
her favorite color—so that's what must have caused me to see her.
That sometimes happens a lot, specially in the summer, specially
when I'm trying hard not to care anymore, specially then."

"If you want my advice," said Johnnie, "what you better
start caring about is keeping yourself clean. I gotta use one of
these old wore-out S.O.S.'s on you now. Won't hurt much though,
and when I get done you won't have no more problems no more
too maybe; maybe not today anyway."

Applebee hadn't heard a word Johnnie Chapman had said.
He was still thinking about Principia. "She made you feel like she
could look right straight inside you and see things," he said, fol-

lowing an airplane across the water. "And whether she saw what
was really there or not, she made you believe that what she saw
was really there. She had some way about her that made you want
to believe more for her than for yourself. There were a lot of
times when she was preaching that people must have felt so sorry
for her that they couldn't help believing. She was just that way:
the most innocent thing I ever came across. She didn't know much
about what was going on in the world, but she had some way
about her that made you think she was all-knowing, and that she
had the power to do just about anything.

"Lots of people didn't feel that way about her though," he
continued while Johnnie slipped his rubber sandals back on his
polished feet. "But it's only because they never really allowed
themselves to know her, I say, it's only because their hearts, what
was left of them, were already hard to what she was saying and
doing. They saw her as a joke. And at times she was. They
laughed at her, and sometimes she deserved it, but it never
seemed to bother her. They saw her as peculiar-looking, and I'll
have to admit that they were right about that too: she was peculiar-looking, damn peculiar-looking; a real sight to this world is
what she was, and that's what made a lot of people uneasy and
caused them to turn their hearts, but it made a lot more of us
open them up even wider."

Johnnie Chapman sat back down between her shopping bags.
Her hem was wet, looked like a dark red brown ribbon running
unevenly all the way around her dress "You talk about her like
she was some kind of giant person," she said.

"She was," said Applebee, admiring his clean feet. Even his
toenails sparkled. "She attracted people who seemed like they
were bigger than life, or else they wanted to be so bad they made
out like they were. That was the bad part. There were people
around her who wanted to be bigger than she was and would do
anything to get that way, but what a lot of them didn't stop to
realize was that she was so wrapped up in what she believed in
she came off seeming like she was just puttin'-on when she really
wasn't. And the rest of us? Well, we were more of the same I
guess. I guess maybe we were all doing some kind of imperson-
ation of who we wanted to be and never got down to realizing
ourselves. I don't know. I can't tell you. But I do know that after it

was all over it never stopped being over for me. I lived with an easy heart for a little while, and then I started thinking about her all over again, and then everywhere I looked I thought I was seeing her, and it was always somebody else or nothing at all.

"What is it," he asked, still admiring his feet, "that makes some people more alive after they're dead than they ever were when they were up and walking around in front of you?"

"That's a mighty hard one to answer," said Johnnie, "and we ain't gonna do it all in one day. Now, what you better do is start thinking more about keeping your feets clean than anything else. What you better do is go on home and prop 'em up on something, maybe in front of a mirror somewheres, so you can see both sides at once, and just sit there and study them a little while. Make you feel better for sure just to sit there and give your old mind something else to think about."

Before they parted Johnnie got back in the water again and rolled up Applebee's pants. "Just past the ankles is far enough," she said. "You need to show off these clean toes and be real glad they're yours."

On his way back across town Applebee felt like his feet were made of glass and that his toes were sparkling like diamonds in the sun. When he got home he propped them up in front of a mirror and started studying them front and back. For a few moments he allowed his eyes to drift deep into the mirror. He could see almost all of the wall behind him. Calendars old and new were hanging on either side of a bookshelf filled with stacks of coloring books and boxes of Crayolas. On top of the shelf was a fishbowl with three goldfish, and over to one side was a picture of Principia, the only one he owned. He usually kept her picture turned to the wall, but that day it was face out. He couldn't remember how it had gotten that way, but he thought it was appropriate that she was on the shelf with all the coloring books. "I never thought of this before," he said, "but all of us wanted to color her the way we saw her, and with some of us she didn't seem to mind. It was pitiful sometimes, and real disappointing too, but the best way I can explain it is that her life was like some kind of strange comedy, that most people didn't have sense enough to laugh at, me included."

He started studying his feet again. He had never seen them

so clean. Then he allowed himself to relax, and while he sat there, almost asleep, everything Johnnie Chapman had said came back to him, and Principia Martindale found her place at the very back of his mind.

PART I

Total Immersion

1957

Things don't fall right out of the blue, but if you
want a certain something bad enough you're liable to
get it, and it might seem like it fell right out of the
blue, so you better watch out what you go around hoping
and praying for, I mean, you better make dead sure you
really want what you're hoping and praying for; if
you don't want it bad, you better shut your mouth.

—Johnnie Chapman

1

Principia Martindale lived in Blankenship Hall on the campus of Hillister Baptist College, founded in 1886 by John J. Hillister, who coined the phrase A *distinctive school for higher learning which takes pride in welcoming students of all races and denominations into the folds of Christian fellowship*, a phrase which was to him proof of his profound magnanimity, but he feared that he would not be remembered for having possessed such open-minded goodness, so he had the statement inscribed on every portal, plate, cornerstone and pew, as well as on the base of his marble statue, which after his death came to grace his private grave site: a triangular patch of English ivy growing near the Hillister Chapel and spreading like the Word of God from one tree to the next but for some reason or other it refused to touch his statue.

Principia Martindale often stood at the foot of his grave and wondered what it must have been like to have lived in the presence of such an inspired man of God. She would stand with her back perfectly straight, her eyes closed, her head bowed, and thank the Lord for giving her the privilege of studying in a Christian atmosphere.

Principia was not only the most promising freshman to have entered Hillister Baptist College in many decades, she was the youngest as well. She was majoring in the New Testament, minoring in the Old Testament and hoping that the Lord would lead her to some far distant place where she could serve him for the rest of her life.

Her strongest desire was to become a foreign missionary and, looking back over the years, she believed that her whole life had been moving rapidly in that direction, even when she was unaware of it. At the age of three she walked down the aisle as the congregation sang, "Jesus is tenderly calling today . . ." She took Brother Callaway, her pastor, by the hand, accepted Christ as her Savior and, then, almost in the same breath, she dedicated her life to full-time Christian service. She *re*dedicated her life every year after that, sometimes more often if she felt like it, and at the age of sixteen, still burning with the fervor of her commitment, she graduated with honors from high school, entered Hillister Baptist College the next fall and signed up for a full load of classes, mostly in the theology department.

Because of her striking appearance, her bright red hair particularly, she became, almost overnight, the most recognizable figure on campus. Her hair was naturally curly, fell to the middle of her back, and, because she had two cowlicks, one on either side, her hair often looked as though it had never been combed.

Her father had always called it "sunshine hair" and said that her widow's peak gave her face the shape of a perfect heart.

Principia wasn't very tall, but she was rotund; "big-boned," her mother always said to get around the subject, yet there was something graceful about her, something that gave the impression that she was much smaller than she actually was. But Principia had never been able to see that quality in herself. She was conscious of her size and for that reason always wore loose-fitting, long-sleeved smocks. Most of them buttoned down the front and were purple—or some shade thereof—her favorite color.

She didn't remotely resemble anyone at Hillister Baptist College, nor anyone in her family, but that never seemed to bother her. "God threw away the mold when he made you," Dr. Norman Truly, her Bible professor, always said. He considered her his best student and so did the rest of her teachers. She felt at home in all her classes, contributed to oral discussions, was a straight A student and happy to be living on campus. All her life she had dreamed of attending Hillister Baptist College, and during her freshman year she could hardly believe that her dream had come true.

The school was located at one end of Sycamore Street, which began at the red light in downtown New Bethel—Principia's hometown—and ended directly in front of Blankenship Hall, a large dormitory of Southern colonial architecture which—in 1957 when Principia lived there—boasted an excellent security system by the name of Miss Lively Hathaway, the dorm mother who would sit in her living quarters day after day and keep a constant eye on the front door, the only way in or out that was not always locked.

Lively Hathaway was a tiny woman with straight gray hair that she always wore the same way: pulled up into a bun and twisted so tight that the wrinkles on her forehead smoothed out and her eyes seemed to be forced wide open. She had false teeth that did not fit, glasses that slid down her nose and fingers that were always working on something, usually a quilt. Every day Miss Hathaway—who had known Principia Martindale all her life—would open the front doors of Blankenship Hall at seven-thirty A.M. and then retire to her apartment just across the hall, where she would gather her patchwork and crocheting around her, and, keeping one eye on her needlework and the other on the entrance, she would, in the course of the day, make three check lists. On one list she would count every girl going out: on another every girl coming in; and on the third she would record every visitor by name, who they were visiting and how long they stayed. Then at ten-thirty after the front doors were locked for the night, she would retreat to her manual adding machine—she hated anything electric—and tabulate her lists, making the necessary additions and subtractions until, at the end of a half-hour, she would emerge either greatly relieved that all her girls were inside where they should be or deeply distressed over the discovery that someone was not merely late but *missing* and that the unfortunate girl had probably been strolling back to the dormitory when she was kidnapped, forced into a van and raped repeatedly, unmercifully and beyond human belief.

"Oh my God in Heaven, I just can't stand to think about such a tragedy as this happening right here on a Baptist campus," Miss Hathaway would say. Principia Martindale had heard her many times. Then she would usually leap to the conclusion that the *missing party* had not been raped at all but, worse than that, was off in some remote parking lot somewhere giving herself willingly and joyfully and without shame to the young man of her choice.

With these thoughts whirling through her head, Miss Hathaway would not waste a second dialing the New Bethel Police Department and then, beating two double boilers together, she would run up and down the corridors until every girl had assembled for another late-night roll call in the sunken living room of Blankenship Hall.

"Now I'm going to call the name of each and every girl living in this fine old dormitory in order to determine who is not among us this evening," Miss Hathaway would say, running her fingers and thumbs all over her face and neck. "And if I catch anyone answering twice, that person, no matter who she is, will be immediately expelled. Is that clear? Honesty is a virtue, and here at Hillister Baptist we each and every one of us pride ourselves on the virtuous life, which is, of course, the Christian life."

Because Principia Martindale believed Miss Hathaway was doing a noble job of keeping track of the two hundred and eighty girls who lived in Blankenship Hall, she tried to assist her dorm mother in every way possible, especially during the late-night roll calls when she always took it upon herself to watch carefully in order to catch someone answering twice, and often she did. It gave her a thrill to be able to report such an observation to Miss Hathaway, who was well aware that she could depend on Principia and therefore gave her special privileges, among them the privilege of watching the front door when Miss Hathaway went to the cafeteria for lunch or dinner or the privilege of calling the roll during a late-night assembly. But better still, Principia was allowed to keep the only key to the broom closet on the second floor. Everyone knew that the closet was never locked, but to Principia's way of thinking that was not the point. Just knowing that she had the one and only key was the honor of it all, and, besides that, she could lock the door from the inside if she so chose, and often she did. It was the only place in New Bethel where she could be completely alone, and there was hardly a day that passed when she did not go there and count her many blessings.

"Lord Jesus, Prince of Peace," she prayed one morning in the darkness of the closet, "I thank you for this most beautiful day. Lord Jesus, I thank you for this privilege of worshiping right here in New Bethel. Yes I thank you for this pretty little town Lord

Jesus and for this Christian college Lord Jesus and for all my friends Lord Jesus and Lord Jesus I just want to thank you for this mountaintop experience I'm having right here in my hometown."

New Bethel was located in the lowlands of East Texas. The town was only sixty miles from Beaumont, a stone's throw from Splendora and less than that from Merryville, Louisiana, where Lorinda Goings was born. Lorinda and Principia were roommates and proud to be living in Blankenship Hall, named for the Baptist missionary Lobelia Blankenship, who lost her life to the cannibals in South America. Both girls had chosen to live in that dormitory because more famous missionaries had lived there than in any other residence on campus.

Principia's parents had always assumed that she would want to live at home as they had done while going to college, but Principia had never considered such an arrangement. She had thought it was understood that she would reside in Blankenship Hall where, since childhood, she had gone to visit her beloved Miss Hathaway, who told her stories about the great people who had lived in that dormitory.

When it gradually dawned on her parents that she was moving out, they were heartbroken over the idea of their only child leaving a spacious brick home for a tiny room where she had little or no privacy and not even a bed that was all her own, but they attempted to live with her decision and their sorrow by covering their walls with her photographs and their coffee table with her scrapbooks. Her mother had even taken to leaving one of Principia's old nightgowns flung across her unmade bed so it would seem as though she had not left home at all but gotten up late and hurried off to school.

By the time Principia entered college, her mother, Wilma Lee Martindale, was one of New Bethel's senior citizens. Her hair was lavender gray, always arranged in tight curls and sprayed stiff. She was tall, had small bones, a long face and nervous energy, and was constantly worried about her daughter living on the third floor of the dormitory.

"That's way too high up there," she said to Lively Hathaway. They were sitting in the sunken living room of Blankenship Hall at the time. "Principia's going to start sleepwalking again and fall right out the window. Oh, why am I the only one to see it is what I'd like to know. You mark my word it's going to happen because it runs in our family. My baby sister, Wilda, used to do the craziest things in her sleep. We never could keep up with her after the sun went down, and my mother took a sick headache almost every time the child closed her eyes for longer than five minutes. Even after she was a full-grown woman, we'd find her sitting in the rose bushes with nothing on but her nightgown and it half ripped to shreds. Thank God Principia hasn't been that bad. She's only walked in her sleep three times; twice she had a high fever that caused it, and the last time we never could figure out just what happened, but when we found her she was in the back seat of the car. Wilda was the very same way only worse, and that's why she ended up in such a fix. And I'll tell you something else too, Lively Hathaway, there isn't a day that goes by that I don't thank God that my sister's dead and gone. Now maybe she can get some rest and so can we. Do I have to say more?"

"Yes, you do," said Lively, rearranging the needles in her pincushion. "Your sister has been dead for years now, so it's high time you asked the Lord to help you bury her once and for all. Just lay your troubles at the foot of the cross is all you have to do to overcome your mental strife. Wilma Lee, if you could only trust in God the way your daughter does, you would find peace of mind. I pray that Principia never loses her faith."

"Well, she could stand to lose a little bit of it if you're asking me," said Wilma, picking a pin up off the floor and handing it over to Lively. "I believe in God too, but I don't believe in going overboard. Wilda did, and turned out to be a raving fanatic, and I'm scared to death that Principia's heading down the same road, and I don't think you're helping her one bit, Lively Hathaway. You and that father of hers have caused her to be the way she is. No one ought to love God as much as Principia does. It's not healthy."

"Some of us have no choice but to love him," said Lively sympathetically. "One day, when you're able to forget about your sister, you might understand what I'm talking about, but right now all you can do is pray. That's all I ask of you."

Wilma Lee took Lively's advice and began praying night and day for her daughter's safety. But praying didn't make her feel that much better so she kept herself busy cleaning house frequently and rotating the stuffed animals in Principia's bedroom window. It was a picture window that looked out onto Redbud Lane, and Principia had always kept it decorated either with her favorite toys or pictures illustrating familiar verses from the Bible which her Aunt Wilda had taught her to draw and paint. Everyone in New Bethel said that it was the most beautiful picture window in town, especially when it was fixed up for Christmas, Easter and the Fourth of July. Drawing manger scenes, wise men and luminous stars came natural to Principia; inspirational pictures of the crucifixion were no strain on her artistic ability either, while chalk paintings of fireworks exploding in midair took the least amount of time to create and were often just as effective, if not more so.

"She's the most talented thing this family has ever seen," Wilma Lee had been heard to say many times. "We're so proud of her we don't know what to do. It takes a real artist to draw a picture to where it looks just exactly like what it's supposed to and Principia sure can do it. It's all natural ability too; never had a lesson from anybody except Sister Wilda and she didn't have the slightest idea what she was trying to teach and I told her so too. I said, 'Lessons'll ruin somebody like Principia; the art teacher up there at the high school told me so.' "

Wilma Lee was quick to take out Principia's portfolios and show them to company, and her father praised her every chance he got. She received so much attention from home that she worried constantly because her parents were becoming much too attached to her. In fact, she suspected them of loving her more than they loved God, and she didn't want that on her conscience too, so she left her parents' home and the prettiest picture window in all of New Bethel and went to live in Blankenship Hall because she wanted with all her heart to follow in the footsteps of great missionaries even if it meant that she must give her life to the spears and arrows of savages in some far-distant land where others had walked before her and had sacrificed their lives to the glory of God.

"A missionary is the last thing in this world I want my daughter to become," Wilma Lee had said when Principia first dedicated her life to Christian service. But her husband told her that it would be best not to interfere with the workings of the Lord. He also advised her to put her mind on other things, so over the years Wilma Lee learned to stay busy.

She became a member of the Garden Club, a Friend of the Library and a hospital volunteer. She was elected County Secretary twice, served on the City Council once, and for five years she worked as the Home Demonstration Agent. She liked having a variety of things to do, but her husband was just the opposite. When their daughter entered college, he was principal of New Bethel High School, had been for thirty-five years, would not consider doing anything else, and almost everyone had called him Principal Martindale for so long it was nearly impossible to find anyone who could remember the man's first name: Sheldon.

He was short, almost totally bald by the time Principia was born and carried all his weight in his stomach, which hung below his belt and put so much pressure on his shirt buttons that his wife had to replace them more often than she thought necessary. It got to the point that she could care less if all the buttons matched or not, but Principia cared very much, and after Lively Hathaway had taught her how to sew a button on to stay, Principia went to work on all her father's shirts. She always wanted him to look his best.

Principia had been born late in her parents' lives. Dr. Carl Milam, the family doctor, had already told Wilma Lee that she was past the age of childbearing, that something else was causing her to gain so much weight, and that he would have to run some tests in order to find out what was wrong. He was certain she was not pregnant, but Wilma Lee, determined to prove the doctor wrong, held firmly to the idea that she was carrying a child. She had dreamed that she was, and the dream had recurred five nights in a row, all the proof she needed.

For nine months the parents-to-be waited in great excitement and expectation. If the child was a boy he would be named Principal after his father, if a girl she would be called Principia and that was that, nothing more could change their minds for they were both out to prove Dr. Milam wrong.

"If you do so," he said, "I'll be ruined for the rest of my career." But Principal Martindale reminded him that he had nothing to worry about because his career had been going strong for fifty-one years and he was the eldest, and therefore the most respected citizen in New Bethel.

Throughout the pregnancy, Dr. Milam refused to believe what was going to happen, for, after all, he had seen Wilma Lee through what he called her "difficult years" and was convinced there was no way under heaven that she could be pregnant. Yet Wilma was convinced she was, and nothing would dissuade her, neither the rabbit test which Dr. Milam had performed five times to negative results, nor the frog test, nor the absence of a brown line on her abdomen which the esteemed physician called the *linea nigra* and said was always present on pregnant women.

"I wouldn't believe a word he told me if I were you," said Lively Hathaway. That was on a Monday morning early in the pregnancy. Carrying her Sunday school quarterly in one hand and her sewing basket in the other, she showed up at Wilma Lee's kitchen door and said that Dr. Milam was full of ballooned-up errors. "I don't care if the man *has* made all those tests plus three sets of X rays," she said, helping herself to a cup of coffee, "my test is absolutely accurate and there are no two ways about it either." She ran a needle and thread through the eraser of an unsharpened pencil, dangled it in front of Wilma Lee's abdomen and stood back as far as possible so her opinion would have nothing whatsoever to do with what was about to happen. "Listen to me," she said. "If this brand-spanking-new pencil starts moving crossways then you've got yourself a boy, but if it starts moving backwards and forwards you've got yourself a girl. Now that's not too hard to remember, is it?"

"Yes it is," said Wilma Lee. "It sounds like something my sister would say."

"Your sister's dead and gone," said Lively, holding the string between her thumb and index finger. "Ask God to put her out of your mind for the next five minutes so we can get on with this little test."

For a long time the pencil just dangled there without moving at all. Then it started going in circles so fast Lively Hathaway said it made her head swim just to look at it. "I sure don't know what's going on here," she said straightening herself up and staring off into a corner of the room as though she might find an answer there. "But I can tell you one thing. Whoever it is you're carrying is going to be a mighty special somebody, and that's for sure."

Before the day was over, the results of Lively Hathaway's test had reached almost every household in New Bethel, and for months thereafter everyone waited on pins and needles to see what was going to happen. Some of the men down at the pool hall started placing bets. Most of them favored Dr. Milam's opinion over Wilma Lee's because he had delivered more babies than anyone in the county and therefore ought to know what he was talking about. The men behind bars in the city jail also began to take interest in what was going on, as did the domino players on the courthouse square, so by the time Wilma Lee went to the hospital, nearly half the population of New Bethel had something to gain or lose.

How well Lively Hathaway remembered that day. It seemed to her that everybody in the county had followed Wilma Lee to the hospital. The afternoon was cold and windy. The waiting room was filled to overflowing, and Lively had to stand on the front lawn with dozens of others. She had been sewing that afternoon when the call came; she left the dormitory in a hurry, forgot her headscarf and then refused to go back and get it. By the time the announcement was made she was chilled to the bone, but so glad she was there.

"New Bethel has seen a miracle this day," said Dr. Milam when he appeared on the hospital steps. A hush came over the crowd and nothing could be heard but the faint sound of Lively Hathaway clicking her purse open and shut as fast as she could. "Wilma Lee Martindale has given birth to a baby girl," said the doctor, "and she has the reddest hair and more of it than I have ever seen on any newborn baby in my whole and entire life."

Jubilation filled the streets of New Bethel that day. It was almost as though a sinner had given up the ways of the world and come home, only it was better than that, according to the way Tumpy Bull remembered it. He swore that her birth had been prophesied in the Bible, but he could not go back to the exact scripture to save his life. "Well, it's either in the New Testament or the Old Testament," reported Nova Ray Lutes as though she had stumbled upon a clue to the mystery. But Marcita Cunningham, who had gone to church all her life, disagreed. "You won't find anything like that in the Bible at all," she declared, "because the Bible prophecies have already come true." After she had spoken, nearly every one of her friends rose up against her. They said that she should stop running around so much and start rereading the scripture so she could find out a thing or two. "That's right," replied Dewey Martin, the postmaster. He believed that Principia's life had been blessed before it ever got started. Lavonia Hicks, secretary at New Bethel Baptist Church, said that that was nothing but foolishness because everybody's life was blessed before it ever got started, and to that Lively Hathaway added: "Principia, like Deborah, is slated to carry the breastplate of righteousness into the battle for everlasting life." Annabelle Winters, swooning with ecstasy, believed that she had witnessed the birth of a saint, and Brother Callaway, pastor of New Bethel Baptist Church, was certain that Principia's birthday would be remembered for a long long time to come, which indeed it was.

Principia was brought up on the word of God as well as her father's lap, and when she was three years old he had already read the Bible to her from beginning to end and was about to start over again when he discovered that she could read some of it all by herself.

"You've gone too far," Wilma Lee had said. "She's got all her life to study the Bible."

"But it's important to get an early start," said Principal. "That way she'll be way ahead of everyone else."

Against Wilma Lee's wishes Lively Hathaway had also emphasized the importance of Bible study as well as memory work. She took an active interest in the children of New Bethel, was not ashamed to let it be known that Principia was her favorite, and that all week long she looked forward to their Saturday morning visits when they would sit around and recite scripture. Lively believed strongly in having something else to do while memorizing verse, so, from Principia's fifth birthday until she entered Hillister Baptist College, she went over to Blankenship Hall every Saturday morning to help cut and piece together scraps of material and practice her memory work at the same time.

"Scripture will stay with you so much longer if you're not aware you're learning it," Lively always said. "It will mean much more to you in the long run too, because all the little verses will seep down into your brain, and when you need them most they'll come popping up to give you comfort."

Lively took great care in choosing the verses for Principia to learn by heart. Likewise Principia took great care in cutting and sewing Lively's patchwork, for it was agreed that Lively Hathaway made the most beautiful quilts in all of New Bethel, even if she did take ribbons off funeral wreaths to do it. Some of her earlier quilts were made almost entirely of ribbons that she had collected in the Garden of Memories only a few blocks from Blankenship Hall.

"Used to we had one hundred percent silk ribbons, and now you're lucky if you can find anything but plastic," complained Lively. She didn't collect the plastic ribbons at all, or the cloth ones for that matter, until they had been on the grave overnight. "Taking ribbons on the day of burial is nothing in this world but stealing," she always said. "But taking them immediately the morning after is not stealing because the dew has already got to them and they're too limp to be used for anything else except patchwork."

Lively could look at any quilt and tell you whose funeral was represented, as well as the date and cause of death. Principia was impressed with Lively's accurate memory, and Lively was impressed with Principia's unusual ability to understand as well as retain.

During their sewing and memory work sessions, Lively would often tell Principia to rest her mind while they listened to the inspirational programs and preaching on the radio. One cold Saturday in the month of December they were listening to a woman from Baton Rouge preach on God's mercy and grace, and after the sermon, Lively had said to Principia, who was eight years old at the time, "I just wonder if you'll turn out to be like that inspired woman of God. Something tells me that the Lord has a very very high place for you, and at times when I close my eyes I can see you standing before a huge crowd. I don't think you're preaching. I can't tell you exactly what it is you're doing, but whatever it is, you're doing it for God, and that's the important thing in the long run."

Each Saturday when Principia returned from Blankenship Hall her father would ask her to repeat all she had learned. If she recited her memory work perfectly he would smother her with hugs and kisses, but if she stumbled over a word, or completely forgot her verse, which rarely happened, he would ask her to begin again until she had recited without an error. Never did he scold her or frown when she had trouble remembering, but she could sense that he counted on her to be right each time, so she tried doubly hard to please him. She was aware that he was living the last quarter of his life, and that he placed great expectation in her.

"Lively Hathaway is right," he always said. "You'll succeed one hundred percent with whatever you choose to do. And you must always remember that your father loves you more than anything or anyone in the whole world."

"If he only loved me a little bit less and God a little bit more, he'd feel so much better about himself he wouldn't know what to do," Principia once told her Bible professor and adviser, Dr. Norman Truly. They were sitting in his small second-floor office. The walls were lined with books as well as photographs of his many trips to the Holy Land, and over his desk was a portrait of his late friend, the theologian and ex-president of the Southern Baptist Convention, Edgar Young Mullins.

"Sometimes I think my parents are going to love me to death," continued Principia as Dr. Truly listened attentively. "I'm all my father thinks about, and I just can't stand it. I don't feel worthy to receive all his love and attention."

"You must remember that you are the miracle in his life," said Dr. Truly. "He has great faith in you, and so has everyone here at Hillister Baptist. There isn't a teacher on this campus who doesn't admire you."

Dr. Truly was right. Since the day Principia enrolled, her teachers had been saying that she was a natural-born leader as well as a scholar and a child of God. Every day it seemed to her that she was being praised above and beyond her classmates, and she was embarrassed by all the attention she received. But it wasn't only the teachers who openly admired her. Midway through the spring semester she had made such a good impression on the student body that she was elected the next year's president of the BSU—Baptist Student Union. She was the only student

elected to that office while still a freshman, and it was agreed that
no one deserved to be singled out as much as Principia because
she had made her freshman year eventful beyond human expectations.

She had been the inspiration behind the successful Adopt-a-
Child Day when every student on campus was urged to entertain
an orphan from the Young Folks Home of New Bethel. After that,
she led a campaign against the Hillister Baptist Drama Club because they continued to produce plays which she said were not fit
for a Christian of any age to see. "How dare they," she said, "put
on a show where everyone is running around worshiping Greek
gods and killing off their children. This is not Christian entertain-
ment if you're asking me. On or off this campus Greek gods are
not to be worshiped and graven images are not to be bowed down
to."

Then she had led an attack on two political science professors, one because he refused to attend the two compulsory chapel
services each week and the other because he did attend but continued to be seen grading papers during public prayer and meditation even though he had been told by students and faculty alike
to bow his head and close his eyes or there would be plenty of
trouble. And trouble there was. Both professors were dismissed
midway through the spring semester, and Principia was given
credit for being the first to speak out against them.

"I hated to call attention to their irreverent behavior," she
said during a meeting of Missionaries-To-Be, a club which she
organized and presided over, "but the Lord put the words in my
mouth. All this year those two teachers have done nothing but
bring disgrace to this distinctive Baptist college."

It was then that she sat down and in the space of five minutes
composed what she later called the Rules of the Majority. She was
especially proud of her wording:

> There shall be no giving in premarital or extramarital communi-
> cation of the flesh. There shall be no partaking of alcohol, ciga-
> rettes or drugs. There shall be no vulgarity expressed in dress,
> language, thought or action. There shall be nothing but happiness,
> peace and Christian love at Hillister Baptist College.

She made two copies of the rules, gave the first copy to her classmate Tawnya Baker, because she, in Principia's opinion, needed some self-improvement, and the second copy she gave to Brother Simon Hemphill, president of the school. He was so overcome by Principia's Rules of the Majority that he adopted the signing of them by each student admitted for higher learning.

It was indeed Principia's year of achievement, but still she was not satisfied and would not be until the question that had been resting like a thorn in her heart was answered. "Lord am I to serve as an Invincible this summer?" she had asked over and over. An Invincible was a summer missionary and more than anything else she wanted to be one, so to make up for the fact that she was too young to qualify, she had submitted along with her application three extra letters of recommendation and had been praying daily that she would be given the opportunity to serve.

"Working as an Invincible would be such good training for me later on in life," she said one day to Dr. Truly. They were both standing at the foot of John J. Hillister's grave.

"I won't think any less of you if you're not called," he said. "You have the unusual ability of being able to serve God anywhere, any time and in many different ways. Because of this you are very special to him, and therefore he's not going to waste your talents." Then Brother Simon Hemphill joined them, and without a moment's hesitation, Dr. Truly turned to him and said: "Not since the glorious days of Lobelia Blankenship have I had a student whom I admired as much as Principia Martindale, and one day I predict that we will name one of our great buildings in her honor."

Oh, I wish they wouldn't say these things, thought Principia. I just know I'm going to be a big disappointment to everyone before I die.

2

On a clear, warm Sabbath in late-spring-early-summer just before second semester was over, Principia woke up early and brushed her hair straight back. She put on a lilac smock, slipped her white Bible into a side pocket and told her roommate, Lorinda, to go on to Sunday school without her because she had something else to do. Then, without waiting for a response, she left their room on the third floor of Blankenship and entered into the broom closet on the floor just below, but this time she was so worried about her immediate future she failed to lock the door behind her.

Once inside the closet she prostrated herself and prayed, "Lord speak to me in the not too distant future, and tell me, your little child, if I'm supposed to be an Invincible or not."

The Invincible Program was created by Miss Corinda Cassy, a wealthy widow from the town of Alice. Each summer she selected twenty-four college students from hundreds of applications, and the chosen, the Invincibles, were trained, paid for their time and sent out two by two to work with pastors and laypeople who needed them. Principia had applied early, had labored for a month over her required essay, "Why I Want to Serve," and during the last week of school she had dreamed every night that she would be selected in spite of her age. She was well aware that the names of the chosen had already been announced in *The Baptist Standard* and her name was not among them, but still she believed she had a chance. She didn't want anyone to get sick and drop out, but it was her constant prayer that at the last minute another Invincible would be needed and she would be called.

"Lord, will I become one of the elect?" she asked, paused, giving time for an answer, and then repeated the question again. In the darkness of the closet, the dampness and dust crept in around her, but still she prayed on and on until Tawnya Baker, an elementary education major, secretary of the Baptist Student Union and a member of the a cappella choir, opened the closet door, and seeing someone on the floor, jumped backward as if something had stung her.

Principia was kneeling with her hands folded and her elbows resting on an overturned bucket. At first all she could see was the silhouette of hair; long, curly and unmanageable, it swept out from a center part like her own and fell below the shoulders. When the shadow moved again, she saw the body was small, almost skinny, and realized that it was Tawnya Louise.

"Can't I have any privacy every once in a while?" said Principia, glaring at the intruder, who was wearing a black, low-cut dress left over from the night before. "You're hair's a mess, and that dress is not only indecent, it's wrinkled to high heaven and I suppose you're going to wear that thing to church because you're just now getting home from last night's date. I know what I'm talking about, don't deny the facts. Tawnya Louise Baker, you have never fooled me for one God-given instant.

"It's clear to me that you slept in that dress and everything else you may or may not be wearing underneath it," she continued, trying not to allow her anger to show because she had always tried to set a good example for Tawnya to follow. "You think you're fooling me but you're not; I'm perfectly aware that you're eaten up with the sins of the flesh and that through animal magnetism you encourage others to take part in your vice. Therefore, I find a place for you in my prayers each and every day, so if you know what's good for you you'll close that door right now and let me finish."

Tawnya was holding her heart as though she had stumbled upon a corpse. "Just what do you think you're doing down there?" she asked.

"Praying," answered Principia. "It wouldn't hurt you to try it sometimes, you know. I came in here to be all alone so I could ask God if I was going to be an Invincible, and he was just about to give me the answer when you opened the door. Now I do wish you would leave."

"Not until I get what I came after," said Tawnya. "Hand me that old cleaning rag. My shoes are filthy. And then, if you don't mind, you can tell me what this silly Invincible business is all about." Tawnya knew perfectly well what an Invincible was, she just wanted to annoy Principia with the question.

"Girl, where have you been all your life is what I'd like to know," said Principia, flying out of the broom closet like a red wasp ready to sting. Her face turned all shades of crimson and made her freckles look like black specks on her nose and cheeks. "I'd be ashamed to admit such ignorance as that if I were you. An Invincible is, for your information, and I hope you're listening because I'm not going to say it more than once, a college Christian carefully interviewed, screened and selected to go out into the remote areas of Texas and teach Vacation Bible School, preach the word of God, pray for the sick, administer to the afflicted and give generously of his or her God-given talents for six whole weeks each summer. Your father's a pastor, Tawnya Louise, and one of the most respected ones around, so you should know these things."

"I've known a few Invincibles in my life," said Tawnya in the most insulting tone of voice she could find. "In fact, I've known more than I ever care to know again."

"I'm going to tell Miss Hathaway you said that, *and* I'm going to tell her the way you said it too," said Principia as her classmate disappeared inside her room. "Furthermore, if you aren't careful, you're going to be transferred to another dormitory, either that or we'll do to you what we did to those awful drama majors. They had no business being here and neither do you. I have asked myself a thousand times: Why on earth did Tawnya Louise Baker enroll at Hillister Baptist College?"

"My father's a preacher. I had no choice," shouted Tawnya from inside her room. "You have all the evidence on me you need. Why don't you use it like you do with everyone else? Why am I any different?"

It was a question that Principia had never been able to answer and did not enjoy thinking about. She knew that Tawnya hardly ever missed church, choir practice or BSU meetings, that she could pray the sweetest prayer ever heard, sing like nobody else on campus and play the piano by ear and by note, and yet she stayed out at night as late as she pleased, had boyfriends who lived off campus and was often seen at the air force base. Tawnya lived in a private room on the second floor, was hardly ever there, and when she was, she was always getting ready to go somewhere else, usually to church, class or out on a date. Most of her dates, Principia knew, were overnight, and the only way she was able to get away with them was by climbing in and out of the dormitory windows, something she had learned to do without snagging her hose. In fact, Principia, although she did not like to think about it, had aided and abetted Tawnya many times, the last incident being the week before when Tawnya was coming home through the laundry room window while Principia was doing her wash.

Just as she had done on other occasions, Principia pretended not to see a thing. Several times she had glimpsed her classmate entering the dorm by way of the sycamore that grew close to the hall window on the second floor; once she had turned her back when Tawnya was coming up the basement stairs, and often she had even answered for her during the late-night roll calls, or, if that was too risky, she would ask someone to tell Miss Hathaway that Tawnya was in the shower. Principia didn't understand why she was so lenient on Tawnya and didn't like being confronted with the question, certainly not by Tawnya herself, but, from time to time, like that Sunday morning of the last week of school, she was forced to question her motives.

"Let me tell you something right now," said Principia, pacing the hall outside Tawnya's door. "I do not appreciate that question you just asked me, and I'm not going to try to answer it except to say that you are basically a good person—deep deep down inside you are good at heart—and I'm not able to say that about everybody who lives in this fine old dormitory. You don't know how good you are, but I do. You're just operating on both sides of the tracks at once these days and you've got to straighten yourself out because you've got too much to lose, and while I'm on the subject let me say this: I have never seen you slipping *out* of this dormitory; I have only seen you slipping *in*. It's the slip-

ping out that troubles me more than the slipping in, and if I ever
catch you slipping out I will not hesitate to go straight to Miss
Hathaway."

"What's the difference," came Tawnya's voice from behind
the door.

"There's plenty of difference, so just think about it awhile,"
said Principia, still swelled up with anger but holding it under
control as best she could.

After a long silence on both sides of the door, she decided
that she was in no mood for prayer after all, so she left Blankenship Hall and started walking toward New Bethel Church, where
she had worshiped all her life. "I just don't know what it's going
to take to get through to Tawnya Louise," she said, watching her
shadow walking on before her like a prophecy of all that was to
come.

For a moment she stopped to pin back her hair with a plastic
barrette. It was yellow and shaped like a half moon. Then she
continued on her way. "I'm just my bouncy self," she said, although her voice didn't sound very happy. "When I'm angry, nobody can tell it. And when I'm worried, nobody knows it because
I just bounce along. That's the way it's supposed to be too, because
a Christian is a child of God and a child of God has nothing to
worry about because everything is already taken care of. That's
why I can't allow myself to worry about whether or not I'm going
to be an Invincible. If I'm supposed to be one God will take care
of it, and if I'm not supposed to be one there's nothing I can do
about it, because 'God is Love,' First John, four, eight, and His
will is always best. He knows what is right for each of us, according to the Bible *and* Mr. E. Y. Mullins."

Dr. Norman Truly had encouraged her to read Edgar Young
Mullins, and after doing so, she said that she would never be the
same again. "His definition of God's love is the best I've ever read
anywhere," said Principia, staring at the steeple of her church.
"In 'Christianity at the Crossroads,' he says that this love is 'the
self-imparting quality in the divine nature which leads God to
seek the highest good and the most complete possession of his
creatures.'

"That certainly is a good thing to know," she said, walking
into direct sunlight. Again she studied her shadow, which was

elongated yet still emphasized her large frame. She had always been conscious of her size and at times it plagued her, for it was true, she told herself, her bones were big, her shoulders broad and her arms a bit long. Yet her waist was small and so were her feet. She was light on them too; at times she even seemed to glide along.

"But my hands are too big, and that bothers me," she said, holding them before her face. "Tawnya has such small hands and so does Miss Hathaway, but mine are big just like my father's and I don't like looking at them."

"Because of her size we'll never have any trouble with her when it comes to the boys," Principia had once heard her mother say. "She'll grow up, get married and have children. There won't be any of this running-around wild business, not with Principia. She won't give us those worries because she isn't the type, physically I mean, and I thank God for it too."

"I'm not like Esther, the beautiful Queen of Persia, that's for sure," Principia sighed, recalling her mother's words. "I'm more like Deborah, who sat under a palm tree and gave comfort and advice to all the people who sought her. Miss Hathaway always said that I would grow up to be mighty in battle like Deborah, who delivered her people from the hands of the enemy. Miss Hathaway always said that I had the hands of deliverance."

Feeling good about herself once again, she walked on a little further, before, without warning, she was seized with guilt over having missed Sunday school for the first time in what seemed like ages. "Everybody will want to know where I was and what I was doing," she said, putting a serious look on her face. "So I'll just tell them that I had to go be by myself because I had something I needed to pray about, and that's no lie either because I've never been known to lie and I'm certainly not about to start now, so when they ask me where I was I'll just say: You know that old closet on the second floor of Blankenship? Well, that's where I've been all this time, down on my hands and knees and praying just about as hard as anybody ever prayed."

A breeze came along and stirred up the lilac and honeysuckle blooming all over the campus. "Oh, that happens to be the sweetest smell I've ever smelled," she said turning her freckles away from the sun and breathing deeply.

Then she studied her shadow again, and even though she didn't like what she saw, she told herself that she did. "I guess I'll keep all this hair after all," she said turning her attention to the white frame church up ahead. "Father would have a fit if I cut so much as a curl to paste in a memory book, and Brother Callaway would never let me live it down. I'll never forget what he said as soon as he baptized me. He said that my hair looked just like the burning bush that Moses saw, and when I came straight way out of the water it still looked as though my whole body was covered with fire. I was three years old at the time. That was the most wonderful day of my whole life, and I'll never forget it as long as I live, which I hope and pray will be forever."

New Bethel Baptist Church stood before her like a promise. "Ask, and it shall be given you; seek, and ye shall find; knock, and it shall be opened unto you," quoted Principia from the book of Saint Matthew, chapter seven, verse seven. It was the first verse from the Bible that Lively Hathaway had encouraged her to commit to memory.

She approached New Bethel Church with a smile on her face and a prayer in her heart. "Oh Lord, I feel just like singing," she said gazing at the church as though it were a vision. Slowly her eyes moved from the single steeple where the sparrows nested to the Gothic windows with purple panes, to the front door, to the columns in need of a coat of paint and finally to the foundation of river rocks. "O Lord," she said with amazement ringing in her voice. "Why haven't I ever noticed those rocks before?" Again she quoted from the book of Saint Matthew. "'And the rain descended, and the floods came, and the winds blew, and beat upon that house; and it fell not: for it was founded upon a rock.'"

She stopped walking for a moment and admired the church, allowing her eyes to fall slowly from the steeple to the foundation. "I realize that there are other churches in the world," she said, "but this one is so special that I never want to leave it. When I'm working for the Lord as a missionary I'll carry this church in my heart and reconstruct it wherever I can. I just want everyone in the world to know that it exists."

3

On the steps of New Bethel Baptist, Principia joined Billy Ray Poindexter, a senior music major standing stiff as a board inside a powder blue suit that swallowed him whole. Billy Ray was blond, freckled and over six feet tall. He had been an Invincible two years in a row but was unable to apply again because he had been called to direct the choir as well as lead the young people's program at Fairview only thirty miles from New Bethel. He was one of Principia's special friends because she could say anything to him that she could say to God, which was just about anything that came to mind.

"I dreamed about you last night, Billy Ray Poindexter. Did you know that?" she asked as though she expected him to know it already. "I dreamed that I was going to be an Invincible and that you were going to be one too. And do you know what else? I think we were partners. I have always believed that we would work together one day."

"That dream means something, so trust it," said Billy Ray. "Being an Invincible was the joy of my life. Sometimes I wish I had applied again."

"Sometimes I wish I hadn't," said Principia. "But I really don't mean that. I'm just nervous because everybody else has been chosen and I'm still left waiting. I just refuse to give up hope though, in spite of the fact that Miss Corinda Cassy has never chosen anyone younger than eighteen."

As they walked into the church, she noticed that Billy Ray smelled of shoe polish and Old Spice; shaving cream was clinging to his ears and his fingernails had been bitten a little closer to the quick.

Lord, pour out your spirit on Billy Ray, for I sense he is struggling, Principia prayed as they sat down in one of the middle pews.

Once inside the sanctuary it was as though the rest of the world had stood still, or did not exist. The air was heavy, motionless, redolent of old hymnbooks aging on hardwood pews, soap-cleansed worshipers in serge, silk and broadcloth, scented, some only for the day, with perfumes, creams, powders and hair tonic, mingling with the almost-no-essence of funeral carnations, tinted blue and green and arranged by Nova Ray Lutes, who had placed them carefully, lovingly before the altar.

Principia's mind was somewhere else that Sunday. She could not concentrate on the announcements, had difficulty listening to the prayers; she had no idea who was sitting in front of her or behind her and did not stand on the singing of the first hymn until Billy Ray tugged at her arm. Slowly she stood up, steadied herself on the pew in front of her and stared intensely at Memory Turner, who was leading the congregation in singing, "All the Way My Saviour Leads Me."

But Principia's energy was down, and she found it difficult to give the hymn her undivided attention. One moment she felt as though she were going into a deep sleep and the next moment she felt as though she were coming out of one. All she could think about was the Invincible orientation, which was to begin the following Saturday in San Antonio, and at one point she turned to Billy Ray and said, "If God doesn't need another Invincible at the last moment I just don't know what I'm going to do. I'm so eager to serve Him. I have prayed a thousand prayers and I'll pray a thousand more if I need to. Aunt Wilda used to tell me to draw a picture of what I wanted and I'd get it, so I drew myself standing on a Bible and put the drawing under my pillow exactly one week ago, and I've been dreaming about serving the Lord ever since."

"God will answer your prayers, Principia," said Billy Ray. "But it's important for *you* to remember that *No* is an answer just the same as *Yes*. Sometimes the Lord even answers prayers through other people, and sometimes his silences are meant to help steer us."

"Oh, you're so wise, Billy Ray," said Principia respectfully. "I'll remember that for a long time to come."

At that moment the choir director asked the congregation to be seated for the singing of the next hymn, number 289: "There Is a Fountain Filled with Blood."

It was one of Billy Ray's favorite songs, but he had always had trouble singing it. Even though he was a graduating voice major with ambitions to become a choir director in a big-city church, Billy Ray had always had difficulty matching pitch. At times Principia worried about this inadequacy and wondered why the Lord had called him into the ministry of music.

After the singing of the hymn came the responsive reading and then the offering, after which Tawnya, still wearing the black dress, took her place at the keyboard. It was her Sunday to provide the special music, and she had chosen a prelude of arpeggios that gradually modulated into "It Took a Miracle," which she sang with her head thrown back and her hands rippling all over the keyboard.

When Principia saw her she folded her arms tightly, bowed her head and said a prayer that Tawnya might make it through the solo even though she had been out all night and had come in with liquor breath and a wrinkled dress and who knows what else.

The Lord works in ways unknown to man, Principia thought as she listened to Tawnya singing like an angel. Billy Ray has to work so hard to learn to match pitch and still can't do it very well and Tawnya Louise is naturally musical. She hasn't had to work a day in her life, and that just doesn't seem fair at all, but we must trust in God and one day his reasons will be made clear.

Everyone always looked forward to Tawnya's specials because she had never been known to miss a note and gave the impression that she enjoyed singing and playing better than anything. That day she sang with more feeling than ever, and after the last line:

> And when He saved my soul
> Cleansed and made me whole
> It took a miracle of love and grace.

the congregation became so quiet it was almost as though the church were empty.

"Tawnya Louise," said Brother Callaway as he came forward to begin his sermon, "is a great blessing to us all."

But Principia, falling into a daydream, was not aware that Tawnya had stopped singing. Slowly her intense stare melted, her eyes began to cloud over and the tension in her shoulders gave way with one long sigh as she withdrew into herself. Billy Ray knew that she could withdraw her thoughts from the world, not always when she wanted to but when she felt strongly that the Lord needed to speak to her. It was something that she had always been able to do, something that Lively Hathaway had encouraged. "You must always allow yourself these little moments of meditation," Lively had advised. "No matter where you are, when you feel the Lord trying to get through to you, you must relax and allow him to direct your thoughts. You must surrender yourself completely to his will no matter what it is."

Billy Ray admired the way Principia seemed to be able to put her total trust in God. In comparison, he often felt like a nonbeliever because he could not surrender his every thought; he could not turn his eyes inward and search his soul, not the way he believed Principia could. He watched her carefully throughout the service waiting for the first sign of her surfacing.

Brother Callaway preached on and on that day. It was Stewardship Sunday, and he said that he had spent the whole week praying that the right words would come to him at the right time. When he finally called for the invitational hymn "Just As I Am" to be sung quietly, and reverently, and with every head bowed and every eye closed, Billy Ray noticed the color gradually returning to Principia's face. Her breathing was becoming noticeably faster too, and her eyes were once again focusing on objects in the church. To Billy Ray it was as though her soul had taken leave of her body and returned fully charged, for the moment she came to her senses she turned to him with an urgency in her voice that he found almost frightening.

"Oh, Billy Ray, I am filled with such peace of mind for the first time in weeks," she said. "Just now the Lord took me up in a pure white light and I was surrounded by doves, and music, and clouds, and sweet baby angels. My grandparents who I never knew were there, and so was Aunt Wilda, just as happy as could be, and so was that poor boy Johnny Murphy, who got his neck broken in that awful car wreck last semester. I just sat there and gave thanks for seeing him once again, and then I promised the Lord that I would never cease to praise His most holy and wondrous name, and do you know what? In turn, He has given me the peace that passeth all understanding. I asked Him, but He did not tell me whether or not I'm going to be an Invincible. I guess He hasn't decided yet, but He did assure me that He has great plans in store for my talents and that you are included in these plans."

"You see," said Billy Ray, speaking over the hymnal, "the Lord does not forget. I'm sure that you and I will work together many times before the Lord is through with us. I just wish I could have as clear a vision as you seem to have had right now."

"Allow Him to lead you," she whispered in rhythm with the song. "It's my feeling that the Lord doesn't want you to become a minister of music, but He is steering you in that direction in order to take you somewhere else, somewhere you might not want to go right now, but when the time is right His plans will be revealed to you, and it will be then that His plans for your life and my life will cross."

She believed that the Lord had revealed only part of his purpose for Billy Ray's life and that when her friend had received and committed himself totally to God's will it might be possible for the two of them to spend their lives together. She had often daydreamed about being married to Billy Ray, and the union as she pictured it was made complete because they were both dedicated to Christian service. Her face turned pale as she thought about it. She felt feverish. Her fingers trembled. Her hands turned bright red and she hid them under the hymnbook.

Billy Ray and Principia had never dated; not really. There was no need to because they knew each other's schedules so well that they met several times a day without planning it. Principia looked forward to their meetings because when they were together, she could feel the Lord's hand resting on her trembling heart, and because of this she believed that Billy Ray was to be part of her destiny. That Sunday she felt the Lord working in a stronger way than ever before, and she almost wanted to jump out of her seat and shout. It was all she could do to contain the excitement she felt.

Her happiness carried her through the rest of the service and for a while made her forget how much she still wanted to be an Invincible.

Two people accepted Christ that Sunday and one rededicated his life because he wanted to be a better Christian in the office. At the close of the service Billy Ray and Principia shook hands with those who had made decisions for the Lord and then left the church together. They had plans to go straight to the college cafeteria, but in front of the church Principal Martindale and Wilma Lee, standing in the shade of a sweet gum, stopped them.

Wilma Lee was taller than her husband. She wore a one-piece dress of black-and-white plaid and carried a patent-leather purse stuffed with Kleenex. Principal was in his standard navy blue suit, the coat of which refused to reach around him. His shirt was yellow, buttoned up tight so the extra skin on his neck fell down around his collar, set off by a string tie held together with a small silver frame displaying his favorite picture of Principia. He had not visited with her in over a week and was hoping that she would consent to come home that day.

"I'd be the happiest man alive if you'd spend the entire summer with us, Prin," he said, holding down what was left of his hair with the palm of his hand. "We're both getting old. We can't live forever you know."

"Oh yes we can if we want to," said his daughter with more confidence and conviction than her father had ever heard coming out of anybody. She put her arms around his waist, snuggled up to him and looked at her mother while she spoke. "In the words of the old hymn: 'No chilling winds, nor poisonous breath, can reach that healthful shore; sickness and sorrow, pain and death, are felt and feared no more.' The Bible also promises everlasting life. We'll be together in heaven and have that to look forward to. There we will know total understanding, happiness and love. There will be no famine or disease. Pestilence will not exist beyond the Pearly Gates. It says so in the scripture, Father, and if you don't remember I can reference it for you in a split second."

She took her white Bible out of her side pocket and opened it on the spot, but her father closed it on her hand. "Sometimes I'm sorry I ever taught you to read God's word," he said. "Now both of you come on home, so Mother and I can visit with you. We'll change around that window of yours and go through the artwork you did when you were little so we can pick out the pieces we want to have framed; then we can look through your high school yearbooks, read all the nice things your friends wrote about you and later on if we don't show home movies, Mother can take your new measurements and work up some dresses for you. We'd both like to see you wearing something that didn't have so much purple on it because we're not sure it goes with your coloring. What you need is something in a pale yellow, Mother thinks, something with a Peter Pan collar and ruffles all around it like you used to wear so much."

"I've got a nice piece of polished cotton print," said Wilma Lee. "It's got a tiny flowerdy design and won't make you look so big maybe. So you two come on home with us and we'll see about it."

For what seemed like eternity to Principia the four of them stood there staring at each other. The last time she had gone home on Sunday afternoon was still fresh in her mind and she didn't want to live through it again, not by herself and certainly not with Billy Ray either. The last time she had taken her friend Delbert Cummings with her. Delbert was a ministerial student from Longview, and she was sure that the afternoon and evening had bored him, even though he would not admit it. After lunch her parents brought out some of her scrapbooks, and they flipped through the pages of Principia's early years. After evening worship they went back home, pinned a sheet to the wall and watched home movies recording sixteen years of surprise birthday parties that had been spliced together so all the celebrations ran into each other, from the very first one to the very last. "Do we have to watch it all?" she had asked that Sunday evening after church. The fifteen minutes of birthday film seemed never-ending, but the worst part of all was knowing that Delbert was watching too.

On their way back to the campus, Delbert had said, "Your parents are wonderful people. What's so sad is that they don't have anything in their lives but you. How did that happen anyway?"

"I don't like to think about that," Principia had said. She was unable to answer his question because she suspected the worst, that she had encouraged the situation until it had gotten out of hand, until her parents could no longer live without her. Matthew twelve, thirty-seven, kept coming to her thoughts. "He that loveth father or mother more than me is not worthy of me: and he that loveth son or daughter more than me is not worthy of me." Lively Hathaway had taught her that verse. It was the only one she wanted to erase from her mind, and she resented Delbert for making her think of it.

Several times after that Delbert asked her out, but each time she refused to accept his invitation. "Are you going to spend your life avoiding people who say things you don't want to hear?" he finally asked, and Principia answered, "My purpose is to serve those who need me most."

"Then you'd better start thinking about your parents," Delbert had said. That was the last time they had spoken.

Every time she saw her parents, however, she thought of what he had said, and then Matthew twelve, thirty-seven, would go spinning through her mind. At times she purposely avoided them, but that Sunday, the last week of her freshman year, they had been waiting for her under the sweet gum, and neither she nor Billy Ray had seen them in time.

"Billy Ray and I . . . we have plans this afternoon," she said, finally breaking the silence that sliced through the hot afternoon like a blue norther out of season. She felt good knowing that Billy Ray was standing next to her. She could always depend on him to be there, even if he had nothing to say.

"Very well then," said Wilma Lee, almost ready to cry. "Daddy and I will just go on home without you, but I hope you realize how disappointed we are because you haven't come to see us as often as we'd like for you to."

After saying goodby as best they could, her parents, still standing in the shade of the sweet gum, watched Principia and Billy Ray walk off toward the Best-Peebles Student Union, named for Jeremiah Best, who had been a missionary to South Africa, and Eula Peebles, who had been a Bible professor at Hillister Baptist and had died teaching the book of Deuteronomy to her eight-thirty class.

On the way to the union building, Principia turned to Billy Ray and said, "The only thing I dread about going to church is having to see my parents. You know they're just foolish about me and always have been, and it makes me feel like I've failed them somehow."

"If you failed them, you didn't go to do it," said Billy Ray. "One thing that's so important to remember is that God forgives all acts committed in ignorance."

"Oh, you're so right, Billy Ray," said Principia with a voice of relief. "I'm ignorant in ways I can't even begin to tell you about, and I feel so much better now that you've reminded me how truly ignorant I am."

Just outside the student union she caught a glimpse of herself in the plate-glass window of the bookstore and turned her head quickly. Her hair had parted itself down the middle, making her already thin nose appear longer as well as thinner. There were times when she hated her hair because it was so crawly it would never hold a barrette or bobby pin for very long; it was wild and untamed, and at times the bright red made her feel cheap. She hated the way men she didn't know sometimes stared at her, and she prayed to God that she didn't give them the wrong impression.

I just can't see what good can come out of me, she thought, catching another glimpse of herself in the window. But if the Lord can take my life and use me in some small way I will be grateful forever and ever.

They entered the building, took their places in the lunchroom line and were waiting patiently when Brother Simon Hemphill, president of Hillister Baptist College, who was himself a retired preacher (but not a retired man of God), came rushing into the building, and, without saying a word, handed Principia a telegram he had just received. It was from Miss Corinda Cassy, Director of the Invincible Program, as well as a lifelong friend to Brother Hemphill. Her message was short and to the point:

MIGHT NEED THREE MORE DEFINITELY NEED ONE SEND MARTINDALE GIRL IF AVAILABLE IF NOT SOMEONE OF YOUR CHOICE

For a few minutes, Principia could not decide if she was happy or sad. Again she saw herself reflected in the bookstore window, this time from inside the student union. The reflection was sharper, her features clearly visible. She noticed, but not for the first time, that her widow's peak was slightly off center, and that her face was, as her father said, "heart-shaped" but not "perfectly." As though in a trance, she stared at herself for a few moments longer, not believing that the Lord had chosen that person she saw, and in spite of the fact that she didn't want to leave her parents, her friends and her church, she knew that she could not say no to God.

"I was able to reach Corinda over the telephone just a few minutes ago," said Brother Hemphill, trying to get Principia's attention by moving between her and the window. "She was at her ranch in Alice. I told her that you were definitely available, and she said you would be working in the small towns along the Mexican border in Southwest Texas."

"Joy!" shouted Principia, as though charged with an electrical current. "The Lord is leading me into the wilderness, but it makes me sad to know that I'm leaving New Bethel Baptist Church, and it makes me even sadder to know that I'm breaking my father's heart. What I must remember is that the Lord wants me. That's the important thing. I will follow him into that barren land, and when I emerge I will be a stronger Christian than ever before."

"Your parents will grow by this experience as much as you will," said Billy Ray.

"Oh, you're so right," said Principia. "Billy Ray, thank God I have you to give me your support. God's will is unfolding before my very eyes, and you're helping me to understand it so much better. At this moment I am reminded of hymn number sixty-three. 'Who is on the Lord's side? Who will face the foe? Who is on the Lord's side? Who for Him will go?' I will, Billy Ray, I will serve the Master. And I promise faithfully to follow Him, and trust Him, and obey Him, even when He leads to strange-out-of-the-way-places. The scripture states that God delivered Sisera into the hands of a woman and that woman was Deborah. I want each person here to remember that I have chosen Deborah, the mighty warrior of the Lord, as my example. I will carry her in my heart all summer long and for the rest of my life."

 4

Principia Martindale's prayers had been heard and answered
and she thanked God for it too. It was on a Sunday afternoon in
late-spring-early-summer that she received her calling to become
an Invincible, and on the following Saturday she boarded a bus
for San Antonio, where she was to undergo six days of intense
training with Miss Corinda Cassy and the other Invincibles, twenty-four in all, counting herself. She had not invited her mother
and father to see her off because she knew they would do nothing
but cry as they had done over the telephone and as she knew they
had been doing all week. Her father was especially upset and had
spent his spare time watching his daughter grow up in eight-milli-
meter footage with no sound except that of a dripping faucet, a
striking clock and a running nose along with the hum of the movie projector, which hurled Principia larger than life upon a per-
cale sheet thumbtacked to the living room wall.

It had been misting rain all week long, but by Saturday
morning it had stopped and rain lilies were miraculously showing
their faces overnight. A warm wet fragrance of wisteria mingling
with early roses settled like an angel's breath over the Saturday-
morning laziness of New Bethel. The sycamores growing next to
the bus station were dripping with leftover rain rolling off their
leaves like a father's tears and falling into an oil drum left out to
rust. Behind the station a stray dog started barking at a squirrel in
the sweet gum; the squirrel began fussing at a house wren nesting
in the eaves of the feed store, and, in retaliation, the wren set up
her own racket against Dr. Carl Milam, who was nearly ninety

and had just rolled out of bed and wandered into the street, where he was laughing to himself as loud as he could. His eyes were still half shut, and he was wearing what he thought was his old worn-out raincoat, but it was nothing in the world but his wife's chenille bathrobe with padded shoulders and a ripped-out hem. "It's so sad to see someone's mind go like that," said Principia when she saw the doctor who delivered her coming toward the station. "Lord, I do pray that you won't ever let me get in that kind of shape." Quickly, she turned her head the other way, and there running toward her was Annabelle Winters with curlers as big as soup cans in her hair and her dress buttoned up wrong down the front. As usual for a Saturday morning in late-spring-early-summer, Annabelle was chasing her pullets through the streets of New Bethel. Once again something had scared them out of their pen the night before, and she had been up since way before dawn trying to run them down.

Following Annabelle down the street was Brother Hemphill. He had come to tell Principia goodby, and behind him came Dr. Norman Truly, Lively Hathaway and Billy Ray Poindexter as well as Lorinda Goings, who was planning to spend the summer back home in Merryville. After them arrived countless other faculty members and students from Hillister Baptist College, and slowly some of the townspeople began to assemble as well.

Lorinda Goings pushed herself through the crowd and gave Principia a wooden cross she had once purchased in Mexico. It was a foot long and carved from a single piece of wood. "I know we as Baptists don't believe in worshiping the cross, but I want you to have this anyway," she said.

"I do not worship the cross, but I do worship the man who died on it," said Principia, tucking the gift under her belt as though it were a sixshooter. "I will take this as my reminder as well as my weapon against the world that might not be prepared to understand my ways."

" 'Put on the full armor of God that you may be able to withstand the wiles of the Devil,' " quoted Lorinda as she hugged Principia goodby.

"Fall not by the wayside," warned Brother Hemphill.

"Place your hands in the nail-scarred hands," advised Dr. Truly, "and remember everything you are and why you're a Baptist."

"I'll never forget that," said Principia, "due to your wonderful lecture on the subject. I am a Baptist because of a home, because of a book, because of a fellowship, a conflict and a program, but most of all, I am a Baptist because of a blessed assurance."

Dr. Truly smiled and stepped aside while Lively Hathaway came forward. "Your folks couldn't stand to come down and say goodby so I'll just take their place right now," she said, forcing something into Principia's hand. It was a little round handkerchief that she had crocheted the day before. "Every now and again, take out this little piece of handwork and let it tell you how much I love you," she said. "And always remember this too: Go with God and he'll go with you. You'll remember that for me, won't you?"

"Yes, Miss Hathaway," said Principia. " 'Wherever He leads I'll go.' You can be sure of that." Then she saw Billy Ray standing in the crowd and went over to him. "You're graduating and going off to work, and it might be a long time before I ever see you again," she said, hardly able to keep from crying. "But I just want you to remember that one day, maybe when we least expect it, we'll be together."

"Follow the King's Highway," said Billy Ray. "I'm sad that I can't go with you."

"So am I," said Principia, without looking him in the face. She squeezed his arm instead and said goodby to some of the townspeople who were standing near them. Then she boarded the bus and, smiling to all the other passengers, made her way toward the back, where she took a seat by herself.

The driver, Handy Spurlock from Hull-Dasietta, started the motor and was just about to pull away when three of Annabelle Winters' fattest hens ran under the bus and stayed there, clucking to themselves for being so smart.

"Turn that motor off fast," shouted Annabelle, grabbing a cane pole that was propped up against the station and using it to force her way through the crowd. "My fattest chickens ran up under that bus of yours, and if you cut their necks off I'll beat you within an inch of your life so help me."

Having been through all this before, Handy, who had recently married a Birdine woman from Honey Island, turned off the motor as fast as he could and waited until the chickens ran off toward the Lone Star Feed Store and Annabelle, arms flapping and curlers falling, ran right in behind them. "I'll knock you chickens crazy if you ever get out again," she said, waving the cane pole in the air.

As soon as she was out of the way, Handy started the motor once more.

Through the window splashed with raindrops, Principia saw a blur of faces and bodies standing against the bus station and separated from her not only by the cloudy window but by words that were growing less meaningful and thoughts that were not what they had been, scriptures she was tired of hearing and phrases she had repeated all her life. Her friends waving her off did not seem to be living breathing people at all but inhabitants of another world, one to which she had belonged and was now leaving. Half expecting everyone to disappear, she rubbed her hands against the glass, but the people were still there, a monstrous mass of heads and arms mixed together on the window. "I better stop thinking these things," she said. "I thought sure I'd be sad to leave, but somehow I'm not sad at all."

Just then she caught sight of Tawnya Louise standing in back of the crowd. Her image came through a raindrop as Principia pressed her face closer to the window. Tawnya was wearing tight jeans and a V-neck sweater that looked as if it belonged on a man. Her hair was tangled, her sleepy eyes were lined all the way around and her wrists were covered with bracelets. Principia could almost hear them jangling as Tawnya waved goodby. "Lord, what will it take to reach Tawnya Louise?" said Principia. She gave a faint smile, returned the wave and settled back in her seat. Handy Spurlock closed the door, looked at himself proudly in the rearview mirror and said: "Here we go, everybody; hang on to your hats." The bus lurched forward, rocking from side to side until it was on the street and picking up speed. At that point Principia refused to turn around, refused to wave another time.

She had the feeling that she would never return. Yet at the same time she believed she would see her church again, perhaps sooner than she expected. But that was a puzzling thought, so she tucked it away in the back of her mind while she stared at everyone on the bus and then down at her hands. They were wide, her fingers were long and there were many wrinkles crossing her palms. She thought they looked like the hands of an old woman and was glad to have pockets in her dress so she could hide them. While she sat there with her hands in her pockets, the bus left the city limits, and only then did she realize that she was glad to be leaving Hillister Baptist College, the town of New Bethel and what started out being a lazy Saturday morning in late-spring-early-summer.

Heading west toward Splendora the bus followed Highway 190, which twisted and turned like a long wet snake crawling through pine savannahs, palmetto flats and hardwood forests. Clouds like angel hair hung low over the pine trees, while the sun, like the eye of God, burned through the rising mist in an attempt to show its face to the world. Puddles of water were standing all over the highway. Some were beginning to reflect a clearing sky. "It's gonna fair off yet," said Handy, aiming the bus at the biggest puddles he could find because he liked to see how high up he could make the water splash.

"Guide us safely, O Lord, to our respective destinations," prayed Principia. "And please have Miss Corinda Cassy waiting for me at the station because now I'm just one in this world and I need you more than ever before."

It was as though Handy Spurlock had been waiting for her to finish praying because the moment she said "Amen," he began singing "Here Comes the Bride," while looking through his wallet for a snapshot of his new wife, Debra. When he found the picture, he held it up so everyone in the bus could see it and then, looking through his rearview mirror, he said, "Here she is, folks. Married her four weeks ago today, and this is the first time I ever left her by herself, so I sure do hope she remembers to keep the dogs fed until I can get back home."

Principia could not imagine what woman in her right mind would have him. His hair, or what was left of it, was greased until it glistened like the wet highway. It was parted horizontally across the back of his head and combed up over his bald spot.

He just about scares me to death to look at him, she thought. I do hope he's not going to be the one to drive us all the way to San Antonio.

In an attempt to put her mind at ease, she opened her packet of materials to be studied before the Invincible Orientation. She disregarded the brochure called "What It Means to Be an Invincible" because she felt as though she already knew everything that could possibly be said on the subject; she had, after all, spent the whole year thinking and praying about God's invincible plan for her life.

The first thing I want to look over is that Vacation Bible School program, she said to herself while flipping through the study guide. Every year they change it around and they have no business fooling with it, especially the main song. Last year's was good enough. I liked it just fine. And I think it ought to be this year's song too, but I know it's not.

Looking over the words to the new anthem, she began singing in whispers into her collar:

> "Come to Bible School-ool
> Come to Bible School,
> Bring somebody with you,
> Come to Bible School.

"Well, that's real catchy," she said. "I think I'm going to like this after all." She went on to the next verse:

> "I shall always come to Bible School
> It shall be my never-ending rule,
> For I am leaning and depending on my
>   Saaa-aaav-yerrr-errr,
> Come to Bible Schoooool."

On the last two lines she got carried away and sang out. Every head on the bus turned to see who was doing the singing, but Principia paid them no mind. She was so absorbed in God's work that she wasn't even aware she had lifted her voice.

To Principia, the daily lesson as expressed through music was the most important part of Vacation Bible School, with the handicraft projects a close second. She was good at working with her hands and always had been. Her mother had taught her how to crochet, knit, hemstitch and smock. Lively had taught her how to sew on ruffles and rickrack without showing a stitch, and her father had taught her how to nail a nail in straight; how to use an electric saw; how to solder and rewire light fixtures. But it was her mother's sister, Aunt Wilda, who taught her to draw and paint. Aunt Wilda had spent her life in and out of the state asylum in

Rusk, and on one of her visits back home she taught Principia how to draw on a blackboard with colored chalk. Not long after that, Principia became one of the finest chalk-talk artists New Bethel had ever seen.

"Lord, I thank you so much for Aunt Wilda, because through her you gave me the art of chalk talk," she said out the window as the bus sped along. She found comfort in knowing that one of her suitcases contained her small blackboard and colored chalk as well as a Western Auto cassette and tapes of her favorite hymns so she would never be without background music when she drew her inspirational scenes from the Bible, each of which took her only fifteen minutes to complete in full detail and living color.

While her thoughts were centered around Aunt Wilda and chalk paintings, the bus, without her fully realizing it, had entered the Splendora city limits and the sun had come all the way to bless the earth. The streets of Splendora were wet and steaming, and for a Saturday morning the town was almost empty of activity. The roads were so muddy the farmers could not come into town to do their trading, so the place seemed deserted except for a dog, a cat and a face at a wet window. When the bus passed the courthouse square, a man waved just as though he were well acquainted with every passenger on board. Milford Monroe liked to do that. It was his way of keeping in touch with the outside world.

"We'll be here for only ten minutes," said Handy as he turned onto Bluff Street and headed straight for the bus station, which was next door to Junie Woods Beauty Cottage and no more than twenty steps from the Smack and Chew Barbecue, also owned and operated by Junie, Splendora's make-up artist and gourmet chef all wrapped up into one.

Handy parked next to another Greyhound. "I advise you to stay in this bus so you won't get left behind," he said. "But if you just have to get out there's nothing I can do about it, is there?" Then he pulled the handle that opened the door and Splendora's Saturday-morning bus station smell—exhaust fumes mingling with hickory smoke, popcorn and hair spray—wafted to the back of the bus and brought Principia out of her daydream.

Looking around to find out where she was, her eye caught a tall man wearing a dark suit. He was standing in the bus station, as though waiting for someone to arrive.

"I simply must give that interesting-looking man one of my religious pamphlets," she said, pressing her face against the window. "He has the most tender eyes I've ever seen on anybody."

In a split second she was out of the bus and inside the station. "Excuse me," she said, approaching the man who was standing near the ticket booth. "My name is Principia Martindale, and I'm an Invincible."

"My name is Anthony Leggett," said the man. "And I'm a preacher."

"I just knew you were a man of God, Brother Leggett," said Principia as though they had been acquainted for years. "Here, I'd like to give you this religious pamphlet. I wrote it myself."

"Well then, I'm glad to receive it," he said, scanning the literature just handed him. "This all sounds very positive to me," he added in a quiet voice that Principia enjoyed very much. "I have the feeling that I'm standing before someone who's just received a calling."

"Oh, I just knew you would understand," said Principia.

"If you don't mind," continued Brother Leggett, "I would like to have at least a dozen of these pamphlets of yours. On my next visit to the Old Folks' Home of Happiness I'll distribute them freely. I doubt very seriously if any of our senior citizens have ever met an Invincible before."

"Oh, I knew I could count on you; I knew it from the very minute I saw you," said Principia, handing over twenty-four pamphlets while noticing out of the corner of her eye that her bus was about to leave. "I've got to go now," she said. "But one day I hope we can meet again. I'd like to hear what's in your heart."

"I don't know if you would or not," he said, looking down at the floor. Principia thought he had the heaviest eyelids she had ever seen. "We don't need to discuss those things now," he added, his fingers nervously fumbling with something in his pocket. "Here, I want you to have this. It isn't much but it might be of some benefit to you in your work." He took a small pocketknife off his key chain. It had a mother-of-pearl handle and two sharp blades, plus a can opener, a fork, an ice pick and a small pair of scissors that folded up. "It's so practical," he said. "Think of me every time you use it."

"I'll do better than that, I'll pray for you every time I use it," said Principia. "And that will be often, too." She shook his hand, turned and ran for her bus.

"I just met a devoted man of God who's going to talk about me at the old folks' home," she said to Handy who was about to close the door. He answered by touching his tongue to the tip of his nose. The sight of him sent Principia flying to her seat.

I just know that man's soul is in great danger, she thought, burying her head in her studies so she wouldn't have to think about him and what he was doing.

On page twenty-six of her study guide, she read that all Vacation Bible School teachers should, at the end of each day, be able to look back and say: "I have worked with my Lord. I have taught His word." On the next page she read: "Three personalities are present during Vacation Bible School: the teacher, the pupil and the Holy Spirit.

"This is one of the many truths I want my students to realize," she said. "It sounds just like something E. Y. Mullins would have written. I also want them to know that the impulse to pray is universal, and even when marred by sin, men still feel the need for prayer. Dr. Truly says that the word 'prayer' is found one hundred and sixty-three times in the New Testament and the word 'love' appears eighty-nine times. I want all my students to know this too, because somehow I think it's very important."

For more than a hundred miles she studied her Vacation Bible School lessons, talked to herself, reflected over the happenings of her first year at Hillister Baptist College and, when she finally looked out the window again, she saw a changing landscape. The trees were gradually getting smaller, and had more space for sky between them. The rain clouds had thinned out as well, leaving nothing ahead but a blue horizon moving in fast, as if to force the timber line further into the distance. Principia turned around to see the tall trees of East Texas disappearing behind her, while up ahead the highway cut a ribbon of blue through the hills and ended in the sky.

It's a mystery how things change before you know it, she thought, daydreaming out the window. Suddenly you aren't where you thought you were. Before you know it everything's different. You look up expecting to see a rain cloud or a big tree and it's all open space and blue sky, or if you're like me you expect a scripture to speak to your heart the same way two times in a row, and it hardly ever happens like that. Sometimes I wish things would stay just one way and not change so fast.

She rested her head on the back of the chair and stared at the ceiling. "I prayed and prayed," she said out loud. "I wanted to be an Invincible more than anything else in the whole world, and now I'm about to be one, and somehow I just don't feel very excited about it anymore. The excitement will come back later on, I guess." .

Handy Spurlock looked at her through his rearview mirror and said, "I bet that girl's got a problem that nobody's thought of yet. That's what I bet."

Principia found the handkerchief that Lively had given her, and she spread it out on her lap. Against the purple dress, the piece of handwork, which was more like a doily than anything else, was clearly defined. Every thread seem to know exactly where it was going; the major ones made a direct line toward the center, and the secondary threads wove around and around the major ones and eventually reached the center as well, at least Principia hoped they did.

Lord Jesus, she silently prayed, I ask for the happiness of everybody and everything in the whole wide world, and I hope that somewhere someone is praying for a little bit of happiness for me as well, for I feel so lost and out of place.

She put the handkerchief away, picked up her memory work and attacked it with added fervor, but after covering three pages she found it difficult to concentrate. "Everybody treats me like I'm special, but I don't feel very special," she said. "And that's part of my problem. Lord, help me to feel the way I'm supposed to, but please keep in mind that I just want to be like everybody else, that's all." Again she picked up her packet of materials and began looking over the outline of each day's activities, but her mind was elsewhere. Isaiah, chapter forty, verse three, came surging through her head: "The voice of him that crieth in the wilderness, Prepare ye the way of the Lord, make straight in the desert a highway for our God."

"Oh, how I love that scripture," she said into her book. "I will take it as my motto for the summer."

She felt as though she was that voice crying in a wilderness from which she might never return. Everything around her seemed foreign. She scanned the arid countryside as if looking for the answer to a question she was afraid to ask, and for a few moments her thoughts returned again to East Texas, New Bethel and her parents, from whom she had never been separated by more than five miles. Realizing that the separation that had been forced upon them was more painful for them than it was for her, she found herself wondering how she might increase her own sense of pain so she might feel better about leaving home against their wishes. The first three verses of Ephesians six entered her thoughts in spite of anything she could do to hold the scripture back: Children, obey your parents in the Lord: for this is right. Honour thy father and mother; which is the first commandment with promise; That it may be well with thee, and thou mayest live long on the earth."

She folded herself up in the seat and rested her head against the window. They always told me I could memorize anything, she thought. There are times when I feel that I've learned more than anybody ought to know, that I would be much better off if I knew a little bit less.

 5

Miss Corinda Cassy started out in life as the daughter of a wealthy rancher and later on, after trying her luck as a dancer in Las Vegas, a popular country vocalist and a leading actress on the dinner theater circuit, she said that she came to know God in a deeper, more personal way, and after that, she began devoting all her time and energy to writing inspirational novels and organizing the Invincible Program, which had been flourishing for the last ten summers and was now leading her into the next phase of her life: The Cowgirls for Christ, a drill team of thirty homeless teenagers who were living on her ranch in South Texas and learning to march in formation while singing such anthems as "Onward, Christian Soldiers," "We're Marching to Zion, beautiful, beautiful Zion" and Miss Cassy's own up-tempo arrangement of:

> Got a telephone in my bosom
> Can call Him up any time
> Got a telephone in my bosom
> King Jesus is on the line . . .

Miss Cassy was truly an inspiration to all dedicated Christians who knew and loved her. She had set up many scholarship funds for underprivileged students who desired to seek higher learning, and she had given generously to building funds for churches and Christian encampments. Many people considered her to be the wealthiest woman in Texas, but she made a point of saying that her riches were not invested in material gain.

At the age of forty-two, when Principia first met her, Corinda had already had a face lift in Argentina and a nose job in California. She had been married once, was a widow and was hoping to be married again. Her business manager, Larry Wayne Johnson, was the man of her dreams. He was blond, had blue eyes that were deep and brooding, was fifteen years her junior, and she was praying that one day there would be no need to hide their love. She was praying that he would accept her proposal of marriage, although she felt like they were already husband and wife. "I just can't live without you," she had told him countless times. She had felt that way from the very beginning, was aware that he did not return her feelings, but she kept telling herself that he loved her deeply and often she found herself believing her own words—at least for a while.

After her husband's death, she had prayed for someone to take his place, and with Larry Wayne she was able, from time to time, to convince herself that her prayers had been answered. Since living with him, however, her faith had been diminishing. When he came into her life she felt God going out the window, but she refused to give up her faith altogether. "I never want to be at loose ends again," she said, recalling the desperate years following her husband's death. "I've got to have something to hang on to. I'm just not quite sure what it is anymore."

Because she could never make up her mind what to believe, Larry Wayne had taken to calling her "Lady Confusion." "Every time you make some wild statement, just stop and ask yourself if you really believe it or not," he told her. That was on the Friday night before she left Alice to attend the Invincible Orientation. "Last year you acted like an idiot. Every time you opened your mouth you made a fool out of yourself and me too."

"The scripture does not allow you to call anybody a fool," she said. "Remember that for me, will you."

"Since when have you started believing in the scripture anyway?" he asked. He was lying on their bed and smoking a cigarette; his boots were on, his shirt unbuttoned and his legs were propped up on the footboard. "One day everyone will find out about you. They're going to realize that you've told yourself so many lies that you don't know what to believe anymore. But it's all right," he added, changing his tone to one of sympathy. "I'm just like you." He got up slowly, walked her into a corner, embraced her, caressed her neck with both hands and was about to kiss her when he pulled away. "The only difference between you and me," he said, going back to the bed, "is that I don't listen to everything I say."

"Please get yourself a fresh haircut and come with me to San Antonio. I can't make it through the orientation this year without you," she begged.

"I'm tired of hearing that silly testimony of yours," he said, lying down again. "If I have to hear that thing one more time, I might start believing it too, especially that made-up part about how you met Jesus on the highway."

"I told you I dreamed that," she said, throwing clothes into her suitcase. "It was one of those dreams that are more real than what happens when you're awake so I consider every word of my testimony to be true whether you do or not. Now I don't want to hear anything else about it because I'm older than you and therefore I deserve more respect than what I'm getting. I don't mean this to be a threat or anything like that, but if you're not careful you're not going to have your expense account renewed; either that or it'll be cut in half this next year."

"And if you're not careful you're going to wake up with nobody in bed with you just real soon," he said with a laugh on his face. "You always said you couldn't live without me. I might like to find out if that's true."

She finished packing her suitcase, put on a pair of creased jeans, a gray silk blouse and sling-back heels. Then she left the ranch for San Antonio, but almost halfway there she stopped and made a phone call. "I didn't mean what I said," she told Larry Wayne. She was in the town of Three Rivers at a roadside café, and two people were waiting to use the telephone, but she refused to hurry. "I know you didn't mean those hurtful things you said to me either, my darling," she continued, in a voice just loud enough for those waiting to overhear.

"I meant every word," he said and hung up without saying goodby, but Corinda, in a voice that was easily overheard, went on talking as though he were still on the line. To nothing but the dial tone, she confessed her love, and then, with her face turned to those who were still waiting, she hung up with tears in her eyes and left the booth slowly.

All the rest of the way to San Antonio she couldn't make up her mind how she felt about him, and the next day, Saturday, the first day of orientation, while she was waiting for Principia Martindale's bus to arrive, she was still unable to decide if she loved him or not. Standing in the Greyhound terminal, she kept trying to talk herself into a better mood while attempting to display an air of tranquillity.

Thank God it's Invincible time again, she said to herself as Principia's bus turned into the station. I've got to have some inspiration to clear my mind. I've just got to find my faith again and get myself straightened out once and for all, so right now I'm going to think about a long straight line and maybe that will help.

While the bus was rolling to a stop, Principia was praying that Miss Cassy was there to meet her. "I don't know what I'll do if she's not here," she said, looking out the window. "This place is so dreary. The streets are just filthy and I do wish that the people who live here could come to New Bethel for a day. That's all it would take for them to see the light."

Still in the bus, she scanned the crowd for someone who might prove to be the Famous Corinda, as she was known to her friends and the press. Then suddenly she spotted her standing in the midst of the crowd, as obvious as a lily among thorns: a tall thin brunette wearing a cowgirl outfit made of denim and decorated with silver studs. She wore white marching boots with cowboy heels and tassels. Her cowboy hat, also white, was embroidered with silver threads, and her short white cape had COWGIRLS FOR CHRIST written in sequins across the back.

She seemed to occupy the brightest spot in the dark terminal, and, when Principia saw her, a warmth which she knew was the Holy Spirit manifesting itself at a time of great need rippled through her entire body.

Principia, the first to leave the bus, rushed up to Miss Cassy, who was standing motionless, as though in a trance, and listening to the Brothers of Temperance singing "Jesus Met the Woman at the Well." The music was coming from a portable cassette, which during Invincible Orientation she carried with her wherever she went, even into department stores, banks and hospitals.

On coming closer Principia noticed that the Director of Invincibles wore no make-up and no jewelry except a diamond ring

and a silver name tag that held her cape together and told everyone who didn't already know exactly who she was: Miss Corinda
Cassy.

"Oh, Miss Cassy, Miss Cassy, thank the good Lord you arrived in time to meet me," said Principia, squeezing the woman's
fingers. "I'm so sorry I didn't wear a name tag too. It would have
made it so much easier for you to find me, but I didn't think of it,
and I realize now that I should have."

Through the cassette, which Miss Cassy was holding to her
bosom, came a piano interlude, and then the Brothers of Temperance were heard again: "Some glad morning when this life is
over, I'll fly away. Oh, glory, glory, I'll fly away."

Still thinking of Larry Wayne and how much she loved him,
the Director of Invincibles turned down the volume and looked at
Principia earnestly. "Peace! Be still, Principiaaa," she said, drawing out her words as was her habit when trying to project sincerity. "I knew our recognition would be instantaneous for Heee . . .
has placed us together."

Her voice rose and fell in pitch and intensity, yet when she
spoke of the Deity, Principia noticed that Miss Cassy's entire body
trembled as though charged with an electrical current.

"Oh, Miss Cassy," she said, "I would recognize you anywhere
in this world because you sparkle with inner peace and light up
this old bus station like it was the palace of a king. How I admire
you so much and everything you have done."

"Word of *your* good work has spread far and wide," continued the Director. "We feel especially privileged to have one so
young and yet so *old* serving as an Invinnn-cible for the very first
time." As she spoke she gestured fluidly, flapping her cape to and
fro like a swan drying its wings or an angel who felt out of place
in public.

She has been placed on earth to do great things, Principia
thought, watching Miss Cassy's eyes flash with a radiance more
brilliant than anything the first-year Invincible had ever seen. "I
know my guardian angel looks exactly like you, Miss Cassy," she
said with worship written all over her face.

"My heart is made glad by your words," responded the Famous Corinda. Her voice was high-pitched, had a windy softness
and a vibrant tremolo that caused Principia to grow weak in her
knees.

"Miss Cassy, I want you to know that I feel like rejoicing," said Principia. "You're an example for us all to follow."

"He . . . has done it all," said Miss Cassy, lifting her hands above her head. "A piano cannot play of its own accord; it requires a musician, and only a musician who is in tune with God can make that instrument truly speak to the hearts and minds of others. I am but an instrument, Principia. Heee . . . has blessed me, loved me, tuned me for His purpose alone." She lowered her hands and began rubbing her diamond ring. " 'Have Thine own way, Lord,' " she whispered as though singing a chromatic scale. " 'Have Thine own way. Thou art the potter . . . I am the clay.' "

"Oh, I've heard so much about your personal testimony," said Principia. "I can hardly wait to hear it with my own two ears."

"That will be today," replied Miss Cassy humbly. "The others are waiting for us now, so we must hurry."

While Principia collected her suitcase, Miss Cassy brought her white Cadillac around to the front of the bus terminal, and soon they were on their way to True Vine Baptist Church on the outskirts of town. "I find that I cannot go a step without a hymn to accompany me there," she said, putting another tape in the cassette. It was her favorite recording by the soul-winning quintet, The All For Jesus Singers. Corinda played the first hymn, "O Master Let Me Walk with Thee," over and over because she thought it was the very best on the tape and never wanted it to end.

While the music played on, they spoke lovingly of their mutual friend Brother Hemphill and what a good job he was doing as the shepherd of Hillister Baptist College. "He serves his Lord with gladness," said the Cowgirl for Christ, "and for that reason I have once again placed my trust in his tender hands. Yesterday I arrived in San Antonio from my office and ranch in South Texas, and today, the beginning of our orientation, I received two telegrams; one stated that Marcos Valdez had broken his back in a fall off a horse and could not work with us this summer—naturally I was saddened—and the other stated that Janet Murphy, who worked with us last summer and was magnificent, has been called back to Star, her hometown, in order to organize a church newspaper, which I'm sure, if the Lord is willing, will be a blessing to all who read and enjoy it. As you can see, this might have created a major catastrophe, but of course, it did not. The Lord led me straight to the telephone and I called Brother Hemphill at Hillister Baptist and I said, 'Send me a girl who can play the piano and a boy who can speak Spanish and my worries will be over.' And praise God, our dear brother said he would act upon my needs that very minute. He said that he would pray earnestly over the matter and by the middle of the week he would be able to send me two Invincibles to fill the gap."

O Lord, Principia thought. Billy Ray is going to be chosen. I just know he is. The future is unfolding before my very eyes, and I thank you for this insight.

Then she remembered that Billy Ray's Spanish was almost as bad as his singing and that Philip Hernandez would most likely be chosen instead. Still, she prayed hard that her friend might have a chance.

"Brother Hemphill is such a hard worker, I'm sure he'll be able to pick the right two," said the Invincible as The All For Jesus Singers moved on to their second song, "Saviour Like a Shepherd Lead Us," followed by "I Am Thine O Lord" and then "Rescue the Perishing."

Before the last song was over they arrived at True Vine Baptist Church located five miles outside the city limits on Interstate 35, across the highway from the Holiday Inn. THE INVINCIBLES ARE HERE! had been spelled out on the motel's marquee just that morning. "It's so nice to be expected," said Principia as she looked over at the sign. Then she followed Miss Cassy into Fellowship Hall, which was located in a Quonset hut adjacent to the sanctuary and bursting with activity.

Many of the Invincibles were gathered around the piano and singing, "Take Me as I Am." Those lifting their voices in praise and thanksgiving were Herbie Stout and Felicita Quintana, who had served as Invincibles the year before. Herbie was nineteen years old, short, wore bow ties and his hair slicked back. Felicita was a foot taller than Herbie and older by two and a half months. Her hair was bobbed for the summer, and she was a second-year student at Sam Houston State. Standing next to them were Beverly Allen Scott, Travis Bacon and Modena Law, who were juniors at Howard Payne College and were serving as summer missionaries for the first time. They were proud to be wearing blue work-

men's shirts that Modena had found on sale and had embroidered
I AM INVINCIBLE across the backs. Beverly Allen and Travis were
planning to enter the ministry of music; they were both tenors,
but Beverly Allen's specialty was the keyboard. He had long arms,
long fingers—could reach an octave and a half—and wore a size
thirteen shoe. Travis, however, was small and self-conscious about
it, but Miss Cassy had put him at ease when they first met by
saying: "God does his biggest things through his smallest people."
It was one of her favorite sayings.

Off to one side of the singers were Robert James, Beth Murphy and Cynthia Sullivan, all wearing white short-sleeved sweat
shirts with Councilor–Alto Frio Baptist Encampment written in
red on both sides. With serious expressions they were sitting on
folding chairs and shedding light on the Book of Revelation while
J. C. Sweeney was sharpening his pencils and Pamela Brown and
Charlotte Cottongame, who had both tied for Homecoming
Queen at East Texas Baptist College, were sharing their favorite
scriptures. Charlotte maintained that her favorite verse in the entire Bible was Proverbs thirty-one, ten. "Who can find a virtuous
woman? for her price *is* far above rubies." But Pamela said that
she had never cared too much for that verse because she felt it
carried a misleading message. Standing near them, Jack Yoakum,
whose hair was falling out at the age of twenty, and Sue Rose,
who was still wearing her lower-jaw retainer, were talking about
the television evangelist Thessalonia Magdalena Montgomery.
Henry Taylor, a ministerial student at Baylor University, joined
their conversation by saying, "You know she had to think a long
time to come up with a name like that."

"Well, she most certainly did not," said Sissy Cisneros, a
Mexican-American who was slight of build and had energy to
burn. "I once met Sister Thessalonia Magdalena and she looked
me straight in the eye and told me that the Lord had given her
that name when she was saved at the age of fourteen, and I know
she was telling me the truth too because a liar will never look you
in the eye when he's trying to tell you something that isn't so."

"But that doesn't sound right to me," said Melinda Young,
who wore her hair in pigtails and refused to put on a drop of
make-up. "I was saved when I was four years old and the Lord
didn't give me a new name."

"He does not rename everyone He takes into the fold," said E. E. More, who was about to enter the seminary in Fort Worth. "Not all of us meet the Lord at the same time, at the same age *or* in the same way. Not all of us have the same relationship with Him either. Surely, Melinda, it has not taken you all this time to figure that out." E. E. More was on his way to becoming a youth director. He was blond, terribly athletic and wore his hair in a flattop.

Miss Cassy introduced Principia to her summer partner, Sissy Cisneros, a second-year Invincible from San Angelo and a speech and religious drama major at Mary Hardin Baylor, where she had recently played the title role in *Ruth*, a musical adaptation taken from the Bible story but updated to the present time.

Before the two girls had time to get acquainted, Miss Cassy asked for everyone's attention, and to the entire group she introduced Principia Martindale as the youngest person to ever serve as an Invincible and one of the most dedicated and celebrated Christians on any campus in the world.

Then twenty-two Invincibles sat down and listened as Miss Cassy gave the official welcome, the one she had given every year for going-on ten years. "Today," she said, "we are going to experience and express some of the spiritual excitement that's ahead of you." She started at a high pitch and gradually allowed her voice to fall and rise again. Principia almost expected to see her levitate.

"Weee are Invinnn-cibles," continued Miss Cassy. "Weee are Invinnn-cibles because *weee* are invinnn-cible, and we are Invinnn-cibles because: the hearts as well as the minds of men, women and children everywhere are hungry for spiritual food; because: men, women and children everywhere of all races and nationaliteees want to know better how to walk with God, how to talk with God, and how to listen to God speaking in their heartsss . . ."

As she spoke, she seemed to be focused on something in the distance, something or someone she could see and Principia could not. O Lord, make me holy enough to be able to see what Miss Cassy is looking at right now, prayed the youngest Invincible with all her heart, soul and might.

Slowly Miss Cassy traced her career as a wife, and widow, as a singer, an actress, a talk-show hostess, a world traveler and, finally, as a Christian. While thinking of Larry Wayne Johnson and how much she missed him, she admitted that it took her a long time to find her place on earth, but she assured each Invincible sitting before her that she was walking with the Lord at last and could not ask for more happiness than she already had.

"I had townhouses and bank accounts in Paris-France, London-England and Athens-Greece," she said, "and I thought I was happy, but I was not. The more I traveled, the more I realized that my automobiles were always running on *full*, but I was always running on *empty* and had been for my entire life. So, on a lonely stretch of road outside Athens, I literally stopped, opened the door to my Jaguar and asked Jesus to sit in the driver's seat. I moved over and asked Him, the Son of God, to release me of my guilt, to come into my life, fill my heart and love me, a sinner turned loose in the world—and before I knew it He had bestowed upon me a thousand blessings and it was then that He led me to create this, the Invinnn-cible Program . . ."

She ended her testimony in the same way she ended all her public speeches: "When I was a child back home in Alice, I wanted to be a star on the silver screen, but when I became a woman I met the Maker of stars and He saved my soul. And now, fellow Christians, I beseech you before it's too late. 'Give of your best to the Master; give of the strength of your youth. Throw your soul's fresh glowing ardor into the battle for truth.' I have given my all; won't you, if you have not already, give of your all as well. The Master is depending on each of us to do so."

Long after her last word, she continued standing there with arms outstretched, an angelic smile upon her face. "She's so personable and dynamic," said Principia to her partner.

"Yes, and I was so impressed to see that you wrote down every word that came out of her mouth," replied Sissy, crossing and uncrossing her legs. "Last year I wrote down Miss Cassy's entire testimony, word for word, and committed it to memory, and I want you to know that she hasn't changed a word of it but has added three new sentences. Isn't that something to think about? I would never have known this if I hadn't taken good notes."

"It's so important to have a pencil with a good sharp point and a clean eraser," said Principia.

"And some paper to write on," added Sissy. "Oh, I'm so glad we're going to be partners, because we see eye to eye on everything. We're going to bring spiritual food to those who need it most."

"I'm so happy I could shout," said Principia.

Miss Cassy called on E. E. More to deliver the closing prayer after which, arm in arm, they all walked across the highway to the Holiday Inn, where a banquet table had been made ready for them. When everyone had sat down, Miss Cassy took her place at the head of the table and said, "Tonight I am surrounded by twenty-two Invincibles. Later on this week we will be twenty-four in all. Our beloved Brother Hemphill is sending us a talented musician, plus a gifted linquist. We will be so happy to receive them, whoever they are, and we will each take turns in briefing them on all they have missed."

"God speed their journey to us," said Sissy Cisneros, while Principia Martindale bowed her head and stared at her hands.

Our Dear Most Gracious Heavenly Father, she prayed. I have the feeling that Billy Ray will be here soon, and if I am right, I thank You in advance.

 6

During the first few days of orientation, all the Invincibles learned to love Principia as a lifelong friend. Her zealous personality was contagious, and besides that she allowed everyone to speak to her at length about his or her calling. She would take her new friends back to her room, three or four at a time, for long midnight discussions and getting-to-know-each-other-better sessions. Everyone noticed right away that her room looked as though it had not been lived in; everything was in its place. Her dresses were arranged in the order she intended to wear them, her study guides were pleasingly displayed on top of the bureau as though they were travel brochures, and her suitcases were carefully hidden in the top of the closet. Charlotte Cottongame noticed that the wastebaskets were always empty, and two soaps, one for the face and one for the hands and body, were prominently displayed in the lavatory, which looked as though it had not seen a drop of water in years. But what struck Sissy Cisneros as most admirable was the fact that Principia had brought her own monogrammed towels, washcloths, sheets and pillowcases.

"It's so important," said Principia, "to feel at home no matter where you happen to be. I also brought two boxes of premoistened towelettes. You never can tell when you'll need to wash your face and hands, so I try to keep plenty of these things around. They come twelve to a box and are individually packaged in foil so they won't dry out."

Beth Murphy was amazed. "You simply think of everything, don't you," she said. "You're the most organized person I've ever seen."

"But I've always lived this way," replied Principia. "Sometimes I get so mixed up inside that I have to have everything around me in perfect order, and this helps me to feel as though I'm getting myself straightened out. Now last night, for example, I washed the windows inside and out because the spots on them bother me, especially when the sun comes up and I'm trying to read my Bible."

"I just love the way she has experienced and expressed her love for God," said Modena Law, who was studying to become a nutritionist and hoping to be called to Bangladesh. It was Monday morning and Modena and a few others had gathered in the lobby of the Holiday Inn. They were waiting for Miss Cassy to come down for breakfast and all they could talk about was Principia.

"She's so personable and dynamic," said Sissy Cisneros.

"That's because she's moved over and put Jesus in the driver's seat," said Herbie Stout, straightening his tie.

"She's the most multifaceted Invinnn-cible we've ever had," said Miss Cassy, joining the tail end of the conversation. "Her personality is sooo strong," she added, trying not to show a growing alarm. She was thinking of Nena Farrell, an ex-Invincible who had almost transformed the program. Nena had wanted to reorganize everything and had rallied much support from the other summer missionaries. This can't happen again, Corinda thought. This program is my creation and I won't have anyone telling me what to do. I have always known what is best.

Then she looked into the eyes of each Invincible standing before her, and, trying to bring a tone of warmth and sincerity into her voice, she said: "There are times when Principia makes me ashamed because I have not done more for God."

"She puts us all to shame," said Herbie Stout. All the other Invincibles agreed with him especially after Principia gave her personal testimony into which she incorporated a chalk talk as well.

On Tuesday afternoon, the third day of orientation, after the session on the proper way to make a visitation in the home of a nonbeliever, Principia asked Beverly Allen Scott if he would play "Softly and Tenderly" while she drew and talked. Beverly Allen agreed, so Principia started her preparations. First she twisted her hair together at the nape of her neck and forced it into the collar of her lilac dress. "I just hate for it to get in my way," she said. Then she balanced her blackboard on a fold-up easel, which she steadied with one hand while she drew with the other.

"The Lord means so much to me I hardly know where to begin," she said, making eye contact with everyone in the room. "So I'm starting with my favorite color, which is purple, and my favorite verse, which is John three, sixteen: 'For God so loved the world, that he gave his only begotten Son, that whosoever believeth in him should not perish, but have everlasting life.' "

She ran the purple chalk over the blackboard several times while speaking above Beverly Allen's piano playing. "I came to know God when I was three years old sitting on my father's lap and listening to the beautiful story of the crucifixion being read aloud by my mother. Now, at this time, I'm going to add some yellow because it reminds me of my mother, and next I'm going to add some blue because that's my father's color."

So far no one could guess what she was drawing, but they all knew, coming from Principia, that it had to be something inspirational.

"At the tender age of three," continued the chalk-talk artist, "God's divine plan unfolded before me and I saw that which He wanted me to do—serve Him for the rest of my life."

Then she added some squiggly orange lines that looked like clouds. "Oh! she's drawing a sunset," exclaimed Modena Law.

"And the most beautiful one I've ever seen, except those that God paints for us each day," said Sissy.

"I have failed Him in so many ways," confessed Principia as she added more orange lines. "My heart is troubled for not living up to His daily expectations of me. For you see, my parents are counting on me. My pastor is counting on me. My friends are counting on me. But what's more important: My God is also counting on me."

She put down the orange chalk and took up the red. Her hand moved more rapidly than before. Beverly Allen sensed that she was approaching the climax and began accelerating the tempo. It was then that she noticed Miss Cassy. The Director of Invincibles was sitting over to one side, and Principia could see her out of the corner of her eye. Miss Cassy's lips were moving, but she wasn't speaking. She was mouthing the words Principia spoke.

"I was the only child," she said, using red chalk in one hand

and green in the other, while Miss Cassy, unaware of what she was doing, repeated the sentence to herself. "I was born to loving parents late in their lives, even after the age of childbearing. I was their miracle; I mean the world to them. In their waking and sleeping I am still their pride and joy, but the Lord takes first place in my life. I have trusted Him all the way. I have taken up my cross and followed Him, even when He has led me to strange-out-of-the-way places. There have been a few times when I seemed to want one thing and God another, but now I realize that my purpose is quite simple: I am but a servant put on this earth; I carry a bucket of water for my Lord."

"Oh, I just love her," said Sissy Cisneros. "She gives simple answers to complex questions."

"Yes, I know," said J. C. Sweeney, gesturing with his glasses —he was on his way to becoming a religious journalist. "Yesterday she compared the Holy Trinity to a chocolate pie cut in three equal sections. 'Each slice is different, but it's still the same pie,' she said, and do you know, that was the first time in my life that I felt like I understood the Father, Son and Holy Ghost."

"Sometimes she makes me feel funny," said Melinda Young, twisting her pigtails. "There's something about her eyes that makes me nervous to look at her."

Then Principia stopped drawing and faced her audience. "It's so hot in here," she said. "Can someone open a window. I can feel my blood pressure going sky-high."

"But the windows are already open," said Travis Bacon.

"She looks like she's worked herself into a fever," replied E. E. More. "I sure hope she's not about to faint."

Principia stood there swaying from left to right. "I just hate it when I get too excited," she said, steadying herself on the piano.

E. E. More moved to the front pew—just in case Principia needed him—and everyone else tried to guess what she had drawn and colored. Robert James said she had depicted the painted desert and a sunset combined, but Sue Rose said she was unable to tell which was desert and which was sky. "That's why it's so meaningful," shouted Jack Yoakum just before Felicita Quintana stood up and said that it looked just like an Easter egg to her.

J. C. Sweeney had a different attitude, however. He had just made an A-plus in Art Appreciation at Sam Houston State, so he told everyone that the painting was an abstraction of Principia's innermost feelings about God.

" 'Place your hands in the hands of the man from Galilee,' " said Principia after the room was silent again. "I believe in the second coming of Christ. I believe that His coming is for sure, but His arrival will be like a thief in the night: unexpected by many." Then she turned the chalk board upside-down and revealed a portrait of Jesus on which she had used every color on the rainbow and then some.

When everyone gasped in unison, Principia felt a surge of energy and knew that the power of God was working alive, filling the room and each Invincible with divine strength. Travis Bacon said that he had not felt so happy in his entire life, Melinda Young said she was speechless and Sissy Cisneros began clapping her hands and shouting, "Praise His most holy and precious name, Jesus!" while Felicita Quintana said the Lord's Prayer in Spanish, her first language, and the one she always used when she prayed.

Miss Cassy noted the reaction, and before she realized it she had leaned over to Herbie Stout and said, "I labor under the strain of toil, the fret of care. If only I had Principia's energy and youth. Knowing what I know right now, I could be of great service to Jesus, who is forever near and dear. I could also bring more happiness into the world as well as my own life."

After she had spoken, her words disturbed her. Precious Larry Wayne is right, she thought. I'm beginning to sound like a broken record and so is everyone else.

"Miss Cassy, we must rest above the troubled waves of life, and rely on God to grant us wisdom," replied Herbie Stout as Principia continued her testimony.

" 'Jesus Paid It All,' " she quoted from one of her favorite hymns. " 'All to Him I owe. Sin hath left a crimson stain. He washed it white as snow.' " Her lips were quivering; she was on the verge of tears, but she refused to cry because there was so much more she wanted to say. She held herself under control as long as possible, but when her arms and legs began trembling, E. E. More jumped up from his seat and gave her all the support he could.

"You feel feverish," he said, touching her brow. "Are you sure you're all right?"

"I sometimes run a low-grade temperature in the summer months," said Principia, accepting the support of his arm. "Oh, E. E. More, it's so good to have a strong Christian to lean on." He guided her to the first pew. She sat down and began drying her eyes on her sleeve.

"You've given so much of yourself you've become weak, Principia," said E. E. "We thank you for your extreme generosity; Miss Cassy thanks you; and what's more important, God thanks you as well."

Miss Cassy stood before the group, and with a serious, almost painful expression on her face, she spoke in quiet tones and carefully chosen words. "It is with deepest concern and admiration that I stand here before you dedicated young Christians," she said with her hands folded reverently at her waist and her cowgirl cape falling over one shoulder. "Never have we ever had an Invincible as totally dedicated as Principia Martindale. Her passionate conviction shames me. For when I was a youth, I did not serve the Lord with gladness as she is doing. I was a greedy, envious young woman, but when I met the Lord, He took the envy and greed away, He washed me white as snow, and gave me peace of mind, and therefore, I am able to say—without envy, without jealousy but with great admiration—that if I had to relive my life I would want to be Principia Martindale. I would want her courage and commitment, her strength and her compassion. In only a few short days she has charged the air around us with her magnetic personality, and I'm convinced that under the right circumstances, surrounded by the right people and with right prayers in our hearts, *we* could assist her in moving mountains singlehandedly."

7

After presenting her chalk talk and testimony, it took Principia
the rest of the afternoon to regain her energy, but by evening she
had fully recovered and was eager to discuss Christian doubt with
her partner, who was of the opinion that doubting increased her
faith and gave her new insights into the workings of the Lord, an
idea that was not unknown to Principia for she too believed that
doubting was healthy and necessary even though she tried not to
allow herself to do it very often.

When Sissy left, Principia did her hand wash and hung it up
to dry on a cord she stretched across the bathroom. She had
brought the clothesline, clothespins and detergent from home. She
had also brought a traveling iron, a can of spray starch and some
spare buttons in case of an emergency. While her hand wash was
drying she stripped her bed, remade it again so the sheets would
fit as tight as possible and then took her bath with her two favorite soaps. After her scripture reading and her prayers she went to
sleep easily and with a sense of well-being, but the next morning
she woke up with a feeling of unworthiness.

"Lord, I feel so useless," she said, standing before the window
and watching the sun rise over the low hills. "Father always wanted to go out west. It seems so wrong for me to be here without
him."

She put on her faded blue bathrobe, which had once belonged to Aunt Wilda, and sat before the dressing mirror without
liking anything she saw. At sixteen, wrinkles were already form-
ing on her forehead and there were lines around her eyes that

were not caused by laughing. "I feel as though I've gone straight from childhood to middle age with no stops in between," she said, examining the hair at the tip of her widow's peak and wondering if it was beginning to turn gray; she was afraid that it was.

Studying her face in the mirror, she realized she was listening to a choir singing faintly. She was unable to course the sound or name the song, but she knew it was a hymn and that Miss Cassy had to be nearby. The music came closer and closer to her room, and when it was just outside her door, she threw it open and there stood Corinda Cassy—tape player in hand—wearing a white cowgirl outfit with a sprig of artificial dogwood in her hat. Next to her stood Philip Hernandez, wearing a BSU sweat shirt over faded jeans, and behind him was Tawnya Louise Baker in a sun dress and sandals. Her toenails were painted bright red.

For what seemed like eternity to Principia, no one spoke. She felt as though she had stopped breathing and that the slightest draft would blow her over.

"Oh look," exclaimed Miss Cassy. "Principia Martindale is speechless. The Lord has struck her speechless. I just knew this would happen when she saw her two friends. Now, before anyone says a word, I want to find the right song for this beautiful moment." She rewound the tape for a few seconds and then pressed Play again. "Just a Closer Walk with Thee," sung by the Melody Masters, filled the corridor. "This song stirrrrs my heart and soul," said Miss Cassy. "I know it does yours too."

"I can feel it all the way through me," said Tawnya with a slight smile.

"I'm going to leave you two girls alone until we assemble for breakfast," said the Director of Invincibles. "Principia, I want you to brief Tawnya on everything of importance that we have covered during the past three days."

After Philip and Miss Cassy left, Tawnya and Principia continued to stand there, one in the hall and one in the room, and stare at each other. God, please help me to love her, thought Principia, even if it's just for the orientation period and not for life. Then she turned on her best Christian smile and said, "Please come into my room, Tawnya Louise. Miss Cassy is so right. I'm overcome with joy to see you here. So far you've missed out on three glorious, Spirit-filled days, but I think I can catch you up very fast."

Lord, make me sensitive to Tawnya's needs, she prayed. Please give me the words to better express how I feel.

"First, I'm going to tell you a few things you might not want to hear," said Principia, trying to smooth down her hair with both hands. She felt dowdy in Tawnya's presence, always had, but she had never admitted it to anyone and not too often to herself. "I'm going to tell you these things for your own good, and nobody else's."

The two girls sat on opposite sides of the bed.

"Tawnya Louise," she said, squeezing her fingers until the ends were blue, "I know you come from a prominent family and that you don't need the money you'll be making this summer, so I'm going to ask Miss Cassy to take us shopping this afternoon so we can buy you some appropriate work clothes. What you're wearing is not right. That sun dress makes you look cheap, and a Christian is anything but cheap. All those bracelets make you look common, and a Christian is anything but common. And those sandals are decidedly the wrong choice because they reveal too much of your painted toenails. Now what I'm thinking is this: In the places where you will be working, painted toenails might mean something entirely different from what you think. They might work against you, Tawnya, so it will be best to cover them up. Don't get me wrong, I'm not going to ask you to take the polish off, but I am going to encourage you to wear some sturdy shoes. What you do in the privacy of your own room is your business alone, but when you come parading around in that next-to-nothing-of-a-dress, and with blood red toenails and all those bracelets, and lipstick, and rouge, and eyeliner, well, people are going to get the wrong idea. The thing you've got to keep in mind is that you're no longer at Hillister Baptist College. Where you'll be working this summer no one will know your father and his fine reputation and if you don't watch out, you just might find yourself in a lot of trouble because of it. What you've got to do is ask God to deliver you from this earthborn taint."

"I don't appreciate your advice," said Tawnya Louise, "and I won't take one word of it. Also, I'm not about to sit here and argue with you because I've argued with your type before and it never does any good." She got up and walked to the door.

"Thanks for briefing me on what's gone on this week. I see that I haven't missed a thing."

That afternoon, Wednesday, Philip Hernandez gave his personal testimony first in Spanish and then in English. He stood before the group and quietly, reverently and with abundant sincerity said: "When I was thirteen years old I met the Lord in a frog pond in South Texas. I was gigging frogs, and the Lord was gigging me, and, as you can see, he got me too . . ."

"I have never heard anything so meaningful and significant in a long long time," said Principia into her praying hands. "I can see perfectly now. The reason why Billy Ray was not chosen is because this experience is going to be so rewarding for Philip Hernandez. Never before has he allowed his inner light to shine forth as it is this very minute."

After Philip sat down, Tawnya Louise came forward and took her place behind the baby grand piano. It seemed to Principia that Tawnya could not wait to strike the first chord and that she started playing before she completely settled herself on the stool.

Tawnya Louise shook her head; her long brown hair fell over one shoulder and touched the keyboard. She always began that way; it was more or less her trademark, as was the song she was about to sing. Her fingers traveled all over the keys before picking out the simple melody and allowing it to stand alone. Then she threw back her head and sang:

> "My father is omnipotent
> And that you can't deny
> A God of might and miracles
> It's written in the sky.
> It took a miracle to put the stars in place . . ."

Attempting to convey God's divine love and forgiveness, Principia stared intensely into Tawnya's eyes. In turn, Tawnya gave the song her total energy, returned Principia's intense stare and sang directly to her as though the words bore meaning for Principia alone.

Miss Cassy noticed that both girls seemed to be overcome with emotion when their eyes met. "Oh look! They're on the very same wavelength," she said to J. C. Sweeney, who nodded his head in agreement. Throughout the special music she watched them carefully, and after the last note, even before Tawnya had left the piano, the Director of Invincibles stood up and addressed the entire group.

"I am proud to be an instrument fully tuned and steered by the strong and mighty arm of Jesus," she said with abundant modesty; she was beginning to believe her own words once again. "There is a *Jesus explosion* going on around us. Do you feel it? It-is-here. This beautiful testimony and this beautiful music have filled me with a true worship experience, and I now know why Janet Murphy was called back to Star and why Marcos Valdez broke his back. They had served as Invincibles before, and through them the Lord was telling me that we need new blood in our midst. I thank Him for sending Philip Hernandez with his gift of words, and Tawnya Louise with her gift of music, for during her beautiful special the Lord saw fit to touch my heart with a prophecy, and at this time I will share *some* of it with you."

When she realized that she had gotten carried away with her speech, she thought of Larry Wayne, considered what he would have said had he been there, and for a moment she wanted to sit back down again, but something inside kept urging her to go on so she closed her eyes and continued speaking as though the words were at that moment being placed in her mouth. "The Lord our God is telling me to change things around," she said, holding the corners of her cowgirl cape and raising her arms above her head as though she were a winged messenger of the Lord. She could feel the Invincibles resting in the palms of her hands; she enjoyed the excitement of standing before an audience and found herself wishing that she had never left the stage.

"E. E. More and Travis Bacon are in my thoughts," she continued. "They are not supposed to work together this summer because they worked together last summer. Travis is to work with our new Invincible Philip Hernandez; E. E. is to work with Beverly Allen Scott instead of Philip and Cynthia Sullivan, who was supposed to work with Tawnya Louise Baker, is now working with Sissy Cisneros, and Tawnya Louise, who was sent by the

Lord at the eleventh hour, has now been called to be the partner of her dear friend Principia Martindale."

"Like hell I have," said Tawnya, but no one heard her.

"I can see admiration in their eyes," continued Miss Cassy. "And because in so many ways large and small, they are so different they will find out before the summer is over that they are so much alike as well. Isn't that a wonderful thing we've just been told?"

"Just thrilling, thank you," said Tawnya under her breath.

Sissy Cisneros broke into tears and ran from the room; Principia stared at Miss Cassy in total disbelief, and finally managed to put a smile on her face, but J. C. Sweeney thought it looked more like a scar made by a dull knife. The Director of Invincibles stood before them in all her radiance, her arms still uplifted, her cape shimmering behind her and the jewels on her winged eyeglasses sparkling like words of God going straight to the heart.

I must try to understand what the Lord means by all this, thought Principia, her lips quivering, her eyes filling with tears. I have never yet lost control, and I never will either. She stood up, but her legs would not allow her to move; not even to take a step. "I'm so happy to have Tawnya Louise Baker for a summer companion," she said. "I'm just as happy to have Tawnya as I was to have Sissy. I'm sure we'll work beautifully together."

"The Lord has spoken," added J. C. Sweeney solemnly.

"Has he now," whispered Tawnya Louise, resting her forehead on the keyboard. "I could be back home on the beach, and if it weren't for my father I *would* be there too."

This must be a big mistake, Principia thought as she sat back down. Either that or it's a terrible nightmare, but if it turns out to be for real, I must remember that God has a purpose for everything He does.

She kept telling herself that she could love and work with Tawnya just as easily as anyone else, and before dinner was over she was beginning to believe it, but that evening in her room she changed her opinion once again. She was down on her knees and praying earnestly over the matter when she remembered that Tawnya had grown up in Baytown. "Now I understand," she said. "Lord, thank you for clearing my mind."

Principia had always been skeptical of anyone who lived too

close to saltwater. Her father had had an elder brother, Simon, who had shot himself on a Galveston pier, and no one in the family had ever been able to determine what he was doing there either. Then, her mother's baby sister, Wilda, went to live near Corpus Christi, and after that she was never known to have uttered a sentence that made very much sense. Principia's mother swore that Sister Wilda completely lost touch with the world when she moved to the Gulf Coast, where the salt air rusted out what was left of her brain. Wilma had always considered her sister a religious fanatic, but was convinced that she had gotten worse after she went to live in a Baptist women's shelter on the Gulf. It was then that she took to wrapping up in sheets and roaming up and down the beaches with a staff in her hand and speaking in an unknown language to her imaginary sheep.

Principia had never believed that her aunt was as crazy as everyone seemed to think, but she did believe that living on the beach had something to do with the fact that she often resorted to cursing rather than praising the Lord.

"Salt air is simply not good for the mind and that's all there is to it," Principia had often heard her mother say. When she remembered that Tawnya was from the Gulf Coast she thought of Aunt Wilda and became so uneasy she decided to tell her partner exactly how she felt.

After their evening class on how to weave potholders in the shape of a cross, how to spatter paint, stencil, trace and skip rope for God, she went back to her room and practiced her speech:

"I hope you don't take me wrong or anything like that, Tawnya Louise, but I wouldn't, if I were you, go around telling everybody where you're from because it's not a very nice-sounding place. Now I know you're a nice person and all that, but I don't want others we might meet this summer to get the wrong impression of us, that's all."

She rehearsed a time or two, then armed herself with her white Bible and went to Tawnya's room upstairs at the opposite end of the hall. Over in a corner were three boxes of art supplies stacked one on top of the other. Tawnya was studying to be an elementary school teacher and during the year she had collected every scrap of anything that could be used again.

Oh, I'm so selfish with my material possessions, Principia

thought, realizing that she had two closets filled with art supplies she had not thought to bring. In some ways I ought to be more like Tawnya Louise. She really does want this job after all.

"I just came here to tell you, Tawnya Louise, that I'm so happy we're going to work together," said Principia. "I think it's wonderful that you've brought all these supplies along. I realize now that I have a great deal to learn from you, and I wouldn't want it any other way."

Tawnya smiled and embraced her partner while motioning for her other visitor to stay out on the balcony, but he did not. Principia turned around to find a man wearing a Texaco uniform. He was either covered with grease or was naturally dark, she could not tell which. His shirt was unbuttoned to the waist. The hair on his chest was thick, long and grew in a straight line into his pants. The sight of him caused Principia to turn her head quickly. She took Tawnya by the arm, led her into the hall and over by the ice machine where they could talk in private.

"Who is he?" she asked. "Where did he come from? What's he doing here? And don't you know better than to wear those tight-looking pants in front of a man? They're the most vulgar things I've ever seen; why just look at the way they ride up on you. Now if we're going to be partners, you go right now and take them off. Do you hear me?"

"I'll do no such thing," said Tawnya Louise, puffing on a Salem. She felt awfully proud to be smoking in front of Miss Cassy's favorite Invincible.

"Don't make light of this," said Principia. "And put out that cigarette because it makes you look trashy. Now, what I want you to do is go right this very minute and throw that dirty-looking person, whoever he is, out of your room, and don't ever let me catch him there again either. Is that clear?"

"You've made yourself very clear," said Tawnya as the man in uniform came into the hall and saluted Principia with a bottle of Pearl. "The best beer ever brewed," he said. "Named after my sister, so it's gotta be good. Be happy to share it with you."

"Thank you but no thank you," said Principia, staring hard at Tawnya.

"Then I'll be happy to fix your flats," said the man, lifting his eyebrows.

"And I'll be happy to save your soul," said Principia Martindale, turning on him face to face. "It needs saving and I'm beginning to think hers does too."

"You can say anything about me you want to," said Tawnya, while the man looked on. "You can even try to get me fired if you want to, but I tell you right now, I will not work with you for one minute this summer because I've had enough scripture quoted in my face. I'm a preacher's kid, remember? Everyone in my father's congregation thought I was sweet and precious and good. God, how I got tired of all that. The good girls were always snobs, little shits, if you know what I mean, and I'm not so sure you do because you're too close to being one yourself."

"I've had about enough of this," said the man in uniform. He went back inside the room and closed the door.

Principia was thankful that they were alone once again. "Tawnya Louise, I'm going to give you some advice," she said, trying to stay calm. "You have lived on that trashy Gulf Coast too long, and you've got to get away from there for a little while. This summer will be so good for you."

"Those beaches saved my life, by God," said Tawnya. "I walked them day and night."

"And," said Principia, staring reverently into Tawnya's eyes, "you were not alone. You had someone to comfort you."

"There have always been men in my life," replied Tawnya.

"But I was talking about God," said Principia, wrinkling up her face.

"Well, I wasn't," said Tawnya Louise. "I was the first to flirt with the boys in junior high. It was my idea to go behind the football stadium at lunch, or to the old culvert that was big enough to stand up inside. It was always my idea to take the boys into the church too. There was a tiny room above the baptismal pool, and that's where we went. My father raised me to be a good girl, and I swear to God I've hated and despised every good girl I've ever met and I hope to Jesus I never have to meet another one of you as long as I live."

"God loves you, Tawnya Louise," said Principia. "He really and truly does; you may not believe it right now but one day you will."

"I'm not sure who he loves," said Tawnya. "What I believe

depends entirely on what side of the bed I get up on, but most of the time I don't believe in anything."

"Mortal mind," said Principia, "is made up of many ignorant beliefs and that's one of them. You make me so sad when you talk that way, and do you know why? Because God gave His only begotten son so *even you* might have everlasting life and what did you do but turn your back on His love and give yourself to every man you've met since you were in junior high. Do you think that's your true mission? Do you think that God wants you to behave that way the rest of your life?"

"I'm not so sure what my mission is," said Tawnya. "I'm not so sure there is such a thing, but back when I was dragging those kids behind the bleachers and working them over, I felt like it was my purpose to save them from growing up to be like you."

"Tawnya Louise Baker," said Principia in a calm straight forward manner, "if I didn't know you so well, and love you so much, you would have angered me just now." She steadied herself against the ice machine and then went on with her speech. "There are times when just being near you makes me so sad I don't know what to do because when I see someone who has such potential and just doesn't love God as much as I do, and when that person has had many chances and still refuses to see the light, then I'm filled with such sadness and anger and disgust that it makes me ashamed of myself to know that some of those feelings are really there. Now, Tawnya Louise, what I want you to do is promise me that you'll remind yourself daily that the forms of immorality are lust, malice, deceit, dishonesty and slander. They are immoral because they advocate evil."

"I'll make you no promises," said Tawnya, "so you better talk it over with Miss Cassy."

"You've given me no choice," said Principia, twisting her hair with both hands. She turned and walked straight down the hall toward the staircase, but halfway there she looked back to see Tawnya Louise still watching her. "I'll leave you with one word of warning," said Principia, pointing her finger toward her classmate. "Hear this, Tawnya Louise Baker, and hear it now. The scripture states that judgment will be worse for those who go forth in His name. I only tell you this because I love you."

"If you're trying to say that your Lord is harder on hypocrites than anyone else, you better tell that to Corinda Cassy too," said Tawnya Louise. "She's the one who needs to hear it."

Before the hour was up, Principia had told Corinda everything. "It grieves my heart sorely to hear this," she said. "I will speak to Tawnya at once. The Lord has put her here to test us, but especially to test you. And you have once again proven your strength, Principiaaa. You are truly an Invinnn-cible able to withstand the wiles of the Devil."

The next morning Tawnya was dismissed from service, but before she left, she wrote Principia a note stating that she could have all the art supplies in her room, and in closing said that the only reason she accepted the job was because she had been given no choice. "My father always wanted a missionary in the family," she wrote. "He got one too, even if it was for only two days."

By noon Tawnya was on the bus heading back to Baytown, and Principia, with the note crumpled up in her hand, was praying that she had done the right thing, while Miss Cassy was searching for reasons to support her feeling that Principia was too dynamic a personality to serve as an Invincible. "I'm afraid she'll throw our program way off balance with her energy," she said to Brother Hemphill. She had telephoned him long distance to ask his advice. "I've never met anyone like her," she continued. "She's so strong she can do her own work as well as everybody else's, and this is not the purpose of Invincibleship. Vacation Bible School is not going to be enough to occupy her."

"Then let her work by herself," suggested Brother Hemphill. "She'll be the only one you can turn loose and forget about."

"I hope I'll be able to do just that," said Corinda. "But you know how I am; I always want to do everything myself. I want to be the only one to do good things for people; I want to make everyone happy; I want them to laugh and feel better and love one another."

"Yes, and you've always put yourself before your works," said Brother Hemphill. "It should be just the opposite. You have always wanted too much glory, Corinda. My advice is to pray for the right attitude, and then you will be able to better enjoy all the truly good things you have accomplished."

She wanted to tell him that she was tired of praying her life away, tired of disappointments and answers that were slow in coming or not at all; she wanted to tell him that she wasn't sure how much longer she could continue holding on to her faith because it wasn't true faith and never had been, but she was ashamed to admit these things because she had invested so much time, energy and money in what she once thought was a lifelong commitment, one that would make her more content and dispel her loneliness and guilt. She also wanted to tell him that her first husband had not died by accident. She had never confessed this to anyone, not even to Larry Wayne, and there were moments when she wanted to tell someone, just anyone, in order to remove part of the burden from her heart.

On the other end of the phone, Brother Hemphill was silent, waiting for Corinda to unburden her soul, but she could not. The prayer she had prayed just before her husband's death was ringing in her head.

Dear Lord, she had prayed as she deliberately drove their car into a tree, kill this stingy son of a bitch sitting next to me because I'm tired of having to beg for everything I want, but please, I beg of You, spare my own life.

The accident happened on his ranch in Alice. She had escaped with only a few scars on her face. They were removed by a doctor in Argentina. And then, after returning to Alice, she was haunted by dreams and visions of her husband lingering around the live oak where she had crashed their car.

By then she had inherited his ranch and fortune as she knew she would, and later on she inherited her family ranch as well, but still she wasn't satisfied and was unable to forget her husband's death, so she took up many careers to occupy her mind and then began traveling the world over until she turned to the Lord to find peace. "Love me, O Lord," she had prayed. "Cast out this unhappiness from my life, and if You cannot love me, please send someone who can."

It was then that she dreamed of Jesus driving her down the highway, and two years later she met Larry Wayne. She wanted Brother Hemphill to know about him too, but the words she wanted to speak were frozen in her mouth. She wanted to confess that she had always had a desperate need to be loved and admired and that all the loving and admiration she had ever received had not been enough. But instead of opening her heart to him she said,

"Brother Hemphill, I hope to profit by your caring words."

"I'll continue praying for your good work, Corinda," he said. "That's all I can do."

After they had hung up she decided he was right about one thing: Principia should stay in the program but she should work by herself. "That way she'll stay occupied and out of everyone's way," she said. "I'm going to break the news to her at once."

"Joy," shouted Principia on hearing the decision. "The Lord is calling me into the field alone. This is to be a proving ground for my faith."

 8

Saturday morning, the last day of orientation, Larry Wayne Johnson showed up unexpectedly. When Corinda Cassy opened the door to her motel room, there he was standing before her like a vision. He was wearing the white silk suit she had bought him in Hong Kong, but it seemed to her that the suit was wearing him. She had tried to teach him how to carry himself in expensive clothing, but it was no use: everything he put on looked as though it belonged on someone else.

"I just thought I'd take a spin, and look where I ended up," he said, backing her up into the room. "Besides, I was getting sick and tired of those skinny-legged cowgirls marching all day long, always marching and singing their damn songs. That's all they're big enough to do. I don't know why Lady Confusion couldn't find some girls who had some meat on their bones."

"I won't have you saying those sarcastic things about my beautiful cowgirls," said Corinda. "And for your information, I chose each of them with you in mind. When I'm away, you're to think of me and no one else, and before I forget it, you can just stop calling me Lady Confusion right now because I may have been confused when I left Alice but I'm not anymore. The Lord has given me many blessings this week and you are one of them."

"You're about to get another one too," he said. He took off his belt, wrapped it around her waist and pulled her toward him. He kissed her on the lips, embraced her for a long time and then, when he felt her body relaxing, he gave her the slightest push— that was all it took—and she fell back onto the bed.

"Not now, my precious," she pleaded. "This suit wrinkles so

easily, and my very last seminar is coming up in thirty minutes."

But Larry Wayne refused to listen, and an hour later, thirty minutes late for her last session, Corinda arrived at the church. Her clothes were slightly wrinkled, but she had a glow on her face that everyone noticed right away.

"She hides not her light under a bushel," said Herbie Stout, "but allows it to so shine that others may see her good work which is to the glory of God."

"'To know her is to love her, and to love her is to know her,'" quoted Sue Rose. "'And I do, and I do, and I do.'"

When the room became quiet, Miss Cassy, dressed in her cowgirl outfit of blue and gold, took a straight pin out of her vest and dropped it on the floor in front of her. After the sound of the pin hitting the floor was heard throughout Fellowship Hall, she rested her arms on the lectern and began her talk entitled: "Everyday Life as an Invincible." While she addressed the summer missionaries, she kept both eyes on Larry Wayne, who had slipped into the back of the room and was sitting under a harsh light that caused him to look older than his twenty-seven years. She was surprised to see that his complexion under that light was so pale she could hardly tell where his white suit left off and his flesh began. She noticed an angry look on his face, and she told herself that he was only a boy trying hard to be a man and that one day he would grow up. Then she continued with her talk.

All the Invincibles listened to her every word, except for Principia, who was staring into space. She was still thinking about Tawnya Louise and wondering if she should have had more patience with her. "Principia," whispered Herbie Stout, "I know you've got your mind on other things, but please try to listen because this is a very important part of our lives. You will find out when you get into the field that an Invincible's work is never done. You will be called on to do things that you thought you would never be able to do, but God will give you the ability when the times comes. Believe me, I know."

While Principia was thanking Herbie for his kind words, Corinda Cassy was punctuating her last remark by doing a side step and a low kick, something that looked as if it had come out of vaudeville but was actually part of the routine she was teaching the Cowgirls for Christ.

When she finished, Larry Wayne, rocking back and forth in

his folding chair, applauded her, and then, pleased to receive his attention in front of the Invincibles, she introduced him as the mathematical brains behind the program. "He's the one who keeps us operating sooo smoothly," she said, staring into the eyes of each summer missionary. "And what's more, he has inspired my every word in today's message."

She was about to tell some of his personal history, but when she looked toward the back again, his chair was empty and pushed aside. "Oh look, he's disappeared," she said. "He just hates to hear anything positive about himself. He's too modest for his own good. Modesty, however, is a virtue, and that's something we must remember on this our last day together."

After a chorus of "Stand Up, Stand Up for Jesus," the twenty-three Invincibles were divided into two groups. Those who were traveling by Greyhound to their first assignment went with Larry Wayne, and Miss Cassy took the other group, Principia included, to the Trailways terminal, where they were given their tickets plus one week's salary of thirty dollars. Principia stood with Miss Cassy, still wearing her cowgirl outfit, and said goodby to her new friends as two by two the Invincibles boarded one bus right after another.

Principia's first week was to be spent in a small town called Judson, her second week in Asherton and then Catarina, Carrizo Springs, Eagle Pass and Crystal City. The first week, according to Miss Cassy, should be the very best of all, not only because the job was new and challenging but because her first assignment was with a pastor by the name of Donald Applebee. "I've never met him," said Corinda as they waved the Invincibles off, "but word of his good work has reached the press as well as my ears. Judson is almost a ghost town, and has become something of a shrine. There's a screen door there which reflects the image of Christ, and many who have been privileged enough to see it have been healed of their afflictions."

"Oh, I've read about that door," said Principia. "I've wanted to see it for a long time. At last the Lord is giving me this blessing."

When the last bus had left, Miss Cassy led Principia out the station and down St. Mary's Street. "Your bus is parked in a loading zone behind Karotkins Furniture Store," she said. "Your driver can only be there thirty minutes so we've got to hurry. His name is Brother Ravenhill; he will take good care of you as he has so many others. He's a beautiful man, and for years I prayed that the Lord would grant us a closer relationship, but the Heavenly Father gave me someone else to cherish instead, Larry Wayne, who has come to be with us today. I'm praying that God will provide us a deeper, more personal understanding of each other and that our love will know no limits. Larry Wayne is so sweet and gentle; a perfect angel, and I do wish you had time to get to know him better. He fell into my life one day as I was driving along the Mississippi coast. He was hitchiking, and although I never pick up strangers, he was blond, and at the time sunburned, and the Lord told me to stop for him, so I did. I leaned across the seat and opened the door, but he came around to the driver's side, so I moved over and he drove the rest of the way. We became friends, well, almost overnight. He's from a poor family in Alabama, lost track of his kin long ago, and now I'm all he has. First I hired him as my gardener, then my chauffeur, then I gave him his first promotion and he became my private secretary. After that I took him around the world many times; dressed him in the finest clothes money can buy and provided him with a car every year. He escorted me absolutely everywhere, but it was in Monte Carlo that he first expressed the desire to know more about business, so I sent him to school and when he finished he became my manager and closest friend. He doesn't express his love for God in the same way you or I do, Principia, but I can assure you that his beliefs run very deep."

"I look forward to knowing better this unusual man of God," said Principia as they crossed Pecan Street against the light. Then they turned left on Crockett, and there in a loading zone behind Karotkins and the Aztec Theater was a silver bus named *Born Again*, and standing in the alley between the two buildings was the part-time preacher, part-time driver Brother Ravenhill, who lived up to the name of his business venture: The Born-Again Independent Bus Company. Like many of his regular passengers, Brother Ravenhill had received the baptism of the Holy Spirit. God had blessed him with a special and private language all his own, and he was willing to demonstrate his love for the Lord in any way possible.

Miss Cassy introduced Principia to her old friend by saying, "You will grow to love him as much as I do. He sometimes preaches right there behind the steering wheel, and every third Sunday he stops the bus long enough to pastor one of our missions out near Pearsall."

"How glad I am to know that a man of God is behind the wheel," sighed Principia, twirling her hair around one finger. She was wearing another purple dress with short sleeves and no collar. Around her neck she had tied a maroon scarf, and in her hair she had fastened three of her favorite barrettes. Two were shaped like red strawberries and all but disappeared into her curls, and the other one was the letter P in purple plastic outlined in lavender. As she spoke to the bus-driving preacher, she held tightly to a bright pink carryall, shaped like a heart. It was canvas, had the initials P.M. embroidered in royal blue on both sides and was a going-away present from her ex-partner and new friend, Sissy Cisneros.

"I'm amazed, thrilled and stirred to have you riding with me on this trip," said Brother Ravenhill. He was a tall, angular man with curls falling into his eyes, below his ears, and down the collar of his black satin shirt, which he had bought second-hand from a thrift store, where he also bought his faded Levi's and cowboy boots with clear plastic heels. He had reached the age when his hair was beginning to gray, but his eyebrows were still jet black and had almost grown together over his nose.

"Oh, Brother Ravenhill," said Principia. "You have the most inspirational eyes I do believe I've ever seen!"

"I tell him that all the time," said Corinda with a tinge of irritation that Principia didn't notice. "You should see how they light up sometimes, behind the pulpit especially or when he gets wound up over something he really believes in. Because our friendship has been so special there have been times when I didn't want to share him with anyone, but the Lord has helped me to overcome my selfishness, and it is with great pleasure that I am able to bring the two of you together."

"Welcome aboard," said Brother Ravenhill. "I trust you won't mind listening to a little of my preaching on the way."

"Well, I just might preach right along with you," said Principia, leaving the two of them for a moment to make sure that her baggage had been loaded. I just wonder if I did the right thing, she thought, looking at the boxes that Tawnya had left behind. Lord, if I've done wrong by Tawnya Louise, I expect to be punished by Your loving hand.

"You, my angel, are the only one I will not have to worry about this summer," said Miss Cassy, leading her to the open door, "and am I glad of that. Now remember, when you step into that bus, you are officially an Invinnn-cible, although you, Principiaaa, have been invinnn-cible since the first breath of life."

"I promise to write often, Miss Cassy," said Principia, "because you mean so very much to me." She stepped on board the bus but didn't feel any different, yet she expected something to happen, something to come over her, sweep her off her feet. Brother Ravenhill told her to sit anywhere she liked. For a moment she thought, looked at everyone sitting there, a total of four people, and then chose to sit alone because she wanted to know who the Lord would place beside her.

I hope I'm not going to be a disappointment to everyone I meet, she thought taking one of the front seats and waiting impatiently for the bus to move. When it did, a trail of black exhaust sent Corinda Cassy running for cover between the two buildings. "She's such a good person," said Principia as she waved to the Cowgirl for Christ, who continued to light up the dark alley like a lost sequin even after the silver bus had left.

When Miss Cassy was out of sight, Principia turned her attention to her white Bible covered with smudges and fingerprints. I like for it to look as clean as new-fallen snow, she thought, taking a bottle of white shoe polish out of her carryall and giving the book a light coat. As the bus forced its way through the city, Principia, eager for her Bible to be dry again, held it close, but not too close to the open window.

It seems like I've been on this bus forever, she thought, and here I've just stepped on board.

When the Bible was completely dry, she unzipped it and opened it at random. "Lord, give me a scripture so I'll know that I'm still on beam," she prayed as her eyes fell upon a verse in the one-hundred-and-second Psalm:

I am like a pelican of the wilderness, I am like an owl of the desert. I watch, and am as a sparrow alone upon the house top.

"Lord," she said, "I can't believe You've sent me this scripture because it's not like You. This verse has given me no comfort. It has only made me feel more alone than ever before. Forgive me, O Lord, for allowing Satan to come between us just now, for I am fully aware that he has sent this verse to cause me fear and loneliness."

Again she closed her Bible, opened it at random to the Book of Isaiah and, ignoring what she was doing, deliberately turned to the fortieth chapter and read the motto she had chosen to guide her through the summer:

The voice of him that crieth in the wilderness, Prepare ye the way of the Lord, make straight in the desert a highway for our God.

"Lord, thank you for sending this scripture," she said, then closed her eyes and repeated it. A smile came over her face. She repeated it again. The bus entered the open highway. Again she repeated the scripture. Somewhere behind her she could faintly hear two women talking. Or were they praying? In front of her Brother Ravenhill was tapping on the steering wheel and whistling. Or was he singing? And was it a hymn, Principia wondered, or just a popular song? With the scripture rolling through her head, she could hear very little of what was going on around her. Finally she opened her eyes. The world seemed brighter than she remembered it, but the verse, even though she was still repeating it intensely, had lost some of its splendor. All of a sudden its meaning seemed obscure, almost pointless, and its message drifted from sight. When her eyes grew accustomed to the brightness once again, she opened her Bible aimlessly and began searching for a verse that would lift her spirits.

Lord, she prayed, send me a scripture that will be meaningful all the days of my life.

 9

Brother Horatio Ravenhill had painted his bus silver inside and
out because he wanted it to look like a bolt of electrical lightning
streaking across the skies on its way to the gates of Heaven, which
he hoped would be standing wide open when he got there with
his passengers, most of them regulars, coming from as far away as
Texarkana or Lake Charles, Alamogordo or Abilene just to ride
with a man whose nature it was to thirst after righteousness and
for the sake of righteousness, a man much sought after by the
bereaved, the down and out, and the betrodden, for his Godlike
reputation preceded him like word of a rain cloud moving across
a parched desert. Twice a week he left San Antonio for a round
trip through the Brush Country and cactus flats of Southwest Texas. Along the way he preached, sang, witnessed and generously
gave drink from his cup of wisdom, filled to overflowing. Great
was his gift for giving, and greater still was his joy in knowing
that he had given his all.

Brother Ravenhill, a confirmed old bachelor, was raised in
the town of Ranger by his mother, a widow who pumped gasoline
at a roadside station and accepted checks from out of town if the
Lord told her to. She never received a bad one either and always
reminded her son of this. He lived at home and helped her run
the station until he was thirty; then she died, he sold the family
business, bought a bus and started carrying people from place to
place. He accepted checks from out of town, out of state and out
of the country, if the Lord told him to, and after twenty-five
years in business he was proud to say that he had never received a
bad one either.

At the time he met Principia Martindale he was fifty-five years old and was known by his passengers as one of the finest preachers in Texas. Principia felt privileged to be riding with him. She was eager to know him better, and if only she could get Tawnya Louise out of her mind she might strike up a conversation. "Oh, I don't know why I can't forget about you once and for all," she said out loud, as though there were someone sitting next to her.

Brother Ravenhill heard her, but didn't know who he was hearing, nor did he understand a word of what she said. "Do I hear the angels talking?" he asked, looking over his shoulder at the passengers, a total of five, scattered all over the bus.

Toward the back was elderly Mr. Elmer Primm, confined to his wheelchair, which was sitting in the middle of the aisle, and in the seat closest to him sat his unregistered nurse Viola I. Dyer, who was accustomed to keeping a careful eye on her patient because he had a bone disease, wasn't expected to live very long and could not walk, even after his last operation, which his doctors had said was ninety-five percent successful.

In the middle of the bus sat Mary Alaska Ragsdale, a grandmother who was on her way to Judson to see her daughter, Joyce Jeannine, and her grandchild, a boy, named Lucky after his father. Mary Alaska was dressed in a pale pink skirt and a matching jacket; her hair was steel gray, had just been washed and set that morning, and her rings, already too large, were sliding to the palm side of her fingers. As usual she was carrying a book and two pairs of eyeglasses, one for reading and one for seeing; both of them were slung around her neck on silver chains.

Mary Alaska read a great deal, and that morning was no exception. She was deeply involved with a little book called *Searching for Serenity* and was enjoying herself thoroughly, but her lifelong friend, Winkie Kermit, sitting on the next seat, was about to jump right out of her skin. Winkie was thin, had black curly hair with white roots and was Mary Alaska's age, fifty-nine, but looked much older. They were both coming from Lockhart.

Mary Alaska was married, had one daughter, no sons and a husband who drank, but Winkie had never been married, said she just hated the very idea of it and didn't need another nasty old man around the house. Mary Alaska was convinced that Winkie felt that way because she had been expected to nurse her father until the day he died, which is exactly what she had done, and, as if that were not enough, her brother Morris moved in on her shortly after their father's funeral, took the best chair out to the front porch and sat there rain or shine, year after year, while Winkie cashiered five and a half days a week at the variety store. Absolutely everybody in Lockhart worried about her because she was so thin, frail, dried-up-looking and scared of anything that moved.

Openly she admitted her fear of airplanes even though she had never been inside one, horses that kicked even though she had never been kicked by one and roofs that blew off in the middle of the night. (That had never happened to her either.) She also bore testimony to her fear of buses; she had ridden on many and already suspected their driver of being a reckless maniac because she didn't like the way he kept looking at her through the mirror, but Mary Alaska, even though she knew she was lying, assured Winkie that nothing was wrong with their driver and that she should sit still and stop worrying.

"But, Mary Alaska, I'm so nervous I can't stand myself today," said Winkie, trying to straighten her white blouse and her black skirt at the same time. She owned nothing but white blouses, black skirts and sneakers, her cashier's uniform. "I simply don't know what's wrong with my nerves; something's went with them, I guess," she said, digging into her purse with both hands. "I sure hope I can remember what I'm looking for; I think I will when I see it."

They had been on the bus a little over an hour and already Winkie had twisted two buttons off her blouse and had wound up her wristwatch so many times she had broken the spring. And besides that, her sinus trouble was acting up again so every breath she drew sounded like reeds in a wind storm, a noise that aggravated Mary Alaska something awful, but she was determined to stand it somehow.

Four seats in front of them sat Principia Martindale, gazing absent-mindedly out the window and feeling the need to rededicate her life. "O Precious Redeemer," she prayed out loud, "I've always wanted to be a simple ordinary person, just a day-to-day servant of God, but everybody else seems to think that's not enough, and now they've got me believing that it's not enough when I know perfectly well that it is, so please, Jesus, help me to straighten all this out."

Winkie Kermit craned her neck to see who was doing all the talking. "Isheee-ma-ha, Lord," she whispered, as though she could reach right out and touch the Holy Spirit. After a few moments she settled back in her chair and waited for something else to happen; she felt sure something would.

"I feel just like I'm grasping at straws," said Principia. "Sweet Jesus, please make me feel better about something. I don't care what it is."

Again Winkie Kermit craned her neck. "Did you say something to me, Mary Alaska, or am I hearing things for sure this time," she said, squeezing her cotton handkerchief and sniffing her nose. "It's so hard for me to course anything these days, especially the human voice."

Principia came out of her thoughts and turned slightly in her seat so she could see the two women as well as listen to their conversation.

"No, I most certainly did not say a thing," said Mary Alaska Ragsdale, popping her gum. "As you can see, I'm reading this little book. It's trying to teach me how to live serenely, and I was just about to learn something new when you interrupted me the way you did."

"Isheee-ma-ha!" said Winkie, twisting another button off her blouse. "I will not say another word to you and that's a promise. Osheee-ma-ha. I didn't go to do it in the first place; something made me like it always does. I was just sitting here and minding my own business and wondering how you manage to stay so calm and something just came over me. OOO-ma-HA-lalalala, I've always wanted to be like you, Mary Alaska Ragsdale. Nothing bothers you and everything bothers me. But I'm determined once and for all not to let the Devil get me down anymore, that is if I can help it. So from here on out I'm just going to sit right here and be real real calm and watch the fence posts go running past this window and thank the good Lord that I'm still alive. OOO-Isheee-ma-ha-la-ma-ha. Ma-ha-la-ma-haaa."

"Winkie Kermit, can't you utter one word without breaking into the 'postolic language?" asked Mary Alaska, trying to be kind. "I do think that might be one reason why you've had so much trouble relaxing on this trip. Somehow or another you've got to keep more of that unknown tongue inside you and not let it go bursting out. You'll frighten my daughter out of her wits if you keep this up and my son-in-law, well, he's liable to throw you right out of the house and me with you. Now if you want my advice, what you should do is read this book because it will teach you how to be serene. God knows you need it."

"God knows everything, Mary Alaska, and I thank you for those kind words," said Winkie, spraying her nose with Breathe-Ease. She squeezed the bottle with both hands. "If I had something good to read it seems like it would satisfy me like it does you, but reading and riding together makes me deathly sick to my stomach."

"Well, it's fortunate then that you have the sense it takes to realize it," said Mary Alaska without looking up from her reading matter. When that woman breathes she sounds just like a percolator, she thought. I wish to God Almighty that somebody would cut her nose off and throw it so far away she'd never find it again.

Principia overheard everything they said. I simply must meet those two women, she said to herself. Tawnya Louise would consider them a waste of her time, but it seems to me they have so much to give.

Without wasting a moment, she put her books and pamphlets into her carryall and moved to the seat across the aisle from the two women, both of whom smiled at her when she sat down, but the one doing all the talking, Winkie Kermit, didn't stop for a moment, not even when she blew her nose. She was telling her companion about the television special "Jesus of Nazareth," which she had seen the week before.

"Lord have mercy on us all," said Winkie as Principia settled herself. "That program was as real as real could be until it came time to baptize Jesus, and then everything fell apart at the seams. They showed John the Baptist scooping up some water in his hands and splashing it all over pore ole Jesus, or the man who was playing him I mean, and I sat there and watched that mess and got madder and madder and finally I looked over to Brother just sitting there and soaking it all in, and I said Brother, that ain't right. That ain't the way it really happened. Somebody ought to have told whoever made this gosh-awful thing to go back and reread the scripture to find out just exactly how Jesus was baptized because I know for fact that he was not sprinkled any more than I was. Baptists don't believe in sprinkling, and John the Baptist was certainly a Baptist and the very first one there ever was at that. What they should'uve done was show somebody going all the way under the water and coming all the way up again, because in order to be saved you've got to get down and go under and soak up some of that water of everlasting life. You've got to be totally immersed in order for the baptism to take."

"You're talking about it like it's some kind of vaccination," said Mary Alaska.

"Baptism is a vaccination," replied her friend. "Ma-ha-ya-ma-HA! It's God's vaccination against the Devil!"

Principia, leaning across the aisle so she could make better eye contact with Winkie, nodded her head in total agreement, a signal that sent Winkie's nerves fluttering and her fingers dancing over her lips as though she were trying to pull the words right out of her mouth. "You see, Mary Alaska," she finally said, pointing to Principia, "that girl with all the red hair over there agrees with me." Principia smiled. Winkie waved to her as though they were far away, and Mary Alaska began introducing herself, but before she could finish, her companion interrupted. "My name's Winkie Kermit," she said, fluffing up her short black curls, "and you'll just have to forgive me because I suffer from what they call a deviated septum, but I'll be all right because I brought along three kinds of nose spray, and one's real strong; lasts nine hours."

"Well I wish to God you'd use it then," said Mary Alaska.

"I'm so glad you're prepared," said Principia.

"Oh, I'm prepared all right," replied Winkie, all smiles and no frowns. "I've got the baptism of the Holy Spirit. Don't I look happy? Mary Alaska has never allowed herself to receive the full baptism, only part of it. She's been totally immersed, of course. I'd worry about her if she hadn't been, but what she doesn't know is what it feels like to have the Holy Ghost come into your life all at once and knock you flat on your face. I know what it feels like though because God came into my life that way and gave me a personal, private and an unknown language, and I use it all the time."

"We've got ears," said Mary Alaska, still searching for serenity.

"It all happened when my father died," said Winkie. "I'd nursed him nearly all my life, and when he passed on I rejoiced that he was out of his suffering, but it wasn't until I saw him in his casket that the Holy Spirit came into my life all at once and gave me a new language to speak. Isheee-ma-HA-ya-ma-HA! I felt such joy and freedom. I fell upon my face right there in the funeral parlor and wasn't the least bit ashamed of myself either."

"My Aunt Wilda received the Holy Spirit when she was in the asylum the second time," said Principia, "and she wasn't ashamed either. She had a nurse who spoke in tongues every day, and pretty soon so did Aunt Wilda. She felt so much happier after that and I know I'd feel that way too if the Lord would only give me the full anointing."

"If you want it that bad you'll receive it," said Winkie, searching the floor for her nasal mist. "Everybody wants to be a born-again Christian whether they know it or not. What you've got to do is find somebody who's already got the total anointing and ask him to put his hands on top of your head and say, 'I baptize you in the name of the Holy Spirit,' and then you're eligible for the full gospel of Jesus Christ to come zooming into your life like a tornado. You'll never be the same again once you've had it."

"That's for sure," said Mary Alaska out of the corner of her mouth.

"Sometimes I feel just like I'm going to sleep when the Lord blesses me with tongues," said Winkie, staring across Mary Alaska and directly into Principia's eyes. "At other times I'm totally aware of what I'm doing, and then there are those beautiful God-filled minutes when I'm taken up in Rapture and my whole Spirit is surrendered to his will. That's when I go completely under the anointing, and those are the best times of all. You'll know what I'm talking about when you receive it because then you'll be set apart from everybody who doesn't have this special blessing. Oh, people will make fun of you, and shun you, and say that you're the craziest thing that ever walked. They have me. I've been talked about up one street and down the other in Lockhart, but you know what? I just don't care because when I'm taken up in the Spirit I'm the happiest human on earth, and when the Spirit leaves me I look forward to getting it again. It's just that wonderful, and I can't live a minute without it, because it makes me feel alive from head to toe. My blood rushes and my heart beats fast, my legs commence shaking and then I just let go and say: 'Lord take over!' And he does."

"Oh, will you please lay your hands on top of my head and give me the full anointing," said Principia. "I want it so bad. My mother wouldn't let Aunt Wilda do it."

"Well, I've never done it before," said Winkie, "but if Mary Alaska will just move her legs and let me get over there to you we'll give it a try."

Visibly irritated, Mary Alaska got up and moved three seats back. Winkie Kermit stood in the aisle, placed both hands on top of Principia's head and said, "Lord, this young Christian has already had the baptism of water. She has been totally immersed in the springs of everlasting life, but now I ask You to give her the baptism of the Holy Ghost. Osheee-ma-HA, Lord Jesus, seal her in the name of the Kingdom. Come into her life and give her Your special blessing. Isheee-ma-HA. Give her a special language to speak, and a special understanding of the full anointing of the Holy Spirit, for we ask it in the precious name of Jesus . . . "

While Winkie spoke, she pressed what was left of her finger-nails into Principia's scalp and shook her head as though shaking the Devil right out of existence. Principia relaxed her neck and let her head fall first one way and then the next, but still she couldn't feel anything except the wind blowing through the open window and the burden of righteousness resting on her heart. She had imagined that her life would be flooded with joy all at once; she had expected her future to unfold before her very eyes, and most of all she had expected a personal language to be given to her without fail. But nothing happened.

She prayed, "Anoint me, O Lord; anoint me."

"Sometimes this takes time," said Winkie Kermit. "And sometimes it happens all at once. It just depends on how the Lord wants to work."

"I want it to happen now," said Principia. "I want the full anointing, and I don't want to have to wait for it. I know I'm being impatient, but I want everything that the Holy Spirit has to offer. Lord, forgive me if I'm rushing you, but I just want you to know how bad I want your special blessing."

Brother Ravenhill, who had been keeping an eye on what

was going on, threw back his head and broke forth with the baptism of the Holy Ghost, "Ooo Cino-me-o-coma-no, give her a song to sing, Cino-me-o. Touch her lips; touch her tongue, breathe into her life a new language that only you can understand. Cino-me-o, our Father. Cino-me-o, our Lord. Cino-me-o-Cino-me-o Keelee-keelee-coma-no . . . "

"Ishee-ma-haaaa," whispered Winkie Kermit as their eyes met in the rearview mirror. "There's a man of God in this bus."

Mary Alaska Ragsdale had endured the situation long enough. "Winkie Kermit," she said, coming out of her seat, "when will you ever learn that not everybody wants or needs the baptism of the Holy Spirit. Now sit down and think about something else if that's humanly possible. I don't know why I agreed to let you come with me on this trip. You've made me a nervous wreck since the minute we left Lockhart, and I won't stand for it any longer."

"Mary Alaska, I'm just about tired of you jumping down my throat every time I turn around," said Winkie. "I can't help it if I can't sit still. The Holy Spirit has given me the heebie-jeebies."

"Then please take your Holy Spirit to the back of the bus and talk to that old man," said Mary Alaska. "He probably needs to hear what you've got to say."

Thinking that a good idea, Winkie went flying to the back of the bus to talk to Mr. Primm, who had just been dismissed from the Veteran's Hospital and was on his way back home to Carrizo Springs. Disregarding the fact that he was still sleeping, Winkie sat down beside him and was about to wake him up when Viola I. Dyer gave her a threatening look, so rather than disturb either of them, Winkie sprayed her nose, put both hands on the invalid's knees and prayed silently for a speedy recovery.

Relieved that Winkie had settled down at last, Mary Alaska took the seat next to Principia and after a few moments said, "You'll just have to excuse my friend. She gets slightly carried away sometimes. She's the only member of my church who behaves this way, and some people think she's gone off the deep end. She's very nervous and I didn't want to bring her along, but my Sunday school class said that a good trip with a pleasant companion would do her the world of good, so I foolishly agreed."

Principia paid her no mind. She turned her back and stared

out the window; Mary Alaska took the hint and returned to her reading matter. Not only was Principia disappointed at not having received the Holy Ghost, she believed that Mary Alaska had stood in her way by stopping Winkie too soon. It seemed to her there was always one person who kept her life from running smoothly, and every time she weeded out one offender there was always another to take his place, always someone to put a finger where a finger should not be, and this time it was Mary Alaska Ragsdale.

For a few miles everyone was silent. Viola I. Dyer had returned to her puzzle, Mary Alaska to her book. Principia was gazing out the window. Winkie was praying for Mr. Primm; and Brother Horatio Ravenhill, imagining himself to be in command of a silver chariot, was driving down the highway like God's favorite messenger speeding across the earth. Occasionally he would look at Winkie through the rearview mirror, and even though she was praying, from time to time she would feel his eyes upon her and would meet them with her own.

Brother Ravenhill felt drawn to Winkie Kermit. He could even imagine her driving his bus. She was the only person who, from the very beginning, struck him as a driver, someone who could understand how he felt when behind the wheel. He wanted her to know that for many years his bus had been his life, his fulfillment. While driving at top speed along narrow winding roads he would begin to feel connected to the sound of the engine. His body would begin to quiver, his eyes dance. He would then feel as though he were married to a streak of lightning and that driver and bus together created a new being charging down the highway in a flash of light.

Already he had sped through Natalia, Devine, More, Pearsall and was coming to Dilly, where he usually stopped for lunch. When they approached the town he announced the lunch stop twice, not to make sure he was understood but to convince himself that he had said what he intended to say, for often it was difficult for him to come out of his thoughts, hard for him to accept the mundane after he had been in such close communion with the highway, the bus and the workings of his soul.

"Here we are in Dilly," he said over one shoulder and then turned around and said, "Here we are in Dilly" over the other. "Dearly beloved, we'll be here for a mere thirty minutes. We'll be here for a mere thirty minutes."

Viola I. Dyer thought he sounded like he was coming out of a deep sleep; Principia thought he sounded like he was pronouncing a benediction and Mary Alaska Ragsdale thought he sounded just like a plain fool.

Winkie Kermit, however, had already decided that she adored the very tone of his voice, so she slipped up behind Mary Alaska's seat and said, "Heavenly days! Have you ever met such a man in your whole life?"

"Oh for God's sake will you shut up," said Mary Alaska, nearly jumping out of her seat. "You've made a complete idiot out of yourself today, and besides that you've pulled every button off your blouse, and here it is gaping wide open just like you've got something to show. Lucky for you I thought to bring along some safety pins."

"Winkie Kermit is a child of God," said Principia. "You shouldn't be so hateful when you talk to her. She has goodness in her heart."

"Yes, and so have I," said Mary Alaska. "But nobody ever takes that into consideration. Never did I dream that I would have to fight for my sanity on this trip. Now let's please try to control ourselves while we go have lunch."

Since Mr. Primm was unable to walk, he stayed on the bus with his nurse. Brother Ravenhill agreed to bring their lunches to them, and Mary Alaska led Winkie and Principia into the Dilly Hotel, Restaurant and Bus Stop, where they took a table directly under the ceiling fan.

"Don't let me have a Coke, " said Winkie the moment they sat down. "It hurts me."

"Now don't start that one again," said Mary Alaska, scratching her leg. "Just remember old Mr. Odell Woodrome. He dipped more snuff, took more aspirin and drank more Cokes than anybody I ever saw and was in perfect health until the day he died."

"He must have been a good person through and through is all I can say," said Principia while cleaning her face and hands with a pink towelette that had been slightly used and was still damp. "I'd be lost without these hand and face wipes," she told Winkie Kermit. "I even brought enough for you and Mary Alaska and whoever else wants one."

"Those things have too much perfume in them," said Mary Alaska. "They've been known to dry my skin, and I wish you'd put them up, they smell too loud." Then she opened her menu and suggested that they each order the same thing because they had very little time to eat. "The cook is probably confused enough as it is; they always are in these places," she said. "So let's just keep it simple so we can have our lunch and get out of here."

They each ordered chicken fried steak, and while waiting for it to be served, Principia explained the purpose of her trip. Both Mary Alaska and Winkie knew what an Invincible was. Winkie was delighted to know that Principia was on her way to her first assignment, but Mary Alaska arched her eyebrows and said, "I sure would be careful if I were you."

When their food arrived, Principia asked Winkie to say grace, but Mary Alaska said that it was ill-mannered to call attention to your religion in public places. "We are going to say grace," said Principia, glaring at her opponent. "I've never sat down to the table in my life without thanking God for all He's given me."

"Then thank Him in your heart, the same way I do," said Mary Alaska, rearranging her silverware. "What's wrong with that?"

"Oh, all right," said Principia, "but we can at least hold hands." She took Winkie's hand and then Mary Alaska's and bowed her head for a few moments. Winkie did the same, but Mary Alaska simply stared at the ceiling fan and wished she had one just like it.

"There's only one thing that bothers me about this trip of yours," said Mary Alaska the instant Principia looked up from the blessing. "Judson is miles from any good-sized town, and it just doesn't seem right for a young girl to be abandoned way out in the middle of nowhere. There's not much to the place anymore, you know, probably not a handful of people living there and the ones that do are about as sorry as you can get. It used to be quite a place, but that was back in nineteen twenty-five when a man by the name of L. J. Judson developed it as a model city. He was a land promoter of some sort, went there when he was forty-one, but nobody knew exactly where he came from. They say he was aiming for a population of ten thousand, but I don't think he ever got it, in spite of all the conveniences he had put in."

"But what about Brother Applebee?" asked Principia.

"That thing may be your brother, but he's certainly not mine," said Mary Alaska. "I don't claim kin to apes, and he's as close to being one as you can get in my opinion, but you're making me go too fast is what you're doing; I'm getting way ahead of myself real quick, so let's go back to that Judson man; he was something else. He built the Royal Palms Hotel, which still stands but is no longer used. He even had full-grown palm trees planted along the main boulevard that leads up to it. You'd think that would have been enough to satisfy them back then, but he didn't stop there, no, he put in waterworks and electric lights, a fire station, a fourteen-acre park with a concrete swimming pool and a Baptist Church. He was a big Baptist, or so I've been told."

"How many Baptists lived there?" asked Principia, salting her food heavily.

"Lots," said Mary Alaska. "Especially after Judson advertised the place as the New Garden of Eden. He said it was the only area in the states where you could grow Bermuda onions and make a profit, so naturally he sold houses and acres left and right until there was nothing left to sell. He was a tall good-looking man and quite a womanizer. There in the café is a picture of him taken in front of the hotel, and all around him are these rich women from Carrizo Springs and their tongues just a-waggin'. He enjoyed showing them around his town on Sunday afternoon, talked them into spending their money too. He had a way with money, a way with women and a way with slick talk; always said what everybody wanted to hear and was doing just fine until he drilled too many irrigation wells and the water table dropped way down. Then the onions rotted in the train going to market, and then the Depression hit and gradually everybody got sick of the Garden of Eden and moved somewhere else. Then one of those rich, high-falutin' sisters in Carrizo Springs found out that she had lost every dime of her investment and the next thing you heard about was how she drove out to Judson one Sunday afternoon and shot Mr. L. J. to death while she was sitting in her car. Nobody ever heard from her after that, and nobody ever figured out where he was buried or even if he was, but after she murdered him the town went empty for a good long time and then a few wetbacks moved in and took over, and then my daughter got married and where did she go to live but Judson. Never in all my life did I dream she'd end up in such a place; she's beautifully educated and could have gone anywhere—was a Kilgore Rangerette, and then went to art school for two years—but she's happy where she is, or so she tells her mother, and that's the main thing, isn't it? She has a good marriage too. Now just before you get into what's left of the main part of town, my son-in-law, Lucky we call him, owns a big cattle ranch. He's very successful and rich so I thank God that my daughter doesn't have to want for anything. Some of the Mexicans who live there work for him, and . . . "

"But what about the screen door?" asked Principia, too excited to touch her food.

"That screen door you hear so much about isn't what it's all cracked up to be," said Mary Alaska, "and neither is your *Brother* Applebee, but he's at least responsible for putting the place on the map, and the screen door is what helped him get it there. I've seen that door at least a dozen times, and I keep going back to see it every time I'm out that way, but I tell you right now, I am not impressed. Not for one minute are you going to get me to believe that the image just appeared there overnight, but a lot of people do. Seems to me like everybody needs a miracle or two these days. Everybody but me that is. I believe, don't get me wrong, but I sure don't need a miracle to keep me believing. I've got enough faith already."

"I've got faith too," said Winkie. "But I want a few miracles every once in a while, because I like them."

"I'd like them too if they were real," said Mary Alaska, "but most modern miracles are manufactured by warped minds and have nothing whatever to do with the Great Creator."

"Why, Mary Alaska Ragsdale, shame on you and hush your mouth right now, do you hear me?" said Winkie Kermit. "What you just said is most certainly not true and you know it. It doesn't matter one bit what kind of mind creates the miracle as long as God has his fingers in on it and it works."

Principia's mind was beginning to spin. She wanted to enter the conversation, but she didn't want to get involved with Mary Alaska with whom she found herself at odds most of the time, so, after piecing on her chocolate layer cake, she pushed back her plate, excused herself and went outside.

All she wanted to do was forget Mary Alaska and everybody else like her and only think about the Holy Spirit, which she hoped would descend as it had on the day of Pentecost and fill her with God's total blessing. How she admired Winkie Kermit, Brother Ravenhill and others like them who had received the full baptism of the Holy Ghost. Their lives were so filled with direction and meaning, so free from doubt. Just thinking about such a state of being filled her with so much joy that at times she felt it was too good to be true.

When she returned to the bus, Mr. Primm was staring into space. Viola was reading the obituaries, and Brother Ravenhill was sitting behind the driver's seat and playing with his thumbs. Principia took the wooden cross from her carryall and told the driver that it had been a present from her roommate Lorinda and that she was going to use it to keep track of her summer converts. Then she showed him the pocketknife that Anthony Leggett had given her and said: "I'm going to notch this cross, and each notch is going to stand for a new Christian."

"By the end of the summer I hope you've got that cross whittled away to nothing but a toothpick," said Brother Ravenhill. "Whittled to a toothpick."

"By the end of the summer I don't think there's going to be anything left of it," said Principia. "And by then I sure do hope I've received the baptism of the Holy Spirit. Winkie seems to think I will. When she laid her hands on me I thought by the Grace of God I'd receive the baptism then and there, but I guess the time wasn't right."

"When the Almighty is ready He will give you the full anointing," said Brother Ravenhill. "He might want to give you the blessing a little bit at a time rather than all at once, so you have to be patient and let Him decide the proper course for you. Very few things come to us when we want them. Sometimes the Lord makes us wait; sometimes He makes us suffer, but never does He give us a burden too great, a cross too heavy to carry."

"With God, all things are possible," said Principia.

"That's right," said Winkie Kermit, boarding the bus in front of Mary Alaska. " 'God can do anything, *anything*, and He will; God can do anything but fail.' "

"That's one of my favorite songs," said Brother Ravenhill. " 'He can laugh; He can care; He can be anywhere. God can do anything but fail.' "

"You sing it just beautifully," said Winkie. "I bet you've got a lot of songs inside you." She took a seat directly behind him.

"And I bet you ought to stay up front and learn some of them," said Mary Alaska, heading straight for the back of the bus where she sat down, near Mr. Primm and his nurse. "My Sunday school class has encouraged me to be a Good Samaritan," she said to Viola. "But it's not a role that comes natural, not all the time I mean."

Before long they were on the open road, and Brother Raven-hill was beginning to feel a strong connection with the sound of the engine. He pressed the accelerator to the floor and the bus in all its glory sped down the highway as if bound for the Pearly Gates.

Winkie Kermit, normally terrified of high speeds, found the ride the most exhilarating experience of her life, and even though her heart was in her throat, she realized they were safe because the Lord's protective hand was at work in Brother Ravenhill. At one point he took a curve so fast Principia was afraid the bus was going to leave the highway, but Winkie, fully confident that their course had already been charted and blessed, assured her that the Lord was leading them safely to their destinations.

"Cino-me-o," whispered Brother Ravenhill before breaking into rapturous song. "Cino-me-o-Cino-me-o-Keelee-keelee-coma-no-Oooo-Oooo, 'The Holy Ghost will set your feet a-dancing. The Holy Ghost will thrill you through and through. The Holy Ghost will set your feet a-dancing, and set your heart a-dancing too'. . ."

"Oh my God in Heaven, they've got him stirred up," said Mary Alaska. "I knew this would happen. Now we'll never get there in one piece. Sit all the way down, you fool, and behave yourself," she shouted. "You're not the only God-fearing person on this bus, and you're responsible for the safety of each and every one of us."

But Brother Ravenhill paid her no mind. The louder he sang the faster he drove. And the faster he drove, the more Winkie Kermit swayed in her seat, clapped her hands, tapped her feet, bounced up and down, until finally she jumped up and danced in the aisle. "I just can't sit still another minute," she said, kicking up her heels and twirling around on tiptoes. "I don't think I'll ever be able to sit still for the rest of my life. Thank you, Jesus, for Your divine and sustaining wisdom. Thank You for making me so happy. And thank You for this wonderful man behind the wheel for he has come not to destroy but to fulfill. Osheee-ma-ha-ya-ma-Ha . . ."

Viola I. Dyer put cotton in Mr. Primm's ears and rubber plugs in her own. "I'm so sorry we took this bus I don't know what to do," she said.

"You'd think they were having a hollering contest," replied Mary Alaska. "You can't tell me that's right."

"It may not be right for you," said Principia, "but it's right for them; now leave them alone." She was on the verge of leaping to her feet and dancing with Winkie, but something held her back. She had never danced in her life. As a Southern Baptist she had been taught that it was wrong, yet she wanted to give in to that rhythm she felt beating in her heart.

"O, Jesus, Prince of Peace," she said, "it's so hard to know right from wrong sometimes. It's like fighting a long battle with a short stick. If Tawnya Louise were up there dancing like Winkie I'd say it was absolutely shameful, but with Winkie, it's different. Her feet are being guided by a power and a love, and I pray that one day I too will know what it's like to burst forth with the glory of the Holy Ghost."

Winkie and Brother Ravenhill settled into a medley of gospel hymns starting with "Oh how I love Jesus. Oh how I love Jesus. Oh how I love Jesus, because he first loved me." From there they sang, "There's Power in the Blood," "Blessed Assurance," "Amazing Grace" and "Glory to His Name."

"Oh, how I love good singing," said Principia, watching a dust storm blow up over the horizon, where some hills were just beginning to show themselves. The sight of something other than scrub brush and cactus breaking up the flatness made her feel better, but only for a moment. She was becoming all too aware that her prayers had been heard and answered and still she was not satisfied; she had been carefully screened and selected, and still she was not content; she was an Invincible at last, something she had wanted to be for a long time, but she felt as though she was going backward, not forward, and that the Born-Again Independent Bus Company was taking her someplace she might not want to go.

PART II

Judson

There ain't no such thing as love. You just
gotta give yourself time to get used to each
other. That's how I believe.

—Johnnie Chapman

1

It was a Saturday evening when Principia arrived in Judson, a town marooned by miles of mesquite, saltbrush and prickly pear, tarantulas, rattlesnakes and scorpions. "This is the part of Texas that bites, stings and sticks," said Brother Ravenhill as they approached the turn-off to Principia's final destination and the end of the line for the Born-Again Independent Bus Company. "We're in the heart of the Brush Country now," he added. "Judson's ten miles down this dirt road. A little bit further and it'd be in Mexico."

"It's not exactly what I expected it to look like," said Principia. "I thought it would be more of a desert where nothing much was growing." For miles around, all she could see was scrub brush, cactus and dust rising up in the distance.

"That's Judson kicking up the sand over there," said Ravenhill, pointing to a row of date palms just coming into view. "It's the dustiest town God ever created."

"Well, I wonder what He did it for," said Winkie, arming herself with nose spray and Kleenex. "I happen to be deathly allergic to dust of all kinds."

The bus rolled into town shortly before sunset when the light was golden and all of Judson was bathed with a radiance it didn't have during any other time of day, for the houses and buildings—frame, adobe and red brick—were crumbling with age and neglect, the streets were paved with sand and the date palms, what few were left, seemed to be standing as far away from the hotel as possible. The place was hot, tired and thirsty; hardly a sunflower or a tumbleweed would take root, hardly a chicken or a dog had the strength to make a sound, and during the heat of the day no one was seen walking about.

The town boasted a population of dogs, chickens, cats and armadillos along with fifteen some-odd human beings, sometimes more, sometimes less, depending on who had moved back or who had gotten fed up and left again. There was one main street, Judson Avenue, which came to a dead end in front of the Royal Palms Hotel, a two-story frame building, falling down in the back and boarded up in the front except for the café part, which was operated by a Mexican woman in her late fifties whom Applebee called Rosita, La Rosita or Rosita the Tamale Woman, but never Rosa Angélica López, her full name. Rosita was short and stout, already had a road map of wrinkles on her face and, unlike her mother, Señora Obdulla Hernandez, who lived down the road and always wore a stern expression, Rosita seemed to be smiling all the time, even when giving orders, arguing or working on a tight schedule in her café. The smile, although sometimes faint, was always there, even when she felt as though she would be better off without it.

Rosita's café occupied only a small corner of the Royal Palms Hotel. It was the central gathering place for everyone who lived in Judson and was more or less in the center of what had been a good-sized town with many houses, stores and streets. But when Principia Martindale arrived, only two of the streets were plainly visible; the others were hidden by cactus, creosote bush and mesquite. Judson Avenue, the main thoroughfare, which had once been lined with date palms all the way from the highway to the business district, ended in a circular drive in front of the hotel and the door to Rosita's café. From there, going back toward the highway (a distance of what amounted to a half block), another street, a smaller one, crossed Judson Avenue, and in the middle of the intersection grew a cottonwood that had been there longer than anyone had memory. The tree as well as the avenue divided the smaller street into two sections, each of which L. J. Judson had named for himself. On one side Lewis Street began, then shortly, without any warning, disappeared into a footpath that led off into the cactus flats; on the other side, Jennings Lane led directly to Donald Applebee's front door.

After years of wandering around in search of a place to live where he could do what he pleased, Donald Applebee had stumbled upon Judson, and, ten years later when Principia arrived, he was beginning to feel like the place belonged to him. By that time Jesus had already been seen hundreds of times on the screen door, the town was once again beginning to acquire some fame and Applebee had given himself the credit, for, after all, he had advertised the shrine in all the local newspapers, had notified church officials of the appearance of Jesus and had placed signs up and down the highway—MIRACLE DOOR, TWELVE MILES—MIRACLE DOOR ELEVEN MILES—MIRACLE DOOR TEN MILES—TURN HERE TO SEE JESUS—OPEN NOON TO THREE O'CLOCK. There for a while Rosita thought Applebee had gone sign-crazy. "Very soon we will all be wearing signs around our necks," she said to Sergio, who worked at the Lucky L Ranch. "Signs will be everywhere."

"There already are," her husband answered.

Principia Martindale thought it was inspiring to see the Son of God advertised on a billboard. "I have the feeling I'm going to like whoever is responsible for this," she said as they approached the town on one of the busiest afternoons Rosita could remember. Standing in the kitchen of her café, she was rolling tamales as fast as she could. Her best customer, a restaurant owner in Carrizo Springs, had ordered twelve dozen by the next morning; she had other orders to fill as well and was not looking forward to a late night in the café. While working she distracted herself by staring out the kitchen window, through the branches of the cottonwood and all the way down the avenue to a point on the horizon where the dirt thoroughfare disappeared into a cloud exploding with flashes of silver and gold as though all the angels in heaven were about to be turned footloose upon Judson. For a moment, because of her fatigue, she convinced herself that she was seeing things, but then she came to her senses, flung a tamale across the counter and shouted: "Mr. Señor Apple, the bus with the crazy driver, he is coming fast."

"I'll take care of him in a minute," said Applebee. Wearing faded Levi's and a matching jacket with the sleeves cut out, he was sitting at his favorite table in deep concentration. His face was round and full like that of a well-fed infant, and his sandy red hair, which was shoulder length, looked as though it were being blown straight back. His beard and hair gave him the appearance of a disciple according to Señora Hernandez, but his bare feet always made Rosita think of a child who had grown too big for his age.

He had, in fact, posed for Manuel's carving for the Santo Niño.

As the bus approached Judson, Applebee didn't leave the table and was determined not to unless absolutely necessary. He was hard at work trying to finish the most difficult coloring book he had ever started: The Knights of the Round Table, complete in thirty-four pages. First he had gone through the book and colored all the armor. Then he had gone back through it and worked on the horses, the castles, the sky and the costumes, in that order. Now, on the last lap, he was attempting to do something with the faces, his least favorite part because he was never able to arrive at suitable flesh tones.

"You are like a little baby with his toy," said Rosita. "You listen to nothing. In Spanish we say: 'Cada loco con su tema.'"

"'Every madman has his subject,'" said Applebee. "I got sense enough to understand that much." But still he didn't get up.

A self-ordained minister devoted to coloring books, gospel songs and the word of God as he interpreted it, he was forty years old, over six feet tall, and even with more than two hundred and eighty pounds to his name, he didn't always appear to be fat.

"You look fat from the front but not from the back," Rosita had often said, calling attention to the fact that all his weight was in his stomach. "It is because you have a face like a little fat angel that you are not ugly all over."

Applebee had not heard anything she said. Like an overgrown apostle, he was hunched over his favorite table next to the back window trying to scrape some of the color off Lancelot's face before the bus arrived with another coloring book, one he had ordered from a company in San Antonio. For years, he had special-ordered his books because there was no place in or around Judson to buy the complicated kind he liked. The one he was working on had come from a mail-order company in Fort Worth, and the one before that had been ordered and reordered more than three times before it ever arrived from Birmingham.

"Hey, Rosita, the new one's supposed to be here today," said

Applebee. "So you better go meet the bus and claim it for me. You know how I get every time I have to go around that driver." Applebee had no intention of ever meeting the bus again and Rosita knew it; she just liked to pester him from time to time because she thought he deserved it. She knew he had come to Judson to get away from everyone and everything that annoyed him, especially all the Bible-beating Baptists he had gone to seminary with and that category now included anyone who acted like, looked like or even remotely resembled Brother Horatio Ravenhill.

After Applebee had settled himself in the Brush Country, he had given up almost all communication with his old friends. No one ever wrote to him, and no one ever sent him so much as a coupon for ten cents off on a box of soap, no one except the companies he ordered from that is, and they all found him to be an easy customer for the latest thing in colored pencils, magic markers, Crayolas and coloring books. But what puzzled him most was how the last company he had ordered from knew the exact day the book would be delivered and that it was going to arrive by bus rather than by regular mail, which was delivered to the box on the highway.

The company's advertisement had arrived three months back, and Rosita had intercepted it, a double postcard, the bottom half of which was an order form to be torn off and returned, all postage prepaid. "Somebody tries to get you to color a book by God," she had said, handing the card over to Applebee. As usual he read it in a hurry:

COLOR YOUR WORLD WITH THE WORD OF GOD
BOOK YOUR INVINCIBLE EARLY THIS SUMMER

Below the large heading had been several paragraphs in smaller print that he had been too busy to bother with, so he tore off the bottom of the card, checked the box marked Yes and gave it back to Rosita so she could send it to True Vine, something or other, a company he had never ordered from and had no idea how they had gotten his name.

"They heard about you in one place, they heard about you in all places," he had said, and for weeks thereafter he didn't give the advertisement another thought until he received a reply stating that his *two* Invincibles would be arriving on the afternoon bus of June the fifth.

"Well, how do you like that," he had said. "Here I've ordered *one*, and now they're trying to tell me I'm getting more than I ordered. I can tell you one thing though, I'm only paying for one and that's it. Rosita, you got your wires crossed and ordered more than I need, and all of them just alike too. A man could go crazy way out here if he had to color the same picture over and over every day of his life."

Applebee had never given very much attention to details, but he did keep track of everything that he ordered, the day he ordered it and when he expected it to arrive. He kept his records on Rosita's picture calendar and would not allow anyone else to mark on it. When June the fifth rolled around, he noticed that the calendar had been marked with a large red letter I for Invincible, and under the letters he had written: "Ordered one, pay for one."

"Hey, Rosita, today's the fifth and that color book order you messed up is supposed to be here. I only wanted one and you ordered two. If I remember right it's on a religious subject."

"I'm very tired of all your religious subjects," said Rosita. "You make me wish I could believe in nothing."

"A little religion never hurt nobody," Applebee shouted toward the kitchen. "But a whole lot of it has sure as hell done a mess'a harm. That's what I have to say."

"And," replied Rosita, "I have to say that my mother is right when she says, 'There is a long distance between saying something and doing it.' For example: The man with the bus is almost here. I have my tamales to roll, and still you do nothing but sit."

"I'll get up and hide in a minute," said Applebee, staring out the back window. In the foreground was a fire hydrant almost covered with sand, and behind it was a lamp post raising its head above the cactus like the ghost of Lewis Judson, who often came back—according to Rosita's mother—to give testimony to what his town had been and might yet become.

"Mr. Applebee, you ask God quick to make you little," said Rosita, watching the bus come closer and closer. "You know how this man crawls under your skin, so you make yourself be little between the table maybe."

"Beneath the table maybe, or under the table maybe," corrected Applebee. A tarantula, sitting on top of the fire hydrant, had captured his attention. The spider was eating an insect, a grasshopper, looked like. Applebee tried to put himself in place of the predator and then the prey. After a few moments he said, "I don't think I'd like to be either one." But still he did not move.

Rosita did not feel like dealing with Ravenhill either, but she knew that someone had to, and it was not going to be her most regular customer. That day she had served thirty-five hot lunches, had rolled more tamales than she could keep track of, and still was not finished. "My feet are tired all day long when I roll tamales for my good customers," she said, hurrying to close the front door before Ravenhill got there.

After hanging the CLOSED sign in the window and pulling the curtains shut, she went out the back way and came sauntering around the building as though she had just come from a leisurely stroll through the cactus. "I hope he is not very hungry this time," she said, wiping her oily hands on her apron and then using the other side of it to mop her face. "I will tell him that I have no food cooked. I will say: 'Give me Mr. Applebee's little book and go have dinner somewhere else. In Carrizo Springs, my good friend Juanita makes enchiladas the way you like them. She will be open tonight too.' "

As tired as she was, Rosita, practicing her speech, stood in front of the hotel and waited for the bus. About a quarter of a mile away it stopped by the side of the road and someone carrying a suitcase got out. "Miss Alaska visits her daughter again," Rosita shouted toward the café. "Now we will listen to her tell us how to paint the hotel pretty colors, and how to wash the dishes clean. In one day she will finish my patience."

Once out of the bus, Mary Alaska told Brother Ravenhill to take Winkie Kermit back where he had found her. Then she got into her son-in-law's pickup truck and they drove off toward the ranch, while the bus proceeded into Judson.

In front of the café, Ravenhill came to a full stop and opened the door fast. Winkie Kermit stumbled out of the bus and into the arms of Rosita López, who was trying to block the exit. "Isheee-ma-ha-ya-ma-HA. I thank Jesus for asking me to stay on this bus," she said to the Mexican woman as though they were old friends. "Ma-ha-ya-ma-HA. God wants me to follow this beautiful driver-man even if he leads me to the end of the world."

"Welcome to that place," said Rosita. "Nobody much lives here now. We have no food and no beds."

"Oh, we can't stay, thank you," said Winkie. "Back down the road Mary Alaska started acting ugly all of a sudden, and now she won't let me stay with her, so I'll be getting back to Carrizo Springs before it gets too dark. There's a Baptist mission there where Brother Ravenhill says we can spend the night and hear some good preaching tomorrow. We just stopped here to deliver Principia Martindale. Your Brother Applebee's expecting her to-day. She's an Invincible, but I guess you know that already."

Inside the café, Applebee's ears caught the word *Invincible*. He stood up for the first time that afternoon, peered through a hole in the window curtain and saw Principia, her arms folded around her heart-shaped carryall, her feet buried in the sand. She was standing close to the door of the bus and appeared to be on the verge of boarding it again.

"You're not supposed to be a person," said Applebee.

"You're the religious subject I ordered?" he heard Rosita ask. She was standing between the café and the bus and hoping no one would ask to go inside.

"Yes, and I'm so excited to be here," said Principia as though she had lost her breath.

Rosita stared hard at the Invincible and wondered if she was the stranger her mother, Señora Hernandez, had said would be coming to Judson to stay a long long time.

Señora Hernandez knew the properties of herbs; she read tea leaves, cards and palms. As a young woman, oil companies had hired her to travel in a wagon over the Permian Basin and predict the best places to drill. Because her predictions had been accurate most of the time she had been called the Prophetess of the Plains, but in her old age she was known to be wrong more times than right; still, Applebee and Rosita continued to have *some* faith in her ability and had been wondering who this dark woman was and what she was all about. The señora had said the woman was not young and not old and had some connection with the town, so it was Applebee's worst dread that one of his ex-wives was going to find him, and it was Rosita's fear that her first cousin Sofina was going to show up for another long visit.

Through the hole in the muslin curtain Applebee was eyeing Principia carefully and also wondering if she was the stranger who kept turning up in the cards. After considering Principia's fair complexion he said, "She's not dark; she's not the right age, but she is a stranger. Señora's never been one hundred percent accurate with her predictions. Getting too old to see things the way she used to. She's probably colorblind too and nobody's ever had the sense to discover it."

Still watching Principia through the curtain, he wondered where she had come from, what had brought her to Judson and what she thought she was going to do there. He noticed her wooden cross tucked under her belt, her white Bible sticking out of her side pocket and her two suitcases and three boxes of supplies on the ground behind her. "She sure does look like she's come to stay awhile," said Applebee. "That might be just fine with me too."

She seemed to be looking at everything at once and focusing on nothing in particular. He wondered what had run off with her mind and if she had come way out there to find it again. There was something about her that made him want to protect her, but at the same time he wanted to send her back where she belonged. "She looks like the type that never fits in anywhere," he said. "She probably came out here to get rid of some weird disease, and I bet it's catching too."

"You're in good hands now, Sister," declared Ravenhill. His voice carried inside the café. "Brother Applebee is the finest man of God I've ever known."

"He's a damn liar," said Applebee, while Rosita, still trying to block the entrance to the café, was telling Ravenhill that she had closed the kitchen a long time ago. "That's right, you tell him a thing or two, Rosita," said Applebee, pointing his finger through the curtain. "The man knows he hates my guts, but he's too good a Christian to admit it. Seminary was full of 'em just like him."

In the past few months Applebee had learned to dislike Ravenhill intensely because he continued to send the wrong kind of people to kneel before the screen door and ask for God's healing power. Only two months before Principia arrived, one of Ravenhill's friends, Melvin Timbrook from La Grange, suffered a fatal heart attack when he knelt down before the image of Christ, and a week before that, another person, Mrs. Oletha Riley, deeply afflicted—also sent by Ravenhill—knelt down and was unable to straighten up again so she had to be taken to the hospital in Carrizo Springs, where she was visited by a reporter who wrote up the story for a San Antonio newspaper.

"You aren't doing us any good," Applebee had said to Ravenhill after reading the article in the paper. "If there's one more *accident* anywhere near that screen door, God only knows how much longer we'll last. Don't get me wrong—we welcome the sick, but we don't welcome the very very sick."

By the time Principia arrived, the two men were unable to agree upon anything and trying to stay out of each other's way. Applebee had already threatened to have Ravenhill's silver bus blown to bits if he sent them one more sick person, and Ravenhill, because he thought Applebee might do exactly what he said, did not linger in Judson any longer than absolutely necessary. He would arrive, drop off packages and passengers, order his tamales to go and leave fast, unless, of course, Applebee was nowhere around, which was not often the case.

Principia thought it was strange that Brother Ravenhill seemed to be in a big hurry to leave, especially when Rosita told him that Applebee was on his way to the hotel. He ushered Winkie back to the bus while saying goodby over his shoulder. "I'll be back at the end of the week to take you to Asherton," he said to Principia. "God bless you until then."

"You have lifted my soul, Brother Ravenhill," replied Principia, following them to the bus. "And, Winkie, you have been a blessing to my life. God will take care of me, and He will take care of you. I'm so glad that He brought us together . . ."

Before she finished, Ravenhill had gunned the motor and was speeding along Judson Avenue as though something were chasing him. The evening light was golden and the bus reflected the setting sun all the way down the road until it disappeared into the brush and Principia could no longer see even the faintest flash of light. Then she turned her attention to the town, or what was left of it.

Beyond the cottonwood the shell of an adobe house stared at her like the sun-bleached skull of a bandit. The roof had already fallen through, the back wall had collapsed and the front door was dangling on its hinges like a lock of hair falling over a dead man's face. Sand drifts, one after another, had invaded the interior, and a prickly pear had inched its way inside until its thorny elbows rested on a windowsill—like a mother too worried to go to bed, Principia thought.

The sight of the house filled with cactus gave her an empty, hollowed-out feeling, so she turned her attention to the cottonwood, the cloudless sky and then the hotel all boarded up for life. "It looks like it hasn't seen a guest since Noah's flood," she said.

"It's been longer than that," Rosita answered. She was still standing before the entrance to the café. "Used to we had many streets and houses in Judson, but that was then."

The hotel stood next to a dry goods store, which was also boarded up. There was a narrow alley between the two buildings and a well-worn path leading toward the back, but along Lewis Street, Principia saw that the vacant stores were standing one against the other. Again the sand drifts and mesquite had taken their toll on what had been the busiest street in Judson.

Hoping to see the image of Jesus, her eyes moved from one door to the next, but after a few moments she realized that the shrine was most likely in the church rather than outside. Then, wondering where all the people were, she found herself staring at a sign pointing the way to Manuel the Woodcarver. "Where does he live?" she asked.

"Oh, my father Manuel, he no longer lives here," said Rosita as though he had recently moved to the next town. "He died two years ago. When he finished carving *santos* for the new church in Laredo he died fast, so we buried him under the hollyhocks, but since then the hollyhocks don't bloom pretty anymore."

"I guess they need some water," said Principia.

"Everybody needs some water," replied Rosita. She moved away from the door and sat down in the old metal lawn chair that was covered with dust. "Three years ago we had a drought, and the water table went further down. Today we get maybe twenty gallons of water from one well. That's why nobody wants to stay very long."

Principia scanned the town for a trace of another human being and found nothing but Applebee's 1950 green Ford pickup with his bantam rooster, Saint George, perched on the steering wheel. Applebee had raised Saint George from a baby chick, had hand-fed him most of his life, and, according to Rosita, he was spoiled rotten. The rooster was blue black with a red and yellow ruff, a trace of orange on his wings, and had the sharpest spurs Rosita's husband Sergio had ever felt. For a few seconds Principia watched the rooster sitting on the steering wheel as though he owned it, and then she looked at the truck. The tires were worn slick, a toy rifle, red and blue, was hanging in the back window, and REVELATIONS 21:1 was written across the tailgate.

If a person didn't know his Bible he wouldn't know what that scripture was all about, she thought, quoting the verse to herself. "And I saw a new heaven and a new earth: for the first heaven and the first earth were passed away, and there was no more sea."

"How many people did you say lived here now?" she asked, coming out of her silence.

"It's hard to answer," said Rosita. "In Judson people come and people go. First there was nothing here, and then there was the town, and then that went away, and then the ranch, and then my mother and father came here and then Sergio who became my husband, and then Rubendella our daughter was born, so that makes five people. Then Sergio's three sisters, Encarnación, Concepción, and Modesta came here, and then Applebee, and that makes nine people in all, and then Sergio's sisters they left, so take away three and that makes six, but then they came back again with their husbands so add six more and that's twelve, and then Rubendella left but then she got divorced and came back so that's still twelve and then Modesta's husband left for good, so that's back to eleven, and then Manuel my father died, so that makes ten plus whoever's here today and plus the ranch people, but they don't live close, and plus the children. We have six little children, and one big children. You will meet the big one soon." Then she smiled as though about to tell a secret and added, "Today he plays with his colors."

"But that don't mean that there's something the matter with him," came a voice from the café.

Principia turned to see a giant of a man standing in the doorway. For a moment she was unable to speak or think very clearly, and she felt as though her power of reasoning had left through the top of her head.

"You know I could have you arrested for advertising yourself as one thing and showing up as something entirely different," said Applebee. "You're not exactly the best-looking thing that's ever come to town either, so I hope you don't think you'll be getting lots of business around here. But if you stay long enough I guess somebody'll have you; looks like it nearly 'bout always works out that way."

"I'm not that kind of woman," said Principia, blushing all the way down to her fingertips. Her hands had always turned red when she was embarrassed, so she tried to hide them behind her back. For a moment she put herself in place of David standing before Goliath. She assured herself that the Lord was with her every minute of the day and there was no reason to be frightened.

"Whoever you are, you're not what I expected," said Applebee. "So I hope you brought some water with you to make up for my disappointment."

The summer missionary drew her carryall up to her bosom and clutched it there with both hands hidden under her arms. Because Applebee's stare was so intense she felt as though she had just been exposed. She wanted to stop blushing, but she could not, so she took several deep breaths and began speaking rapidly.

"My name's Principia Martindale, and I did not come here with the kind of intentions you seemed to imply just now. For your information, I attend Hillister Baptist College; the Lord has called me to be a full-time missionary, and I happen to be one of the two Invincibles you requested, but at the last minute the other girl was sent back home so I'm here all by myself, and I didn't bring any water with me, but I did bring the Word of God."

"We got the Word of God already," said Applebee.

"Well, I'm going to add a few more words to what you already have then," replied Principia.

"You're real sure about that I see. I got a few ideas on the subject myself. Come on in and let's talk it over."

When he realized that Principia wasn't about to move, not even to take a step, he added, "You don't need to be scared. I'm just messin' with you. That's all. Never been known to hurt anybody yet." He smiled, rubbed his stomach and turned to go inside. "I ain't seen anything like you since I left the Ozarks and I ain't too sure I ever seen anything like you back there. Don't get me wrong, I'm real glad you came, but I was led to expect something entirely different."

Principia felt herself begin to relax, but she wasn't too sure she wanted to. Never in all her life had she met anyone like this man, and she wondered if there were many more like him in the world. Rosita realized that the summer missionary needed some encouragement, so she got up from the lawn chair and gave her a little nudge toward the door. The first step Principia took was hard, but the others came easy because a cool breeze, like a giant sigh of relief, started in the branches of the cottonwood and followed her inside.

2

Even though Rosita López had only one daughter, Rubendella Hinojosa, twenty-eight, divorced and determined once and for all to become an actress if it killed her, Rosita felt as though she had given birth to everyone in Judson plus a few cats and dogs, a pet rooster and three baby armadillos that Carlos Sánchez, the seven-year-old son of José and Encarnación, turned loose in the café and then refused to catch so Rosita had to do it herself and ended up feeding them for two weeks before she decided it was best to let them go. According to Rosita, Carlos had a lazy streak inside him just like everyone else in Sergio's family, everyone except Sergio, that is. Rosita had taught him to do a little bit of work and was proud of that achievement, but she was convinced that the others would never learn anything.

"You take care of too many people," her mother, Señora Obdulla Hernandez, always said. "You must get Sergio's sisters to do something besides argue so much." But Rosita always told her mother that the three sisters were the biggest babies of all. When they first came to Judson, Rosita swore that she would never have anything to do with them, but before long she was settling their disputes and giving out advice. Then when they got married she told them not to expect her to take care of any children that might come along; again however, she went back on her word, and, just as she had done with Rubendella, Rosita accepted the children as her own: fed them, clothed them, got them up in time to catch the school bus, took them shopping in Carrizo Springs, never tolerated a moment of disrespect and insisted that they speak English as well as Spanish. "They are good children in spite of where they came from," she always said. "And in time they might learn a thing or two, like Sergio."

When Principia arrived, she looked so lost and frightened that Rosita's heart went out to her without any effort at all, but then she told herself that she didn't need another responsibility because she was already taking care of Carlos, Rafalita and Antonio; Romero, Isabel and Maria Luisa. She counted them on her fingers. She was taking care of their parents as well, and then there was her own mother, her daughter, her husband, Saint George and of course Applebee, who was always hungry. She told herself that she would not take care of Principia even if she had come to stay a long long time, even if she had come to stay one minute.

"This time I will not be responsible, Mr. Señor Apple," she whispered as the three of them went into the café.

Applebee had expected Rosita to welcome Principia and make her feel at home, but instead she went straight back to her tamales. Applebee left Principia standing in front of the counter and followed Rosita into the kitchen, where he asked her what she thought she was doing, and without a moment's hesitation Rosita informed him—although he didn't really believe her—that she was tired of taking care of the whole world.

"Listen to me," she said. "This little girl will be a nice friend for you, not like Miss Gloria Sleaze-ball who comes here to sit on your lap. If you are very very nice to this person, she may even wash your clothes while she's here. Now go back out there and tell her how happy you are that she's come to see you, and in a few minutes I will bring you a cup of coffee and maybe a nice tamale to go with it."

Applebee returned to the café, sat down at his favorite table, which was always cluttered in order to keep everyone else away from it. Coloring books by the dozen were stacked up on one side, Crayolas on the other; in the center were several hymnals both old and new and on top of them was a dirty plate, a beer can and a pencil with the eraser chewed off and teeth marks up and down the shaft. On the chair next to him was a fiddle that had once belonged to Manuel.

Because of his threadbare Levi's and his messed-up hair,

Principia did not realize he was the man she had heard so much about. She saw his name written on the coloring books and hymnals—every letter was a different color—and decided that he was Donald Applebee after all, but she hoped that he was not.

"Brother Applebee, you look like you didn't know I was coming," she said, sitting on top of a stack of coloring books. "What were you expecting?"

"I was expecting what you're sitting on, that's what," he answered. "And you can lay off that brother shit, you understand?"

"Don't be vulgar with me," said the summer missionary as though commanding a regiment. A blush swept over her face and continued all the way down to the tips of her fingers. "I don't know how this misunderstanding has occurred, but just let me say this: If you aren't a preacher I am firmly convinced that your soul needs some attention, and if you *are* a preacher your soul needs even more attention for backsliding in your beliefs. And if you think I've come all the way out here to sell my body and soul you're absolutely wrong, because I happen to be here to bring committed individuals into a deeper personal relationship with Jesus Christ and firmly establish those who are not yet committed into a local church. I am also here to teach Vacation Bible School to the children in your congregation, if you've really got one, and that's just what I intend to do. I'm here for only one week and then I'll be going to Asherton to do the same thing and after that I have four more assignments before I go back home. I've already been paid for my time, and I'm ready to work, so you might show me where I'm supposed to live and tell me how many children I can expect in Bible School tomorrow morning. I want to get started at eight o'clock and will keep the first day short because I don't want to interfere with your regular Sunday morning service. I brought my wind-up with me so I'll be sure to be up and ready." She took her alarm clock out of the carryall and reset it to match the café clock.

Suddenly conscious of the time, Applebee sprang to his feet. "Come with me. I got something to show you." He picked up the two suitcases and was out the door before Principia realized that she was supposed to go with him.

As the sun was sinking into Mexico she followed him down one of the side streets. "If we don't hurry we'll miss them," he kept shouting to her. They ran past store fronts covered by mesquite and prickly pear, passed many sandy trails leading out through the brush to houses with only a flicker of lamplight coming from within, for there was no electricity in Judson except at the café, no telephones except at the Lucky L Ranch and no radio that would pick up a clear station. There was very little at all except sand, last year's tumbleweeds standing motionless in abandoned doorways, a few graves, a few houses still holding their own tucked away behind cactus and brush and a few families who made their living not from what Judson had been but from what it had become.

Principia, thinking she was being led to the sacred screen door, followed Applebee down the dusty street to a tall narrow building of sandstone and adobe, where he stopped fast, spat in front of him as far as he could and said, "That's the church. It was designed and built in nineteen twenty-five by L. J. Judson. He was a devoted Baptist, and this is all that's left of it."

Principia rubbed hair and sand from her face, gazed at the wet spot on the ground and for a few minutes was unable to tear her attention from it. Applebee put her suitcases down, took her head in his hands and forced her to look up at the church, a fortress with five steps leading to double doors of weathered oak.

His hands were rough against her face, and she pulled away from him fast. "What's the matter," he said. "You not used to being touched?" She put her hands behind her and stepped backward several times. Her skin was burning, her fingers were nervously twisting her dress. She felt embarrassment and shame, and a sharp stinging sense of comfort when Applebee said, with kindness, almost in whispers, "I didn't mean to upset you. I'm just that way, I guess."

Principia could still feel the print of his hands burning on her face; she could feel her heart trembling, as though something in her was about to break and there was no way of holding it together, but it was not just his hands on her face that upset her, it was also the way he kept staring. In the evening light the blue of his eyes had faded away, giving the impression that he had no pupils, just two large gray openings that seemed to be seeing her from the inside out.

"I was just trying to get you to look up at the building," he said. His voice was friendly, had a soothing quality to it, but still she could not bring herself to look at him for very long, so she turned her attention to the church.

On one side of the double oak doors was a crumbling bell tower, and on the other a blue century plant, its leaves sharper than any two-edged sword, was facing the last days of its life. Its twenty-foot stalk and cluster of flowers was in full bloom against the sunset, streaked with purple and gold like one of Aunt Wilda's finger paintings or an illustration from the Rainbow Bible.

"They call it a century plant because it blooms once every hundred years, or that's what I'm told anyway," said Applebee. "Can't never count on what you hear and only half of what you see, but if it's the truth I think it's one more sad story. Just imagine what it must be like to sit around for a hundred years waiting for yourself to bloom and as soon as you do, you drop dead and that's the end of it." Applebee eyed Principia carefully while he spoke because he always judged people by what they thought of the century plant. If they agreed with him that it was a sad story, he would scratch them off his list without another thought, but if they said that it was not a sad story, he would assume (and rightly so, he came to learn) that they were worth his time.

Principia thought it was a beautiful story and that Applebee had failed to see its deeper meaning. "It's not the end of it at all," she said. "It flowers and goes to seed and comes back again, so in a sense it's like dying and going to heaven."

Applebee found her answer about seventy-five percent satisfactory. "It's more like dying and coming right straight back to where you started and doing it all over again only in a different way," he said. "But don't get too hung up over it because that's not what I brought you out here to look at. You want to see something really beautiful, you just stand here and don't make a sound. Don't even clear your throat, you hear me?"

Principia nodded her head in obedience and stood perfectly still waiting for something to happen. She hoped to see Christ materialize on the church door, but it wasn't a screen door, so for a moment she felt confused and looked to Applebee for an explanation, but he returned her stare with an enigmatic grin. She had not yet decided what she thought of him, but one thing was sure, she felt uncomfortable in his presence. Yet there were moments when there was something reassuring about him that she could respond to, something easy underneath his appearance.

They stood in silence looking at the church. The evening was hot and dusty and the only sound that could be heard was the wind whistling through the mesquite on its way to the bell tower, where it died slowly and then could be heard coming back to life again somewhere on the other side of town. Principia looked up to see a full moon rising above the church, stars just beginning to flicker against the evening sky and tiny specks like cinders flying from the building. Before she knew it, the sky was alive with a windy fluttering, the stars were obliterated, the moon turned gray and the bell tower almost disappeared against a black cloud passing behind it.

"Mexican free-tail bats," said Applebee. "They're coming out of a back room, and pretty soon they'll be coming out of everything."

There were five frame houses around the church. They were small, had pitched roofs and were barely visible over the brush. Applebee had boarded them up so the bats could have dark places to live in and had made holes in the roofs so they could come and go. "In a minute or two you'll see more bats than you can shake a stick at," he said. "I got five houses, plus the back room in the church, that's six places where they like to live. When I first came here they were only in the church, now they're everywhere, and when the sun's hot, or the wind's just right, you'll know it too; can smell 'em all over town."

When the bats started flying from all the houses, Principia folded her arms around her, placed her legs close together and admitted to herself that she would like to be anyplace in the world other than where she was. Before she realized what she was doing, she reached out to put her arms around Applebee, but she stopped herself before he saw her. All she wanted was someone to assure her that she had been led to the right place, and for a moment, only a moment and no longer, she found herself believing that she might find that kind of comfort in Applebee. Then she told herself she was mistaken, and, feeling completely alone in the world, she began wondering why the Lord had led her to such a place and what good she could possibly do there. Rosita's words "We have six little children and one big children" rang through her head like the bells of an asylum, but she was unable to voice her feelings, so she stood perfectly still and stared at the heavens while the bats flew off in clouds that gradually thinned out over the brush. Then she felt something crawling up her leg. She lifted her skirt, attempted to brush whatever it was away, but there was nothing there except a few grains of sand, her imagination and a weed clinging to her slip.

"Something caught you?" asked Applebee with a grin that made his face light up like a jack-o'-lantern. "I got two things to say. One, before you leave this place you'll know how much faith you've really got, and two, the next time you feel something crawling up your leg, you better watch out, it just might be a hairy ole spider or a hand about like mine."

"I didn't come out here to listen to that kind of talk," said Principia, fingering the wooden cross. "If Miss Cassy knew you were using that kind of language around me she would never send another Invincible to help you out. Now let me remind you of this: If you lust after me, then you have sinned in your thoughts, and if I cause you to lust after me then I have sinned in mine, but you can be sure that I will not give you that cause, not ever."

"I got a woman," said Applebee, "and don't need another one, but I can still lust if I want to, and I just did, and you made me by hiking up your skirt, so you better bow your head and close your eyes real tight and ask God to forgive you for your many sins and iniquities. Ask him before it's too late now."

"If I thought you were serious I would," said Principia. "I happen to talk to God every minute of the day, and I know for sure that I did not cause you to sin because I'm not that kind of person. Now will you tell me where I'm supposed to live while I'm here. I'd like to get settled."

"That's a good idea," said Applebee reverently. "You'll enjoy serving the Lord after you're settled."

"I've enjoyed serving the Lord from birth, thank you," said Principia, her hands clutching the wooden cross under her belt. "I have served him gladly, and I have served him with the devotion of Deborah, and, furthermore, I will not work in a church that's full of bats because that's the most disgraceful thing I've ever seen."

"They're in the back part and it's all closed off," said Apple-

bee. "But you might get to liking them and move back there before it's all over." He had also been known to judge people by
what they thought of his favorite nocturnal mammal. "You'll hear
everything in the world said about a bat. If one flies into all that
hair of yours, you'll go stark raving mad, or so they say. Won't
ever recover either."

Principia ran her fingers through her hair, nervously twisted
it around and forced it into the neck of her dress. A cold chill ran
through her as one lone bat fluttered its way over the church and
into the darkness beyond.

"They got a built-in sense of where they're going," Applebee
said. "It's like radar. You can put one's eyes out, and he can still
find his way around without bumping into things. Bet you can't
do that."

Principia did not answer.

"Some people think bats are evil; some people think they're
sacred. The Mayas even built a city in their honor, Izinacent Lan,
Bat City, they call it."

"Well, I don't think I'd like to go there," said Principia.

"You won't have to," replied Applebee. "You got all the bats
you need right here. But the worst part is that they go away in
the winter, hibernate somewhere, and that's when I feel all alone,
feel like everything's left me suddenly. I get that empty gnawing
feeling and can't go to sleep at night and can't get up in the
morning because there's no bats to watch. What I'm about to say
is going to sound funny to somebody like you because you don't
know anything but what's in the Bible, but the bats keep me believing that there's still a Spirit even though a lot of people will
tell you different these days. They say there never was such a
thing, or that it's forgot all about us, or won't come back to earth
anymore, but I say it comes back every once in a while just to let
some of us know it's still alive and kicking. I know what I'm talking about because every now and then when everything gets real
still I can hear the wind blowing low across the earth and know it
can't be the wind because there's nothing moving so I say to myself: Well, I guess that's the Holy Spirit stirring things up this
evening. It's come back to earth to remind us there is such a thing
after all. But it won't come back as often as it used to, so you've
gotta have all the reminders you can get. The bats are my re-

minders. I come out here every evening and watch them fly off. First I see them a speck or two at a time, and then I see them in a cloud going off together, and I hear their wings flapping, and it sounds like the wind, but there's nothing moving, and my flesh gets cold and my bones get hot, and I know right off it's just the bats, but it reminds me of the Holy Spirit, so that's what I say it is, and to me that's exactly what it is too because it makes me feel that way."

"'The wind bloweth where it listeth,'" quoted Principia, "'and thou hearest the sound thereof, but canst not tell whence it cometh, and whither it goeth: so is every one that is born of the Spirit.'"

"Saint John, three, eight," said Applebee. "You don't need to be quoting scripture right and left, because I know a few myself, went to seminary in Fort Worth, you know; didn't finish but went there just the same and didn't learn a damn thing about bats either."

A dark cloud rose from the furthest house, drifted over the church and left behind a stale odor that seemed to hang in the air like dust in an empty closet. Applebee watched the cloud of bats fade out of sight. "When they all fly up like that," he said, "they make me believe in things I used to believe in and then quit believing in, and found out that I could believe in again if I just stayed away from the wrong people. People like that bus driver, people who've lived all cooped up in their fancy churches all their lives and don't know how to do anything but drive two blocks to the store, too lazy to walk, too lazy to think, too lazy to wonder what all this is really about, even too lazy to feel anything. They're content to say the same old tired, worn-out amen, amen prayers all their lives and don't know one thing about the Spirit. I say they ought to come out here to live, but probably wouldn't do any good because nothing seems to reach them in their tired, scared-to-death states of mind, not even the bats, but they sure help me a lot; they keep me feeling and believing that there really is something you can't see moving low across the earth."

"Maybe I'm going to like bats more than I thought," said Principia. Again she was feeling at ease with Applebee, was beginning to believe that she had been led to the right place after all, and that her work in Judson would be blessed, but she didn't agree with him that the Holy Spirit made itself scarce, for she hoped that she was in constant communion with it and thought that Applebee could be too if he would only try.

"I think you're too hard on people," she said. "Brother Ravenhill is a wonderful man and a devoted Christian. Winkie Kermit has been blessed with a special language, and if you want it you can have it too. The Holy Spirit will give it to you if you really and truly want it and ask for it. I want it very very badly. I've asked for it and when the time is right I'll have it, you'll see. Brother Ravenhill agrees with me too."

"I don't believe in taking advantage of a good thing," said Applebee, going toward the church. "People ought to keep most of that emotion inside them where it belongs."

He sounds just like Mary Alaska Ragsdale, thought Principia. If I told him that the gift of tongues is the most beautiful and precious gift a Christian can receive he'd just laugh in my face, so I just won't tell him anything and let him find out for himself, that's the best thing to do in this case, except of course, pray.

Applebee started up the church steps. Principia, believing that she was at last going to see the sacred screen door, followed him. She imagined that the door would be on display behind the pulpit, or perhaps above the baptismal pool, and that the aisles would be worn slick by the footprints of thousands who had visited the shrine and been healed. But when he opened the doors they stepped inside what appeared to be a garden with plants growing everywhere, corn taller than her head, tomatoes, peppers, squash and a single sunflower blooming earlier than usual and growing in the middle of what seemed to be an aisle. They were standing in the main sanctuary of the church; the walls were still intact, there were three windows on the east and west sides, but the adobe floors had crumbled with age and constant gardening and the roof had been missing for so long no one could remember what had happened to it. Applebee said that as long as he was around the roof would never be replaced either because one was not needed. He explained that the walls not only kept the armadillos from rooting up the garden, they also blocked off most of the winter cold; the open roof let in the sun, and the old adobe floors made it easy to convert the interior into a winter and summer garden.

In the middle of the aisle, the sunflower faced them as though they had intruded upon its sleep and it expected to be rewarded by another dipper of water from the baptismal pool. Ignoring its silent request, they walked to the front of the church, where there were a pulpit and five pews placed one in back of the other, but toward the entrance where the congregation once sat there were eight rows of corn standing in reverent formation, and behind the corn marched several stands of chili peppers for Rosita, and then the tomatoes, and next the squash and then the speckled butterbeans growing on strings up the back wall. Somewhere in a far corner a single watermelon plant was sending out its longest runner; the vine had inched its way between the rows of vegetables until it had entered the main aisle, where it was making a slow pilgrimage toward the altar. Applebee had not wanted to plant watermelon because of the lack of space, but the children of Judson wanted watermelon more than anything else so he planted one seed, which produced a plant that was about to take over the entire church.

"This is the second garden we've had in here since January," he said. "We usually grow three to four crops a year, got plenty of sun, plenty of warmth, but now we're running out of plenty of water. All the wells but one went dry and that one can't last much longer. Been watering the garden with what's left in that old baptismal pool and when that runs out we'll have to haul every drop we use."

"We'll have to pray for water," said Principia. She was not aware of speaking because she was slowly coming to the realization that the church had been abandoned and that she was not going to see the screen door there. The building, in such a state of disrepair, made her feel lonely and out of place.

"We've already tried praying for water," said Applebee. "Got to get the money to drill a well is what we got to do."

He took a kerosene lamp off the top of the upright piano and sat it on the floor. Then he pulled a blanket and a pillow out of the instrument and closed it up again. "This was L. J. Judson's piano," he said. "Everything around here either belonged to him or got named after him. He was shot to death right out there in front of the church. Some rich woman from town did it. She claimed he tried to run off with all her money and he probably did too. For a long time Señora Hernandez kept saying he wasn't dead and would come back one day, and then she started seeing his ghost drifting around, so I guess she's right about part of it, he did come back, one way or another. She says she's seen him six times and touched him on the leg once, even says she hears him in here banging out some old hymn late of the night too, but you know how it is when you get that old. I don't say she's wrong, but me, I ain't never seen him dead or alive and don't want to neither."

While Principia was trying to tell him that she didn't believe in ghosts, he was leading her over to a bench that was cushioned. He said that a lot of visitors had slept on it and she could too. She accepted the bedding and said she wanted the children in Bible School at eight o'clock. Applebee promised that Rosita would round them up, and before he left the church he said, "If you need some drinking water you can get that in the café, and if you need the *necessary* you'll find it back behind the church, but if you get lonesome, or just can't sleep, you can always come on down the road. I live in the first house on the left. I named it Rapture's Heights and I sure will be happy to put up with you if you know what I mean."

"I know exactly what you mean," said Principia, "and the answer is *no*. I'll be just fine right here by myself."

After Applebee left the church, she felt more alone than ever, and for a moment she wanted him to come back, but instead of calling out after him, she looked up at the stars and wished for a proper church, a proper pastor and a parsonage to sleep in that night. But most of all she wished that Applebee would stop looking at her as though he knew her thoughts before she knew them herself. There was a look in his eyes, however, that came through only occasionally; it was a hollowed-out, lonesome expression that made her cold all over.

"Loneliness is the worst disease in the world," she said, dragging her suitcases through the garden. "It can cause us to do so many things that we might regret in the long run. Sometimes I wish there was no such thing as regret; that's something that Tawnya Louise ought to know something about but doesn't."

Attempting to put her mind to rest, she unpacked her suitcases onto a pew, arranged her clothes in the order she intended to wear them, made the bed with her own sheets and then set out to find a place for her soap and towels. She realized that somewhere near the baptismal pool was the logical place, since that was the only water supply readily available, but she didn't like the idea of using a drop of it, not even to water the plants. "If I have to I guess I have to," she said as she climbed the steps to the pool, which was elevated no more than four feet, built partially into the back wall and encased with a Mexican mosaic depicting the birth, death and resurrection of Christ. The moon and stars reflected in the dark water, as did the walls of the church, Principia's dirty face and the kind words of Herbie Stout:

"You will find out when you get into the field that an Invincible's work is never done. You will be called on to do things that you thought you would never be able to do, but God will give you the ability when the time comes."

Quickly she heeded his advice, and without thinking too much about what she was doing or trying not to think about it anyway, she dipped her washcloth into the pool and wrung it out. Not wanting to use more than her share of water, she rubbed her arms and legs with the wet cloth and squeezed the water that was left in it on the sunflower. Then she bathed her face with a towelette, put on a cotton nightgown and, for the first time in her life, went to bed feeling dirty. Sand was still on her face and arms, her legs were covered with grit and her hair was matted and tangled. "The Lord is testing me; from this experience I will learn strength," she said as she tried to sleep with the moon shining in her face.

But sleep did not come quickly, and she spent hours watching the shadows of corn stalks that the lamplight made on the back wall. "What kind of person would it take to allow a holy place to get so run down," she said, pulling the sheet up close to her head. Then she thought of Deborah leading the armies into battle and the hardships that she must have endured for the Lord. She also thought of her own relative Aunt Wilda, whose faith Principia believed had always been misunderstood. "All Aunt Wilda wanted to do was live as close to her Maker as she could get, and nobody wanted her to," said Principia, remembering her aunt's death in the state asylum. She had been there three times, knew her way around better than anyone thought, and one night she wrapped herself up in a sheet and climbed to the roof. She told everyone on the ground she was going to jump to prove her faith, and that's exactly what she did. "The Lord will save me," she said, as she fell to her death.

"'Thou shalt not tempt the Lord thy God,' Matthew four, seven," said Principia, staring up at the stars. "Lord give me the strength to succeed where Aunt Wilda failed."

Then she thought of Deborah again and wondered how many times she had slept outdoors. She thought of Lobelia Blankenship, who gave her life to the savages while attempting to bring them the teachings of Christ. She thought of Lottie Moon, and Annie Armstrong, Ruth and Naomi, and Esther, all of whom had loved the Lord with heart and soul and had endured unspeakable trials and tribulations in order to prove their faith. "Lord, thank you for these good examples," she said, gazing into the heavens. "And thank you for these hardships I am now enduring, for I too wish to be a shining example so others might see my good work and glorify my God who lives in heaven."

Although she felt honored to be chosen to suffer discomfort, there was no denying the fact that it was going to take some getting used to, for there was no roof over her head, no protection from insects or from all manner of creatures that might find their way into the abandoned church, and, besides that, the bench was hard and narrow, so she asked God to help her believe that she was in her own bed back home in New Bethel.

With that in mind, she finally drifted off to sleep, but in the middle of the night she awoke, remembered where she was and began to feel homesick. Nothing around her struck a familiar chord, and she longed for the sight of something, just anything, that would remind her of home. Most of all she longed for New Bethel Church resting on its solid foundations of river rocks, with its roof intact and its pews filled with worshipers. She longed for the soft humid air, the faint smell of rain and the delicate fragrance of mimosa. But she was awakened to sand and a dry wind blowing across her face, the smell of dust and the rancid odor of bats drifting in through the west windows, falling upon her from the open ceiling and lingering around her bed like the breath of Satan waiting to be blown away.

"This place is not a church," she said, trying to sit up. "Maybe it was at one time, but it's not anymore." She looked all around her for the sight of something that was familiar, but there was nothing, not even the baptismal pool looked as though it belonged there, encased with mosaics as it was and rising up from the floor like a cement box placed directly behind the pulpit where she was accustomed to seeing the choir. "The baptismal pool should be built into the wall back behind the choir," she said. "That's where I've always seen it, and one side should be partially glass so the congregation can witness the total immersion of the body." Again her eyes wandered around the church in search of something familiar; the old upright piano looked as though it belonged in a bar, and the pews looked more like benches that had been taken from some city park. There was nothing she could see that gave her comfort except the garden, so to compensate for her loneliness and feeling of desperation she decided to move her bed up near the front door, where she would not be separated from the plants by five rows of pews. But the moment she placed her bare feet on the floor something scurried across her toes; it was small and felt as though it had many legs. "O Lord, give me your protection," she said, lifting her feet onto the bed and then slowly placing them on the floor again. Satisfied after a few moments that she was safe, she began dragging the bench up the center aisle toward the sunflower.

Before she made it all the way there, however, she felt something crawling under her left foot, and then a pain like a hot coal seemed to travel through her bloodstream, up her leg and to all parts of her body, even to the ends of her hair, which seemed to bristle. Something was crawling all over her; she felt it moving up her leg, up her back, across her shoulders and down her right arm. It was as though her whole body had caught fire from the inside. She doubled over with the pain. A scorpion crawled out of the long sleeve of her nightgown, danced across her fingers and fell to the floor. She ran to the baptismal pool and threw herself into the cold water, but the fire consuming her body was not so easily extinguished.

"Lord, why hast Thou forsaken me?" she cried. "Give me comfort." But the pain did not leave. It lingered throughout the night, and finally when fatigue crept over her she managed to climb out of the pool, inch her way along the center aisle toward her bed, and, for a moment, for just a moment and no longer, she had the feeling of being in another place, a place much like New Bethel but it was not New Bethel, a place much like the church she had grown up in but it was not her church. She was still in Judson, but everything was different. "The Lord is trying to tell me something; he is speaking in whispers," she said as a light breeze rattled the corn stalks and whistled through the bell tower. "I must obey his every word." She tried to listen carefully to that small, faraway voice, tried to understand what she was being told, but she was unable to stay awake another moment and, like a fallen angel, she sank into her bed and slept in the company of the sunflower, its head bowed for the night as if in prayer.

 3

Donald Applebee had always given his life to busy-work because he, like Lively Hathaway, believed that important decisions could be made while performing some repetitive task such as cutting out patchwork, knitting, crocheting or, in Applebee's case, coloring, something he had enjoyed since early childhood. He swore that his concentration had been improved because he was able to allow his mind to roam freely while his hand chose colors at random and his eyes unfocused upon the page, a method of working that didn't always create a pleasing end product as Rosita could testify, but to Applebee's way of thinking it wasn't the end product that was so important but the process of arriving at it and his total involvement with the materials. Almost every afternoon he could be found at his favorite table in Rosita's café. There he would usually sit and color, drink his beer, or, when the mood struck him just right, he would try once more to find another tune on the fiddle that Manuel had left him. Manuel had made the fiddle out of mesquite, had often played it for the visitors and had been of the mind to teach Applebee how to play it too, but he died before he got the chance. With a lot of effort, however, Applebee had managed to compose one tune, but Sergio said that it sounded just like noise. "I'm tired of hearing the same old thing," he complained. "Now play something else, something pretty for a change."

Sergio was Rosita's height, only smaller around. He had a thin mustache, sunk-in cheeks and eyes so small that when he opened them up wide no one could tell much difference. He was convinced that Applebee had no musical ability whatever, and Applebee was convinced that Sergio was dead wrong.

As a child in Calico Rock, Arkansas, Applebee had taken two piano lessons from a one-eyed teacher, Mrs. Dorothy Summers, who insisted that he learn to read music, but Applebee had no intention of doing such a thing. Playing by ear was more enjoyable and making up melodies as he went along was almost as good as coloring because he didn't have to think too much about what he was doing and therefore could lose himself completely in the music, the coloring, and his own thoughts, which seemed to soar. There were moments when banging out a tune on L. J. Judson's piano that he almost felt as though he were flying, and he was beginning to feel the same way when playing the fiddle.

"You will drive us all out of our heads trying to be so musical," Sergio had said many times. "Your problem is that you need more attention than anybody else, and my wife's problem is that she gives you this attention and then you go off and make more noise. Your other problem is that you were the only child like my crazy daughter, Rubendella. Rosita and I, we should have had more babies."

Donald Applebee was well aware that he had been the only child, but he didn't see that it made any difference, not really. He had fond memories of both parents, even though they had been difficult to live with at the time. His father, also a Donald, was a part-time preacher for any denomination that would have him, and his mother, a devout Christian laywoman, worked at the old folks' home, where she was eventually fired because she had the old people up singing and dancing, clapping their hands and believing there was no such thing as death. Most people thought she was putting fool ideas in the old folks' heads, but what she said she was doing was making their last days happier than they would have been otherwise. Her first name was Myrtle, and, next to praising the Lord, songwriting was her biggest love. She wrote both the words and the music, had some of them published, and eventually they ended up in the new hymnbooks, but she never lived long enough to see that day arrive, and what a shame too, Applebee thought, because now everybody in Calico Rock had to sing her songs whether they had liked *her* or not.

The members of her church thought she was too happy to be

trusted because she took a tambourine with her everywhere she went, claimed it was the very hardest instrument in the world to play and liked nothing better than to give it a good shake and kick up her heels for the Lord. No one could agree on whether her husband should be pitied or admired for having the fortitude to put up with her, but when she died first it was the general consensus that the Lord had taken Myrtle in order to give Donald Senior a few years of peace before it was *his* time to go.

Applebee had vivid memories of both parents. His mother had lived and breathed the word of God, and carried it on her lips at all times, but his father had not been so quick to discuss his beliefs, except when behind the pulpit. As well as preach, he had been able to repair radios better than anyone in Calico Rock. He had been called on to do minor house and appliance repairs, and in his spare time he had read the *Encyclopedia Britannica* from beginning to end, but was unable to remember very much of what he had learned. He said that all the learning went into his head somewhere and got lost like everything else except the word of God, which came pouring out every time he preached, which was twice a month until his wife died, and then he went on the revival circuit as a full-time minister until he was killed in a traffic accident in Oklahoma City.

Applebee did not learn of his father's death until two years afterward—he had been in Panama at the time—but he would never forget the day his mother died while attending a service his father was preaching in a small church just outside Calico Rock. She had a bad heart to begin with; her doctors were watching her carefully, and during the invitational hymn when everyone was standing up, she fell over on the pew in front of her, gave her tambourine one last shake, and was dead.

"Mother Myrtle was something else," Applebee always said. Rosita had heard him many times. "Too bad not enough of that songwriting rubbed off on me."

He had written one song, however, not much of one in Sergio's opinion, but at least it had been published and recorded. That was way back when he was in the seminary, and at the time he had been proud of his effort, but now he considered his success beginner's luck because he had not been able to write anything else. By the time Principia Martindale arrived, he had discarded numerous attempts, but he had managed to come up with two lines that he liked and was determined not only to finish the song but sell it, record it and, with the money made, help drill a deep-water well, then take a long-overdue vacation. After ten years in Judson he was beginning to feel locked up; even his occasional trips to Laredo did him very little good—he dreaded the drive there and back—and his visits with his old friend Gloria Marshall, a waitress at a roadside restaurant twenty miles away, were not as enjoyable or as frequent as they had been.

Gloria was thirty years old, blond and sometimes spent the weekends with Applebee, but he had not seen her in nearly a month and was beginning to have moments when he could care less if he ever saw her again because the last time they were to-gether she talked about marriage and nothing but. Applebee had already been married twice and had no intention of marrying Gloria because he sensed that underneath it all she was a carbon copy of his ex-wives. Rosita thought so too. She had never met the ex-wives but said she didn't need to in order to know what they were all about. "All the time you end up with the same type and don't know it until it's too late," Rosita once said, long before Principia Martindale arrived. "Your friend Gloria, she tries too hard to be beautiful, she wants to be sixteen forever. She has a selfish streak that is longer than this." Rosita stretched her arms to either side as far as they would go and then added: "Don't tell me I am wrong."

Rosita had never taken to other women rapidly, but she did like Principia. Applebee could tell that right away, but he could not imagine why she would feel that way so quickly unless it was because she thought the summer missionary was young and lost and didn't have what it took to hurt anybody or stir up trouble. "I better tell Rosita that it never took much sense or anything else to stir up trouble," said Applebee after he left Principia in the church.

He had thought of driving over to Highway 85 that evening and visiting with Gloria until she got off work. He had also con-sidered bringing her back to Judson for the night, but on second thought he decided that he was in no mood to put up with all her talk, and besides that he kept hoping that Principia would get scared in the church and come knocking on his door, so he went home to work on his new song and wait.

"Shout the message clear; Hosanna! He is here" were his first two lines, but something told him they were not original, so he settled himself in the kitchen, and, while Saint George was roosting on the cabinet door above the sink, Applebee tried to remember when he had heard the lines and where.

Applebee and Saint George shared a four-room house, but there was only one room that they considered worth living in and that was the kitchen. Applebee had always done his best thinking there, and after he settled himself down and took another look at the song, he decided that he had also done some of his worst thinking there as well. Because he was almost positive that the lines he had written had come from another hymn, he found it difficult to continue working, so he turned up the kerosene lamp, skimmed through a few hymnals and was unable to find the lines or anything like them, but he still had the sneaking suspicion he was using someone else's idea, so he threw the paper on the floor and started all over again.

The floor of his house was covered with paper, discarded attempts at songwriting, but Applebee didn't care because with Saint George living with him, he needed paper on the floor anyway. Rosita said that he was the messiest person she had ever known, and often she would clean house for him, but her efforts did very little good because the next day the house would be messy again.

"I would hate for the visitors to see where you live," she once said before tackling the job of cleaning up after him. "If they knew you lived in this messy house and named it Rapture's Heights you would never be able to convince them that they were not sick. 'Cleanliness is next to Godliness.' If you listen to me you will learn something, but 'He who does not listen to advice will not reach old age.'"

But Applebee hardly ever listened, not to talk like that anyway. He had furnished his four rooms out of the old hotel; had helped himself to two double beds, a couch, several easy chairs and three bureaus which he had never used because he liked hanging his clothes on door knobs and nails so he could find everything easily. He had no window curtains, no trash cans and no shelves for his coloring books, which were stacked haphazardly in every corner. He never did much in the way of straightening, said he liked rooster feathers clinging to cobwebs, refused to make his bed more than once a week and had the habit of sleeping with his kerosene lamp burning all night long because he had never gotten used to total darkness.

He liked his home the way it was. He was comfortable there and saw no reason why it should not be called Rapture's Heights, the name he had chosen with great care and had written in blue and red Crayola above the front and back doors. From time to time he did get dissatisfied with the place though, and on occasions he would go sit on the roof just to get away from all the clutter. Every now and then he admitted—but only to Saint George—that he would like his house much better when he finished painting the jungle scene Manuel had drawn on the walls and ceilings just before he died. Manuel had also drawn a continuous Southwest Texas landscape on the outside of the house, and Applebee had already colored it with all-weather paint. The landscape extended onto the tin roof, and from a distance he was pleased that his house blended in with the rest of his world.

If the house were finished, the inside mural completely painted, he believed he would be able to work better there, but he finally realized that that was only an excuse; he sometimes found it hard to work in the café too. After several attempts on a new song, he got tired of looking at the unfinished mural and began wishing he had gone to visit Gloria after all. "If I'm lucky she'll come see me," he said. "That way I'll save the gas." He fell asleep over his work, as was his habit, and woke up shortly before dawn with Principia on his mind. He went to the church to check on her and found her sleeping near the rows of corn, so he closed the doors without making a sound and went to the café to get the rest of the supplies.

When he returned with her three boxes, he placed them on the ground in front of her, sat down on them and watched her sleep.

She looked entirely different when she was sleeping; he had thought she would and was glad to know that he had been right about her. She slept carefully, was relaxed, perfectly balanced on the narrow bench and, unlike Gloria or his two wives, her movements were slow and smooth. Applebee imagined that she could go to sleep in a large bed and wake up in almost the same position; he had been told that he could do that, and it was one of the things he admired about himself—he could sleep easily and without worry. Gloria was so restless when she slept. He was tired of that, and thought it would be pleasant to be with someone who was languid. He turned the lamp wick up, allowed the light to shine directly on Principia's face, and in spite of her size, in spite of her large bones, her masses of hair, she appeared to be weightless. Watching her in that dim light, he was unable to decide exactly how he felt. At first he wanted to make love to her, and then he just wanted to sleep with her, for there was a quality about her, not just her lack of experience, but something else, something that made Applebee think she was almost too fragile for lovemaking, and yet he could not completely dismiss the idea of their being together. She was so different from the others; that was part of the attraction, but there was something else creeping into his thoughts that he could not understand: he was filled with the desire to put her in his truck and leave town, not so much for his sake, but for hers.

He was amazed at the way she slept. There was no tension in her face, and her expression was softer than he remembered it. Her eyes and forehead were free of lines. She looked younger, much younger, and he was overcome with the desire to touch her but was afraid she would wake up, so he just sat there on the boxes and watched her sleep.

On the garden floor next to her bed he noticed three barrettes. He picked them up and carefully pinned them in her hair. His fingers were agile; this surprised him, but if she had been awake he realized that he would have been his clumsy self all over again. After he replaced the barrettes, he arranged her hair so it fell over the bed and almost to the floor. He felt as though he were playing with a doll that might wake up and catch him, so he took shallow breaths and held them as long as possible. He had never felt timid with the other women in his life; they were forceful, came on strong, and no exchange of words was needed, but with Principia it was different; just the thought of being in bed with her frightened him, made his heart feel like it had skipped a beat.

When her barrettes were in place and her hair arranged, he sat back down on the boxes and wanted to do it all over again. He wanted the dawn to last longer, but the sun was rapidly showing itself, the bats had already returned one by one, and soon he realized that she would open her eyes and he would once again make a mess of everything.

"She's closer to her real self when she's asleep," he said, walking over to the baptismal pool. "Maybe she just ought to sleep forever." He took a bucket off the wall, filled it with water and, while the first rays of light were streaming through the window, he pulled a few weeds, watered the garden and prepared another row for some purple hull peas. He wasn't sure they would grow there, but he wanted to find out.

By seven-thirty the day was already getting hot. The sun, shining through broken stained glass and onto Principia's face, woke her up, but at first she was unable to move. Her whole body was stiff; the throbbing in her leg had turned into a dull ache, which she felt all over, and her tongue was swollen, tingling; felt as though it was too big for her mouth.

Somewhere in the church she heard water splashing, and slowly she sat up. She saw the boxes of materials Tawnya Louise had given her stacked in the aisle, wondered how they had gotten there and gradually remembered what had happened the night before. "Oh Lord, I'm so thankful Tawnya Louise isn't here," she said, looking at the supplies. "I'm not sure she's strong enough in her faith to endure such hardships. This would have been enough to turn her against You for life." Then she looked toward the baptismal pool and saw Applebee splashing around in the water. His flesh was pink. Red hair was plastered to his wet chest and stomach, scarred with stretch marks and resting on the edge of the baptismal pool like a sunburst. With the sight of him bathing, not only in her presence but in the water intended for baptizing the children of Judson, her pain increased.

Applebee had hoped he would be able to have his bath and leave before she woke up, but he had not been fast enough. When he noticed she was awake and staring at him in disbelief, he felt embarrassed but tried not to let it show. "Don't worry," he said, sinking into the water so only his head was visible, "I don't use much soap, so we can still use the water for the plants. It won't kill 'em. When I get through you can jump in too. That ought'a make you feel better. Wake you up anyway."

Instantly the pain disappeared, leaving her filled with rage. "I have never bathed after a man or anybody else in my whole life," she screamed. "And I never will either. You're defiling that sacred water, and now I'll never be able to baptize with it because it's dirty; do you hear me? Filthy! Right now I'm going to the café, and when I return I want you to be out of here so I can teach Vacation Bible School because that's what I'm supposed to do."

While getting out of bed, she wrapped the monogrammed sheet around her until only her head and tangled hair was sticking out. The next thing Applebee knew she was flapping her way down the road.

From the café, Rosita saw her coming. "The religious subject is wearing her bedclothes this morning," she said. "The Apple must be taking his bath."

She gave Principia coffee and breakfast, told her that Applebee was a little crazy, but everybody loved him anyway because he had good intentions and was generous. "He put this place on the map," she said. "He is always thinking of more ways we can make our living, and as long as the Applebee is here, everybody else will be here also. You will learn to like him too, much better than his girlfriend Gloria, I hope. She wears the rodeo queen make-up and walks like a sleaze-ball; you will see for yourself and tell me what you think."

"I don't think I'm a good judge of those things," said Principia. "I just wish someone would persuade—whatever that man's name is—not to bathe in the baptismal water. That's the most disgusting thing I've ever heard of."

She was unable to call him by any of his names. She could not bring herself to say Donald, or Applebee, or Mr. Applebee and certainly not Brother Applebee, for she had made that mistake already and was hoping that she would not have much dealings with him and therefore it would not be necessary to call him by a name at all, for all the ones he went by didn't seem to fit the image she had expected, so, as far as she was concerned, he was nameless.

"Right now he makes you feel uncomfortable like two in a shoe," said Rosita, wiping off the checkered oilcloth that was tacked to the counter. "But you will get used to this, I think."

"I'm not so sure of that," said Principia, trying to find her balance on the wobbly stool.

Before she had finished breakfast, Applebee came into the

café, told her that the tub was hers and he would have the children at the church as soon as he could round them up. "I'll take the children, but I will not take the tub," said Principia, and in a flash she was running down the road toward the church. The throbbing in her foot and leg was coming back, and against the warm sand the pain seemed to be renewing itself in full force. When she got back to the church, she collapsed on her bed, and an hour later when she woke up, six dark-eyed children were sitting before her; two of them were less than a foot from her face. They had been watching her sleep, could not imagine who she was or what she was doing there, but they knew she was going to be doing something, so they waited for her to wake up. When she did, they crowded in closer and said their names and ages as Rosita had instructed them: Isabel, six; Carlos, seven; Antonio, three; Romero, six; Maria Luisa, seven; Rafalita, four.

In one glance Principia took them in; they were all barefoot except Maria Luisa, who was wearing her mother's rundown high-heel shoes. Their clothes were dusty, threadbare in spots, and had neat patches sewn on here and there. Isabel and Rafalita had on pastel dresses with puff sleeves and nylon lace; their ears were pierced with tiny gold rings, and their hair was long, straight, and in the direct sunlight it was so black it was blue, almost purple in spots, Principia thought, Maria Luisa's hair especially. Maria Luisa was the eldest. She was wearing her mother's slip, a baseball cap with flowers all over it and a white silk stocking tied around her neck. She wanted to look her best for the first day of school so she had smeared her face with make-up and insisted that her three-year-old cousin, Antonio, do the same. She had pinned bow ribbons in his hair, had given him one of her old dresses, a purse and a string of pearls, and he was as happy as could be until Principia said, "What a pretty little girl you are," and then he started crying and nothing anybody could do would stop him. Realizing her mistake, Principia rolled out of bed, tucked the sheet securely around her lilac nightgown and took Antonio in her arms. She removed his dress and beads, took the ribbons out of his hair and, in spite of the fact that he still had on make-up, she told him he was the most handsome young man she had ever seen. After he was quiet, she brushed Isabel's hair out of her eyes and pinned it with a barrette Lively Hathaway had given her. She tied

Rafalita's sash, touched Maria Luisa on the cheek and then turned
her attention to Carlos and Romero. They were dressed in T-shirts
and denim pants held up with suspenders made of rope, and they
both had toothless smiles. To Principia they were the most beautiful children she had ever seen because in their dark, curious stares
she believed she saw a burning desire to learn about Jesus.

"My name is Principia Martindale, and I love you so much
already," she said. Then she hugged the children one by one, and
on having their faces buried by masses of red hair, they each
laughed out loud and rubbed their noses. Maria Luisa had never
seen hair like Principia's, and she had a hard time trying to keep
her hands out of it. Antonio said it was scary-looking, Isabel
wished hers was the same color and Carlos could not believe that
it was real.

"What kind of a person are you?" he asked.

"I am a Christian," answered Principia. "That's the best
thing in the world to be too."

Oblivious to her difficult night and morning, she welcomed
the children to the first day of Bible School by giving them each
an all-day sucker. She had ten of them stashed in her carryall and
was so thankful that she had brought enough.

"Boys and girls," she said, "there are two things I love better
than anything. I love all-day suckers, and . . . I love Jesus. One will
last throughout the day and the other will last throughout eternity." After she spoke she smiled as hard as she could, and the children just sat there staring holes through her and squeezing their
suckers as though they had no idea what to do with them.

"Boys and girls," she continued, still holding her smile, "I
don't know how many of you children have ever been baptized,
but I can tell you one thing: Before this week is over, I'm going to
baptize the living daylights out of each and every one of you, and
if you don't like it at the first, you're going to like it at the last,
because the Lord is good, we are all His little children, and He
wants us to sing our praises unto Him. Now, if you had created
this beautiful world in all its glory and perfection, you too would
wish to be praised, so I ask you at this time, at this place, raise your
voices and praise Him, praise Him, I say unto you, praise His most
holy and precious name, praise Jesus Christ, the Way-Shower."

The children were silent; their eyes and mouths were wide

open, and their hands did not attempt to unwrap their all-day suckers. Principia was pleased to see that they were so attentive, so eager to learn about God's love and grace. She had planned to begin the first day by following the outlined course, which meant beginning with the "Bible School Anthem," but at the last moment she decided to start out with a chalk talk, because Lively Hathaway had always encouraged her to use this talent as much as possible. She unpacked her chalk, blackboard and cassette recorder, chose a medley of old hymns for background music and began depicting the life, baptism and crucifixion of Jesus in living color while telling the story in her own words. The children were mesmerized by the way Principia conveyed her message. Carlos liked the part about Jesus coming straightway up out of the water like a little bird flying toward heaven, so Principia went back to that part, lingered over it awhile and drew several different pictures of the baptism, the dove, John the Baptist and Jesus floating above the River Jordan.

O, Jesus, Lamb of God, she silently prayed. Once again I just thank You so much for giving me the gift of chalk talk.

Without realizing it she had convinced Carlos to be baptized also. "Do me that way," he kept saying while pointing to the blackboard and the picture of Jesus floating in the water. Principia's heart was filled with joy when she realized that he wanted to be baptized like Jesus. Our Precious Redeemer, she prayed, You truly do care about each and every one of us. You continue to show us Your love when we least expect it. She hugged Carlos and told him how happy he would be for the rest of his life because he had accepted the Son of God and was about to follow Him into Holy Baptism.

Then she realized that it was impossible. "Our Dear Most Gracious Heavenly Father!" she said. "How could I get so carried away? There's no water fit for baptism."

She had always been taught that total immersion was the only true way to baptize, but she was afraid that the water in the baptismal pool was contaminated, so she excused herself for a moment, went to the nearest corner and prayed in earnest over the problem. While praying, the pain returned to her leg. She shifted her weight, prayed harder, forgot about her discomfort and finally, when her mind was still and she had stopped worrying about what to do, the answer came to her.

Returning to the class with her heart-shaped carryall, she addressed her pupils again. "Boys and girls," she said, "because we have a water shortage in Judson, and because the water in the baptismal pool is unclean, the Lord has instructed me to modify things a little." She took a silver packet out of her carryall and held it up before the class. "This is a premoistened towelette," she said. "They come in handy when you're traveling and there's no place to wash your hands and face. They're also very refreshing on a hot day. Now I'm going to open it up and show you what I'm talking about." She ripped into the package and unfolded the pink cloth. "It smells so good and clean and it will feel good too. Because of the special way in which we are about to use it, it will feel good in more ways than one. Now I want you to bow your head and pray with me for a few moments.

"O Heavenly Father," she said. "We realize that there is only one true baptism, but under the unusual circumstances we are in You have led us to accept and believe in another method. Thank You for bringing us here on this most beautiful of days, and thank You for Carlos, who has just now accepted You as his personal savior. Amen."

Kneeling down she took Carlos in her arms and said, "Because you have accepted Christ as your personal savior, and are willing to follow him into Believer's Baptism, you are and will be a child of God, even if you live to be a hundred and five, for there's on old saying in the Baptist Church: 'Once saved, always saved,' and I'm so happy to say that it's true." Then she wiped the cool wet cloth over the child's face, held it there a few seconds and said, "Carlos, I baptize you in the name of the Father, Son and Holy Ghost. Now, don't you feel better?"

"Yes," said Carlos, all smiles. "Do me that way some more."

Gladly, Principia repeated the baptism, then sent Carlos back to his seat and asked if there were others who needed to meet the Lord in a private and personal way.

"Me," said Isabel, stepping forward.

Principia took her in her arms and sponged off her face. "Little precious Isabel," she said. "I love you so much and so does Jesus. I now baptize you in the name of the Father and the Son and the Holy Ghost. From this day forth you are cleansed through and through."

Happy as could be, Isabel touched her face as though she

expected it to feel differently, and then sat back down while Romero came forward. Principia opened another towelette and brought the wet cloth down to rest on Romero's face while he giggled and blew it away. "No, no," said Principia, "you must let me do this, and remember, it is not my hand at work here but God's. Romero, this day you are baptized in the name of our savior Jesus Christ, who died on the cross so we might have everlasting life. Because you have come forward and asked for God's love, you will now have it forever more; even when you backslide the Lord will be there to show you the right path. You're saved now and so are Carlos and Isabel."

She baptized Antonio and Rafalita in the same manner, and after she had finished she threw back her head and shouted, "Lord God, this is the most joyous day of my life! What started out so bad is turning out to be so good." Then her voice became soft again. "The Lord, children, takes us over many hills and through many valleys," she said, almost singing. "We must always be prepared for whatever He puts before us. We never know what's next. We just never know. But with God on our side, life is never as bad as it may seem, so we must leave ourselves wide open to have a total experience with our Maker."

Before she had finished sermonizing she realized that Maria Luisa had not come forward for baptism. She turned her attention to the child and asked if she had a decision to make. Maria Luisa sat there without saying a word and then got up and ran. "Girl, don't you ever run from God like that," shouted Principia as the rest of the children gave chase out the door and down the road where Maria was caught and held down.

When they left the church, Principia took the moment of privacy to take off the sheet and nightgown and put on a faded purple shift. Outside the children were calling for her to come quickly, and, before they knew it, she was standing over them waving her pink towelette as though it were the word of God made manifest.

"Maria Luisa, we're going to have to get one thing straight right now," said the Invincible, kneeling on the hot sand where the dressed-up child was pinned down by her cousins. "Have you or have you not accepted Jesus Christ as your personal savior, is what I'd like to know, and have you or have you not confessed your sins before man?"

"I don't know," said Maria.

"What do you mean you don't know?" asked Principia. "Maria Luisa, this is very important, and you've got to be sure if you love Jesus or not."

"Yes," said Maria Luisa. "I'm sure. I'm sure. I love Jesus too."

"That's all in the world I wanted to hear," said Principia. "Now I'm going to baptize the living daylights out of you just like I promised." She wiped the towelette across Maria's face and said, "I baptize you, my little angel, in the name of the Father and the Son and the Holy Ghost. After today you'll never run from God again, but you will walk in step with Him all the rest of your life."

The moment Maria felt the wet towel on her face, she started giggling.

"Joy," shouted Principia. "Only a Christian can know such happiness as this. You're saved, Maria Luisa, don't you know it? God has seen fit to save your soul. You didn't want to be baptized at first, but now you're so glad you were, and you'll never be sorry either, even when times are hard, because the Lord will always be there for you to fall back on. And now there's something else I've got to tell you too. Maria Luisa, don't you ever come to Vacation Bible School wearing that much make-up because it makes you look cheap and trashy and you don't want that, not now that you've become a Christian you don't. You'll give people the wrong idea of you, even at your age, and if you start out on the wrong foot now, you'll keep going on the wrong foot for a long long time to come, just like somebody else I know and am worried sick about."

She ripped open another towelette and rubbed the wet cloth over Maria's face until she had scrubbed away every trace of rouge and lipstick. Then she stood up and said, "You can just consider that a second baptism because I do. Maria Luisa, now you look like a child of God! If I only had a mirror I'd let you see yourself."

She took the child by the hand, helped her up, and they returned to the church, where Principia made six notches on her wooden cross. "Lord," she said, "please bless that beautiful man who gave me this little knife. And bless my friend Lorinda for being thoughtful enough to give me this cross on the day I left New Bethel."

She wanted to carve the names of her first converts on the cross as well, but there was no room, so she assured the children that their names would forever remain in her heart. "This has been one of the best days of my life," she said, smiling with no effort at all. "I have led you to the Lord without stirring you emotionally, and without using human pressures you were each brought to a decision for God. I did nothing. I am but a vessel containing His words, and He uses me as He sees fit."

The children were sitting on the first pew, and Principia was leaning against L. J. Judson's piano. The sun was beating down upon them and because there was no shade in the church Principia asked the children to help her construct a canopy for protection against the sun. Using four bean poles and one of her purple sheets, they erected the shelter near the pulpit, and after they had finished, Principia sat down under it and gathered all the children around her.

For a moment she was silent. Her eyes were glazed over as she stared beyond the children, out the front door and across the flat countryside, where nothing grew very tall except an occasional mesquite or a century plant in bloom. Then her mind went blank; then it filled up again with thoughts rushing at her so fast she could not recognize them. But this much she knew: She suddenly had the feeling she was sitting in her church in New Bethel, although nothing around her had changed. She was still in Judson, but the feeling of being in New Bethel was there, and it was so strong that she turned to the children and told them the Lord was depending upon her to build a better place of worship on that dry and rocky ground.

"In His own quiet yet powerful way, He has instructed me to build a church here," she said, "and already we have begun by erecting this canopy as protection against the sun. But that's not all we're going to do. We're going to make this building into a place of worship again. I don't know yet how we're going to do it, but when I leave Judson, you will each be able to say: 'I have a church home.'"

At last she believed she was being of service to mankind and was spreading the word of God to those whose hearts were prepared to hear it. While the children licked their all-day suckers, she sermonized on the importance of Holy Baptism, the Lord's

Supper, constant prayer, witnessing and daily devotion. She was not sure how much they understood, but she prayed that through the grace of God her words would find a way into their hearts and lodge there forever. A feeling of well-being came over her as she spoke; the tension left her shoulders, her hands no longer twisted nervously at her hair, the lines around her eyes gave way to a softer expression and her lips broke into a gentle smile that showed no trace of doubt.

 4

After the first session of Bible School the students refused to leave the church until Principia agreed to do another chalk talk. She erased her blackboard and began drawing flames, and within the flames she drew three men. "Boys and girls," she said, "in the Book of Daniel we are told that Shadrach, Meshach and Abednego were three devout men who ruled over the province of Babylon. Because they refused to bow down and worship pagan images as was the law of old King Nebuchadnezzar, Shadrach, Meshach and Abednego were 'bound in their coats, their hosen, and their hats, and their other garments and were cast into the midst of the burning fiery furnace.'"

While Principia delivered her chalk talk, Applebee, wearing a threadbare navy blue suit, slipped into the church and took a seat on the bed, which was still in the garden. He was carrying a bouquet of wild poppies and wondering if she would like them. During her chalk talk, he never once took his eyes off her. He just sat there and squeezed the bouquet of poppies until he had crushed their stems.

Principia, involved in her presentation, didn't realize he was there. "Now, children," she said, trying to keep as much of her face to the audience as possible while still drawing, "the Bible tells us that Shadrach, Meshach and Abednego worshiped Jehovah, the one and only god, and therefore they didn't burn up. Not a single hair was singed, their coats weren't one bit scorched and they didn't even have the smell of fire or smoke on them anywhere. This was truly a miracle and old King Nebuchadnezzar was smart enough to recognize it, so he made a decree. Now, you will read this in the third chapter of Daniel, in the next-to-the-last verse. The king made a complete about-face. He said that 'every people, nation, and language, which speak any thing amiss against the gods of Shadrach, Meshach, and Abednego, shall be cut in pieces, and their houses shall be made a dunghill: because there is no other God that can deliver after this sort.'"

As she was nearing the end, Rosita rang the cowbell that signaled the coming of visitors, and the children jumped up together and ran down the road. They knew exactly what was expected of them and that they had better not be late.

"I guess you know by now that we don't have Sunday services around here," said Applebee, gazing down the aisle at Principia, who was standing by herself in front of the baptismal pool. "But we do have visitors, not as many as we used to, but they're still coming and some of them are here right now so you better come on out and be sociable."

Principia followed him down the road to a chartered bus that was parked in front of the café. She was surprised to be thinking that he looked almost handsome in his blue suit and was about to tell him that he would look even nicer if the suit were cleaned and pressed, but she stopped herself from saying this because she was afraid he might get the wrong idea. Again her foot and leg were throbbing and she found it difficult to match Applebee's pace, but she refused to ask him to slow down because she believed that she was on the verge of seeing the screen door, and this time she didn't want anything to stop her. In the back of her mind, however, she was becoming apprehensive. Something told her not to expect too much, yet she could not help expecting all the radiance and glory of the Son of God, who lived in her daily thoughts. She felt as though she were about to discover a great secret, and although the seeds of doubt were present, she refused to allow them to take over, so she continued matching Applebee's pace and channeling her thoughts on the image of Jesus. The pain in her leg made her want to slow down, she wanted to limp for just a few steps, but she refused to allow herself this comfort.

I will suffer gladly, she told herself, that which the Lord gives me.

"They've come to see Jesus, or what's left of him anyway,"

said Applebee as they hurried toward the bus filled with people from the First Baptist Church of Brownsville. "If we're lucky we get three or four busloads in here every week. Some of them come because they're just curious, some are sickly and want to be healed fast, others are out to disprove everything, but we don't let them get that close, not the skeptics anyway. Used to we asked for a dollar a head, but we found out we can make more money if we take up a love offering right after a dramatic healing. Here lately, we've started selling everything we can think of, souvenirs and junk like that, because healings have been scarce and we need a lot of money fast."

As they approached the intersection where the cottonwood grew, Principia saw that folding tables had been set up in the shade. "Looks like good business today," said Applebee, straightening the lapels on his suit and trying to walk with the self-assurance of a country preacher. "Pretty soon we might have enough money to make a few improvements around here."

For a moment Principia thought she was at a county fair, and her heart sank with disappointment. She realized that the visitors were there to see the screen door and be blessed, but at the moment they were buying trinkets, eating tamales, arguing over prices and reminding her of the money changers that Christ threw out of the temple.

Rosita, in a blue cotton dress and a white bib apron, was selling holy tamales. A new penny was hidden inside one of them, and whoever got it was sure to be blessed. Sergio, dressed in striped overalls without a shirt, was selling wooden crosses he had carved himself and chalk Jesuses he had ordered from Mexico. His three sisters, Encarnación, Concepción, and Modesta, all younger than he, were ignoring their customers and arguing over who was supposed to sit where and how much space they each needed to sell their merchandise. As usual, they were attempting to share a long table and were not too happy about it either. They were all three large women, larger than Rosita, and were wearing rubber thongs on their feet, dresses that were too small, sunglasses and lots of make-up that Applebee's girlfriend, Gloria, had taught them to apply. Encarnación had her hair pulled up in an almost-top-of-the-head ponytail that was being held together by a ribbon with plastic flowers on each end. Concepción had on a sparkling hair net over pink foam rollers.

"Forty is too old to wear your hair in a ponytail," said Concepción, forcing a roller back under her hair net.

But her sister would not take the advice. "You should tell this to Modesta," she said. "At her age she should never have dyed her hair that color. It makes her look like a big grapefruit is on her head."

"I told you it was an accident," shouted Modesta across the table. "Now leave me alone. Today my business is good."

Modesta, the youngest of Sergio's three sisters, was selling small cactuses she had gotten out of the desert. She had potted them in Dixie cups and tin cans, and they were selling for fifty cents each if they were not blooming, seventy-five cents if they were. She also had a few resurrection ferns, a crown-of-thorns begonia and an *Aloe vera*, said to be blessed in Juárez and guaranteed to heal anything. Next to her was Encarnación, whose merchandise, painted rocks and postcards, was not selling, so she blamed her two sisters for not giving her enough room to spread out, but Modesta said that the amount of space had nothing to do with business because Concepción was using only a square foot to display her miniature *ojos de dios,* and she was selling them as fast as she could put them on the table.

"I do not have a husband to help take care of me and little Antonio, so I need more space than the two of you," said Modesta, oblivious to the fact that they were arguing in front of the visitors. Her husband had run off the year before and she had been known to say that she was glad he had left her—but had never admitted that to her sisters.

"My three sisters," said Sergio, shaking his head at the cottonwood. "They get along by not getting along. It has always been this way."

There was so much happening at once that Principia hardly knew which way to look. José Sánchez, husband of Encarnación, father of Carlos and Isabel, was organizing the visitors into a single line so Señora Obdulla Hernandez could read their palms. José, a muscular man, dark and handsome, was forty years old and appeared much younger. He had a handlebar mustache, hair so black and shiny that it almost looked silver in spots, and, as usual, he was trying to make a good impression by wearing a dark suit in front of the visitors, but it seemed to Principia that his pants had caught all the dust in Judson and then some.

Roberto Galvan—who preferred to be called Robert, or better still, Bobby—husband of Concepción, father of Romero, Rafalita and Maria Luisa, was helping José line everyone up when he realized that Señora Hernandez was not there. He kept asking Sergio if he had seen her and finally Sergio broke down and answered: "The Señora will be here when you see her here! You better calm down or the heat will get you."

Robert and Sergio were the same size and about the same age but had opposite dispositions. Sergio was patient and enjoyed taking life easy, but Robert Galvan had too much nervous energy for that. He was known to be extremely excitable, and even though he knew Señora Hernandez was often the last one to greet the visitors, he somehow never expected her to be late.

Señora Hernandez, almost ninety, could not walk as fast as she used to and was only halfway to the cottonwood when Robert and José stopped what they were doing and ran down the road to get her. She was as thin as a bolt of lightning and under the bright sun seemed too frail to be alive. She was wearing a faded black dress, a maroon apron, tennis shoes that had once been white and a blue rag wrapped around her head. Her face appeared to be covered with only a thin layer of skin, and the fire in her eyes was brighter than the opals dangling on silver chains from her ears.

"You're late again," complained Robert Galvan, as he and José made a chair out of their arms for the old woman to sit on. "You must learn to start earlier."

"And you must learn that I am very old and will not be here much longer," said the señora, slapping the men on their heads as they ran with her toward her table where she told fortunes and gave advice for a dollar a person. Long ago she had made the practice of telling only the good things and ignoring the bad. That way she got more customers and didn't feel quite so responsible.

Señora Hernandez captured Principia's attention right away, but it was Rubendella Hinojosa who caused the most commotion among the visitors. Wearing earrings and necklaces she had bought at Stuckey's, and a bright red dress, the neckline of which had been stretched to fit off the shoulders, she stood on the back of Applebee's pickup truck and sang, "He's the Flower on the Mountain, my Savior and my Lord . . ." the song Applebee had written when he was in the seminary. Rubendella was as slim as a pencil. Her black hair fell to her waist, and her arms moved gracefully in rhythm with the song.

Federico Chapa and Herman Gonzales, both wearing Levi's without shirts, were accompanying Rubendella on their guitars, and occasionally they sang along with her. The two men were supposed to be working at the Lucky L Ranch that day, but when they saw the visitors arriving in a packed bus, they knocked off early and took the short cut through the brush in order to reach the cottonwood before all the activity started.

When Rubendella started singing, Rosita turned to her husband and said, "Your daughter should not be wearing her dress stretched over her shoulders. You must tell her that this is not show business, she will listen to you. You must say to her: These people are very religious and you must not make them angry." But Sergio was selling his crosses as fast as he could and paid his wife no mind.

Mary Alaska Ragsdale and her daughter, Joyce Jeannine, were standing off to one side and surveying all the activity. Joyce, a younger version of her mother, was tall and slender, with a long sharp nose and a lantern jaw. She had just told her mother that she sometimes regretted not having graduated from art school and to make up for it she was going to paint some flowers on rocks and weathered wood and see if she could sell them to the visitors.

"My God in heaven, have you lost your mind, Joyce Jeannine," said Mary Alaska, smearing her lipstick. "That's so far beneath your dignity, I'm going to try my best to forget that you even suggested it. We didn't spend all that money for you to come out here and take part in this disgraceful sight."

"Oh, Mother, you've always taken things too seriously," replied Joyce. "Now stop it before you make yourself sick."

"I'm already sick, so what's the point of stopping now!" shouted Mary Alaska. "I arrived here sick, and I tell you right now, so help me God, I will not take that bus back home. You'll either have to drive me yourself or I'll walk. Look, there's Principia Martindale. I'm scared to death to ask her how she's doing but you know I'm going to."

Principia, anxious to see the screen door, didn't want anyone standing in her way. She thought Rubendella was singing too fast and the guitar accompaniment was wrong for the occasion. She didn't think too much of the children running around with hand-drawn maps of Judson for a dime, and she was disgusted that Applebee was selling pieces of the true screen for twenty-five cents each.

"Don't worry," Applebee told her. "There'll always be enough screen to go around. There'll always be enough of Saint Peter's bones, enough splinters off the true cross and enough hair direct from the head of Jesus himself. Gives you something to think about, or ought to anyway."

"Principia Martindale," shouted Mary Alaska, forcing her way through the crowd. "You come here to me!" She took Principia by the hand and led her away from all the activity. "I want to tell you something right now," she said, blotting perspiration from her face with a used Kleenex wrapped around two fingers. "I'm going to give you some advice and this is it: If you listen to one thing that man tells you I'll slap your face; I swear to God I will. I've been worried sick to death about you but haven't had the nerve to come out here all by myself. I want you to meet my daughter, Joyce Jeannine; we can't stay long, but I just had to come see this circus again. The last time I was here they were only selling tamales. Now they look like a regular five-and-dime, and if I thought calling the law would do any good I'd have already done it a long time ago."

"Oh, Mother, will you stop it," said Joyce, shading her eyes with a paper plate. She had already eaten seven tamales and Mary Alaska was convinced that she would be poisoned before nightfall. "You've just got to get hold of yourself, Mother," Joyce added. "You used to tell me that all the time. You've got to stop finding so much fault with everything too."

"And just where would I be then?" asked Mary Alaska. "Sitting up in bed and begging everybody to wait on me, that's where. If you wanted me to behave some other way, you shouldn't have invited me to come all the way out here again."

While they argued, Principia slipped away, the business died down and Applebee began leading the visitors around the Royal Palms Hotel to an open space where thousands had already left their footprints in the sand. Principia didn't want to be anywhere near Mary Alaska or Applebee so she stood far away from them, but Applebee saw her and insisted that she stand with him while he addressed the crowd. Mary Alaska spotted them together, and, feeling protective, she decided that her place was at Principia's side, and even though her daughter was against standing in the sun, Mary Alaska insisted and was victorious.

The back wall of the hotel was covered with crutches and wheelchairs, leg braces, neck braces, eyeglasses and photographs of those who had been healed. Letters of thanks had been tacked to the wall and prayers had been scribbled in pencil around the back door, which at first appeared to be nothing special at all. The frame was coming apart, the screen was rusting, even had holes in it here and there, and the steps leading up to it were covered with candles. Applebee checked his watch and looked up at the sun. He asked those who had come to be healed to kneel before the door, and three people came forward; two were on crutches, and the other walked upright and without aid but was obviously burdened.

"No wheelchairs today," Applebee said to Principia. "Kind of unusual."

"I'm witness to the fact that he'll lie to you faster than anything," whispered Mary Alaska. "So you better watch out."

But Principia didn't listen to a word either of them said. She had never witnessed the ministry of healing before and was hoping she was about to have her first opportunity. She had always believed in healing, even though many of the members of her congregation back home did not, and over the years she had managed to hold on to her belief that, according to the scriptures, two or more people, who gathered together in the name of God, could bring about miracles. Lively Hathaway believed that way too, and for Principia that was proof enough.

While she watched the three visitors struggling to kneel before the door, she asked Applebee when Christ would appear. He looked at her with a smile and said, "We gotta have some sunlight on the back wall first. Won't be long now."

Principia stared at all the crutches and wheelchairs on the wall and wondered why the Lord had chosen a rusty screen door to display His only son. Studying the screen carefully, she saw that the rust had almost taken on a human shape, and, using her imagination as a chalk-talk artist, she could fill in the missing parts with her eyes, but was unable to give the face distinct features.

As the sun slowly moved toward the back of the hotel, the door began to shimmer, almost as though it were moving, and then an iridescent image appeared and flickered slightly as though about to ignite, or as though the figure were on the verge of stepping from the screen and walking among the people. There was no question in anyone's mind who it was. The Son of God was standing, His robes were falling to his side, His eyes were staring into the distance, and His overall image was somewhat muted in tone as though He too had been a product of rust and neglect.

To Principia's disappointment, the image appeared to be much like a charcoal drawing that had an extra spark of life added to it. Around the body she thought she could see a faint trace of silver and blue. And was there or was there not a golden halo around Christ's head? She could not be sure. But the most disappointing thing of all was having to squint hard in order to bring the entire image into focus, and even then it wasn't too clear.

"If you stare at the sun for a second and then look at the door, you'll be able to see him a lot better," said Applebee. For Principia, that didn't work very well, but some of the visitors said that it made the image much brighter. One woman said she could see Jesus as clear as day and fell to her knees; three of her friends knelt with her, but in general the crowd was not as appreciative as Applebee had hoped.

Principia stared into the faces of almost everyone there; some were visibly moved; some were sneering; others walked away shaking their heads as if wondering why they had gone to all the trouble to make the trip. Both Mary Alaska and Applebee were watching Principia carefully, and neither was sure how she was reacting.

Principia felt that everything she had ever believed in no longer existed except in her own mind, and she wasn't too sure it existed there. She wanted to believe she was witnessing the Son of God return to earth in a recurring vision that everyone could see. She wanted to believe God had chosen that particular door and that particular time and place to reveal His son, but on seeing the image she could not believe the God she had worshiped all her life had anything to do with it because from certain angles she could see brush strokes on the robes; or was it only the sunlight playing on the rusty screen wire, some of which looked as though it had been scrubbed clean in order to allow the Son of God to shine forth.

Applebee offered a blessing for those who were kneeling at the door. "God of our Father," he said, "bless these poor afflicted ones kneeling here before you, and if you see fit, give them your healing power . . ." After he had prayed, the two visitors on crutches walked away still using them, but one said that she felt a warm tingling in her leg for the first time in months. Applebee assured her that that was a good sign. The woman with a heavy burden left with a slight smile on her face, and the other visitor on crutches said he had not felt a thing. "But you may feel something before the day is over," Applebee said. "Sometimes miracles don't happen all at once, but over a period of days, weeks, months, sometimes ever years."

"If it takes longer than a day it's not a miracle in my book," Mary Alaska whispered to Principia. "I don't know what you think, and I don't really care, but I think this is outrageous, and I swear to God this is the last time I'll ever come back here."

"But, Mother, you say that every time," said Joyce Jeannine. "Let's have lunch and you'll feel better."

"Lunch will not make me feel better any such of a thing," shouted Mary Alaska into her daughter's face. "I don't want you to even suggest it. I'm going to stay right here until this mess is over with. I always do."

"Why?" asked Principia.

"Because, Principia Martindale," said Mary Alaska, "just because I wish I could believe in anything that's stuck before me. I could be the happiest fool on earth, so help me God, if I had that kind of simple blind faith. Oh, I've got faith alright, don't try to say I haven't, but it's a different kind of faith than what you're used to seeing. My faith is more practical than most people's."

"Well maybe that's your problem then," said her daughter.

"How many times do I have to tell you that I don't have any problems, not any big ones anyway," said Mary Alaska, turning on her daughter as though she could eat her alive. "I happen to be very happy most of the time. Your father doesn't drink as much as he used to. He hasn't torn up the house in over a month, and I'm thankful for that. We've got good neighbors, good friends, a bank account, a good church and a darling of a pastor who gives excellent advice." Then she focused her attention on Applebee and said, out of the corner of her mouth, "I just wish you'd look at that fool standing up there. What does that thing think he's about to do anyway."

Applebee was standing on the steps leading to the door, and getting ready to collect the love offering in spite of the fact that many of the visitors had moved back to the shade of the cottonwood. He found it difficult to ask for money if a healing had not occurred, and since there had not been a single healing in several weeks, he was especially nervous about passing the offering plate.

"Brothers and sisters in Christ," he said. "There have been many healings before this screen door. As you can see, the walls of this hotel are covered with the evidence of God's love and mercy. We also have, for any of you who want to see it, a scrapbook of letters from all over the world, telling about the various healings that have happened right here in Judson, Texas."

"They wrote those letters themselves, you know they did," said Mary Alaska.

"Maybe they didn't," said Joyce. "You've got to give people a chance."

"At this time," continued Applebee, "I know each of you want to thank the Lord for making this shrine possible so we're going to pass the offering plate to give you the opportunity to express your faith and love. But right now I want to see you waving your offerings high in the air. Just lift your hands and wave your dollar, or five dollars or whatever you can spare, and say to yourself: Lord bless this offering for the ongoing of your kingdom."

"They won't get one penny out of me," said Mary Alaska Ragsdale. "I don't believe in any of this and I'm leaving." She took her daughter by the arm and was about to walk away when Carlos Sánchez tugged at her skirt and lifted up the offering plate. He gave Mary Alaska a toothless smile; she brushed hair out of his eyes and put a dollar bill in the plate. "Oh, I don't know what's wrong with me," she said. "I always have to give something even though I don't want to. Someone has to keep these poor children alive. All they need is someone to take them home and love them, and, Principia Martindale, while you're here all I ask is that you see to it that my dollar goes to the right place."

After Mary Alaska and her daughter had left, Applebee approached Principia, who was standing by herself again. "This is an off day," he said apologetically. "Too many skeptics for people to get themselves all worked up, and besides it's a Baptist group, and they never do respond like some of the others. You ought to be here when the Pentecostals arrive. They get so excited they leap out of their wheelchairs and dance around. Sometimes they throw their crutches at the wall and walk away completely well." Noticing that there was a fair amount of disappointment on her face, he added, "I guess you expected a little more, didn't you?"

"I'm not sure what I expected," said Principia, squeezing her fingers in an attempt to forget about the pain coming back to her leg. The image of Christ was beginning to fade from the door, and the crowd was dispersing in all directions. "It doesn't look like I thought it would because I expected something more lifelike and it's nothing but a drawing that shows up better when the sun hits it."

"That's exactly what it is," confessed Applebee. "If you're going to stay around here you better know it sooner or later. Everybody else who lives here knows it. Manuel and I first saw the image made by rust, so we just helped it out a little; acted like the hand of God, or the instrument of God if you want to look at it that way. With the world in the shape it's in these days, God needs every little bit of help we can give him, you know."

"No, I didn't know that," said Principia in a solemn whisper. She had never experienced such a letdown in all her life. Every bone in her body ached with disappointment, and her thoughts were spinning so fast she could hardly stand up. She couldn't believe that anyone had ever been healed by the door and wasn't going to believe it until she saw a miracle for herself. Yet Applebee swore it worked; he promised her faithfully that he had not hung the crutches on the walls for show, and neither had anyone else.

"Of course," he added, "it did take a man like Manuel to come up with the mechanics of how to do it. He had the good sense to know exactly how to bring out the image that was already up there and give it the impression that it hadn't been touched by human hands. He used old house paint for one thing, not much, just a little here and there to give you the idea of two eyes, a halo and some long flowing robes. Then he rubbed candle wax all over it, and then sewing machine oil, and then something else, dirt, looked like. After that he stood back and let the sun melt the wax and run everything together until the image that had been there kind of disappeared. Everybody who was watching him said that he had made a mess out of everything, but Manuel said that he was through. He said that Jesus would appear in his true glory only when the sun was at a certain angle and the screen was wet. He was right too. We have to rub a little wax on it from time to time, and before we bring the people back here we have to spray it with a little bit of oil and water. We've always got enough water for that; but we haven't figured out how to maintain the picture the way Manuel did. He used to touch it up every Saturday morning. Right now it's not nearly as impressive as it was two years ago."

Applebee followed Principia over to the shade of a mesquite tree, where she sat down on a white rock and stared at one of the biggest disappointments in her life.

"If you hadn't expected so much you wouldn't feel so let down," said Applebee. "Everybody who comes here expecting to see a lot is always disappointed, and everybody who comes with no preconceived idea leaves uplifted and sometimes they're healed too."

"I realize that God uses us as instruments," said Principia. "He uses me every day. I allow Him to, and have given my life for that purpose, but I don't think you have."

"I admit that I have to put away some of my beliefs in order to come out here every day and do this show," said Applebee.

"I didn't realize you had any beliefs to put away," said Principia.

"Well, it looks that way, I guess," Applebee replied, ignoring her sarcasm. "I get carried away and act like a real fool sometimes. Just can't help myself either."

"If I knew how to get some help to you I would," Principia said, trying to hide her anger. "But you don't take anything seriously. These people who come here aren't looking for a trick. They want something to reaffirm their faith. They're Christians and you aren't, and that makes a big big difference."

"Makes no difference at all," said Applebee. "Everybody believes the same thing in the long run. So that makes one religion just as good as another. Me, I believe them all."

"Then you can't be a Christian," Principia said, twisting her hair with both hands as she spoke.

"Good thinking on your part," said Applebee, a grin stretching across his face. "I'm not a dyed-in-the-wool Christian anyway. Let's say it like that." After a pause he added: "It would be better for all of us if while you're here you could try to believe in the door the way we do."

"I can promise you that I will not turn my back on a single belief that I know to be true," said Principia, staring at the door. The image of Christ had already evaporated and from where she sat all she could see was the rusty screen. "In a strange sort of way," she continued—almost ready to preach—"what you have asked me to do is bow down to a graven image. If an inspired Christian had painted that door I might be able to believe in it, but I know that you're behind it all, and therefore it's not a miracle to me."

"But it might be a miracle to somebody else," said Applebee. "Ever thought of that? Right now that's all that counts. You don't have one thing to judge a miracle on, but some of the people who leave Judson do. Lots of them claim to be healed, and if they are, or even if they think they are and really aren't, it's still a miracle in my book. And besides that, you never knew Rosita's father. You don't know if he was inspired or not, but I do."

"Let me tell you something right now, and don't you ever forget it either," said Principia, her face almost as red as her hair. "I have always been able to recognize divine inspiration in, and in the works of, others. It's one of my gifts. Lively Hathaway has always told me that the works reveal the soul, and so do the eyes. I can look into anybody's eyes and tell you what that person's all about."

"Well, ain't that something now?" said Applebee. "Wonder what you see when you look into your own."

"I make a practice of never looking into my eyes," she said, "because I'm not self-centered like you are."

"Maybe it's because you don't enjoy seeing yourself," said Applebee. "Now tell me. What do you see in mine?" He pulled his lower eyelids down as far as they would go and pressed his face up against Principia's.

She stood up quickly to put distance between them. "I'll be absolutely truthful," she said, "because you give me no choice. You don't have focus. You're looking at too many things at once. God didn't mean that. He wants you to have eyes for Him only."

"God didn't mean for us to be as nearsighted as you are either," said Applebee.

"I'll have you to know," said Principia, almost shouting, "there's not one thing wrong with my eyesight and never has been."

"Then you better go look at yourself in the mirror real real soon," he said. "That's all I got to say."

He left her alone to think, but she didn't have a clear thought in her head. She watched him walk away, watched the crowd disperse, and by three o'clock the visitors were gone and the town was, or seemed to be empty again except for Applebee, who was talking at the top of his voice to Rosita, who was trying to count the money they had made that day, and Carlos, who was chasing Applebee's rooster along Judson Avenue. Everyone else had gone home for a siesta, but Principia was sitting under the mesquite and staring at the crutches and wheelchairs hanging on the back wall.

Her mind was so cluttered it almost felt empty; not a scripture came to her, not a prayer, not even a single word of comfort entered her head. Only Lively Hathaway's favorite saying kept surging through her mind: "Any fool can count the seeds in an apple, but only God can count the apples in a seed." Then Applebee's idea that the Holy Spirit did not visit the earth very much anymore kept coming to her thoughts, as did his statement that God needed all the help he could get. But those thoughts troubled her, so she put her mind back on Shadrach, Meshach and Abednego, who refused to worship idols. How she admired them for their commitment. Then she studied the screen door again and thought it was very strange that God would allow His only son to be used as a graven image. "There is so much good here that's gone astray," she said. "This man who claims to be in charge is like King Nebuchadnezzar before he saw the light. Right now he is not a shining example, especially for these children." She was watching Carlos, who was still chasing Saint George along the palm-lined avenue, and she was wondering how she could *reach*

Applebee. No plan for his salvation came to mind, and she was glad to be distracted by the child, who obviously needed her example.

Applebee looked out the back window of the café and saw her still sitting on the rock. The shade had already moved away from her, and under the blazing sun her purple dress and red hair seemed more brilliant that ever, but her arms, legs and face were so pale they were almost white. "She looks like a ghost who just stepped out of a beauty parlor," he said, looking for some clean paper to write on.

"You are the one who needs the beauty parlor," said Rosita. "Tell the little one to come inside before the sun burns her up."

Applebee lingered over his songwriting, and by the time he got around to calling Principia in he was unable to find her. Rosita said that she had probably run off, but Applebee was not satisfied with that answer. He looked for her all over Judson, asked everyone if they had seen her and was beginning to believe that Rosita was right until he heard Principia laughing at him. "We're up here," she said. Applebee looked up in the cottonwood, and there she was sitting on one of the highest branches. "I'm coming up there too," he said, and before Rosita knew it they were all sitting in the tree together: Applebee, Saint George, Carlos and Principia, who was looking out at the world as if for the first time in her life.

5

Rosita López could not imagine how Principia and Applebee had climbed the cottonwood, but she was glad they were there. She hoped Carlos and Saint George would stay there awhile too; she was sure Applebee would because he was pointing west toward Mexico and she knew that he was talking about his travels, in which case he could go on forever. He was, in fact, doing just that. After he had been expelled from the seminary, he had traveled all over the United States, Mexico and Central America and liked nothing better than to talk about where he had been. He said that he had climbed the Pyramid of the Magician in much less time than it took him to climb the cottonwood; said that he led a blind girl to the top of the pyramid, and when they got up there her sight started gradually coming back on her.

Principia could hardly listen to a word he was saying because of the way he was making the tree shake; even the rooster was beginning to act nervous, but Carlos didn't seem to mind.

Applebee paid no attention to Principia's growing alarm. He shifted his weight onto a larger branch and told her he ended up marrying the no-longer-blind girl. "But there was a catch to that one," he said, taking Principia's hand as if he needed the support to steady himself. "She ended up being a religious fanatic and insisted on prayer and scripture reading before and after intercourse."

"I would have been just like her," said Principia, quickly withdrawing her hand. "I approve completely."

"Well, I don't," answered Applebee. "Wouldn't cooperate

with her either, so she ran off with a two-bit preacher and must have found him obliging because the last I heard they were still together and still praying, about twelve times a day I 'magine, and for every little thing too."

"You can never address the Lord too many times in a single day," Principia said. She made her voice firm to stress her point.

Applebee propped his feet on the branch Principia was sitting on and continued his speech. "Don't believe in boring God to death," he said. "Don't believe in boring myself either." He moved his legs as if they were uncomfortable where they were and touched Principia's arm with a bare toe.

"Don't touch me with your feet," she said, moving closer to the center of the tree. She regained her balance and asked him to tell her more about the blind girl, but Applebee said that he would rather talk about his second wife.

"Beverly Kay was wife number two. She started off as a waitress and ended up in religious vocation. To her that meant taking a job as a nurses' aide at the Baptist Hospital. We lived in Longview then. I worked in a pawnshop, and all I went home to was scripture and more scripture, and God this and God that, and Jesus and angels, and miracles. Made me just about sick to my stomach."

"O Blessed Redeemer," prayed Principia. "Speak to this man's tormented soul and give him peace."

"You sound just like her," said Applebee, "but you'll get over it."

"She was a guiding light in your life," said Principia. "She might have even been an angel."

"An angel she was not," said Applebee. "After two years of it I hit the road again; carried a truckload of junk from one town to the next and sold it cheap. Wherever I went I looked for something I could pick up for nothing and sell to anybody who'd have it. Then I stumbled on this place. Been here ever since."

He inched a little closer to her, but she tried hard not to notice. She was afraid he was going to put his hands on her, and he was afraid she would fall if he did, so he eased away again.

"Right after I got here," he continued, "I read in the newspaper about Jesus appearing on a convent wall over in New Mexico. Thousands of people were flocking to the village to see him so

Manuel and I, we decided to go have a look too; couldn't hurt anything is the way we felt about it. We drove all day and all night and couldn't get a parking place when we finally got there; had to park two miles down the road and walk."

Principia became interested in the story, but she didn't trust Applebee to give it the kind of ending she thought it should have; neither did she trust his hand, which was slowly moving toward hers.

"We saw him too," said Applebee, looking pleased with himself. He was about to put his hand on top of hers, but she moved it before he had the chance. "There he was, just as plain as day up there on that old adobe wall; had probably been there for years and nobody thought to look for him. The building had been painted at least a half-dozen times, and all the coats were bleeding through each other so the wall was filled with stains, and along about sunset when the light was just right there he was, good ole Jesus, looking just like himself. He even showed up plain on television for the folks too sick to make the trip, and one woman in Albuquerque said when they showed the image of Jesus her set went into living color and stayed that way until they took the ole boy off again."

"Jesus is not an ole boy," interrupted Principia.

"My point," continued Applebee, "is this: You can convince yourself of just about anything as long as you want to, or need to. By the time we got to the village everybody had turned out to sell tacos and enchiladas, and every kind of trinket you could think of. The local priest even set up a confessional booth next to the holy wall, but when the Archbishop of Santa Fe came to have a look he made everybody go home; said Christ was nothing but a stain on the wall, wasn't distinct enough to be called a miracle and that the state of New Mexico had no use for another shrine."

"I'm inclined to agree with the archbishop," said Principia.

"Well, I'm not," said Applebee. "He deprived all those people of a new miracle and a new source of income is what he did, so we decided before we got started that that couldn't happen to us. Manuel chose the spot. He said that Christ had never to his knowledge appeared on a screen door, and it was about time he did, especially since there was already an image on it; nobody would have ever seen it who wasn't looking for it, but it was there just the same, so like I told you, we helped it out a little, advertised ourselves in the papers, and pretty soon word of mouth did all the advertising we needed."

"That's just one more way of taking the dear Lord's name in vain," said Principia.

"Lots of people thought that at first," said Applebee. "Even Rosita. But after the first healing some minds were changed, and after the second healing some more minds were changed, and after the third and fourth some heads were turned completely around and mine was one of them. I never expected this place to catch on like it has."

"Mercy healing is the only logical explanation," Principia said. Applebee propped his legs on another limb; the rooster lighted on his head, started pecking at his hair, and Principia tried to inch her way to the other side of the tree without snagging her skirt, but it was impossible to move gracefully with Applebee's eyes on her so she ended up staying where she was. "If the Lord sees the need to heal somebody," she said, "He's going to heal them no matter where they are, or what they're doing, or what they believe in, simply because He's a god of love and mercy."

Applebee shooed the rooster off his head and agreed with her only in part. "It's all owing to what you believe and how deeply you believe it," he said. "Hysteria can cause illnesses so it makes good sense to me that hysteria can heal them too. Now, getting back to wife number one, she went blind watching her father die a slow horrible death, and she stayed blind until I took her to the top of the pyramid. When we got up there she got all red-faced and commenced wheezing on me. I thought for sure she was about to pass out, but she didn't. She started seeing colors and vague shapes and over the next six months her sight gradually came back. Today she sees just fine, even without glasses. Clearly a case of hysteria. But some healings you just can't explain so easily, and if I ever had to face it myself, I mean if anything bad ever got the matter with me, I wouldn't take any chances, I'd find the highest roof, or the highest hill or the highest something-or-other and stretch out on top of it and try my best to get well again. I wouldn't want a doctor, a preacher, a nurse or anything except to be way up high where everybody's gods could find me."

"I've never heard of anything so sad before in my whole life," said Principia. "Ask the Lord to deliver you from this yoke of sin, and ask Him this very minute." She wanted down fast, and was looking for the best way when Applebee put his hand high on her leg and said, "Be still, I'm not through yet."

"You take your hand off me and take if off right now," she said, but Applebee refused.

"If you're not perfectly still you'll fall," he said. "I just want to put my hands on a pretty girl and tell her how I feel, that's all."

Principia felt a hot current traveling from Applebee's hand all the way up one leg and down the other. For a few seconds she lost her balance but then managed to regain it long enough to pull Carlos up to her lap for protection. Then she clapped her hands over the child's ears and whispered: "Lively Hathaway told me about men like you. You would like to lead me beyond the point of resistance, but you're not going to because I have more resistance than you've ever heard of."

"Can I find out for sure?" he asked, slowly removing his hand.

"You've lost all your beliefs is what you've done," said Principia.

"I haven't lost anything," said Applebee. "I just figured out a long time ago that it's more comforting not to know exactly what I believe rather than go around saying I'm absolutely sure and spend the rest of my life trying to convince me and everybody else that I have no doubts. Don't get me wrong, I still believe in something, but most of the time I haven't got the faintest idea what it is."

"No one is born into a state of confusion and disbelief," Principia preached. "You get that way as you grow older. If you had only gone to school with me you would know, even today, exactly what you believe. I would have stood by you every step of the way to see you through that difficult time of doubting. Somebody should have done that. Somebody, I don't know who, failed you."

There was a growing feeling inside her that Applebee was not as lost as she thought, but she stubbornly buried her flickering doubt and filled herself with the urge to witness to him.

"There are wars in our families and wars in our communities and wars in our hearts because of sin," she said. "Sin, that's what it's called. Sin is a disease and you are a sinner so therefore you are diseased."

"Oh, I've got a disease," joked Applebee. "Wonder what I can do about it."

"You can repent, that's what," said Principia earnestly. "Just bow your head and close your eyes and tell Jesus how much you love Him. It won't hurt you, so go on and bow your head and confess that you want to play ball with the Lord. That's what it's all about you know. We're all on the same team and looking to the same quarterback for inspiration and guidance. Just tell Jesus how much you love Him; do it right now."

"I can't do it," Applebee said. He had slipped his hand into hers, but because of her fervor, she had not noticed that their fingers were beginning to interlock.

"There's no reason for you to be stingy and grudging with God. Don't throw Him the crumbs. Give Him the whole loaf. Accept the word of God as it is being given to you, because in the next moment we might fall out of this tree and kill ourselves instantly. Now how do you think that would make you feel? Where do you think your soul would go after that? I've made my peace with my Maker, but it's clear to me that you haven't, so you better tell Him right now that you love Him or you might not live to get another chance."

Applebee bowed his head, but no words would come out. Principia's hand was very warm and he enjoyed holding it, but he knew the moment was coming when she would realize he was touching her and pull away. He wished that she could be more responsive; wanted her to be more like Gloria so he would not be afraid of hurting her, but still he didn't want her to possess any of Gloria's aggravating qualities either.

Without realizing what she was doing, Principia shifted Carlos' weight to the other side of her lap, slipped her hand away from Applebee's and touched him on the back. For the first time she called him by name. "Applebee," she said, almost in whispers, "I'm placing a hand of faith on your shoulder. Carlos and I are sitting here praying for you."

The moment she touched him, he felt as if he had been struck with something sharp and hot. He felt her hand all the way to his heart, which ached as though it could split in half. "There's nothing to be afraid of," she said. "You can talk to God the very same way you can talk to me, or Carlos or Rosita. Now come on, give it a try."

"God is great . . ." said Applebee with his eyes half shut. The weight of Principia's hand on his back pleased him and he didn't want her to remove it, but she sensed that he was misinterpreting the way she was touching him so she withdrew her hand and brushed her fingers through Carlos' hair. "Try again," she said without showing as much concern as before. "There's so much at stake here."

"God is great, God is good," said Applebee, "and I thank him for his son Jesus, who died on the cross for all my sins, and I really do love him a lot for it too, but, dear Lord, right now, I love this young woman sitting next to me. If she could only return a fraction of that love it would make me so happy, and if Carlos will just run on home, I'll show her how much I really do care."

"You won't do any such of a thing, because I won't let you," shouted Principia. "You speak of love with a little 'l' and I speak of love with a capital 'L.' There's a difference, you know." Her voice seemed to shake every branch of the tree, and her blood rushed to her face all at once, causing her freckles to grow dark and menacing as she frowned through the branches at Applebee, who had withdrawn to another limb. "You're the sneakiest person I've ever met," she said. Carlos wiggled out of her lap and swung to the ground. Saint George flew over to the truck, and Applebee just sat there and wondered how anyone could get so angry so quickly. "You're just like the Devil," she continued. "You don't understand that it's impossible to divide your love if you're going to be a full-time servant of the Lord."

"I think being a part-time servant is good enough for most people," said Applebee, trying to keep as much distance between them as possible.

"Lord have mercy on you for even thinking that!" exclaimed Principia.

"You don't even know the meaning of the word 'mercy,'" said Applebee, trying to find a stronger branch.

"I most certainly do and that's for sure!" shouted Principia. Her voice was so loud Applebee could almost feel her words hitting him in the face. "Mercy for your information, and I'll only say it once so you better listen carefully, is 'love expressing itself in forgiveness and remission of penalty from the guilty.' Edgar Young Mullins said so. And now I'd like to tell you something else: Mercy is used twenty-two times in the New Testament alone, and the Greek word for grace, which is *charis*, appears one hundred and fifty-four times, sixteen times that I know of in the Gospel of Saint Luke and one hundred and thirty-eight times in the Epistles of Paul."

"What'd you do, count them or something?" asked Applebee.

"No, I did not," Principia answered while slowly climbing to a lower branch. "I didn't have to because Dr. Truly, my Bible professor, counted them himself. He even wrote a paper about often-used words in the Bible."

"And how many times does the word 'passion' appear in the Gospels?" asked Applebee. "Any idea?"

"If you're speaking of the Passion of Christ it appears fairly often I'm sure," said Principia. "But if you're speaking of the passion of the flesh, which I think you are, it doesn't appear at all."

"I suppose you're sure," said Applebee, watching her descend.

"I'm sure," said Principia. Before she realized it, she had swung to a still lower branch and jumped the rest of the way to the ground, leaving Applebee in the tree to get down the best way he could, but what she didn't realize was that he was not far behind her, and halfway back to the church he managed to catch up.

"Don't let me bother you," he said, walking backwards in front of her. "I'm just messing with you again, that's all. I haven't been around anybody I really care about in so long I just don't know what I'm doing until after I've done it. But if you'd stop depending on the scripture so much and what everybody else has said about it, and get inside your own head awhile, you might find out that you know a lot of things that can't be said or written down because there's no language to express what's there. Most people are afraid of turning their minds loose like that because they think it'll make them crazy and sometimes maybe it does, but you ought to take the chance anyway."

"I think you're hopelessly lost," said Principia, "and my only regret is that I didn't know you earlier in your life before your mind was so jumbled up. I could have helped steer you, and I would have too."

She refused to say anything else until they reached the church, and then she realized that the sun was going down rapidly; the sting of the scorpion, although the pain had left her leg, was still fresh in her mind, and she dreaded being inside the dark building, so she asked Applebee for a safer place to sleep. He knew better than to suggest his house, and didn't want her to stay with anyone else, so he assured her that the church was as safe as any place in Judson because scorpions were everywhere, even in his own house, and had been on earth almost unchanged since they came out of the water three hundred million years ago, which made them older than the cockroach. He advised her, if she had to be stung or bitten again, to choose the tarantula first, the scorpion second and the rattler third, to check her shoes and clothes before she put them on, and, as an extra safety measure, he decided to hang his Guatemalan hammock from one side of the church to the next.

"If you sleep up high," he said, "it'll be harder for anything that bites or stings to bed up with you."

While hanging the hammock, the first cloud of bats passed over the church. The interior became so dark that Applebee had to stop what he was doing until it was light enough to see, but as soon as he started hammering again, another dark cloud moved across the sky. Standing on top of a stepladder, he peered through a hole in the east wall of the church and watched the bats fly off into the horizon and vanish like a trail of smoke into the dusk. When the third cloud passed over, there was again the sound of wind, but nothing was stirring; the century plant was motionless as were the scrub oaks and the mesquite. Then there was a sudden upward draft in the church. Applebee didn't know if it was caused by the bats or not, but he did know that he had the feeling he had left his weight behind on the stepladder and was floating up through the open ceiling, when another gust of wind swept him away with a cloud of bats.

After he had regained his senses, he turned to Principia and said, "That's the Holy Spirit."

"It's just the bats," said Principia. "That's all." She was sitting on the first pew and trying to finish a letter to her parents before it got too dark to see. She told them that she was fine, that she was happy and that the Lord had given her a thousand blessings already. She did not tell them about Applebee, nor did she mention the screen door because she knew how easily upset they became, so she wrote at length about her pupils and how much she loved them all.

Before she had finished the letter, Applebee lit the kerosene lamp, said he was sorry if he had offended her and left. On his way home he decided to visit Gloria, but he changed his mind before he could turn around. He had gradually been losing interest in her anyway, and now that Principia had arrived Gloria interested him less than ever before.

After he had left the church, Principia realized that it was Sunday. Back in New Bethel her friends were going to evening worship, and for a moment she wished she were there with them. She closed her eyes and saw her father in his dark suit and string tie and her mother with her tightly curled hair and handkerchief in her hand. "Lord Jesus," she said, "please bless my dear parents and keep them safe until I return. Bless Lively Hathaway, and Brother Hemphill, and Billy Ray and all the people I'm forgetting about, and, Lord, just please bless Tawnya Louise wherever she is right now, and, whatever she's doing, just reach over and give her a hug and let her know that You care."

While praying for her friends back home she washed her face and arms with a towelette, changed into a fresh nightgown— she had brought three along—and, moving carefully through the church, carried the kerosene lamp and her Bible to the top of the stepladder Applebee had left behind and slid into the hammock. Oblivious to the candle moth circling the flame, or the scorpions dancing like mad saints in the garden, she read of the Passion of Christ, wept over the crucifixion and rejoiced over the Resurrection, the promise of everlasting life.

It was her second night in Judson; a cool breeze entered the church, swung the hammock to and fro, while Principia, feeling safe from the creatures of the night, closed her eyes, prayed for the salvation of Applebee, for the happiness of her parents, the success of her work, and then, before saying Amen, she drifted off to sleep suspended above the corn, the dancing scorpions and a tarantula, crossing the moonlit garden like a wise man who had lost his way.

 6

Applebee woke up at dawn on that Monday morning in June,
Principia's first Monday in Judson, and celebrated the new day by
playing, over and over again, the only song he had been able to
compose on the fiddle Manuel had left him. Applebee had grown
to love the fiddle because of the same old tune that kept coming
out of it, a song that, according to Rosita, took some getting used
to, mainly because there wasn't much to it, but even still, she had
to confess that she had grown fond of the song and said that it
sounded much better early in the morning than it did late at
night. "In the morning it's a happy song, but at night it's so sad,"
she always said, but Sergio thought it sounded the same all the
time. Applebee thought it sounded the same too, and that was one
reason he liked it so much, it was dependable; another reason he
liked it was because it was a jealous tune, one that seemed to take
control of him as well as the instrument and wouldn't allow another song to come near. Applebee had tried for a long time to
pick out another melody, but finally he had decided that it was
impossible, so he named the song "Jealousy," and several times a
week he woke up Judson by playing it over and over until he felt
completely relaxed and ready to start the day.

Rosita had grown to depend on the tune almost as much as
Applebee, and it was always a disappointment for her to get out
of bed without hearing it. She believed her days went much better
when she started out with the music because it was fast and repetitious, a good tune to work by.

"It's not a very pretty song until you've heard it as many

times as I have," said Rosita, pulling Monday morning's bedcovers away from her husband. "Sometimes Mr. Apple plays it all day long right there in the café, and if you don't get up I'm going to ask him to play it right here in the bedroom. When I hear it so much I am able to do a lot of work, and because of that you should listen too. It is very fast and will help you get out of bed."

In the next room Rubendella was keeping time with the fiddle while putting on her clothes; across the way, Modesta was trying to sleep with a pillow on her head; José Sánchez was fussing at his children because the fiddling had made him wake up too fast, and in the house down the road, an old crumbling adobe, Señora Obdulla Hernandez was sitting in her garden drinking a cup of nettle tea, which she took three times a day to provide energy and purify the blood. She sat in her wicker chair and rocked gently, while the sun threw shadows of the hollyhocks across her lap and the hummingbirds came to visit her garden as they did each morning before the heat of the day drove them to cooler places. Señora Hernandez noticed that some of her herbs were wilted; the ground around them was parched, and she wondered if Rosita could spare a quart of water; if so, the señora intended to spoon it directly on each plant so nothing, not even a drop, would be wasted. Rocking in the still, almost-no-air of dawn, she stared at her husband's grave and missed him; she sipped her tea; told herself that she felt as though the world were drawing its last breath, and then she rested her head on the back of the chair while the tune Applebee played washed over her like a soft wind and made her feel as if she were going to sleep for the last time.

On the other side of Judson, Principia was also awake. At first she found the fiddling annoying because it kept her from concentrating on her daily scripture reading. After a few minutes, however, she hardly noticed it at all, but when the children entered the church she became aware of the repetitious tune again because it seemed to her that the children were marching to it. "I might like it after all," she said. "If he doesn't play it too often that is." Before the children had time to sit down she put them to work constructing two more purple canopies, one over the altar and the other over the piano to balance the one that was already shading the classroom. "Right now that's all I know to do to make this place more worshipful," she said to Rafalita, who was unfolding a sheet.

As they worked, Principia quizzed them on the verses they were to have memorized the night before. Applebee continued playing the fiddle. Sergio tried again to stumble out of bed, Rosita started an order of tamales for Mary Alaska's daughter, and Señora Hernandez went back to sleep sitting among her hollyhocks.

Rubendella, still swaying to the music coming through her bedroom window, was almost dressed and ready to begin her own work; she had planned a full day and was hoping that she would not be disturbed.

As everyone in Judson knew, Rubendella wanted to be an actress more than anything else she could think of. She had spent most of her teens reading plays and most of her money going to the movies in Carrizo Springs, but after having graduated from high school in that town, she gave up her ambitions in order to marry a bank teller, Richard Hinojosa, and went with him to Laredo, where they made their home. There she took a job as a secretary and was content until the age of twenty-five, when she woke up one day and decided that she wasn't doing anything special with her life. It was then that her aspirations to become an actress returned; she signed up for acting lessons at the community theater, and after that she was always rehearsing and had very little time left over for her husband. Two years later she divorced him. She was twenty-seven and already feeling very old, so she moved back home to cut her expenses and, investing her last dollar, she began studying method acting by correspondence from the Wynona Langford Institute of Speech and Interpretation in Tulsa.

Once a month the institute would send her a new lesson, and the latest one, number fourteen, was her most challenging assignment to date. She had received a small rock in the mail and was supposed to carry it with her wherever she went, which she had been doing for the past three days. According to the instructions, she was supposed to get to know the rock, learn its rhythms and character. She was supposed to imagine changing places with it, and then, when she was totally familiar with every line, shape and color, she was supposed to clap out the rhythms it contained, discover something about its hidden personality and, finally, tell in her own words how the rock made her feel, what images it brought to mind and what it was like to *become* an inanimate object.

On Principia's first Monday in Judson, Rubendella woke up ready to study her new lesson and was glad to have some music to dress by. She put on tight black pants, black heels and a red nylon blouse she enjoyed wearing when she piled her hair on top of her head.

The night before she had slept with the rock under her pillow, and although she could not remember dreaming about it, she did have the feeling that she knew more about her inanimate object than she had the day before, so, still keeping time to Applebee's fiddling, she walked over to the house where her grandfather had carved statues, faced a full-length mirror and began telling herself everything she felt about the rock. So far she considered it her most sensitive assignment and intended to work on it until the visitors arrived, but secretly she was hoping that no one would show up that day.

Applebee was hoping for just the opposite, however; he always wanted more visitors than they got and was concerned because the crowds were not as large as they once were. Throughout the morning he played the fiddle and entertained the thought that the music would find its way out on the highway and persuade the people passing by to visit the shrine, but around eleven-thirty he stopped playing and went to the café to drink coffee. When the music stopped, Rosita found herself suddenly very tired from her morning's work; Principia felt as though something were missing but could not decide what it was, and Rubendella was so involved with her lesson that she didn't miss the music at all; she continued clapping out the rhythms of the rock and then created an interpretative dance to further express her feelings.

In the café Applebee drank his coffee with an uneasy mind because something told him there would be no visitors that day. He was determined, however, to think of a way to give the town more good publicity but he had nothing to color, was tired of fiddling and therefore wasn't able to think very well, so he started flipping through the hymnbooks and reading song titles at random.

While he sat there attempting to pass the time, Principia was

bringing the second day of Bible School to an end. The lesson of
the day had not interested her pupils as much as she had hoped.
All they wanted was more chalk talks, so after a lengthy consulta-
tion with the Lord, she came to believe He was leading her to
present the entire week's worth of lessons in pictures, which
meant she needed her afternoons to prepare for the next day.

Because the afternoons were so hot, she decided to work in
the café, but after she carried her first box of supplies there, she
wasn't too sure the arrangement was going to work because of
Applebee.

"Somebody needs to help this man find peace of mind," she
said when she came into the café and heard him reading the
hymnbook out loud and shouting for Rosita to bring him a tamale.
He was barefoot, wore Levi's and a matching vest with nothing on
underneath it and his hair tied behind his neck with a piece of
string that came off a package—he was a string saver from way
back. He also wore a cartridge belt—a toy from his childhood—
slung high around his waist and fastened with added elastic. The
two holsters were filled with broken crayons and protruded from
his sides like the wings of a deformed angel.

"Listen to this, Martindale," he said. "Back in Calico Rock,
we used to play this game in church to keep from getting too
bored." He began reading hymn titles as fast as he could: "'Softly
and Tenderly,' 'Love Lifted Me,' 'In the Garden of Gethsemane,'
'Where We'll Never Grow Old'—'Hark, Hark, My Soul,' 'I Am
Coming Lord,' ''Neath the Old Olive Trees,' 'While Shepherds
Watch Their Flocks,' 'On Jordan's Stormy Banks,'—'Joy to the
World,' 'In Tenderness He Sought Me,' 'Beneath the Cross of Jesus.'"

"Yes, I know every one of those hymns," said Principia.

"Yes, and you don't get the joke either," said Applebee. "Let
me make it a little bit easier for you." Again he turned through
the hymnbook and read song titles at random: "'Savior Like a
Shepherd Lead Us' between the sheets. 'Take Me As I Am' between the sheets. 'Love Lifted Me' between the sheets . . ."

"Stop," cried Principia, throwing up her hands. "You shall be
severely punished if you continue this much longer, and if I stand
here and allow you to do it there's no telling what might happen
to me either. Merely by the tone of your voice and nothing else I

can tell that you're an unhappy person. You have just now defiled this precious and most holy songbook with your blasphemy and I want you to know that I understood every word and nuance of what you just said, although I'm sure you don't give me credit for such understanding, and I also want you to know that I realize that you are hopelessly and aimlessly in love with wrongdoing. A real Christian would never have thought to do what you just did."

"Is that so?" said Applebee with mock astonishment in his voice. "I thought you'd be able to see the humor, but it went right over your head and didn't even mess up that hair of yours."

"I'll be back in a few minutes," said Principia. "And by then I expect you to be in a better mood."

When she returned he was still sitting in the café, but he had put down the hymnal and was trying to find a coloring book that needed some work.

Principia thought there was something endearing about him as he sat there fidgeting and trying to find something to color. She realized that she had caught him when he was worried about something, and was glad of it because she believed he would be more vulnerable and therefore easier to reach with the word of God, so she settled herself across the table from him and began working on the preliminary ideas for her chalk talks on the parable of the sower.

Before long she was hard at work with her usual intense concentration. The furrows in her brow were deepening, and her mouth was beginning to draw up as she sketched her scenes. She just knew that the children would love what she was going to do, and she felt sure God would be pleased too.

As she worked she kept one eye on Applebee and was noticing that he was unable to find anything to color. He seemed to be more interested in what she was doing, so she selected one of her own sketches, marked the areas to be colored and the color to be used and handed it over to him.

With a gleam of approval in his eyes, Applebee started coloring the sketch. "You draw 'em and I'll color 'em," he said. "I guess you're thinking that we'd make quite a team."

"No, I wasn't thinking that at all," said Principia casually. She saw that he had abandoned her color scheme and had used all bright colors, which gave the picture a gaudy look, but rather than object she gave him another sketch and complimented him on his good work.

When he was deeply involved she looked up from her sketch pad and said, "You ought to start preaching again you know. I'd really like to hear one of those sermons you used to preach when you were in school. I haven't had any preaching in over a week, and I'm getting starved for it, so you ought to get all worked up and tell everyone exactly how you feel, deep down inside I mean."

"You might be right," said Applebee. His mind was so far away he only heard part of what Principia had said. He wanted her to stop talking so he could think better, so he repeated himself—"I think you might be right"—and hoped that she would be satisfied and close her mouth because he found her voice irritating when he was trying to do his serious thinking. He was about to arrive at a solution to the problem they were having with the visitors, and every time the answer was about to surface the tone of Principia's voice caused him to lose track of his thoughts.

Principia continued to advise him until her voice got on his nerves so bad he put down the coloring, picked up the fiddle and began drowning her out. Before long she was coloring as fast as Applebee was playing. Rosita was rolling her tamales to match the rhythm. Señora Hernandez was making tortillas faster than ever, and Rubendella, off in her grandfather's studio, began adding dramatic flourishes to the interpretative dance she was creating.

After a few minutes a smile came over Applebee's face, and he began playing faster. He had thought of a plan that would bring them good publicity and increase the number of visitors to the shrine. He would need Rubendella's help, however, and he was sure she would cooperate. Still fiddling at top speed, he continued to make his plans. He had the biggest smile on his face Principia had ever seen; his eyes were dancing and his fingers were moving along the fiddle with more agility than ever before.

"Music is the most wonderful thing God put on this earth," he said after he had stopped playing and calmed down. "The best medicine in the world is for a man to have something to fiddle with. Sometimes I get to going so fast that I get carried away, transported is what I mean. Before I know it I'm up in the clouds, and the best part of all is knowing that anybody can go up there with me. All you got to do is fiddle and fiddle and fiddle until you fiddle your way up there, and when you're there you'll know where you are, even if you never been there before. I call it Rapture's Heights; don't know what you call it."

"I call it the love of God," said Principia, matching his smile.

"I call it that too sometimes," said Applebee, winking at her. "I gotta go now. I thought of something and now I better go see about it."

"I understand," said Principia, thinking he was leaving to prepare a sermon. "You need to be alone now."

After Applebee had left, Rosita sent her mother home to rest; then she gave Principia a tamale that had just been steamed. While she ate it Rosita took a bucket of water off the stove and prepared a bath. "This will make you feel much better," she said, leading Principia to a galvanized tub secluded behind the stove. "While you wash I will go get your clean clothes."

After her bath, Principia put on a fresh cotton shift with red and blue checks and sat back down at the table to finish her work. It felt good to be clean again, and she enjoyed the way Rosita combed her hair until it was dry. "I'm going to miss you very much when I leave," she said, almost ready to shed a tear. "My days in Judson have already been the most rewarding and the most difficult of my whole life." She believed that the Lord had reasons for everything He did, but some of the reasons she believed were special. With each passing hour, she was more convinced than ever that He had one of those special reasons for calling her to Judson, and she was beginning to believe the special reason was Applebee.

The night came and then the morning of the next day dawned clear and hot. Principia, still in her hammock, admired the canopies in the morning light, and then wondered what else she could do to make the church more conducive to worship. Slowly she rolled out of the hammock and descended the stepladder to the garden floor. The first thing she noticed was that the sunflower had already turned its head toward the east, as if, she thought, in anticipation of the second coming of Christ. Then she threw open the double doors and looked out over miles of prickly pear in full bloom. The solid patches of yellow glistening in the morning sun made her think the Lord had taken gold from the streets of heaven and thrown it down to earth as a reminder, as well as a promise, of all that was to come.

"Thank you for this most glorious of mornings," she said, as Applebee's jealous tune found its way into the church before a sandy hot wind carried it off to the other side of Judson.

While she stood there admiring the morning, Applebee and a woman Principia had never seen before strolled by, and for a few seconds they were framed by the portal, then by the broken stained glass in one of the side windows. They were leaving the café and now seemed to be on their way back to Applebee's house. The woman was carrying an armload of hymnals, and Applebee was carrying his fiddle. In front of his house, he started playing a few bars of his song, and the woman squealed, dropped all the hymnbooks and said, "That thing makes my ears hurt so bad I don't know what you want to play it for. You play it every time I come here and I just hate it and you know I do too."

"I bet that's Gloria, the one Rosita told me about," said Principia, moving to another window to get a better view. "I just can't stand the way she rotates her shoulders when she walks. That makes her look cheaper than what she is."

Gloria's hair was platinum, teased to the top of her head and falling down her back in long sausage curls. "It can't be real, can it?" said Principia, twisting her own hair around one finger and remembering that some people thought hers was artificial too. For a moment the couple turned around and looked toward the church, and Principia could see the woman clearly. She was wearing short-shorts and sandals, was plump through the middle, but her legs were skinny, her breasts small and her fingernails bright red.

"Rosita's right," said Principia. "She looks like a rodeo queen with all that make-up on, and here it is not even eight o'clock in the morning. It's so pitiful to see Applebee giving his life to the wrong people. He needs someone who can feed his soul, but he just doesn't know it yet."

As she watched them, she felt her eyelids twitching uncontrollably and her heart racing. "If only he would listen to me," she said, as they disappeared into Applebee's house. The idea that Gloria had spent the night there angered her. "How could he do this, especially after he seemed to respond to my advice yesterday," she said. "Lord, I feel Satan at work here, and I ask You to help me cast him out. Help me to run him out of town for we don't need his presence in this place."

While she was staring out the window, the children arrived for Bible School and sat down in the shade of their canopy. Principia felt prepared to do her series of chalk talks on the parable of the sower, but she realized that it was going to be hard to get Applebee out of her mind long enough to teach. She asked God to clear her thoughts and steady her hand so she could draw the four pictures.

With a few deep breaths she felt as though she had regained her confidence. She no longer felt angry at Applebee, and the disappointment of a few moments ago was no longer noticeable. Teaching the children was uppermost in her mind and she was ready to begin, but when she turned around and saw Rafalita scribbling on the clean blackboard, her anger returned.

"Don't do that," she yelled, clenching her fist behind her back. "I've already cleaned that board and I don't want you or anybody else touching it. You're never supposed to bother things that don't belong to you."

The children had never seen Principia angry before and never wanted to see her that way again because she looked like an entirely different person. Her face turned red, her eyes glazed over and her lips trembled as though she could go out of control at any moment.

Rafalita sat down and hung her head, but Principia could not bring herself to apologize for her anger, even though she was ashamed of it. She told her class she didn't always know why she lost her temper so quickly, but she believed it had to do with a feeling of not really knowing what she was supposed to do next. "I don't always trust the Lord as much as I should," she said, regaining her composure. "And sometimes I get angry with Him because I feel as though He is leading me rapidly in the right direction, yet I don't know where it is I'm going."

Principia's voice was calm, and she was beginning to feel better, but the irritation of only a few moments before was still there; she could feel it, a ball of anger that she had twisted and knotted and forced to the bottom of her stomach where no one else could see it.

The children responded with a silence that Principia felt like a cold wind against her back. The only thing she knew to do was to get started with the lesson, which, in spite of the way it began, proceeded successfully until she turned around to address the class directly, and, gazing down the center aisle that divided the garden, she saw Applebee, Gloria and Rubendella Hinojosa. All three of them were looking into the church and waving. They were framed by the rows of sun-dried corn, by the butterbeans wilting on their string trellises and finally by the portal and the glaring sun that seemed to fall brighter on them than anywhere else. Smiling and frowning almost at the same time, Principia waved to them, but on returning to the chalk talk she found that she was so nervous her hand went sliding across the blackboard. After she had finished there was a smudge across the picture; the children noticed it at once, and Principia apologized for the carelessness of her strokes.

"I feel as though I should be stronger in the presence of the Father," she told her class. "But His strength is so overpowering that I tremble when I feel His hand resting upon my heart, for I am so unworthy of His goodness and love."

At twelve o'clock she dismissed the class with an uneasy feeling. Something told her not to leave the church, that in spite of the sand and hot wind blowing through the windows, she would be better off staying there the rest of the day, but, rather than obey that warning, she took Rafalita by one hand, Antonio by the other, and, with the rest of the children running on ahead of them, strolled to the café where Joyce Jeannine was eating chili rellenos and Mary Alaska, sitting across the table from her daughter, was refusing once again even to take a sip of iced tea. "They never have enough water here to wash the dishes like they should," she informed Joyce, who was reading a back issue of *McCall's*. "God only knows how they made that tea, so if you come down with something bad and I'm not anywhere around, you go straight to the nearest hospital and demand that they pump your stomach. If you're lucky that's all they'll have to do."

The children sat down around a long table and waited for Rosita to serve them. Principia sat next to Mary Alaska, and before long Rosita was passing out plates of chicken enchiladas.

When Rosita turned her back, Mary Alaska pointed to Principia's fork and said, "That's absolutely filthy, and you'd be better off using your fingers to eat those enchiladas with."

"Oh, Mother, you wouldn't be happy unless you had something to complain about," said Joyce Jeannine, looking up from her magazine.

"That's not true and you know it," said Mary Alaska as Principia bowed her head and returned thanks.

Before long Rosita spotted a bus coming their way and sent Carlos out front to ring the bell.

"The visitors are almost here and nobody is ready yet," Rosita said, touching her cheeks with both hands and forcing her lips to smile. "We will all need help today."

"I'll help you, Rosita," said Principia, pushing back her plate and leaving Mary Alaska and her daughter at the table. Although she could not approve of what was about to happen, she helped carry six pans of tamales to the cottonwood where Sergio was wiping the tables and his three sisters were once again arguing over the lack of space.

"When will the three of you learn that 'no flies can enter a closed mouth,'" said Rosita, but the sisters were too busy talking and arranging their merchandise to listen.

That day Concepción was selling small yucca baskets as well as *ojos de dios*, and said that she needed more room to spread out. Encarnación had decided to sell paper flowers as well as postcards and painted rocks and needed more room too, so she told Modesta to sell her cactuses out of the Safeway shopping cart she had taken from a parking lot late one night in Carrizo Springs. Modesta had taken the cart in order to have something to transport her plants in, but she wasn't willing to sell them out of it because people would think she had stolen it.

"You *have* stolen it," said her two sisters. They had argued this point many times.

"But no one will know it is stolen," said Modesta, covering the cart with a tablecloth. "It is my shop that makes all the money here, so I need room. Today I will sell the large begonia, and if you don't watch out, I'll keep all the money and you will never see me again."

"Good," said Concepción. "We never want to see you again, so goodby." But Modesta settled herself behind the table and would not budge. The three sisters continued to argue until the visitors stepped off the bus and then, once again, they were all smiles.

In a matter of minutes the shade under the cottonwood was filled with activity. Señora Hernandez had already been carried to her table and was beginning to read palms. Sergio was trying to keep Saint George off the tables and out of the crowd, and José Sánchez, with his hair slicked down and his mustache curled, was strutting around in an aquamarine sport coat with iridescent threads and telling the visitors that a tamale would taste very good and a late lunch in the café would taste even better.

"When he walks like that," Rosita said to Principia as they arranged the plates of tamales, "I can't tell sometimes who is Saint George and who is José, they are so much alike." Principia was about to agree when Federico Chapa and Herman Gonzales, who had run all the way from the Lazy L Ranch, started strumming their guitars and shouting for Rubendella to hurry up.

"She will not be here today," said Rosita, wiping her hands on her white bib apron. "She is practicing her lessons for the Apple. He will be a little late too I imagine, so you go home and put on your shirts and come back."

The two men smiled at Rosita and didn't give her another thought. They strummed their guitars and started singing by themselves while watching Applebee running down the road toward them. Applebee always made an attempt to greet the visitors as they stepped off the bus, and if possible find out what illnesses they had brought with them, but that day he had not gotten dressed in time. He had been at Modesta's house when he heard the bell ringing, had to run all the way across town to put on his suit and was so out of breath when he got home that he fell down putting on his pants and ripped out both inner seams. While the visitors were getting out of the bus, Applebee was safety-pinning the pants back together again and trying to decide which hat to wear if any at all. By the time the two ranch hands started singing, Applebee was running down the road, stirring up the dust behind him. "What a day for this to happen," he said, straightening his string tie, held in place by a small brass frame displaying a picture of Jesus on the cross. Again, his shoes were unlaced, his collar twisted and his umbrella hat kept blowing off his head. At the last moment he had decided to wear the hat because it had three colors on it, red, yellow and blue, which he intended to say symbolized the Holy Trinity.

He was hoping the press would be there that day, and he was nervous. So was Rubendella. They had gone to the ranch the day before and telephoned six small-town newspapers and three city papers, plus a dozen local pastors, and invited them to Judson to witness a rash of healings. "The Lord has been good to us," Applebee had said. "People are being healed before they even get out of their cars . . ." Rubendella had repeated the same speech to the reporters she called, three of whom had hung up in her ear, but Applebee was still sure that some of them would show up.

When he reached the cottonwood in his ripped-out pants and umbrella hat, there were no pastors and no reporters standing in the crowd, and, after waiting as long as possible, he gave up on them and led the visitors around the hotel just as a Tuesday afternoon wind began blowing sand and dust everywhere. The ground was burning through the thin soles of his shoes, and he was beginning to wonder if there was any danger of sunstroke. All the visitors were elderly; that always bothered him because they were more sensitive to the heat. "What we don't need is for somebody else to fall out and die on us," he said to José Sánchez, who had just finished spraying water on the door and was trying to hide the insect sprayer under his sport coat. "So you better keep an eye out. If you see anybody who looks sickly, get 'em back to the bus fast."

Applebee stood before the crowd, gave a brief history of the door and then offered up a prayer that Principia thought was one of the most inspired deliverances she had ever heard. Before he had finished praying, Mary Alaska left her daughter sitting in the café, took her place next to Principia and, after Applebee had said Amen, she agreed with the summer missionary that it was a good prayer, but coming from where it did she was unable to believe one word of it. Principia was willing to give Applebee more credit that than, however, and was certain he was about to preach a fiery sermon, but again he disappointed her by asking for the afflicted to come forward and kneel before the door.

An elderly woman in a wheelchair was pushed forward. Something in her eye caught Principia's attention, and before she realized it she had turned to Mary Alaska and said, "That woman can be healed because she has the right faith. You can see it in her eyes. The sad thing is that she's not being prepared to fully receive the hand of God."

"Of course not," said Mary Alaska, rubbing Tan Fast all over her arms. "This is a circus, not a hospital. Haven't I told you that before? I don't know what you expect."

"I expect a great deal," said Principia as she listened to the woman in the wheelchair, Mrs. Clara Pruitt, declare her faith. Mrs. Pruitt was from San Angelo. She had been confined to a wheelchair after smashing her Buick into a truck, fatally injuring the other driver and a horse that happened to be standing near the road. She said her doctors had never been able to pinpoint the exact cause of paralysis, had given up on her after months of physical therapy, but because of her devotion to God, she was sure she was going to be healed that day. Such was her faith that, before she left San Angelo, she told her husband to dress her in her Sunday best, because she was certain she wouldn't be coming home in a wheelchair.

While she was talking, a station wagon with two people in it slowly drove around the back of the hotel and stopped. The driver, a woman in a nurse's uniform with short brown hair, got out, pushed a blond curl back under her wig and helped the other woman balance herself on a pair of crutches. The woman on crutches had a drawn look on her face. She was wearing a white nightgown with a red chenille housecoat, slightly off the shoulders; her hair was tucked into a sleeping cap; she had dark circles under her eyes and was moving slowly on her crutches, while the nurse walked attentively by her side.

At first Principia didn't recognize them, and Mary Alaska, without her eyeglasses, couldn't tell if they were men or women. She had both pair of glasses dangling on fashion chains around her neck, but she refused to take off her dime-store sun shades, and Principia thought that was fortunate. "I think you should go home right now, Mary Alaska," she said, realizing who the visitors were. "It's too hot out here and I don't want you to make yourself sick."

"Principia Martindale, what kind of fool do you take me for," said Mary Alaska. "I'm strong as a horse." She unwrapped a piece of Doublemint gum, folded it in half and put it in her mouth without touching anything but the tinfoil.

"I wish you would listen to me just once," said Principia. "If you'll leave now, I'll leave with you."

But Mary Alaska refused to leave, so Principia stood as close to her as possible while Rubendella took Applebee by the hand and told him she had been striken with the dropsy. She was supposed to have said she had been striken with polio, but at the last moment she had decided to change her disease and had resorted to Rosita's Bible to find something appropriate. She had skimmed her way through the New Testament until her eyes fell upon a verse in the fourteenth chapter of Saint Luke, where she read of Jesus healing a man of dropsy. "This is my kind of disease," she said. "I like it because I don't know what it is, so maybe I won't catch it."

When Rubendella announced her new disease, Applebee, hoping that no one had heard her, folded his hands reverently and leaned forward as if to pray in her ear, but instead he whispered, "I've got a lot invested in this. Now don't mess me up, you understand, just do what I told you, and let's get it over with, even though there's nobody here to write us up."

Then he faced the visitors and said, "This poor woman has been striken with polio, and her recovery has been slow."

"I get up and go two steps and I drop," said Rubendella, tears running down her cheeks. She had always been able to cry easily, but now, thanks to her correspondence course, she could cry on cue.

Gloria wiped Rubendella's eyes with a Kleenex and helped her turn around to face the screen door.

"Well, what on earth is going on," said Mary Alaska, putting her seeing glasses over her sunshades. When she brought the two women into focus all the color seemed to leave her face at once. "Now I've seen everything," she said.

Rosita was standing behind her. She took Mary Alaska's arm and said, "Don't worry, my daughter is not really sick. She pretends to be sick and then to be healed so the ones who are really sick can find the faith to believe. The Apple thought of this. Tomorrow he wants me to be healed of a stiff leg, but I said, 'No, Modesta is the best actress,' so she will take my place, and you should see her practicing. She is so good. Mr. Applebee says she will convince dozens of people that there's nothing wrong with them."

"Principia Martindale, I wish to God Almighty I had left when you told me to," said Mary Alaska, putting another piece of gum in her mouth. "You knew perfectly well what was going to happen. Why in God's name didn't you drag me away from this evil place?"

Before Principia could answer, the image of Christ appeared on the screen and a continuous sigh was heard rippling through the crowd as Rubendella hobbled toward the door on her crutches. First she dropped one, took a few steps, dropped the other, and, for a moment, stood there swaying. As planned, Gloria rushed to her side and offered support, but Applebee took Gloria by the arm and pulled her away. "She can do it," he shouted. "She can walk with God all by herself."

Mrs. Clara Pruitt was about to leap out of her wheelchair with excitement. She shouted for Rubendella to keep going, but she took a few more steps and fell face-down on the sand. "Somebody wheel me over there to her," said Mrs. Pruitt. "This sand's too deep and I can't make this chair move by myself." Applebee pushed her over to Rubendella. "Get up in the name of Jesus and walk," she shouted, leaning over her wheelchair and touching Rubendella on the back.

Slowly Rubendella came to her feet again and walked feebly, yet she walked all the way to the door, where she dropped to her knees and gave thanks to God for healing her. "She's healed," cried Mrs. Pruitt. "God has healed her. And he will heal me too." She struggled to lift herself to her feet, but her legs would not move or support her weight.

Applebee ran over to Principia and whispered in her ear. "This is what I mean when I say God needs every little bit of help we can give him. Pretty soon that woman in the wheelchair is going to jump up and dance, just you watch." Then he ran back to Mrs. Pruitt and commanded her to "stand up in the name of Jesus Christ of Nazareth."

Again Mrs. Pruitt struggled to stand, and again she was forced by the paralysis in her legs to sit back down.

Principia was astonished by the extent to which Applebee

had gone to convince people of the power of God. She thought he was a disgrace, and she held firmly to her belief that the God she had worshiped all her life needed no assistance except love and constant devotion.

While Mrs. Pruitt struggled to stand, Gloria held her arms outstretched, as though coaching a baby to walk. Rubendella took slow wobbly steps toward her. "She walks into the loving arms of her nurse," shouted Applebee. "And into the loving arms of her God."

"I have seen my left leg grow two inches to match my other leg," said Rubendella as she steadied herself on Mrs. Pruitt's wheelchair. The woman tried once more to stand. She was able to lift her body off the chair, but again her legs would not support her.

"This has gone on long enough," said Mary Alaska, nearly choking on her gum. "Principia Martindale, you're an Invincible, you've simply got to do something before that poor woman kills herself."

Principia took a step forward, and then another. She didn't know what it was that was forcing her into action, but for a few moments she thought that it could be the Tuesday afternoon wind blowing sand and heat on her back, or the musky odor wafting from the bat houses and for an instant falling upon her like the breath of a demon she was determined to expel.

"Mrs. Pruitt," said Principia, kneeling beside the wheelchair, "I don't know if what I'm about to say will make you feel any better or not, but you can't force the Lord to work, you can only pray that He will, when the time is right, place His hand upon your troubles and take them away. When you least expect it, He'll come to you. It may be in the car going home, or it may be in your sleep tonight, and there is always the possibility that it might not be His will to heal you at all. But it is my belief that if you have the faith of a little child, the Lord will listen and be merciful. It is possible if you have the faith of a grain of mustard seed the power of God will come into your life like a bolt of lightning and you'll never be the same. That's never happened to me, but I believe it anyway, because it has happened to a lot of people and it can happen to us too."

In spite of the heat reflecting off the sand and the hot wind blowing across the plains, Mrs. Pruitt was almost put to sleep by the soothing quality of Principia's voice. "I feel so much better," she said, "even though I can't get up. I have surrendered to my affliction now, and if I'm supposed to be healed, I just want to go home and wait patiently for it."

Principia wheeled Mrs. Pruitt back to the bus, where her friends helped carry her inside. "If I only had someone like you to talk to everyday," she said, "I could get well faster. I know I could." While Principia continued to offer encouragement, Applebee and Mary Alaska, standing in the alley between the hotel and what had been the dry-goods store, were engaged in a heated argument.

Applebee was convinced that the woman was suffering from hysterical paralysis, and if Principia had left her alone she would have leaped out of her chair and walked, but Mary Alaska said that nothing he could ever do would put the woman back on her feet again. "You're the one who's hysterical!" she screamed. Her voice carried inside the café, where the visitors were gathering and where her daughter was still eating enchiladas. "You're the one who's the disgrace to the human race," she shouted, shaking her sun shades in his face. "I'm going back to Lockhart today, and I don't care how I get there, but I have one more thing to do before I leave. Joyce Jeannine, get yourself out here right this very minute, do you hear me?"

Joyce, who had seen her mother in action more times than she liked to remember, came out of the café with an exhausted look on her face and a paper plate stacked with tamales balanced on the palm of one hand. She led her mother over to Lucky's pickup, and they left without saying a word.

But later on that afternoon, after Gloria had gone back to work and while Rubendella was rehearsing her lesson, Mary Alaska returned by herself.

Rosita was counting the money they had made that day and didn't notice the truck coming down the road and turning into the lane that circled behind the hotel. Applebee and Principia were too busy to notice it either. They were sitting at the back table near the window and arguing over what had happened that day. Principia was telling Applebee that his soul was in grave danger because he was behaving like a false prophet, and Applebee was telling her that she had no idea what a false prophet was, and that she would be wise to pack her bags and go home.

"Everybody is always fussing," said Rosita. "I don't know who are the children anymore, so don't ask me. The nice woman in the wheelchair went home feeling better. We now have five hundred and eighty-three dollars for a water well, nobody got hurt and here you sit arguing." It was then that she looked out the window and saw the truck parked behind the hotel, and while Principia continued to preach, Rosita went out the back way to see what was going on. In a few seconds she came running through the café and out the front door.

"Miss Alaska paints the door!" she screamed while ringing the bell. "Miss Alaska paints the door white all over."

By the time Applebee and Principia got there, the door had been completely painted and not a trace of Christ could be seen, but Mary Alaska was still standing on the ladder and slinging her paintbrush. "I'm so sick of this one-horse show, I don't know what to do," she shouted. "I've wasted hours of my precious time to come here and watch people be disappointed."

When she started down the ladder, nearly everyone in Judson was looking at her. Concepción Galvan, feeling as though all her blood had evaporated on the spot, sat down quickly before she fell. Modesta sank to the ground next to her, said that their days were numbered without the door, and they would have to go someplace else to find work. Rubendella said if that were true her career was doomed and she would have to return to being a secretary, something she despised even to think about. But Robert Galvan assured her the situation could be worse than that because they might be forced to go pick spinach in Crystal City, the spinach capital of the world, where there was nothing very interesting to look at except a statue of Popeye on the courthouse square. Then José Sánchez, who always tried to be optimistic, told everyone that all was not lost, because he too had watched Manuel paint the original image, had even seen him touch it up a few times and believed that he could do it too.

"You can do anything you want to," said Mary Alaska, getting back in the truck, "but you'll never have another shrine here, and I'm glad of it. You've harmed thousands of people and now it's all over. My bags are already packed and I'm ready to go home to common everyday problems. I've got a husband who drinks and tears up the house every chance he gets; he parks his car in the middle of the sidewalk, and spits on the floors when he feels like it, but that's all right because he's better than any of you. And as far as my daughter is concerned, I hope and pray to God in heaven that she has the sense it takes to persuade that husband of hers to move to a decent, God-fearing community."

After Mary Alaska left, Applebee wandered over to the shade of the mesquite, sat down on the white rock and stared up at the door. "It's all over now," he said, almost choking on his words. "It was good while it lasted, but nothing like this can go on forever." He remembered the disappointment on Principia's face after she first saw the image of Christ and wished he had given her more comfort.

"I can't stand any more of this," he heard her say. She was standing over near the door. Her back was turned toward him, and she was leaning on Rosita's arm. "I just can't stand any more."

While Applebee sat there staring at the door and telling himself it was time to move on, Robert Galvan went into the hotel and dragged out a box of paint Manuel had used. José Sánchez took off his shirt, flexed his muscles and started up the ladder with a brush in his hand when Rosita tried to stop him, but Applebee called out to her to let him have his fun because the door was already destroyed. "But I can fix it," said José. He practically ran the rest of the way up the ladder, and, after wiping off some of the wet paint, he worked diligently for a few minutes and produced a face that Modesta said was bigger than the body.

"That thing won't heal a sick fly," said Concepción. She was still sitting on the hot sand. "You have made Jesus look like a moron."

"Maybe he was," shouted Encarnación. "You leave my husband alone. What he's doing is very good."

"But he is no artist," argued Concepción. "Someone help me up. I can fix this problem."

"No one will help you do anything anymore," said Modesta. "It's my turn now."

José, embarrassed over his failure, climbed down and told Modesta to take his place if she thought she could do any better.

Modesta was positive she could rectify the mess he had made, but Rosita was not so sure and begged her not to try. She would not listen to reason, however, and before anyone could stop her she was standing on top of the ladder and painting eyes that were smaller than Concepción said they ought to be, shaggy hair that was blood red, and lips that were so purple they were black.

"Jesus does not look that way," screamed Encarnación, running up to the door and shaking her fist at her sister. "My husband's picture was much better."

"Everybody in his head has a different picture of what Jesus looks like," argued Modesta from the top of the ladder. "If you do not believe me, ask Principia Martindale what she thinks."

"There is only one Jesus and He has only one face," said Principia, attempting to catch her breath.

"You're not telling me this," said Concepción, attempting to stand up without assistance. "I know exactly what Jesus looks like, and now it is my turn to paint."

Rosita stepped in front of the ladder, told Modesta to come down and refused to allow anyone else to go up. "My father painted this picture," she said, her face wrinkled up with a mixture of pride and sadness. "I'm glad my mother has already gone home today, so she cannot see the way you are acting."

"Jesus is very displeased," Principia managed to say. She was bracing herself against the corner of the hotel.

"But He will get over it," said Concepción. "He always does."

"I don't believe there's power in the door," said Principia, "but I do believe that the image of Christ, no matter where it is, should be respected." Her voice was so weak from shock that hardly anyone heard her. She was hoarse, almost too tired to speak, and her head was throbbing. "I have never known Jesus," she continued, almost in whispers, "when He was more displeased with everyone."

"I heard what you said," shouted Concepción, finally making it to her feet. "And I want to tell you something very important: Jesus likes to forgive people, and so do I. Now I'm going to try to paint Him a pretty face and if I fail, I will just say, Ooooh"—she put both hands on her cheeks—"I am sooo sorry and then he will tell me in my heart, he will say, 'It is all right, Concepción. You tried very hard and your intentions, they were sooo gooood.'"

"As long as I'm alive no one will ever touch that door," said Rosita. Concepción sat back down on the hot sand. She felt as though someone had pushed her.

"It was as wrong for Mary Alaska to destroy this picture of our Savior as it was for you to misuse it the way you have," said Principia, speaking to no one in particular. Her voice was much stronger. Her stare was intense. "I don't know if I can solve this problem or not, but I would like to try."

There was a calm urgency in Principia's voice that Rosita had not heard before, so she stepped aside and allowed her to go up the ladder. After a few minutes of studying the door, she asked Rosita for an apron, and, using it as a rag, she began smearing the wet paint around until it was possible to see part of the original picture. Rosita handed her another apron, and with it Principia removed more paint until the face of Christ was visible, more visible than before, Sergio thought. The body seemed to disappear into the screen, but the face was haunting, the expression sorrowful, and when Principia added a few touches of color around the eyes and mouth, Rubendella thought she was witnessing a miracle. "Suddenly it looks so real," she exclaimed.

Applebee, still sitting under the mesquite, took a look at what Principia had done and said, "Now it's just another picture of Jesus."

But when Principia stepped back and looked at the door she began to weep, and would not allow anyone to comfort her. What she saw was a mass of swirling paint that vaguely resembled robes, and above it was a face of sorrow and disappointment. What she heard was the voice of Jesus: "I am come not to destroy but to fulfill." The more she wept the more Applebee began thinking she might not have destroyed the shrine after all. "I guess we'll have to give it a try and find out," he said, getting up from the rock and taking a closer look at the door.

"Now the image will be there without the sun," said Sergio, trying to comfort Principia. "And it will be better too."

Everyone, even Concepción, agreed with him that there was something about the door that was better, but they could not decide what it was.

"I didn't remove the paint so you could have a shrine," said

Principia. "I simply did it out of love for Jesus."

She cried her way back to the church, locked herself inside, would not even allow Rosita to enter and for the rest of the afternoon tried to put her mind in order again by straightening her clothes, rearranging everything in her suitcase and planning her lesson for the next day. Then she climbed into the hammock and watched the cutworms eat what was left of the tomatoes. "O Lord, I need a change from this place, but my work here isn't even finished yet," she said, looking over the garden. There was hardly any water left in the baptismal pool and hardly a plant that didn't look thirsty. The corn was drying rapidly, the climbing butterbeans were hanging limp on their string trellises, the peppers were drooping, the squash had already turned brown and the watermelon vine was beginning to dry up from both ends. Only the sunflower seemed to be holding its own. Principia looked at the flower and wondered how it could keep going in the face of such odds.

She closed her eyes and tried to sleep, but she could not relax long enough to allow herself to drift away. For a few moments she opened her eyes and stared at the cracks in the church wall. Matthew chapter ten, verse twenty-three, came to her with a gust of sand blowing through the garden. " . . . when they persecute you in this city, flee ye into another." She drew a deep breath and, expelling it slowly, said, "'All our enemies have opened their mouths against us,' Lamentations, three, forty-six." She could not recall having learned the scripture and had no idea why she had remembered it.

"O Lord, that scripture does not comfort me," she said. "Please remove it from my thoughts, and please, God, don't let it be true."

Again she tried to sleep but could not. She closed her eyes, said the Lord's Prayer over and over, and when she opened them up again it was evening. The sun was sinking rapidly over the horizon and the dark was creeping over the walls of the church; the scorpions were coming out for the night and the bats were passing overhead like a tornado that refused to touch down.

Off in the distance Applebee was playing his fiddle. The music penetrated the evening with a slicing clarity that made Principia's soul ache. It's not an unpleasant sound at all, she thought, but it's not very pretty either. While listening to the repetitious tune, she forgot about the troubles of the day and was transported into a half-sleep, where everything seemed right again, but the moment Applebee put down the fiddle she woke up suddenly and with the feeling that something was missing from the world, something that had been missing for a long long time. She was unable to say what it was.

7

On Wednesday morning Principia Martindale got up slowly, slipped into a lavender dress, brushed her hair straight back and tied it out of her eyes with a purple ribbon. She had not slept well that night, could not remember when she had been more exhausted, and the thought of teaching Vacation Bible School did not make her feel any better. "I'm not so sure I make a good Deborah after all," she said, looking at the cross with six notches. It was lying on top of her suitcase, which reminded her that she was ready to leave Judson even though she had not finished her work. The sunrise that morning was scarlet, unsettling at first, but as the light faded into golden rays drifting through the three east windows, she began to feel better about beginning the day.

While she was reading her Bible under the classroom canopy, the children arrived with hot buttered tortillas and flowers they had picked on their way to school. Principia unbolted the door and let them in. A breeze followed them through the garden, and, after they were seated under the canopy, Sergio came in to water the plants.

"Boys and girls," said Principia, smiling with her whole face and making eye contact with each child, "today we're going to take part in a wonderful Bible game. In case you don't know what a Bible drill is, let me give you a brief explanation. Each of you will be given a small New Testament. When I say *Attention!* you will stand up straight, as if you're about to do battle for the Lord. Now, do you follow what I'm saying? Let me repeat: *Attention!* simply means that you come to attention, you stand erect and wait for the next command, which is *Draw Swords!* Now, boys and girls, the Bible is a Christian's weapon against the evils of Satan, and when we draw our special swords or weapons we hold our Bibles straight out before us and get ready to charge. Then, I will give you a Bible reference, such as John three, sixteen, which we all know by heart. I will repeat it three times—three is such a symbolic number for a Christian—and after the third time I will say: *Charge!* At that time, you will each rush to find the scripture and the one who finds it first will step forward and read it with all his might and in a loud voice so we might each one profit by the inspired word of God. The person who finds the scripture first will be given one point, and at the end of the Bible drill we will tally the points, and the winner will be given a certificate which I have hand-lettered myself."

For the next hour Principia drilled them. Sometimes she used the same passage two or three times, especially if it was one that she thought they would profit by, or one of her old favorites such as Ephesians six, ten through seventeen, which she called out four times and which Maria Luisa was the first to find. Principia was pleased to know that Maria was so comfortable with the Bible and even more pleased to present her with the winning certificate.

After the Bible drill, Principia had planned to teach the lesson in a series of chalk talks, but by then the sun's rays were falling over the church wall and onto the canopy, which by mid-morning offered very little protection from the heat or the stale odor of the bats that was entering through the west windows and filling Principia with a nausea that the children had grown accustomed to. She took deep breaths to alleviate her dizziness, but that did no good so she sat down, and after silently asking for guidance she stood up and began the chalk talks.

While working on the first drawing, the wind shifted and once more the air around the canopy smelled clean, hot and dusty, but free of bats. Principia thanked the Lord for the fresh air, but before she had finished the drawing, the heavy, almost sour odor had moved back into the church, and again her head began to swim. She believed that Satan was causing the wind to blow in the wrong direction, so she prayed for guidance and strength. "Lord, I place this lesson into Your loving hands," she said. "Use me as the mouthpiece for conveying Your love." Suddenly the air around the canopy was clear, and, with her first breath of fresh air, she felt another hand take over for her. From there on she surrendered the lesson into the hands of her Lord and spoke with a steady voice of assurance.

The children, captured by her intensity, sat without uttering a word and watched her illustrate the selection of the twelve apostles while she told in her own words who they were, why they were called and what some of them were doing on the day they met Jesus.

On completing the lesson she could not remember what she had drawn and very little of what she had said. The children could remember almost all of it, however, and when Principia questioned them, she found out that they could name with little effort all twelve apostles.

Even after hearing the lesson outlined, Principia still could not remember teaching much of it. I must let this be a lesson to me as well, she thought. I must always rely totally on the Lord to help me out of the troublesome places. I must learn to completely surrender myself to Him.

The class was almost over, but there was a little time left, so Principia asked the children to sweep the floor of the church and add some green leaves to the poles that were holding up the purple sheets. "I regret there isn't more we can do," she said. "Sometimes the Lord doesn't allow us to do as much as we would like to because He wants us to more fully use and appreciate what we have to work with."

At noon, after she had dismissed the class with a prayer, she confessed that she was too exhausted to walk to the café for lunch, but the children refused to take no for an answer. Tugging and pushing, they forced her out the door and were halfway to the café when Rosita rang the bell to signal the arrival of the visitors. Up until then Principia had tried not to think about them, but the thought of their arrival had been in back of her head all morning. The bell reminded her how tired she was and that she didn't feel prepared for what the afternoon might bring.

"Lord help me to get through this," she said. It was a voice of calm desperation.

The Wednesday visitors arrived in a minibus, two cars and a van especially designed so one side folded to the ground to form a ramp down which rolled a wheelchair with Mr. Elmer Primm, whom Principia remembered from her bus ride with Brother Ravenhill. Mr. Primm, dressed in a maroon plaid bathrobe over white pajamas, was carrying a walking cane just in case he needed it. "Everything in the world that can go wrong with a human being has gone wrong with me," he told Applebee, but his nurse, Viola I. Dyer, said it was worse than that. "He's got a terrible bone disease," she said to Rosita, "and he's simply wasting away to nothing. It's so sad to watch him dry up, but what can you do. He's tried everything but this."

Principia greeted them as long-lost friends, but neither of them returned her friendliness. "I don't believe in any of this, you understand," said Viola when she saw Principia. "I uphold the medical profession all the way, even if I am unregistered, so I don't want to have my arm twisted into believing something else. I think the doctors know what they're doing or they wouldn't have the jobs they've got."

While walking to the other side of the hotel Principia told Viola there were a lot of arms she wanted to twist but hers wasn't one of them. "I don't believe in this either," she confessed. "Not the way they're conducting it, that is, but please don't tell Mr. Primm that. I just don't think I can stand to see one more person disappointed, not after they've expected so much."

When everyone assembled behind the hotel, Applebee explained to the visitors what had happened the day before and called their attention to the fact that the image was still visible, thereby proving that Christ cannot be destroyed, not by fire, not by water, explosion or earthquake. "He is almighty," said Applebee. "He's the fairest of ten thousand morning stars and will exist when nothing else does."

Five people came forth to be healed that day: Mrs. Adelle Riley, clinging to her Bible and praying for her bursitis; Mr. C. M. Hollis, who came from Dumas and suffered frequent and acute migraines; Mrs. Etta Hawkins, who came from Port Arthur and had rheumatoid arthritis so bad she could hardly walk, and her granddaughter, Noveline, who was ten years old and able to see only out of one eye. Mr. Elmer Primm was the last to come forth. Viola I. Dyer, with a newspaper tucked under her arm, wheeled him to the door, and during the service she put on a green sun visor and worked the crossword puzzle standing up.

"All you have to do is believe," said Applebee. "If you don't believe, it's impossible; you'll go back home the way you came." Principia didn't agree with this theory or his presentation. In her opinion he was speaking too rapidly, giving the impression that he was in a hurry to get out of the sun. Again that day she felt something pushing her forward, but it wasn't someone, neither was it the wind that for a moment had died down, nor the odor of the bats that had not yet begun to seep into the afternoon. A cloud passed overhead, providing a few minutes of shade, and when the sun shone upon them again, Principia felt herself moving forward.

"This is not the way it's done," she said, so low only Applebee could hear. "You're forcing me to take things into my own hands." There was something so urgent in her voice that Applebee stepped aside, while Principia, like a saint burning to deliver the word of God, approached the five who had come from such long distances to ask for the healing power. With an agitated heart and a smile on her lips, she addressed them with such peace and understanding in her voice that even Viola I. Dyer was forced to put away her crossword puzzle and listen.

"Be still and know that I am God," quoted Principia as though she were speaking of herself, but no one took it that way. "We glorify God for bringing you here today. We are touched by your faith and commitment and if the Lord sees fit to heal you we will rejoice in His glory. In the words of Jesus, 'If you cannot believe in me, believe in my miracles,' and today we hope to see those miracles performed."

For a moment she felt unsteady. Applebee noticed that she was beginning to sway back and forth, but when she looked over the low brush and miles of prickly pear, she seemed to find her balance again. She could see heat waves rising from every bush, every cactus; everything and everyone seemed to be outlined by the glaring sun. She told herself that she could not lose control as she had done in Bible class, that she must remember what she was saying and what she was doing; she told herself to stand up straight for the Lord, to remain in control yet allow herself to become His mouthpiece.

"We are about to lift our voices in praise of the Almighty," she said. "But one thing you must realize is this: I cannot heal you. This image of Christ which was painted by a man and which was almost destroyed yesterday cannot heal you, but the Holy Spirit can and will heal each and every one of you. It is my belief that even a nonbeliever can be made well through the goodness and mercy of God, who has a purpose for everything He does.

"Try the Man of Galilee," sang Principia, wishing someone would join in with her. "Try Him . . . Try Jeee-zus. Love that won't grow old, a faith that won't grow cold; Try Jee-zus Man of Gaa-la-leee."

As she sang, the visitors began swaying to the rhythm, but after the second verse she realized that the brush was moving also, and so was the lamp post, the old fire hydrant and the back wall of the hotel. When the horizon line began to tilt back and forth, she stopped singing, and with all her energy she concentrated on making the world still again. She told herself it was the heat that made her head swim and that during such moments of weakness it would be easy for Satan to step between her and the Lord and put false words in her mouth.

When her world was level again, she looked everyone straight in the eye and continued singing. No one spoke, no one moved, not even Applebee, who was captivated. Again he felt protective; he wanted to run away with her that minute; he wanted to believe that with time she would become more like him, but he was beginning to think it might be the other way around and he was just realizing it; he could not decide which it was, but the thought was there just the same; perhaps he was more like her after all.

He admired her commitment, but the intensity of it frightened him, especially that day, Wednesday, which began with a violent burst of light and faded into a golden dawn that suddenly disappeared into the bright, clear, almost startling light of mid-morning and then afternoon. Applebee had gotten up feeling as though something was going to happen and watching Principia conduct the healing service convinced him that he had been right, for she had at some undetermined time, like the morning sun, slipped into a new color and a new voice. She spoke with a different kind of authority; there was a peacefulness about her, and for a moment Applebee found himself believing that the Lord had

truly taken her into His bosom and put not only the right look in
her eyes but the right words in her mouth and the right way of
speaking them so they penetrated like daggers into his heart. Being in her presence that afternoon was for Applebee as awesome
as watching the bats fly off in the evening. She made him aware
of the Holy Spirit, and he believed that she might have the power
to call it back to earth.

As she continued singing, someone joined her. It was the
voice of a twelve-year-old boy who had come with his parents,
John and Jewel Pedigo, from Odessa. The boy, Andrew, had a
voice as clear and penetrating as the afternoon light, and to Principia it was the voice of an angel.

Earlier in the service his parents had tried unsuccessfully to
persuade him to go forward and declare his affliction, a speech
impediment he had suffered since the year he started talking.
When he began singing with Principia, his parents were not surprised because when he was younger he had been able to sing
without missing a word but had not been able to speak clearly.

After the last verse, his mother asked him to talk, but for her
he would not; still she believed that her son had been healed, so
she declared her belief to Principia. "There was a new strength in
his singing voice," she said. "I think he can speak properly now."

"Go on, let's hear you say something," said his father with a
tone of sarcasm in his voice that astonished Principia's heart. The
boy hung his head and did not look up until Principia approached
him, took aim with her entire arm and pointed her finger accus-
ingly: "Speak in the name of the Most High," she commanded,
"for the Person of Christ is here today."

To Andrew, Principia had an evil look in her eyes, and in her
presence he felt as though he had no choice but to do what she
said, but he could not move; his legs were frozen into place and
his jaws felt as if they were locked. Principia extended her arms as
though about to embrace the boy, but instead she slapped him on
both sides of the face at the same time and shouted: "Speak in the
name of Jeee-zus."

Andrew remained perfectly rigid. He was too frightened to
cry or move, and his mother was about to intervene when Principia slapped him on both sides of the face again and nearly lifted
him off the ground. "Speak!" she said. "The Lord is waiting for

you. You may keep man waiting, but don't anger the Lord with your silence. Don't ever give Him second place in your life."

"My name is Andrew Pedigo," he said. "And I don't know what you want me to say." His voice was trembling, but he did not stutter on the P as he had been known to do.

"You've been healed," said Principia. She was surprised to hear herself saying it; she was surprised that the words came out as easily as they did.

The boy's father, still disbelieving what had happened, even though he had come there to believe, came forward and asked Viola I. Dyer for her newspaper. Turning to the comics, he asked Andrew to read aloud, and he did, without missing a word.

"You've been healed," said Principia, again shocked by the sound of her words, and almost afraid that what she was saying was really true. "Anyone who has the faith of a little child can be healed." She spoke with a joy that did not explode but was quietly contained within her heart, tucked away where her doubting mind could not find it, at least not for the moment.

With her arm resting on Andrew's shoulder, she turned her attention to the five who had come forward and who were praying to be made well, but when she looked upon their suffering and the expectation in their eyes she felt incapable of helping them. Along with that feeling of helplessness, she felt something twisting inside her; something within had broken and a cool fragrance no one else seemed to notice was evaporating into the air and being carried away by the south wind. She could almost see it, almost determine what it was she had felt come upon her. "Don't go yet," she whispered into the wind. Everyone thought she was talking to Andrew who was still at her side, but Applebee knew that she was not.

"Lord, take not Thy Holy Spirit from me," she said, but it was already too late. She felt as though she was waking up, yet she remembered everything that had happened, and, again gazing upon the five who had come to be healed, she felt powerless. "I believe in miracles," she said. "But I cannot perform them. Miracles often happen when we least expect them, and when we feel as though the Lord has no use for us. It is in an hour when we do not expect to be blessed that the Lord will send His Spirit upon us. We must be patient and wait for those times and not question who is healed and who is not healed. My message to you is to continue believing. God has a purpose for all His people, and you must trust in that purpose, even if you don't know what it is."

Principia took the addresses of the five who had not been healed and promised to write them encouraging letters. She embraced Andrew, reminding him that he carried the name of one of the twelve apostles and that she had not healed him: "It was Jesus."

After the visitors had left, Principia sat under the cottonwood and wept while everyone came to her with comfort she could not allow herself to receive. Again doubt was creeping into her heart. She did not believe or disbelieve the boy had been healed. She felt as though the Devil had led her into a state of confusion where she would never be able to believe in anything. She accused Applebee of trying to fool her; she accused Rosita, Rubendella and Sergio, but they told her they had had nothing to do with the healing. Rosita truly believed that the boy had been blessed and told Principia that she, whether she would admit it or not, was responsible. Sergio agreed, as did Rubendella. "It was not a performance that little boy gave," she said. "Believe me, I can tell if someone is just acting."

But Principia didn't want to believe them, and Applebee knew it. He could sense she was beginning to feel the dreadful weight of something that with the coming years would grow heavier. But he could not match what he felt with words, and, like Principia standing before the five visitors, he felt a helpless rattling in his bones. He sat down under the cottonwood with her, and, after watching an ant crawl across his foot, he said, "You're the one who ought to preach, not me. With you around I think I could do without the bats."

"But do you believe the boy was healed?" she asked, and Applebee answered her truthfully: "Yes, he was, and he will be for as long as the image of Principia Martindale is alive in his mind. You've heard about people being scared speechless, well this time it happened in reverse. It's still a miracle in my opinion, but it's more of a miracle to some of us than it is to others and that's okay too."

"You seem to think I had something to do with it," said Principia.

"You had everything to do with it," he said.

Principia thought that Applebee's answer made God seem awfully small and insignificant, and she could not accept his viewpoint at all, yet no matter what the real answer was she dreaded receiving it. But she knew she could not live without the truth, so she left him sitting under the tree and went from house to house and pleaded with everyone to tell her if the boy had been healed or not. Robert Galvan was of the opinion that a healing had occurred, and José Sánchez agreed with him. "You don't know your own power," Jose said, pointing a finger in her face. It was the answer that Principia decided she wanted to hear, but it filled her with an unspeakable and soundless terror.

"But there is no reason to be so afraid," said Concepción, who was sitting on the porch with her sisters and trimming the wick on an oil lamp. "We have seen these things happen many times; we cannot explain them, but we are not afraid." Encarnación and Modesta agreed with her, and as far as Principia knew it was the first time all three sisters had seen eye to eye on anything.

Still Principia was not satisfied. Beyond Encarnación's house was one more, a small adobe tucked away behind some cactus and brush at the end of the trail. In the back of the house was an herb garden where Señora Obdulla Hernandez, sitting among her hollyhocks, was gathering spider's webs to stop the flow of blood where Rafalita had cut her foot. The child was sitting on the ground with her leg propped up on a chair, and the old woman was covering the wound with webs and yarrow from her garden.

When Principia asked her if the boy had been healed, Señora Hernandez shook her head as if she knew the answer but could not tell it. "I was not there," she said. "How can I say. But I will tell you this. The truth is inside." She touched her heart with fingers that were covered with webs.

It was not the kind of answer that Principia wanted, but for a while it put her mind to rest. She returned to the church and closed the door behind her. When the bats began flying overhead, she went to bed, but for a long time she could not sleep due to the heaviness of her heart. Finally she closed her eyes and, thinking of Luke seventeen, twenty-one, " . . . for, behold the kingdom of God is within you," she drifted into a peaceful sleep.

That night she dreamed that the image of Jesus stepped from the screen door and walked the dusty streets of Judson to the church where she slept, and there, standing among the corn stalks, his robes falling to the garden floor and His arms outstretched, He asked: "But whom say ye that I am?"

And Principia answered and said, "Thou art the Christ, the Son of the living God."

And Jesus, answering her, said, "Blessed art thou, Principia, for flesh and blood hath not revealed *it* unto thee, but my Father which is in heaven. And I say also unto thee, that upon this rock I will build my church and the gates of hell shall not prevail against it."

It was then that she was taken up in the Spirit.

For a few moments she watched herself lying in the hammock. Then a strong wind transported her from the church in Judson to the church in New Bethel where she had worshiped all her life. Unlike Judson, the air in New Bethel was humid, heavily laden with the fragrance of mimosa and pine. The night air was as she remembered it, and so was the church, a white frame structure resting on the solid foundation of river rocks. It was her home, her idea of a place of worship, but not the church the Lord wanted her to build. "You must take your mind away from this building, Principia," she was told. "You will never see it again, for already you are a servant in a new church."

She was then brought back to Judson on a cool breeze, and just before returning to her body the church of the future was revealed to her. It was not an adobe, brick or frame structure but one made of glass and steel with spires and towers and heavenly music playing both day and night. "This is the church you are to build," said the Christ. "Look carefully and forget not what you see."

From the hammock, Principia opened her eyes and marveled at all that was revealed to her. She wanted to ask how the new church was to be made possible and was almost able to speak, when the Son of God, saying, "And if I be lifted up from the earth, will draw all men unto me," ascended from the rows of corn, through the open ceiling and the gates of heaven while Principia Martindale lay in her hammock and, for a while longer, slept peacefully.

But later on that night she began dreaming again.

She dreamed that Satan blew into Judson on a hot wind and set fire to everything in sight. He was determined to stop her work from going any further, and she was determined to drive him out of town. From the gates of heaven the Lord looked down upon her, and she heard His voice as if He were standing in the church: "Attention, Principia!—Draw Swords!—Charge!"

With a fine purple blanket, which was the raiment of her Savior, she beat out the flames, and with the word of God on her lips and the Bible in her outstretched arms, she drove Satan to the far reaches of Judson, where they met face to face. The Devil, clothed in a mantle of fire, took her to the top of the bell tower and revealed unto her the New Judson, a holy city paved with gold and filled with worshipers of Christ. "All these things will I give thee," he said, "if thou wilt fall down and worship me."

Then Principia answered, "Get thee hence, Satan: for it is written, thou shalt worship the Lord thy God, and Him only shalt thou serve."

She pushed the Devil off the tower, and he fell to the earth, bounced like a flaming ball and disappeared into the night. "The earth shall be full of the knowledge of the Lord as the waters cover the sea," shouted Principia as two silver-winged angels appeared and stood watch over the road into Judson and a third with wings of blue and gold hovered above her hammock, where, for a while longer, she slept peacefully, but then she began dreaming again, not of the Son of God, and not of the Devil, but of the visitors who had come there that day and were not healed. She saw their faces clearly, watched their expectation dissolve into disappointment, and in her sleep she wept out loud for them.

Not far away a wind, blowing low across the earth drifted into Judson and carried Principia's cries to every corner of the town.

Señora Obdulla Hernandez, who at her age did not sleep very much or very well, got up from her bed and went outside to listen to the cries and say prayers. "There are evil ones in the air tonight," said the old woman. She went back inside her house, lit an oil lamp and looked for some sage to burn.

Applebee was also awakened by Principia's crying. Stealing

into the church, he watched her sleep as he had done before, only this night she tossed so violently in the hammock, he was afraid she might fall out, so he folded her arms over her body and held them there until she was calm.

It was then he realized she had fever. Knowing that Señora Hernandez would know what to do, he left the church, the doors standing wide open, and ran down the road past the cottonwood, the café, and the house where Manuel had worked on his carvings. He thought he saw the old man sitting at the window as had been his custom, but after blinking many times he realized it was only the moon shadow of a bucket hanging on a dead limb.

Rather than walk in front of the house he took the longer path behind it and continued on his way when a light flickering through the brush made his heart leap before he realized it was only Señora Hernandez. She was carrying a pot of burning sage and walking as fast as she could but came to a complete stop when she saw Applebee. The old woman was wearing a black dress that disappeared into the dark, but her eyes were clearly visible. "There are evil ones in the air tonight," she said.

"I was coming to get you," said Applebee.

"I know," Señora Hernandez replied. "She is not well."

After they entered the church the old woman added more sage to the pot and walked around the hammock three times while mumbling something Applebee could not understand. Then she took Principia's hand and looked at her palm. "It is good and it is bad at the same time," she said, her fingers trembling across the hand. Applebee turned the lamp wick up so she could see better, and with her index finger Señora Hernandez indicated a place where two lines came together in a point. Then, still with her finger, she counted five points, a perfect star. "This is the mark of something very special," she said, "but she has been born under two stars and will never receive the kind of satisfaction she expects. Her happiness will come only in moments, not hours, not days, not weeks, so it is good that her soul will be put to rest early. There is a three here, three days, three weeks, three months, three years, I don't know, but when she is no longer here, people will keep her alive in their thoughts."

Señora Hernandez folded Principia's arm over her body. She threw more sage on the fire, said another prayer that Applebee could not understand and placed the knotched cross in Principia's hand. "The fever will leave soon," she said. For a few minutes they watched her sleeping peacefully, then Applebee followed Rosita's mother out of the church and closed the doors behind them. She would not allow him to walk her home, however. She said she had made friends with the dark long ago, but before they parted she told him that there was something else in Principia's palm, something or someone who would influence her in a strong way and possibly interfere with her fate. "It could be someone she already knows," said the old woman, tapping Applebee on the arm. "But I am not sure."

Heat lightning was on the horizon when they parted, and before Señora Hernandez reached her house she felt a strong wind blowing down the road. The branches of the cottonwood caught it, spun it around and hurled it toward the church. The double doors swung open and the night wind, like a restless spirit, whipped through the garden, rattled the dried corn stalks and left in an upward gush through the open ceiling.

Then the wind changed its course, and again the air was heavy with the smell of bats. Principia dreamed that Satan, disguised as an angel of the Lord, had slipped back into town and blown all the fresh air away. She saw him clearly; he was standing in the garden where Jesus had stood; he had white robes and silver wings, hair as light as clouds and eyes burning with the fires of hell. Struggling for her breath she rolled out of the hammock, tore a corn stalk from the garden floor, and with it she whipped the Devil out of the church, chased him down the road and into the brush, where he disappeared into a mesquite that had died the year before.

Still in a half sleep, she wandered around Judson and blessed each house until she came to Applebee's kitchen window. She looked in on him. The oil lamp was burning on the kitchen sink, and Applebee, sitting toward the window, had gone to sleep with his head on a stack of books. His yellow shirt was buttoned up around his neck, but the rest of the buttons were missing. I sure wish I could sew them back on, Principia thought, noticing stacks of paper all around him. His fiddle was propped up against a straightback chair, and Saint George, perched on an open cabinet door, was sleeping with his head under his wing. The mural on that outside wall was a landscape of mesquite and prickly pear, and for a moment Principia felt as though she were looking through the brush into a house that had no walls, but her thoughts did not linger there. She stared at Applebee and wondered who he was, why he was so familiar and if she would ever see him again.

"Our Precious Redeemer," she prayed, whispering through the window. "Please bless this man, and help me to love him more. Help me to see the good that is buried within his heart and help him see it too." She wanted to reach out, put her hands on his head and pray for the Holy Spirit to fill him, turn his life around and put a new look in his eyes. "O Heavenly Father, I think I could love this man if he had more of You inside him," she said, reaching through the window with both arms, straining to get just a little closer so that she might at least touch the sleeve of his garment, but he was too far away. In her half sleep, she stretched herself as far as she could, but still she could not reach him, not even with her breath.

He moved slightly, stretched his arms across the table toward hers, and only then did the tips of their fingers barely touch. While Principia asked for the Holy Spirit to come into Applebee's life, she felt a warm current flowing through her arms and entering him, filling him with a new life. He then moved his hands back, only a few inches beyond her reach, but still she felt as though something were connecting them, some current that was flowing from her into him and back again. With joy in her heart she pulled away, watched him sleeping for a few seconds, and then she felt the Spirit come upon her in full force. Her whole body trembled, and her heart raced; she tried to speak, but no words would come out. As if something had pushed her, she fell backward on the ground and for a long time she lay there shaking. Then she felt the Spirit moving through her again, caressing her, lifting her up and leading her off through the night.

She wandered west toward Mexico, did not question her course, but kept her eye on something bright in the distance that occasionally came closer and then led her a little further away until she reached an arroyo several miles from Judson. There she slid into a ravine and slept peacefully until, shortly before dawn, a stray dog cuddled up next to her and rested his head on her arm.

When the dog began to scratch, Principia, imagining that Satan had returned and bedded down next to her, rolled over on the animal, wrapped her arms around it and would not let go. "I'll kill you if it's the last thing I do," she said. "I'll wrestle you until there's nothing left but goodness and mercy on the face of this earth." The dog broke away howling and ran off. Principia sank again into a deep sleep and was awakened not by the hot sun of late morning, not by the white-tailed hawk nesting in the yucca just over her head, but by the voice of her Lord, calling to her, saying:

"Principia, arise. Wake up, Principia. I have work for you to do today. Get up and follow me."

 8

During the night Señora Obdulla Hernandez dreamed of Principia many times; once she was sitting on the front porch, the second time she was flying over the house. It was then that the señora got up and went outside to find out what was going on, but there was no one in the front yard and no one on the porch, nothing but the *Aloe vera* sitting in the chair where she had left it to catch the morning sun. The wind storm had blown on across the border, and it seemed to Señora Hernandez that it had taken all the air with it, for the night was still as death, and because there was something in the atmosphere she didn't like, something besides the dust settling in her yard, she was unable to draw a satisfying breath.

Inside her house again, she lit an oil lamp and shuffled the cards, cut them three times and spread them out on the kitchen table. The dark-haired woman who had been turning up for months was still there only she was much closer; was it two hours, two days, two weeks? Señora Hernandez could not tell, but according to the cards, the person on her way had some connection with the town; she was bringing a man with her, and it was the señora's worst fear that relatives of L. J. Judson were about to show up and claim everything in sight. She put the cards away, pushed the dark lady to the back of her mind and went to bed with Principia in her thoughts.

Many times before dawn Señora Hernandez saw a white-faced girl with long purple hair sitting in the corner of her bedroom, but each time the girl appeared, the señora woke up and realized she had been dreaming. The last time it happened she thought she went outside again, but she didn't leave her bed; still she was aware of being outdoors where there was no wind, and no air and nothing moving except a long-haired girl floating over the brush like the ghost of Llarona and wailing almost in whispers.

As a child Señora Hernandez had often heard her mother tell the story of Llarona, a Mexican woman who murdered her children and after her death wandered aimlessly in search of them. "La Llarona will get you if you're not good," Señora Hernandez had been told, and many years later she heard herself saying the same thing to her daughter, Rosita, and then to her granddaughter, Rubendella.

Three times in her long life, Rosita's mother claimed to have seen the ghost. The first time was in Mexico City. Llarona, dressed in black, drifted across the Plaza de Garibaldi and disappeared into a wall. The second time was a Sunday night when the Señora was walking across the bridge at Piedras Negras and Llarona, as transparent as a piece of fine silk, was sitting on a rock with her feet in the river. The last time the ghost appeared was three nights after Señora Hernandez and her husband, Manuel, moved to Judson. That time Llarona, weeping loudly, was floating above the cactus and brush.

Señora Hernandez was aware that the ghost of her dreams was not Llarona because the next morning when she awakened she was holding in her mind an image of Principia floating over the brush, ripping her nightgown and tangling her hair in the mesquite.

"She is trying to catch up with the wind," said the señora, getting out of bed and moving faster than usual.

Applebee had also slept with an uneasy feeling and knew something was wrong when he looked out his kitchen window that Thursday morning and saw Señora Obdulla Hernandez coming up the road. He met her at the church and together they went inside, but Principia was not there; the hammock had fallen to the floor and Saint George was scratching in the garden.

Applebee followed Principia's footprints out of the church, down the road to the cottonwood and on toward the house of Señora Hernandez, back again to the hotel, the screen door and finally to his kitchen window, where he found the place in the sand where she had lain. He wondered how long she had stayed there watching him sleep and what she had been thinking. In his mind he could see her face staring at him through the window, and he hated himself for not waking up.

He searched for her all morning as did Sergio, José Sánchez and Robert Galvan, who was sure she had vanished into thin air because her footprints kept disappearing into the brush and reappearing again a little further on until finally they disappeared altogether. By eleven o'clock the men gave up and went back to the café, where everyone else had assembled. It was then that Señora Hernandez cut the cards three times on Applebee's favorite table, but she could not see Principia in the spread, so Rosita brewed a pot of desert tea, spooned extra leaves into a cup and gave it to her mother. After the señora had finished drinking she stared for a long time at the formation of leaves in the cup. Then she turned it upside-down in its saucer and covered it with her hands while she mumbled something no one could understand.

After the señora had studied the new formation of leaves she looked up and said, "It is very clear. You will find her not where there is water, but where there used to be water." Then she stood, said she was very tired, and walked home by herself.

Everyone else left the café too and started searching again. The men looked in all the dry wells in Judson, but found nothing in them but garbage; Modesta and her sisters thought of the baptismal pool, but Principia was not there either. Rosita thought of the swimming pool that L. J. Judson had dug behind the hotel. It had never held water, was covered with sand, and she wasn't too sure she remembered exactly where it was, but after searching the area where she thought it had been, she was forced to admit that Principia was nowhere near that spot.

After a while everyone returned to the café. Rubendella said she had been to the old dry cattle pond on the ranch and while walking back she had thought of a plan. "I am psychic, just like my grandmother," she announced with abundant pride. "I will go off somewhere all by myself and hold something that belongs to Principia. Then I will be able to tell you exactly where she is." She went to the church, found a barrette on the floor and took it home. In her room papered with pages out of movie magazines, she sat in the center of her bed, held the barrette in both hands and closed her eyes.

While Rubendella was secluded in her bedroom and Señora Hernandez was resting in her garden, everyone else sat in the café and tried to decide what to do next. It was then that Encarnación Sánchez, pacing the floor, looked out the window and saw a parked bus with dozens of visitors standing around it and looking as though they were lost; some of them had already found the door, others were milling around the front of the hotel and a mother was changing her child's diapers on the table where Rosita sold her tamales.

"We'll give them what they want as best we can," said Applebee. "Then we'll ask the ones who are well enough to help us look for her." He went outside and greeted the visitors. Modesta ran home for her shopping cart full of cactus, and her two sisters helped Rosita set up her tamale stand.

"We will not take their money today," said Rosita. "If they are not hungry they will be more likely to help us."

Sergio tried to arouse Señora Hernandez, but she said she was too troubled to work. Rubendella refused to work too. She was still sitting in the center of her bed believing she was about to receive pictures in her mind. "In not too long I will be able to tell you where Principia is," she said, still holding the barrette and trying to make her mind go blank so she could receive a message.

There were many visitors in Judson that day, but only two of them professed their faith in miracles. Mr. Clarence Durham from Texarkana was the first to come forward. He had had a hurting in his left leg for months, and because he had never been sick a day in his life—he was fifty-five—he could not determine the origin of the pain, and neither could the physicians attending him, so he decided to lay his burden at the foot of the cross.

Applebee told him he had made the right decision.

Mrs. Kathleen Montgomery was the next to declare her belief in miracles. She was from Waco, had arrived in an ambulance behind the bus and was carried around the hotel on stretchers and placed on the hot sand with her head propped on a pillow so she could view Christ with ease. Applebee explained to her that the door had been badly damaged by a lunatic and that the colors were not as bright as they had been, but Mrs. Montgomery would not listen. "Jesus never fades," she said. "He just keeps getting brighter and brighter."

She was forty-five years old and for the last ten years had suffered from arthritis and was unable to move without pain. She was convinced that her condition was growing progressively worse, even though the doctors had told her she was getting better, and because of her newfound faith she was sure the Holy Ghost was about to touch her soul.

"I led such a reckless youth," she told Applebee. "The Lord has punished me a thousand times over for my sins. I was young and didn't know any better, but that's no excuse. I slept with more men than I can remember; I was unfaithful to my husband five times that I know of; I lied on my job, stole money from my friends, and now I'm ready to serve God, and if I can just get on my feet again I'll never stop praising His name."

While Applebee was standing before the visitors attempting to conduct a healing service, he looked over the crowd and there, no more than thirty feet into the brush, stood Principia. There was dried blood on her legs, and her arms and face were badly sunburned. She was dragging her bathrobe behind her, and her purple nightgown was reduced to shreds around her ankles. She was walking with her head thrown back and her eyes wide open like a blind person, Applebee thought. He was unable to tell if she was focusing on anyone or anything, yet she seemed to be staring at, or through, something.

In spite of Applebee's efforts to stop her, Rosita approached Principia, tried to lead her toward the back door, but she would not be led. She looked into Rosita's eyes, but her stare was blank. "I have work to do," she said, brushing Rosita to one side and walking to the front of the crowd. "These people need me.

"Last night I wrestled with the Devil," she said, taking Applebee by the hand. "I fought the battle and won, but the victory is not mine but God's. I have met him face to face, and now I realize more than ever before that the riches of God's Grace in Christ are far greater than silver or gold."

Her voice was calm, soothing, but Applebee noticed something else trying to break through.

"It has to do with the stomach," Principia said, turning to the crowd. Her face wrinkled up as though she had grown old instantly, and her voice was no longer calm. "You have lived with this pain for years and today the Lord has taken it away from you and given it to me. Our Father, I rebuke this pain. I cast it out into the desert to die." She doubled over, spat up a red fluid, then stood up straight again and calmly listened to a man, John Simmons, a bricklayer from Amarillo, tell her that he had suffered from a stomach ulcer for years and that when Principia rebuked the pain, he had felt a warmth in his entire body.

"That warmth was the Lord healing you, Mr. Simmons," said Principia. "I have also felt the Lord working inside me that way. He gave me your pain and I cast it away. You will not have it any longer. Go home and tell everyone what has happened to you."

For a few moments Principia stood there without speaking, then turned her attention to Mrs. Montgomery lying on the ground. "There is a woman here," she said. "There is a woman here who is confined to her bed and cannot walk. In the name of Jesus I rebuke her pain. In the name of Jesus I say that she will be able to walk again."

Slowly she approached the arthritic woman, kneeled down and spoke directly into her face: "Jesus loves you. He loves you more than you will ever know; He really does. And if you'll allow Him in your heart and love Him back, He will return that love by making you well again. So I beseech you in the words of the old old hymn: 'Only trust Him. Only trust Him. Only trust Him now. He will save you. He will save you. He will *heal* you now . . .'"

"I, Kathleen Montgomery, ask to be healed in the name of Jesus," cried the visitor, staring at the painting of Christ. Principia touched the woman's temples, removed her fingers quickly as though she had burned them, and, throwing back her head, she shouted, "Heal in the name of the man of Galilee."

Mrs. Montgomery swooned, rotated her head as she had never been able to do in many years, while Principia took her by the shoulders and shook her mightily. "In the name of Jesus, Pain, come out of this woman."

Mrs. Montgomery wanted with all her heart to be well again, and at any price; oh, how she had prayed and was still praying for the mercy of God. "Lord, have Thy way in my life," she shouted until she felt a tingling sensation up and down her spine. Then

Principia rebuked the pain again and Mrs. Montgomery slowly turned her head, shook her arms and without assistance sat up and looked around. She felt as though her whole body were waking up after a long sleep. Her husband fell to his knees and gave thanks while Principia commanded his wife in the name of Jesus to stand; and she stood, not without someone's shoulder to lean on but even still she was standing. Principia commanded her to bend from the waist. Slowly she did so. Principia commanded her in the name of the Lord to run, and Mrs. Montgomery, wearing her best Sunday dress and hat, ran in circles around Principia, who commanded her again in the name of the Son of God to touch her toes, and even this Mrs. Montgomery did with the greatest of ease.

"You're healed. You're healed," shouted Principia as Mrs. Montgomery dropped to her knees, took her husband's arm and thanked God for her miracle. "The door has not healed you," said Principia. "I have not healed you. But God has, on this day, at this time and place seen fit to deliver you of your great and long suffering."

Mrs. Montgomery threw up her hands and rejoiced, but Mr. Durham still had the hurting in his left leg, and even after Principia touched him he said it was still there. Over and over she rebuked the pain, but the man still declared its presence until Principia, helpless in the face of he who had come from so far away, began to feel the power leaving again. It was as though something were evaporating into the air, leaving through the top of her head and floating off into the distance. She felt as though she had no blood, that her veins were dry and her body was turning to dust.

She fell on her knees and wept because of her helplessness and had to be carried to a cot in the back room of the café. There Señora Hernandez placed cold towels on Principia's forehead, rubbed *Aloe vera* into her burns and applied spider's webs to the cuts on her arms and legs. Then the old woman brewed a sedative tea from the root of angelica, which had been steeped in wine, distilled in a glass and stored in her kitchen cupboard until needed. "This will kill all pain," she said, pouring the tea into a small wooden bowl. Then she cooled it with her breath and was spooning it into Principia's mouth when Rubendella came into the café to say she had received a message.

"I have seen Principia in my mind," said Rubendella, touching her temples with the tips of her fingers. "She's right now hitchhiking on the highway, but don't worry, no one is going to pick her up. Don't ask me how I know this, I just do." Without saying a word, her father led her into the back room and when she saw Principia lying on the cot, she said, "This must be some kind of crazy mistake; I saw her so clearly."

"I have heard my mother say this too," said Rosita, leaving the room to get more towels.

When Rubendella entered the back room, Principia began to toss and turn. "Leave me alone," she said in her delirium. "I am not worthy to be administered unto." Occasionally she would open her eyes and look around, but nothing would come into focus; the café, the people around her were reduced to a blur of color and indistinguishable shapes moving in slow motion. But out of the blur one figure began to emerge more than the others.

"Tawnya Louise," said Principia, motioning to Rubendella to come closer, "'I will show thee the judgement of the great whore that sitteth upon many waters; with whom the kings of the earth have been made drunk with the wine of her fornication.' Tawnya, the Lord carried me away in the spirit into the wilderness; 'and I saw a woman sit upon a scarlet-colored beast, full of names of blasphemy having seven heads and ten horns.'"

"Drink this," said Rubendella, taking the tea from her grandmother. "It will help you feel better."

"Take heed of what I'm saying," said Principia. Her voice was forceful, loud and angry. She sat up straight and took Rubendella by the shoulders. "The Lord showed me the shadow of a woman arrayed in purple and scarlet and with gold and precious stones. At first I thought she was Esther the Beautiful, Queen of Persia, and then I thought she was Deborah, but when the Lord told me to take a better look I saw that she had your face and your hair, which was also scarlet, and on your forehead it was written, 'Mystery, Babylon the Great, The Mother of Harlots, and Abominations of the Earth.'"

"Don't you tell my mother these things," whispered Rubendella, as Rosita came back with more damp towels. "She will think you're talking about me."

Rubendella tried to get Principia to take more angelica tea, but she refused. "Bring me my sketch pad," she said. "I want to show you great things." Applebee went back to the church for her drawing materials, and when he returned Principia, propped up on the cot, was talking about the New Judson the Lord had shown her. "I'm going to show you what it's supposed to look like," she said, taking the pad and pencils. She began sketching rapidly, at times with her eyes closed, for in her mind she was seeing it all over again, from the top of the bell tower where Satan had tempted her and from every corner of the new church. After she had drawn a dozen angles of a modern building with a high vaulted ceiling and spires that seemed to reach all the way into the clouds, she said she was very tired and fell into a deep sleep.

Rosita sat next to the cot and held Principia's hand while she slept. Applebee examined the drawings and admired their architectural detail. Señora Hernandez sat quietly in a corner. Sergio went home to bed, but his sisters decided they should lend a helping hand, so they sat around the cot and argued over who was pulling the most cactus needles from Principia's arms and legs, while Robert and José played cards and Rubendella applied wet towels to Principia's face.

"I am like the Nightingale woman," said Rubendella. "If only I had a costume I could do a better job."

Sergio's sisters got tired of playing nurse and went home early, but Rubendella refused to leave Principia's side as did Applebee, Rosita and Señora Hernandez, who asked Applebee to bring her biggest *Aloe vera* to the café, which he did, and many times before dawn the señora cut the plant and drained its thick fluid onto Principia's burns.

At an early hour of the morning, Principia called out in her sleep: "Applebee, are you there?" He came to her bedside and held her hand. She didn't open her eyes, nor did she close her fingers around his. "I see the bridegroom," she said. "But I can't see the bride. Don't you know who she is?"

"I know who I'd like her to be," said Applebee, squeezing her fingers.

She opened her eyes and looked at him. "Where I'm going," she said, "there can be no giving or taking in marriage. You must try to realize this."

Then she closed her eyes again and drifted away.

At dawn that day, Friday, the sky was thick with dust blowing in from the northwest, and for a while Rosita had to close all the windows in the café, but before midmorning the heat was such that she had to open them up again. Principia seemed to be no better, and around noon, when the dust began to settle like brown powder all over Judson, Applebee considered calling a doctor, but Señora Hernandez said a doctor would not know how to treat someone like Principia and it would be best to allow her to recover slowly.

That afternoon two carloads of visitors arrived, and in her sleep Principia became restless. "She knows someone needs her," said Rosita, "but she is not strong enough to wake up."

Applebee sent the visitors home by telling them that the door had been partially destroyed and had been taken to Laredo to be repaired. "We sure hope you'll remember us in your prayers," he said as he waved them off.

After they had left, Judson settled into a quiet uneasiness. The dust storm had already blown over leaving everything covered with a thick layer of grime, but no one seemed to notice it that day. Hardly anyone said a thing. The children stayed outside and waited for word of Principia's condition, while their mothers, unable to think of anything to fuss about, sat in the café and watched Sergio, José and Robert Galvan play cards. Rubendella, Rosita and Señora Hernandez stayed with Principia in the back room, and Applebee sat at his table and colored some of the books Principia had given him. They were not difficult enough to hold his interest though, and toward late afternoon he moved to the shade under the cottonwood and played his fiddle until Rosita came outside and asked him to stop. "Your music is too sad right now," she said. "I know it's not nighttime yet, but it's too sad anyway."

Applebee put down the fiddle, went back to the café, sat on the floor with Rafalita and played jacks until it was time to watch the bats. As he was leaving the café, Brother Ravenhill drove up in his silver bus, came to a full stop, and Winkie Kermit leaped out the door and started shouting for Principia. Brother Ravenhill was reluctant to get out, but Winkie, who was now his wife, said that he must go with her to find the Invincible.

Ravenhill and Winkie had gotten married in Laredo, gone to

Mexico on their honeymoon and were hoping that Principia was ready to leave so they could spend a day together. Winkie was no longer dressing in her cashier's uniform, said she would never put it back on again either because she liked Mexican blouses, pleated skirts and lots of silver jewelry. "I've never felt better in my life," she said to Applebee, as she led her new husband toward the café. "Isheee-ma-ha-ya-ma-Ha. I've got all the buttons on my blouse, a wristwatch that winds itself up and a love in my heart that I never knew existed. Osheee-ma-ha. Praise His most holy name. I raise my hands in the air to signify that I have surrendered my all to Him, and now I can breathe again, because this week the Lord working through my husband healed me and I threw away my nose spray for good. Praise God! I can't wait to find Principia Martindale and see what the Lord's done for her. I just know it's something wonderful."

"She's sick," said Applebee, stepping in front of them. "You two better go on your way. We don't need you here. Not right now anyway."

But Winkie wouldn't take no for an answer. She pushed Applebee to one side, telling him she was going to find Principia and no one was going to stop her either. Ravenhill followed her into the café but kept looking back to see where Applebee was and what he was doing.

When Rosita brought them into the back room, Principia became restless. She was aware someone was there, either someone she knew or someone who needed her help. She opened her eyes, squinted, and after a few seconds regained her focus. "Oh, Winkie, you look so happy," she said. "And, Brother Raven, you look so happy too." Then she went back to sleep.

Applebee refused to allow Ravenhill and Winkie to stay any longer. He was angry with Rosita for showing them to the back room, and he was sure they would try to make trouble of some kind. But Winkie didn't want to leave. She thought Principia had been poisoned. Rosita assured her it was only a bad sunburn, and then Sergio ushered Ravenhill back to his bus. Applebee, with Winkie by the arm, was right behind them.

Ravenhill drove at top speed until he reached the highway, and once they were in Carrizo Springs he stopped at a filling station and called Corinda Cassy.

Corinda arrived the next morning in her red and yellow mobile home, parked it under the cottonwood, the only shade she could find, and while the Melody Masters' new rendition of "Heavenly Sunshine" was playing at top volume on her tape deck, she got out and stretched. She was wearing creased jeans, cowboy boots and a maroon silk blouse with COWGIRLS FOR CHRIST embroidered in silver across the back and front. Applebee thought sure he was seeing things. "She's got the shortest waist and the longest legs of any human alive," he said. "I don't know where she came from, and I don't want to know either."

The first thing she did was move Principia into the trailer house, and, along with Rosita and Rubendella, she helped nurse her Invincible back to health. For over a week Principia drifted in and out of consciousness. She dreamed of the holy city that she had been shown, and from time to time she woke up asking for her sketch pad and drew until she had illustrated every avenue, every fountain, every prayer garden and every last detail of a tabernacle that spiraled into the sky.

"The Lord is directing her," said Corinda Cassy as she looked over the drawings.

During Miss Cassy's first week in Judson, Principia woke up each time the visitors arrived and insisted on conducting healing services, but no one was healed. After each service she had to be carried back to the trailer home, where she cried out in her sleep that she had failed those who needed her the most. Even though there had not been a single healing, Miss Cassy felt an energy in the air when Principia was conducting a service and said that under the right circumstances and at the right place Principia could do great things for humanity. She was not convinced that Judson was the right place, however. She was not moved by the image of Christ on the screen door and thought the landscape lacked inspiration, but after she witnessed the healing of a deaf man her opinion changed.

That happened during her second week in Judson. Principia sat up in bed and said, "There is a man out there who has a bad ear, but it's beginning to open up. He will hear again." Miss Cassy went to the window, but no one was there. A few minutes later, however, a car stopped in front of the hotel and a man, Frank

Johnson, who had been deaf in one ear for many years, got out with his sister, Clarice. The moment the car stopped, Principia left her bed and went out to meet them. "You've arrived," she said. "We were expecting you." The man was startled by her appearance. She had on a lilac gown and Miss Cassy's scarlet robe; her hair was tangled; her face was peeling; and in spite of the burning hot sand she wore no shoes. He backed away from her and toward his sister, who had come to be healed of eczema. Principia paid no attention to his alarm, and when she was close enough she reached up, gave his right ear a hard jerk and the man fell into a dead faint. After he was revived he said his hearing had returned, and as far as he was concerned there was no explaining it except to say it was a miracle. His sister, however, was not healed, and because of this, Principia returned to bed and cried herself to sleep.

Corinda Cassy was astounded by what she witnessed, but she believed Principia needed guidance in developing her "miraculous gift." It was then she decided that she had a spiritual affinity with Judson. There was something about the landscape that struck her as being very ancient, and she could compare it only to the Holy Land. "It's a little bit different," she said to Rosita when the visitors left, "but the feeling is still the same. This land is sooo sacred."

After Principia was resting again, Rosita took up her kitchen work, Applebee sat in the café and played his fiddle and Corinda brought a folding chair from her mobile home, sat under the cottonwood and studied Principia's drawings. She could see herself standing in the center of the city Principia had conceived, she could see the Cowgirls for Christ prancing up and down the avenues and she could see Larry Wayne at her side, guiding her, encouraging her and giving generously of his financial wisdom.

"I will see this into fruition," she said as Applebee wandered over to ask what she thought of the drawings.

After a pause, she answered him with carefully enunciated words: "They are beautifully . . . and . . . delightfully visionary. I have always dreamed of possessing such a gift, but the Lord has never seen fit to bestow it upon me. He has, however, given this divine power to Principia, and I will dedicate my life to seeing that she uses it properly. I was the first to recognize her specialness. I saw it in her eyes the day we first met, and I will stay by her side at all times, because I believe I have been put in her life to guide her."

"Well, I don't think so," said Applebee. "And I don't want her holding any more services until she's completely well."

"May I remind you of one thing," said Corinda, stuffing her jeans into her cowboy boots. "Every time the visitors arrive, Principia wakes up and insists on meeting them. If the Lord didn't want her to have fellowship with these people, He would not wake her up. It is His will at work here, not yours."

"You better remind yourself of that," said Applebee. He left her there, returned home, sat on his front steps and played the fiddle until the bats flew away into the dusk. Then he fiddled for a while longer before falling asleep against the desert landscape painted across his porch.

The next morning he was awakened by Saint George crowing in the kitchen. He got up, fed the rooster a bowl of corn flakes and walked to the café, but Rosita had not yet opened it, so he sat on the metal lawn chair out front and waited for her while Miss Cassy's voice drifted out of the trailer and into the morning sun.

"I fell asleep studying your drawings," she said. "And praise God! During my sleep, I dreamed that Larry Wayne and I were standing in the very city you have illustrated. I saw myself standing in the temple before a large audience. I spoke to them at length and prepared them for your gift. Then I heard the music swell, I lifted my arms and suddenly there you were standing beside me and giving your all to those desperate people who needed you so much. While you administered unto them I stood there beside you and prayed in earnest. We were both wearing flowing gowns, and I was beside you the entire time, guiding you and encouraging you. The Lord spoke through me to you. There were times when my words were your words, and our words were the words of God. Together we can make this miracle happen. Together we can be known and loved the world over. I know I'm on the right track this time, I don't know if Larry Wayne will think so, but I've never been more certain of anything in my life, for I can feel God guiding me the same way he is guiding you, in the same direction and with the very same hand."

"All she wants is an audience," said Applebee, still sitting in the lawn chair in front of the café. "She knows a crowd gatherer when she sees one too."

He walked over to his truck, kicked the tires, checked the water, the oil and the gasoline. "Over half full," he said. "Rubendella hasn't been using it as much as I thought." The truck started on the first try, and when Saint George heard the sound of the motor he came half running, half flying down the road and perched in the window on the driver's side. "You think we're going somewhere, don't you," said Applebee, scratching the rooster's red and yellow ruff. Then he ran his hand down the bird's back and wiped the dust off his tail feathers. "Well, we are going somewhere, but not today. She's got to get better first, then we'll leave, just load her up and drive off. That's the best thing."

Saint George crowed again, and Applebee said, "I'm glad to know that we see eye to eye."

Applebee stayed to himself most of the day and made plans for leaving as soon as possible. Corinda Cassy had plans of her own though, and that afternoon she started making arrangements to buy up as much land as possible. After making a few telephone calls she found out that most of Judson had reverted back to the state. "I have friends in high places," she said to herself. "I have used their services before, and I will use them again."

In less than a week she had purchased forty acres of land immediately surrounding the hotel and was disappointed that the Lucky L Ranch was not for sale, but she believed it was only a matter of time until it would be. She telephoned Larry Wayne and told him that if he really loved her he would figure out some way to buy the ranch. "Our future depends on it," she said.

During Corinda Cassy's third week in Judson, Principia said she felt like herself again, but Applebee noticed there was something about her that wasn't the same. Her mind seemed to be elsewhere all the time, and when he questioned her, she told him she was focusing entirely upon the Father. "He has given me my direction," she said. "It's not the way I thought He would lead me, but I have no choice."

"You do have a choice," said Applebee. They were sitting under the cottonwood and staring not at each other but down the palm-lined avenue. "You can come away with me, and when you're fully recovered we can sit down and try to figure out what's going on here. There's no rush to find the answers, and there's no rush to heal people; you got to think about yourself first, but as long as that Cassy woman's here you're not going to have a say in anything. People like her are dangerous because they just play around with religion and don't have any kind of deep belief, but they pretend they do and pretty soon they almost convince themselves they're saints. At first you might think they've got a lot of faith, but what they've really got is a lot of problems they're trying to cover up. Cassy's got all that greed and envy bottled up inside her. She's got just enough sense to know it's there and not quite enough sense to know what to do about it. She wants to be you so bad she can taste it, but she knows she can't ever have what you've got, so she's going to run your life her way."

"She'll run it the Lord's way," said Principia without looking at him. "You can be assured of that. If you were in her place . . . if you were trying to help me see clearly which way to turn, I'm not so sure you would help me run things God's way, but she will. Every word she speaks is encouraging because her eyes are always on the Master."

"Her eyes are always on herself," said Applebee, remembering one of Rosita's favorite proverbs. "'He who does not listen to advice does not reach old age.'" He said it aloud, but Principia did not respond, and still he could not bring himself to look at her. He wondered if he would kidnap her in the middle of the night, or if he would talk her into leaving. He decided that he would try persuasion first, so he turned to her and confessed: "All I want you to do is leave with me." Still she didn't look his way. "I wanted you to the first day I saw you; I don't know why, but something told me to take care of you, and I still want to. You won't have to worry about a thing, and I won't ask anything of you, I promise. I won't ever touch you unless you ask me to, and I realize that might be never. If it's marriage that's stopping you, then we'll get married. Today if you want to. I'd like that. And we might come to find out that we're not worlds apart after all."

"Sometimes when I look into your face, I see so much comfort and understanding," said Principia as she followed the road with her eyes until it was no wider than a piece of twine. "But that comfort and understanding is not always there, and that bothers me about you. I never know what you're going to say or do, but I can always trust the words of wisdom that come from Miss Cassy. Her love for the Lord is consistent and yours is not, not the way I see you anyway. There are times when I'm able to picture you the way you used to be and the way you might be again. I wish you were that way now. I wish you were still a preacher and that your whole career had been spent in the same church. Then I believe I could love you. But things aren't that way and I'm coming to believe that the Lord put me in the world to love Him and serve Him and glorify Him alone. I have tried give Him what He wants, and in turn He has given me my direction and a great task."

"Don't get hooked up with Cassy," warned Applebee. "All she wants to do is steal your thunder. You'll see. All these things you say God wants you to do here can be done without her; these things can be done anywhere without her."

"But God wants his holy city here," said Principia. "And He wants it now."

"Then let him have it," said Applebee. For a few minutes they stared at the road. Then he looked up into the cottonwood, traced the major branches and decided that he would have to force her to leave. He had hoped he wouldn't need to.

He left her sitting there and went home to play his fiddle and think. After the bats flew away and the world was dark once more, he went to the café, where everyone except the children, Corinda Cassy and Principia had gathered. The men were playing cards; the sisters were eating tamales. Rosita was cleaning her stove; Señora Hernandez was making tortillas for the next day and Rubendella was reading a movie magazine. There were only two electric lights in the café, a naked bulb that hung from the ceiling in the kitchen and another one like it over the table where Rubendella sat.

Almost in whispers Applebee told Rosita's mother that he wanted to take Principia and leave, but the old woman shook her head, wiped her hands clean and reached into her apron pocket for her cards. "Nothing will ever be the same again," she said in a low voice so Rosita would not hear her. "Come, I will show you." She led him over to a far table where they could talk in private. Applebee cut the cards three times toward him and after Señora

Obdulla Hernandez had spread them out on the table, she gathered them up rapidly, returned them to her apron and refused to tell him what she saw except to say: "'Opportunity makes the thief; greed tears the sack.'"

She got up, kissed her daughter and granddaughter good night, would not allow anyone to walk her home and with slow feeble steps she left the café and made her way through the dark. From her front yard she discovered she had left her oil lamps burning. "I am very old and forgetful now," she said to what was left of the *Aloe vera* sitting on the front porch where the morning sun could find it. Once inside she turned off her lamps and told herself she would never leave her house again because beyond her walls the world was changing. Then, with a troubled heart, she went to bed, and, early the next morning when the world was still, she heard angels breathing in her garden and went out to meet them. That afternoon Rosita found her lying near the hollyhocks, and the next day they buried her beside her husband.

PART III

The New Heaven/New Earth Inc.

1957-1971

Things ain't never the way you thought they were
at first. You gotta take into consideration that
you don't know much about anything at all. You gotta
take into consideration that it's real easy to get
fooled sometimes, even by your own self.

—Johnnie Chapman

 1

"We're just going to change a *few* things," said Corinda Cassy, putting on a pair of purple cowboy boots. They had red stars on each side. Señora Hernandez had been buried the day before. The café was closed for the first time in years, and no one but Applebee could be seen milling about. It was dawn. Principia was asleep in the bedroom of the mobile home. Rosita was in the kitchen cooking breakfast, and Corinda, listening to the Melody Masters sing "Christ Receiveth Sinful Men," was sitting on a stool in the living room and struggling with her new boots. "They look just like me, don't they?" she said, lifting up one leg so Applebee, who was standing outside the front door, could get a better look. He didn't answer. "Now don't just stand there with that long, sad expression on your face, you're too old for that," said Corinda. "I'll say it one more time and that will be enough. We don't want to change a lot but we do want to change a little." She had a gleam in her eyes that Applebee was suspicious of.

"Some people will want to stay here for longer than a day," she said, "so eventually we're going to have a hotel with kitchenettes in each room, a parking lot and a grocery store. But first things first. First we've got to heeeal Principia, and then we've got to arrange a place for her to hold her services. I think an old-fashioned tent, one with stripes, of course, will do just fine until we can construct something more suitable."

"First things first," said Applebee. "You better do something about the water problem."

"How right you are," said the Cowgirl for Christ. "I will

enter that as problem number one on my list of things to be achieved."

"The well should be drilled and paid for by the people who live here," said Applebee. "They are the ones who have been working for it."

"But there's no time for such foolishness as that; not when you have me around," said Corinda. "A well is needed and needed now, and we're going to have one fast. You'll see."

While Principia was regaining her strength, Corinda Cassy hired a company out of Uvalde to drill in less than a week what she called the deepest water well in Texas, and after she had sipped the first glass of clear water that was brought to the surface, she carried a glass of it to Principia who was in bed, exhausted from having prayed for an hour with three victims of polio. "They came here crippled, and they left crippled," she said. Tears were in her eyes. "Sometimes I expect too much from the Lord."

"Drink this divine substance and you'll feel better," said Corinda. "This water surely contains rejuvenating powers. I predict that people will come to Judson from far and wide to see my cowgirls perform in drill formation. They will come from all walks of life to seek your advice, Principiaaa, to be heealed and to drink from the Fountain of Eternal Looove."

Principia drank the water. It had a metallic taste that she was unaccustomed to, but after she had drunk, she said she felt cleansed through and through. "I would like to sit outside a little while now," she told Rosita, who was standing at the foot of her bed. "I hope that will be all right."

"That will be just fine," answered Corinda as Rosita, in a state of exasperation, went back to the kitchen. "But before we go outside I have another surprise for you. Larry Wayne, who was sent to me by God, has just assisted me in making the biggest investment of my career. I've just purchased the Lucky L Ranch, over one hundred thousand acres in all, and eventually we're going to use it as a permanent home for the Cowgirls for Christ."

Principia clapped her hands with joy. "Mary Alaska will be so happy that her daughter's moving," she said, gradually leaving her bed. Every joint in her body was stiff. "I just hope Joyce Jeannine goes back home to Lockhart. Children should always be with their parents whenever possible."

From the kitchen, Rosita watched Principia walking feebly

through the mobile home. "You're moving around like an old woman," Rosita said, putting down her dishrag and helping her through the front door.

"I knew that water would have her on her feet again," said Corinda as she sat down on the couch with her hand mirror, make-up and hairbrush. She expected Larry Wayne to arrive that morning, and she wanted to look her best.

By noon he still had not arrived and Corinda was becoming more and more anxious. She had already applied and retouched her make-up; washed it off and applied it all over again. She had combed her hair several different ways, sprayed it stiff, washed it hurriedly, reset it and styled it in what she said was a more youthful look. "I feel just like I'm going out of my mind," she kept saying. "He's never here when he's supposed to be."

"All this primping is making me very nervous today," said Rosita. "That's why I'm going back home. You can wash the dishes yourself."

"I'll do no such thing," said Corinda. "I'm going to sit right down and pray for that man to get here fast."

Finally, late that afternoon, after Principia had received and prayed over two schoolteachers who suffered bouts of nervousness and after Corinda had managed to calm herself with a pill, Larry Wayne did arrive. "Oh, just look at you," said Corinda when he got out of his Chevrolet pickup. "I suppose you're going to tell me that that T-shirt's white and those Levi's aren't the filthiest things I've ever seen. Here I've made myself all pretty and you can't even button up your pants properly."

"I'll take care of you later," said Larry Wayne. "You can't have everything you want when you want it." He spat on the sand and waited for the truck that was following him to stop. It was a long-bed truck carrying two bulldozers, and behind it came a bus full of workmen who had brought tents to live in. Before sunset Judson looked like an army camp with olive drab tents pitched everywhere space allowed.

"Larry Wayne and I are going to have our hour of joint prayer and meditation now," Corinda told Rosita after the camp was organized. "I suppose we'll pray in his tent for lack of a better place. This is our time together with the Lord, and we must not be disturbed."

They disappeared into his tent, and an hour later Corinda,

looking refreshed, returned to the trailer home.

"Close communion with the Lord is always good for the soul," Rosita said from the kitchen. "I am sure you are not so nervous now."

Ignoring Rosita's comment, Corinda—armed with her cassette—took Principia by the hand and led her outside. They walked over to the truck, stood on the back of it and looked out over the heavy machinery and the army of tents. Principia, dressed in a purple robe that Corinda had just bought for her, lifted her arms to embrace the whole scene. "'Onward, Christian Soldiers. Marching as to war,'" she quoted. "I feel just like Deborah, who led her army into battle for the Lord."

"So do I," said Corinda. She was dressed in her cowgirl outfit of blue denim trimmed in red leather. Her hat was cocked to one side of her head. "What we need is the right hymn," she said. "And I think I've got one at my fingertips." She pressed Play on her cassette and the Brothers of Temperance were heard singing their new rendition of "Lord Send a Revival."

"God is truly sending a revival," said Principia.

"And weee are standing in the midst of it," said Corinda, flapping her cowgirl cape to and fro. "Weee are bringing it about."

The next morning Applebee was up at dawn. He was sitting on his roof and watching the sun come up when he saw Corinda Cassy leaving Larry Wayne's tent. Her long black robe dragged the ground behind her as she hurried back to the mobile home.

Before long the whole camp was awake, and Larry Wayne, wearing the clothes he had arrived in, was giving orders to the workmen. Applebee could hear every word. "We need a track of land one hundred yards long and one hundred yards wide cleared and leveled," he said. "There's no time to survey it off. Somebody will do that later."

For the next hour Applebee watched the workmen clearing the land directly behind the hotel where L. J. Judson's swimming pool had been. Dust rose up from the two bulldozers and nearly obliterated the hotel and the landscape behind it. Out of the swirling dust, Applebee could almost see the figure of a man—a giant. "There he is," he said, pointing a finger. "Old Man Judson him-

self. He's not one bit pleased either." Then the dust cleared, the
figure disappeared into the sky and Applebee started down the
ladder. "It's getting too hot up here," he said to Saint George, who
was waiting for him on the ground. "Besides, my imagination is
about to carry me plumb off."

Applebee spent the rest of the day coloring. That evening he
climbed up on the roof again and waited for the bats to fly off. At
that hour, Rosita was busy in her kitchen preparing supper for the
workmen and Sergio was in their front yard setting up tables for
the food. His three sisters, bursting out of their polyester dresses,
were attempting to sell trinkets and souvenirs, while Rubendella
and her back-up band were standing to one side singing: "I don't
want a Ricochet Romance . . ."

"I will take any kind of romance you can give me," said
Modesta, putting down her tray of hand-painted rocks and twirling to the music. "I am so lonely sometimes, I can't stand myself
anymore."

"I feel the same way about you," said her sister Encarnación.
"Sometimes I can't stand you either."

"Both of you have the same problem," said Concepción.
"You are not pretty anymore. You will have to learn to live with
this too."

"People who argue are never pretty," said Principia. She was
holding hands with Rafalita and Carlos. "I wish the three of you
would keep this in mind, if not for yourselves, at least for me. I
also wish you would take some food to Applebee. He won't join
us, and I know he must be hungry."

Still fussing, the three sisters, each with a covered dish in
hand, left the yard, and while everyone else was busy entertaining
or being entertained, Corinda and Principia walked across the
land that had just been cleared. The earth was soft and spongy
beneath their feet. "This is where it's all going to take place," said
Corinda, "and weee, Principiaaa, are the instruments that are
bringing it to fruition."

"My vision of building a church is coming true," said Principia. "I want my pulpit to be right here where this rock is. I want
the tent to be erected around it, and while I'm preaching I want
to be looking toward the east from whence cometh the Lord."

"This and even more will be done," said Corinda. "We are

going to build a whole city of glass and steel. There will be sparkling fountains and plazas of gold-colored bricks; there will be gardens and shops with wonderful names. Lowery, Murphy and Smith, the famous architectural firm out of Houston, has already begun work on the project. The hotel will be constructed first and then a church of some sort. I have already given them your drawings, and I intend to supervise every detail to make sure that *our* vision is carried out."

"Judson is going to become a city of God," said Principia.

"In many ways large and small it already is," answered Corinda Cassy. "While the construction is going on, you will be able to hold services in a striped tent that will be erected tomorrow. It's purple and gold, Principia. Oooh, wait until you see it!"

As they spoke a cloud of bats flew overhead. There was the sound of wind, but no breeze could be felt and nothing was moving, not even the hair billowing from Principia's head. She felt her hands getting warm and a cold tingling running up her arms. "I just can't get Applebee out of my mind," she said, wondering why she was feeling so weak all of a sudden. "He loves those bats. He says they remind him of the Holy Spirit."

"That's because he's got too much of the Devil in him," said Corinda. "But we're going to take care of that. We don't need the Devil around here. Had I known this man was a worshiper of bats, I'd never have sent you here, but now I'm so glad I did. The Lord had his hand on my heart all along. He steers us through his special people, Principiaaa. You are one of them. I am one of them. And, of course, Larry Wayne is one of us too."

"Every day now is so exciting," said Principia. "I can hardly wait to see what tomorrow will bring. I plan to be up early."

Applebee was up early the next morning too. Again he was sitting on his roof looking out over the army of tents. Smoke from campfires was drifting like a cold breath over the cleared land, and the smell of boiling coffee seemed to settle around Applebee's house and stay there. "Rosita tried not to ever let her coffee boil," said Applebee to Saint George, who was sitting next to him. "If it did, she'd throw it out, even if she didn't have any more."

Before long the growling sound of bulldozers was heard, and then a wrecker seemingly came out of nowhere and headed toward the church. A cable with a steel ball hanging from the rig swung back and forth until it crashed, first into the bell tower and then into the outside walls. Off in the distance the bulldozers were knocking down the frame houses and the bats were fluttering into the bright sunlight. Some of them fell back to the ground and were plowed under, others scurried about helplessly attaching themselves to cactus, brush, anything that seemed remotely stable. It took little effort to demolish the church, and the five houses seemed to collapse before the dozers gave them the first nudge. To Applebee it was as though the houses were already aware of their fate and chose to die by their own will, but the bats almost refused to give up. Thousands of them fluttered into the bright light and then, after what seemed like eternity to Applebee, they settled close to the earth like the remains of a dark cloud.

The tent where Principia would hold services was going up behind the hotel, but the mobile home was not there that morning. Neither were Principia, Rosita, Sergio or Rubendella. Corinda Cassy had gotten up early and taken them on what she said would be a little drive, and they ended up at her ranch in Alice, where she intended to keep them until the demolition was completed and the earth packed firm again.

While Applebee was on the roof a moving van arrived to take Sergio's three sisters and their families to Carrizo Springs, where Larry Wayne had arranged for them to live, and a second van, a smaller one, stopped in front of Applebee's house. Two men got out and looked around. "Can't tell where the brush ends and the house begins," said one of the movers. "Who in the hell would go to all the trouble to paint their place up like this."

"I would, that's who," said Applebee. He was still on the roof. Saint George was perched on his shoulder.

Startled, the movers looked up.

"You don't have to look up here like you ain't never seen two human beings before in your life," said Applebee. "Want you to meet my partner, Saint George. He's got more brains in his spurs than you got in your heads so you better go on back where you came from. We're capable of moving ourselves, thank you."

"Easiest day we ever got paid for," said one of the movers. They got back in the truck and left. Applebee climbed down his ladder. It seemed to take him longer that morning than ever before. Saint George flew ahead of him and waited. "Too bad I don't have wings like you, George," he said when he felt ground beneath his feet again. "I could'uve already been down too."

Saint George flapped his wings and stuck out his neck as if he were about to crow, but no sound came out.

For the next hour, the rooster stood on the front porch and watched Applebee load his coloring books into the bed of the pickup. Then he put his clothes in a paper bag, anchored it under some of the books and put Manuel's fiddle in the front seat. On the fourth try the truck started. When Saint George heard the engine running, he came half running, half flying and perched in the window on the passenger's side.

"I'm not about to leave without you," said Applebee, throwing a handful of corn on the floor. Normally Saint George would be pecking at the kernels until they were all eaten, but that day he just sat in the window and looked around. "You know something's up, don't you," Applebee said, rubbing the rooster on the neck.

Saint George didn't move, not even to make a sound. He just sat there in the window as Applebee drove down the road, passed the ruins of L. J. Judson's church and through the clearing where the striped tent was going up. Behind the hotel he stopped, took the Jesus door off its hinges and put it in the back of the truck. "I consider this mine," he said. Again they were moving. He made a complete circle around the hotel, took one last look at the cottonwood and, when he turned onto the main road which would soon be paved with glistening asphalt, the screen door blew out of the truck and landed in a clump of prickly pear. Unaware of this, Applebee drove on.

"The truth is," he said, not believing a word he was saying, "I always knew that little red-headed girl was a fool, and the biggest one that ever lived."

Then he turned onto the highway. Saint George crowed twice, fluttered down to the floorboard and started eating the corn as fast as he could. After he had swallowed every kernel, he perched on the steering wheel as if he owned it. Applebee scratched the rooster's neck and kept on driving down the long straight highway. He refused to look back.

 2

When Corinda Cassy returned to Judson, she brought the Cowgirls for Christ with her. Larry Wayne had rented six expandable trailer homes for the cowgirls to live in until the Lucky L Ranch could be vacated. He had not wanted to bring the drill team to Judson quite so soon, but Corinda had argued with him over the telephone. "I simply must have my girls near me so I can coach them each and every day. Rubendella and I have created new marching formations and new costumes. What we need now is a new audience and, of course, a stadium, or a very large stage, preferably one that revolves."

One week to the day after Applebee left Judson, the Cowgirls for Christ arrived. All except five of the newest members came in a chartered bus. The five new girls rode in the mobile home that Corinda pulled behind her station wagon, and along the way Rubendella taught them how to execute a countermarch, a right-face, a left-face and an about-face. Principia rode in the front seat of the station wagon; Rosita and Sergio were in the back. As they approached Judson the only familiar landmark Rosita could recognize was the row of date palms leading into town.

At the turnoff to the Lucky L Ranch, Rosita spotted the screen door propped up against the cactus. "Let me out right over there," she said. "I can walk the rest of the way."

Corinda stopped the car, and Rosita got out. She rescued the door from the prickly pear and carried it through the shortcut to her house, the only structure still standing. Everything else had been demolished and burned. From her front porch, Rosita could see fires blazing against the sunset and stiff columns of smoke rising up as if to support the sky. The palm trees and the cottonwood looked out of place, and the striped tent, which she could see rising above the brush, was much bigger than she thought it was going to be.

"Now we are a circus," Rosita said, taking the screen door into the bedroom. "I think my mother knew this would happen." She propped the door against a blank wall and went back outside to inspect her parents' graves. "It's too sad," she said, standing in front of the two mounds of earth. "I am very glad both of you are not here anymore. I'm glad the Apple is not here to see this too. Sergio and I, we are here because we need to be. But it is going to be very hard." She turned and walked away toward her house. "I cannot leave my parents behind," she said. "Not yet. And then there's Principia. She's about to start needing me very soon. And maybe Rubendella will start needing me again too."

Off in the distance Rosita heard the sound of a whistle, and she knew that Corinda Cassy was calling the cowgirls to attention.

As the girls stepped off the bus, they fell into rank and file formation. They were dressed in their everyday uniform: gore skirts of denim with red gingham shirts and brown leather vests. Their cowboy hats were also red and decorated with silver stars, and their cowboy boots, red as well, were rundown and scruffy. COWGIRLS FOR CHRIST was hand-tooled across the back of each vest, and at their waists they carried silver lariats, which they were just learning how to twirl.

After they had stood at attention for a few seconds, Corinda Cassy, baton in hand, blew a long and a short on her whistle, the Forward March signal. Then the Cowgirls took off marching toward the tent. Halfway there, Miss Cassy, twirling her baton awkwardly, gave the signal to sing, and the girls broke forth with:

> "When we all get to heaven,
>   What a day of rejoicing that will beeee,
>   When we all see Jeeesus,
>   We'll sing and shout for vic-tor-reee."

Rubendella marched alongside the cowgirls and singled them out: "Charlene Simms! Guide right! Do you think you're marching all by yourself or what? Lisa Gail! Hold your head up high and keep it there, and don't make me have to tell you this again. Dana Pullen! March like you're glad to be alive, girl!" Then Rubendella stood back and watched the cowgirls from a distance as they pranced around the tent. Larry Wayne stood next to her with an arm around her waist. He was about to lean over and give her a kiss on the cheek when Corinda saw them.

"Cowgirls, halt, one, two!" she commanded vehemently. Some of the girls relaxed. "I most certainly did not give you the at-ease signal," shouted Corinda. "Come to attention this instant. Lisa Gail, you're forever wearing that suffering expression on your face and it's catching. Now stand at attention, and be glad you've got two legs to stand on; some people don't, you know, and you should be thankful for what you've got. All I want is for you girls to stand up perfectly straight and look like happy, beautiful young Christians whether you are or not. Some of you look like you're hurting all over and you can't be because beauty knows no pain."

Then Corinda Cassy, baton on her hip, marched through the cowgirls, across the cleared land and up to Rubendella and Larry Wayne, who were now facing each other and involved in conversation. "Take over for me, will you," said Corinda, thrusting the baton and whistle into Rubendella's hands. "You obviously need something worthwhile to occupy you right now."

Visibly annoyed, Rubendella took over the drill team while Corinda reprimanded Larry Wayne.

"I will not have you staring at her that way," she said. "Nor will I have you putting your hands on her in that suggestive manner. The next thing I know you'll be holding her instead of me. You have never fully realized that I am the woman who has made you the man you are. In my arms you're a god, but in her arms, you're nothing. Your place is with me, always, and I truly believe that the Lord brought us together for a reason."

"Who knows what you're going to find to believe tomorrow," said Larry Wayne, a smile crawling across his face. "If you're jealous of Rubendella, you better get rid of her. I still got those skinny-legged cowgirls to mess around with and some of them are big enough to get branded where it counts."

"Oh, you think you're such a man," said Corinda, flouncing her cowgirl cape. "If you lay a hand on one of my beautiful little cowgirls, I'll have you murdered, and that's a promise."

"It wasn't exactly a hand I was thinking of branding them with," said Larry Wayne.

"I can see that I'm going to have to keep you busier than I thought," said Corinda, leading him over to his tent.

They disappeared inside it.

The next day Corinda was up early making plans to send Rubendella away. "We've got to have somebody to travel throughout the state and tell everyone what Judson was, what it now is and what it will become," she said. "Rubendella, you're just the person for this. I'm convinced that the Lord has put you in my life for a reason."

They were sitting on director's chairs outside Corinda's mobile home. Rubendella was dressed in a red nylon blouse, tight jeans and stiletto heels.

"What you must do," advised Corinda, "is learn to dress more conservatively while you're representing Judson. With a few phone calls, I can promise that you will be well received on radio and television. We will also approach the press. I know so many people who will help us. I intend to put together a slide show about our work, and you will present it to church-related groups all over the state. You'll receive all travel expenses, plus a salary, and at the end of the year a bonus that will make you very happy. But you must be convincing when you speak about the Lord's work in Judson."

"I am not an actress for nothing," said Rubendella seductively.

"I knew you'd say that," said Corinda. "In many ways we're so much alike."

Within a week, Rubendella had left on her campaign, and shortly thereafter the groundbreaking ceremony for the new hotel took place. Reporters from all over the state were in attendance. The ceremony started with the Cowgirls for Christ decked out in their silver costumes. Silently Corinda Cassy marched them around the site of the hotel. Four times, five times, six times they circled the area, and on the seventh time around, on signal, they burst into song:

> "Blessed assurance Jesus is mine!
> Oh, what a foretaste of glory divine . . ."

Winkie Kermit and Brother Ravenhill were in the crowd that day. They were determined to be part of the new city as well and had promised to continue transporting as many people as their bus would hold. When the cowgirls moved into their next song: "Jerusalem! Jerusalem! The faraway city of God . . ." Winkie Kermit broke forth with the unknown tongue, and Brother Ravenhill did the same.

"Oh, now they sound just alike," Principia said to Larry Wayne. "I do pray the Lord gives me this special anointing."

"If you pray real real hard," he said, "you just might get turned on to something even better,"

"There's nothing any better," answered Principia. "Winkie Kermit knows that better than anybody."

"Oh, joyous day!" shouted Ravenhill, rolling his eyes skyward. "Cino-ma-ha-ma-HA!"

"Ma-ha-ma-HA-Cino-me-oooo," shouted Winkie Kermit. "I see Jesus everywhere I look."

"Even the birds overhead are flying in reverent formations," said her husband, clapping his hands.

"And they're doing it on purpose too," declared Winkie. "You can't tell me they're not either."

Then Winkie and Ravenhill fell into line behind the cowgirls and marched with them. Some of the reporters did the same. When Corinda gave the command to halt, Principia stepped forward with a short-handed shovel. She forced it into the sand; Corinda lifted it up and the photographers moved in closer. Then Corinda Cassy gave a short speech as the reporters wrote furiously.

"We're not going to call it a hotel," she announced. "The Lord doesn't want that. We're going to call it The Residence, and it's going to be a home away from home for many people who come here to exercise their faith in miracles. This land we are standing on is sooo holy . . ."

That week Rubendella was also quoted in the press. "The new city," she said, "is being built around the visions of Principia Martindale, who has healed many people, young and old, Christian and non-Christian. She receives visitors each and every day, and on Sunday night she holds services in a large tent that will one day be replaced with a beautiful church. Her power is great, and it does my heart good to know that the Lord still works in ways unknown to modern science."

"Very good," said Corinda when she read the papers. "Rubendella is saying exactly what I told her to. For this she will be richly rewarded."

Every day visitors came to Judson to see Principia. Corinda felt the trailer home did not provide the appropriate ambience for receiving them, so she erected a small army tent under the cottonwood. She had Sergio paint it purple and gold to match the large tent, and then she started thinking about the interior. On the floor she unrolled indoor-outdoor carpet in royal blue. She placed two overstuffed chairs draped in white linen just inside the entrance, and against the back wall she placed a day bed covered with gold lamé and accented with purple pillows.

"Oh, this is perfectly perfect," Corinda said to Principia after the tent was decorated. "Now I must find something appropriate for you to wear while you receive the less fortunate of this world. I have a silk caftan that Larry Wayne bought me in Morocco, and I'm sure he won't mind if you wear it too. It's all white except for purple embroidery around the collar and hem."

"I like it," said Principia, when Corinda showed her the garment. "I imagine that Deborah wore something like this when she sat under the palm tree and gave advice to all who came her way." After Principia put the garment on, she said she felt so comfortable in it that she never wanted to take it off again.

"Then I'll have a dozen made up for you," said Corinda. "Surely there's a talented seamstress somewhere around these parts."

Each afternoon Principia wore the caftan while reclining on the day bed and receiving her visitors. And on Sunday evenings she insisted on wearing it during the group services in the large tent. At first there were no more than fifty or sixty people attending these services, and most of them were brought there by Winkie and Ravenhill, but Corinda Cassy was sure the number would soon increase. "What we need," she said "is for The Residence to be completed so these people can stay overnight and all week long if they feel like it. And then we're going to need a bigger space to show off my cowgirls. But all this will come in time."

The Sunday evening services began with the cowgirls marching down the center aisle. Since there was no room to perform a routine, they would then take their places on a raked platform shaped like a cross and sing a medley of hymns until Principia made her entrance. During the first few services there were no reported healings. Principia was so nervous she could hardly speak and said she preferred lying on the day bed and receiving her visitors privately.

"Suddenly everything seems too organized," she said. "That scares me."

"In time you'll overcome your stage fright," said Corinda. "All of us who have enjoyed life in the public eye have gone through this."

Then one night several weeks after the groundbreaking for The Residence, after the land had been leveled and the foundation poured, a woman who was brought there by Winkie and Ravenhill stood up in the group service and said she had been healed of psoriasis the moment she stepped inside the tent. "My name is Thelma Prescott, and you have healed me," she said, pointing to Principia.

"I have done nothing," Principia answered softly. "I haven't even prayed for you."

"Up until tonight I have not lived in step with the Lord for many years," the woman said.

"What she says is true," shouted Brother Ravenhill.

"But," she added, "when I walked inside this tent, suddenly the desert wind started whipping against it, and at first I thought I was inside a great heart that was beating fast. Then I was given the vision of Jonah, and my body began burning all over. I saw myself as the sinful woman I was years ago when I was swallowed up by a great whale that took me far away from where I was supposed to be, and tonight that creature has died and been washed ashore, but I am living for the first time in many years. When my skin stopped burning, I looked into my compact mirror and my complexion was beginning to clear."

"Praise His precious name," shouted Winkie. "One hour ago her face was red as a new potato, and now look at it."

"Jesus is washing her white as snow," shouted Ravenhill.

"And He's doing it before our very eyes," said his wife.

Ravenhill held his Bible in the air with both hands and started shaking all over. "We have seen the Lord at work," he declared.

Winkie grabbed a tambourine away from someone sitting in front of her and commenced dancing in the aisle. Larry Wayne took her by the arm and led her to the front entrance. "What do you think we've got here, a sideshow?" he asked.

"You speak like the Devil," shouted Winkie. She bopped him on the head with the tambourine and danced back down the aisle again. "Jesus, lover of my soul; You're here tonight; I can feel You," she sang.

On stage, Principia was receiving a man who had suffered a stroke and could not speak or open his left eye. Corinda Cassy was sitting with the cowgirls. Her head was bowed, but she was not praying. She was filing her fingernails and hoping that Larry Wayne would be in a good mood after the service. Sergio was standing to one side with the offering plate in his hands; the organist, Lenore Jackson, was rearranging her music, and Rosita, standing behind a blue curtain, was watching Lisa Gail, who had been sitting on the back row, leave the stage and slip out the rear exit.

Rosita followed the girl, who had just turned thirteen, around the front of the tent where Ravenhill and Larry Wayne were arguing.

"Anybody who would stop a Christian from singing praises has to have Satan in him somewhere," said Ravenhill.

Rosita stood to one side and listened.

"Being a Christian is one thing, and a circus freak is another," said Larry Wayne. "You better decide which one you are."

"I'm a child of God," shouted Thelma Prescott, dancing out of the tent. "It's the most beautiful night I've ever seen, and I've never been so happy in my entire life, for the Lord has restored my beauty."

"Son," said Ravenhill, "you've got a great deal to learn from this woman." Not far away he noticed Lisa Gail disappear into a worker's tent. Rosita saw her too.

"He has a great deal to learn from me, and I have a great deal to learn from God," said Thelma, as Larry Wayne left the scene.

"There's too much going on here tonight," said Rosita.

"I feel the hand of Satan at work, Sister Rosie," said Ravenhill. He pointed his finger at the tent where Lisa Gail had gone.

Larry Wayne was approaching it. At the entrance he hesitated. Then he ducked his head and went inside. "That's just what I'm talking about," said Ravenhill, still pointing toward the tent.

"It is only the beginning," said Rosita. "Sometimes it's very hard to live around here now, and too often I listen to myself say: Where did the Apple go, and why didn't he take Sergio and me with him."

Thelma Prescott returned to her home and told everyone that Principia Martindale had saved her from a life of ruin. She preached the power of Principia Martindale wherever she went, and she was only one of many who did this.

"Our fame is beginning to grow, grow, grow," shouted Corinda. It was a few weeks after Thelma had been healed of psoriasis. The Sunday service had just turned out and Principia was already in bed. Corinda was pacing the floor. "One woman told me that she had a vision of her cancer leaving through the fluids of her body," said Corinda. "So naturally I told her to go home and drink plenty of water and come back again next Sunday. Winkie and Ravenhill brought her here. They were responsible for sixty-eight people being in the congregation this evening, and forty-three more came all on their own. Very soon every seat in the tent will be taken."

"But I still prefer seeing the people privately," said Principia, pulling the sheet around her. "I like being able to reach right out and touch them."

"When you feel more confident, you'll be able to do this in the large services," said Corinda. "I can see you running out into the congregation and touching people, singling them out, and praying over them, individually, yes, but in front of everyone. This will be sooo meaningful to witness."

"I enjoy people one at a time," said Principia, drifting to sleep. "I just pray we'll have visitors every day."

But there were days when no one would show up, and she would feel as though she had failed the entire world. And there were other days when as many as twenty people would be standing in line outside the tent. Sergio was given the duty of guarding the entrance and allowing the visitors in only when Principia was ready for them. "You also have the authority to turn visitors away," Corinda told him. "And if there's any trouble you must call me immediately. I, of course, will be working with my darling cowgirls, but if you blow three longs on a whistle, I'll come running and so will Larry Wayne, unless of course, we're having our afternoon meditation. We pray together at three o'clock and must not be disturbed until after four."

At five minutes till three every afternoon, Corinda Cassy would march her cowgirls into the large tent. Blowing a long and three shorts on her whistle, she would give the baton signal to halt and then shout the command: At ease!

"Cowgirls, this is your hour of discipline and my hour of prayer," she would say, hardly ever rearranging her words. "In a few moments, I'm going to call you to attention, and you will remain at attention until I return. Remember, the tape recorder is on, and if you speak or move around the sound will be recorded and you will be subject to dismissal." Then she would call them to attention and blow three shorts on her drum major's whistle, the signal for Larry Wayne to meet her in his tent.

At three o'clock each afternoon, Principia would be involved with her visitors or still waiting for them to arrive. Sergio would be guarding the entrance to the tent and Rosita would be washing dishes in her kitchen at home. It was her job to prepare lunch for everyone, and since her sisters-in-law were living in Carrizo Springs, she had to clean up after each meal all by herself. From her kitchen window she could look out through a clearing in the brush and see Corinda Cassy half marching and half running toward Larry Wayne's tent. Shortly after that Larry Wayne would follow her and for an hour or more they would not be seen.

"The lovebirds are about to pray for each other again," Rosita said one afternoon when she was caught up with her work. "I'm going to find out more about this."

As Rosita approached Larry Wayne's tent, she heard music: "Softly and tenderly, Jesus is calling . . ." modulating into the Melody Masters' rendition of:

> "Love lifted even me,
> Love lifted even me,
> When nothing else could help,
> Looooove lif-ted meeee . . ."

When she peered into the entrance, she saw Corinda and Larry Wayne, half undressed, writhing on the floor next to the cassette turned up loud. Rosita stepped back before they saw her. "I never knew such a man existed," she whispered into her clasped hands. "He is big like an animal."

"I used to feel so guilty for this," said Corinda—Rosita overheard her—"but now I realize the Lord has sent you to give me strength and confidence. You are the earthly god in my life. Our union is sanctified because God has placed you here to reassure me that I am loved and am carrying out His divine plan."

The music played on, but Rosita had seen and heard enough. She walked away shaking her head. "As long as he makes love to her she is not so crazy to be around," she said. "May God look after us if he ever stops."

Then she thought about Applebee, but it made her sad to bring him to mind. She missed him more than she would admit and at times became melancholy for the old days when Judson was nothing but a few houses and store fronts, a dilapidated hotel, a café and a screen door. On her way back home, she passed the construction site for the new hotel. The foundation was poured and the walls were going up, but she refused to turn her head to make note of the progress. She walked directly to her parents' graves and stopped. "Life with Mr. Apple was much easier," she said, dusting off the wooden tombstones. "Or was it harder? Sometimes I can't tell. But whatever it was, it was much better than this."

3

Early one morning, Corinda Cassy flipped a tape into her cassette. "Faith of Our Fathers," as sung by the Armstrong Family, filled the entire trailer home. Then she burst into Principia's bedroom. "We're going to call it a tabernacle, not a church," said the Cowgirl for Christ. "This just came to me in a flash. In fact, we're going to call it The Tabernacle in the Sky. It's going to be all glass and steel, just like The Residence, and it's supposed to look like it's floating up to heaven."

"I feel as though I'm hearing a prophecy," said Principia, closing her Bible and sitting up in bed.

"You are," said Corinda. "Our hotel is well into construction, so it's time to start thinking about our next project. You can't preach in a tent all your life. It wouldn't look right. Groundbreaking will take place in the next few weeks, and in the meantime I've got to get my precious girls settled in their new home. The Lucky L Ranch is now vacant. Rosita and Sergio are over there cleaning it up, and I intend to march my cowgirls over there as soon as they're out of class. Then later on this afternoon we're going to start rehearsing our groundbreaking routine."

"Lord, how good You are to give us this opportunity to serve," said Principia. "I woke up this morning and didn't know where I was or what I was doing. I felt lost and unworthy, but now I feel as though I've received a thousand blessings and haven't even gotten out of bed."

"I have known such mornings myself," said Corinda, thinking of Larry Wayne. "After we break ground for the tabernacle, we'll have two buildings under construction at once. Judson's going to be so noisy no one will be able to sleep past six-thirty, but some of us are awake much earlier than that anyway."

The groundbreaking ceremony took place as scheduled and was reported in major newspapers throughout the state. In the Sunday edition of the Fort Worth *Star-Telegram*, there was a color photograph of Corinda and Larry Wayne with the cowgirls standing around them and the new hotel going up in the background. Principia was shown standing in front of the small tent. She was holding the architectural renderings for The Tabernacle in the Sky and staring into the clouds.

Other newspapers ran similar picture stories on the hotel and tabernacle under construction. In the *Christian Reporter* Principia was shown lying on her day bed and receiving a man from Longview who had growths on both sides of his face. The newspaper credited her with five healings in the past two months. "But I can't remember any of them," she said after reading the article. "I'm going to have to start writing everything down. I want to know who these people are and why they think I healed them."

She began receiving letters from all over Texas and nearly half the population of New Bethel. All her friends back home promised to visit her and bring Principal and Wilma Lee with them.

"I don't want my parents visiting me until we've got more to show them," she said to Rosita, who was sweeping out the bedroom. "It would disturb them to see that I'm living in a trailer home. They always told me: 'Nice people don't live on wheels.' "

"Children should listen to their parents," said Rosita, pointing the broomstick at Principia. "Then they might learn something. But it's impossible to tell you this. My daughter, Rubendella, she has always listened to the wrong people."

A few days later, Rubendella was in the news again. She had given a talk at Baylor University and had presented slides of the way Judson had been, the way it was and the way it would be. She used architectural renderings to depict the Judson of the future. From Baylor she drove to Southwestern Baptist Theological Seminary in Fort Worth, where she was scheduled to give the same presentation.

Applebee's eye caught the notice in the paper. He was sitting on the curb in front of the Golden Rule Pawn shop where he worked and lived. It was Sunday morning. Downtown Fort Worth was quiet. There were few cars on the streets. Saint George was scratching in the vacant lot not far away, and Applebee was keeping one eye on him. "Rubendella's in town," Applebee shouted. Saint George stopped scratching and lifted his head. "I got just enough time to get there and hear what's on her mind."

At the assembly hall, Applebee sat in the back row and waited impatiently for the first glimpse of Rubendella. When she walked across the stage, he almost didn't recognize her. She was dressed in a black tailored suit, wore no make-up and her hair was fashioned into a bun at the nape of her neck. "She looks a good fifteen years older than she really is," Applebee said to the man on his right, who was wearing an Odd Fellow Lodge tie tack.

"You better not tell her that," the man answered.

"I don't even intend for her to see me," said Applebee. "Wouldn't know what to say to her anymore. That's why I'm sitting way back here in the back."

Applebee stayed for only half the presentation. When he saw slides of the buildings under construction he got up and left the hall. "A little bit of mediocrity goes a long way," he said when he was on the street again. It was a cold February Sunday, but sweat was pouring from his brow. "She's really got her act down is all I can say, but, then, that's Rubendella."

In the next few weeks Rubendella gave her slide show at the First Baptist Church of Dallas, Hardin-Simmons University in Abilene and several Hispanic Baptist congregations in El Paso. She gave herself three days off each week and on those days she put on her high heels and tight pants, a nylon blouse and Indian jewelry and drove to the nearest city to see all the movies. She would sometimes see the same picture over and over until she had memorized the lines and could act out all the parts while driving from one place to the next.

She sent Rosita postcards from every city she visited and clipped out her newspaper interviews and sent them home as well.

"There is too much happening too fast," Rosita said, after she read the clippings about her daughter addressing the Southern Baptist Convention in Houston. "I never know where my Rubendella is going to turn up next." She was sitting in front of her parents' graves and glancing at the article in her hand. "I never know where Sergio and I will turn up either. Now we are living in the Lucky L Ranch because our house is going to be a parking lot, but where we are is not home. The little cowgirls we live with are too silly, and the big one is worse. They will grow up to be just like her too."

Every day Rosita visited her parents' graves, sat there a few minutes and talked to them about all the changes she was witnessing. During the construction of the tabernacle, the graves were almost covered over, but Rosita threw herself between the wooden crosses and refused to get up. "I'm going to be buried right here anyway," she said. "You might as well cover me up right now and get it over with."

Corinda Cassy was marching her cowgirls up and down the dusty road when out of the corner of her eye she caught a glimpse of Rosita lying between the graves. "Stand up before you're covered up!" Corinda shouted. The drill team dispersed in all directions, but Rosita did not move. Corinda rushed over to the construction site. She stopped the workers and told Rosita it was all a mistake.

"This is only one of many mistakes," said Rosita, still lying on her back. "I will stay here until I have proof in writing that these graves will not be covered up."

Corinda dismissed the workers for the day. She left Rosita lying between the graves and went to the ranch to telephone the architect. Together they decided to incorporate the graves into a rock garden adjacent to the tabernacle.

"Let's get started on the garden right away," she said. "I want a bubbling fountain in the very center of it, and a few trees, whatever kind will grow here, with lots of twinkling lights in them. If we're going to have to do this, we might as well do it up good."

After hanging up the phone, she wrote a letter stating that the graves would not be destroyed. Rosita, still lying on the ground, read the letter three times before she was satisfied. Then she got up and went about her work.

"It's going to cost me a great deal of money to make this slight change," Corinda said to Larry Wayne that afternoon during their "hour of prayer." "But I can see no way of getting around it without bad press."

"If there was a way of getting around it," he said, unbuttoning her blouse, "I'm sure you would have thought of it."

When the garden was completed, Sergio made a wooden bench and Rosita placed it in front of the graves, but Corinda Cassy replaced it with a bench of her choice, one made of stone, which she said was more in keeping with the total environment she was trying to create.

"What does it matter," said Rosita, "just as long as there's something to sit on? What does it matter?"

There were days when she was so busy caring for Principia and the cowgirls she was only able to sit on the bench for a few seconds, but according to Rosita a few seconds were better than none at all. She often passed her time there looking back; retracing everything that had happened from the time Applebee arrived in Judson to the present. While reflecting over the years that had passed all too rapidly, she sometimes took refuge in a strange, almost comforting sadness that obliterated the once constant smile on her face.

Sergio didn't think it made his wife any happier to linger over the past. "Her eyes get sadder by the day," he told Corinda, who said Rosita would get used to the changes in time.

"A few changes are good, but not so many," said Rosita when Corinda suggested naming the town Jericho. "I will dig up my parents and leave with their bones if you change the name. I'll never stop cursing you either."

After some thought, Corinda decided Rosita was right, the town was known as Judson and should go on being known as Judson, but the main street leading to the yet unfinished tabernacle should be called the Avenue of the Redeemed. In order to have the avenue widened into a glistening thoroughfare, she had the date palms cut, then the cottonwood, and after that she started wondering what she could do to improve the smaller street. Finally she decided to have it paved as well, and on the north side of the intersection she called it the Pathway to Eternity. On the south side it was known as the Road to Righteousness. Miss Cassy told a reporter from the *Baptist Standard* that the Lord had spoken to her in a dream and instructed her to make these changes. "And if He's willing," she was quoted, "I will make even more."

"How could she make any more changes than what she already has?" said Applebee. "There's nothing left of the place as it is." He folded up the *Baptist Standard* and stuffed it into one of Johnnie Chapman's shopping bags. They were sitting at the Water Gardens. It was Sunday, and there was a wind blowing through the business district. "The only one who's getting the good end of the bargain is Rubendella," Applebee said. "She covered Texas last year, and now they've got her traveling around the south. Newspapers says she's going to launch a campaign in California next, and if I know Rubendella she won't come back after that."

"She'll just keep on a'going," said Johnnie Chapman, lifting her feet out of the water. They were just beginning to wrinkle from being under so long. "Best not to think about all this. Try not to anyway."

She had told him this before, dozens of times, but it had never done any good. He didn't enjoy reflecting on his years in Judson, but there were times when he could not help doing so. "Too much reflection on some things is poison," Johnnie had told him, and for that reason he stopped playing the fiddle because the old jealous tune brought the past too close to the present. Yet without any effort at all there were moments, sometimes whole days, usually in the summer when there was sand in the air, when his thoughts would go rolling like a ball of twine unraveling down a hill. Then he would usually sit on the curb just outside the entrance to the pawnshop or walk down to the Water Gardens to soak his feet and think of Judson.

During those times, he would also think of Principia, but it would only be a painful half thought, a thought that registered without completely making itself known, for the truth was he did not enjoy thinking about her at all, but there were times when Judson would come back on him all at once and he would search for a way to make the past crumble from his memory and drop to the hot sidewalk like beads of sweat pouring from his face.

The Golden Rule Pawnshop, owned by Applebee's ex-brother-in-law, didn't always provide the necessary distraction because it was located on the north side of downtown Fort Worth, a district that was under reconstruction most of the time. The shop was in a corner red brick building of three stories. In the back behind the display cases was an archway covered by a chintz curtain, and behind the curtain was a large room where Applebee lived. All around him old buildings were coming down and new ones were going up. Sometimes during the night he would be awakened by an explosion of dynamite, and the next day the hull of a building that had been standing the day before would be nothing but a pile of bricks. With each building that was ripped to the ground he would think of Judson and wonder if he were destined to live within the sound of demolition for the rest of his life.

From time to time he would consider moving to a quiet section of town, but he was never able to make that move because there were a few good things about living in the pawnshop, and he reminded himself of them every day: he was close to F. W. Woolworth's, his favorite place to have lunch or a cup of coffee, and he wasn't too far from the bus station where he knew he could find Johnnie Chapman, when she wasn't in the pawnshop that is, or down at the Water Gardens washing out her rags and waiting for him to show up.

But most of the time he endured long, unavoidable afternoons in the shop. He dreaded those days most of all because invariably he would have a difficult customer, something would be stolen or someone's voice would remind him of Corinda Cassy, Principia or Rosita, and then either a quiet internal rage or a long brooding sadness would sweep over him. When that happened he would often leave the customer to browse, or from time to time he would attempt to tell the story of Judson, but less than midway through he would usually stop himself, finish the business at hand and go out front with his coloring book and sit on the curb.

Applebee was never far removed from Judson, and before long he realized he never would be, not only because it occupied a large part of his mind but because the *new* town was too often in the news. When The Residence was completed there was a grand opening. Newspaper reporters and television anchormen arrived from all over Texas to inspect the new seven-story hotel: a stair-stepped pyramid of mirrored glass, the top floor of which was a penthouse occupied by Larry Wayne and Corinda.

In a press conference held in the lobby of mirrors, Larry Wayne, dressed in white silk, told reporters the hotel was run by a staff of thirty devoted Christians and every room was booked for six months in advance. Corinda said she was certain they would need to expand their facilities in due time. "I have," she added, "purposely designed The Tabernacle in the Sky bigger than what is now necessary, for midway through the construction of the hotel the Lord gave me the vision of growth and I want to allow much room for expansion."

"Speaking of expansion," said Larry Wayne, "our station, The Radio Church of God, will begin broadcasting in about a month."

"Oh, yes," said Corinda, wrapping herself in her cowgirl cape, "we will be on the air waves with music interviews and, of course, Principia's healing services. She's now living in a modest apartment on the ground floor of the hotel. There's a tape recorder by her bed, and when she feels the spirit leading her into communication with her followers she will simply record herself for future broadcast. None of her talks will be edited very much, but some of them will be spliced together so we can create one long program, which will be like a medley of beautiful songs."

After the press conference, Corinda and Larry Wayne relaxed on the terrace of their penthouse. "The Radio Church of God will become known in religious circles throughout the world," Corinda said, "but this is not enough. We've got to televise Principia during her healing services. We've got to televise my precious cowgirls prancing across the stage too. Sooo many many lost souls can be won this way."

"And yours might be one of them," said Larry Wayne.

"One day you'll ask me to forgive you for saying that," said Corinda. "You never take me seriously on anything that has to do with my inner strength. I want this to be the most inspirational program on television. I want it to speak to the minds and hearts of *everyone*. Even you will be moved by it."

When The Tabernacle in the Sky was completed, Corinda delayed the opening ceremony until television cameras could be installed and checked out. The tabernacle, connected to The Residence by an underground passage, was a dome-shaped structure with three spires of varying heights and three steps leading to three front doors. The main auditorium could seat three thousand, three hundred and thirty-three people, and the proscenium arch, shaped like a heart, was draped with a silver curtain.

A few days before the grand opening, Corinda invited the press to tour the building. "I just want our holy city to be uplifting," she told the reporters, but a writer from the San Antonio *Sun* said it was anything but. "The Residence," he wrote, "is a modern-day pyramid, which, unlike the ancient structures of its shape, does not appear to be in relationship to the guiding forces of the universe, and as for the much-talked-about Tabernacle in the Sky, all I can say is that it can be seen for miles around. The mirrored glass is constantly doing battle with the blazing sun. If visit you must, a cloudy day is recommended."

"That happens to be the silliest, most stupid journalist I've ever read," said Corinda, stomping through the penthouse in her purple boots. It was the day of the grand opening. She was wearing a red cotton dress with a ruffle around the hem and a concho belt slung low around her hips. "This man obviously suffers from cleverness," she said to Larry Wayne, who was sitting on the couch with a towel wrapped around his waist and his feet on the coffee table. "Principia is not allowed to read the newspapers today. She is not allowed to answer the telephone or turn on the radio or the television. She is not to have visitors, unless I approve of them. She's nervous enough about the first service in our beautiful tabernacle, and I don't want anything or anybody to upset her."

Principia spent the morning and afternoon in her apartment. She read Edgar Young Mullins, listened to tapes of the Armstrong Family and lunched with Rosita and Sergio, who had been instructed to keep the conversation light.

When it came time to leave for the opening services, Rosita combed Principia's hair, which had grown to her waist, and pinned it out of her eyes with silver barrettes shaped like musical notes. She had chosen to wear a gown with cathedral sleeves and silk slippers that clung to her feet as though they had grown there. "I feel so unsure of myself tonight," she said when they left the apartment. Sergio gave her an arm to lean on as they walked through the tunnel to The Tabernacle in the Sky, and along the way Principia's thoughts kept turning back in time. "I wonder what Aunt Wilda is doing right now," she said as they approached the double doors leading into the tabernacle.

"Your aunt is no longer living," said Rosita.

"Oh, that's right," said Principia. "I must have been thinking about someone else. Sometimes it's hard to remember who isn't living anymore."

When they arrived backstage, Larry Wayne said the tabernacle was only a third full, but no one was expecting a full house on the first night anyway. Still, he delayed the opening until he was sure everyone had arrived and was seated.

Principia stood in the wings and swayed back and forth, finding her balance first on Sergio and then on Rosita. "I feel weak all over," she said, peering through the curtain at the congregation. "Why do I keep looking up and expecting to see the stars instead of a ceiling? It looks like they could have left the roof off this church, doesn't it?"

Rosita turned to Sergio and whispered in Spanish, "All things resemble their owner." It had been one of her mother's favorite proverbs.

"In this case it's true," said Sergio.

"New Bethel Church was nothing like this," Principia continued, still looking through the curtain. "There you could look up and see the clouds and stars."

"Now *you* are the star," said Sergio, trying to make pleasant conversation. "And all these people have come here to see you."

"If only I knew what to expect I'd feel better," said Principia. "I don't like all this waiting around."

At eight o'clock the curtain went up and the cowgirls, each carrying a Christian flag and singing:

> "Do Lord, Oh Do Lord,
> Oh, do remember me,
> Hallelujah!

> "Do Lord, Oh Do Lord,
> Oh, do remember me,
> Forever . . ."

pranced across the stage with Corinda Cassy in the lead. On command and still singing, the cowgirls executed countermarches and gate turns, pinwheels and left flanks, right flanks and a series of diagonals before returning to rank and file formation. The congregation broke into applause as the drill team left the stage. Corinda returned to take a bow for the entire group, and then, waving the Christian flag, she marched off with her head held high and her cowgirl cape flapping behind her.

For several minutes after that, the stage was empty. Principia was still standing in the wings, but she didn't feel led by the Spirit to make her entrance. "I don't think I can do this tonight," she said.

"Oh yes you can," said Larry Wayne. "You can't let us down now." He gave her the slightest push—that was all it took—and suddenly she was standing on the stage. The audience broke into thunderous applause as she walked to the microphone, which was surrounded by white lilies. She stood there and for a long time, did not speak. She stared at the paying audience, but she couldn't see beyond the first row. The spotlights were blinding, yet she continued to stare directly into them.

"I don't know what to say," she finally said. Her voice was weak. "So I'm going to stand here for a few minutes. I hope you won't mind."

The congregation was silent. Principia didn't move. She stood there and allowed her mind to drift far away. She had no idea what she was thinking. The spotlight seemed to burn away her thoughts before she was aware of them. Then, when she had lost track of where she was, something happened. It was as though an electrical current had shocked her into life, for she began speaking with an authority that the *Christian Reporter* said could only issue from the mouth of a saint.

"If you came here to see Principia Martindale you came here for the wrong reason," she said. Her voice was angry. "If you came here to see this building, you came here for the wrong reason too. This building is nothing but a shell, and so is Principia Martindale, but the Lord God who created life is all . . ."

While she preached members of the congregation walked down the aisle and up on the stage to touch her. People kissed the hem of her garment, touched her arms, her hands, her hair. But she was so absorbed in her sermon and the blinding light that she wasn't aware of their presence until she felt someone tugging hard at her sleeve. Then she realized she was surrounded by people. They were sitting at her feet, or standing, straining to get a better look, or to touch her, any part of her. Some were on crutches, one was in a wheelchair and others appeared to be perfectly healthy. "What have I been saying?" she asked.

"It's not what you say that's so important," someone said. Principia started twisting her hair with both hands. The people began closing in. They touched her, kissed her, stroked her hair and ripped off pieces of her dress. Corinda and Larry Wayne tried to form the mob into a single file, but it didn't work. Finally Principia broke away and ran. Before she made it to the wings, she fainted. Sergio and Larry Wayne carried her offstage, and when she was revived she said she felt as if she were living inside a nightmare. "Suddenly everything was so scary," she said. "I wish I was still in the tent. It was so old-fashioned and comfortable."

"But you weren't comfortable there at first either," said Corinda. "In time you will find comfort with this new place."

Two days later the newspapers were filled with accounts of Principia's first service in the tabernacle. One reporter called her "hypersensitive" and "neurotically religious." Another said that her power, if she had any, was located in her little finger, and that she possessed an insane stare which convinced some people she was a mystic when in reality she was anything but.

"Hide the newspapers quick," Corinda Cassy screamed over the telephone. She was talking to Rosita, who was about to serve Principia breakfast. "We simply can't have her reading these idiotic articles about herself."

Then she hung up and called Larry Wayne in the ground floor office. "We're going to publish our own inspirational magazine each month, and we're going to call it *The New Heaven*," she instructed. "Right now you've got to find me some able editors and some writers who can communicate our true worth and intentions."

Within two months the first issue of the magazine was printed. By then Principia was more comfortable with her Sunday evening services and *The New Heaven* announced that very soon she would be giving two healing services each week. The first issue also contained an article about the wheelchairs, crutches and eyeglasses left behind as proof of a healing. These objects were hung on the back wall of the tabernacle. Corinda Cassy had written the article herself, but she did not mention that some of the wheelchairs had been retrieved, some of the crutches had been taken back and that a lady from Kerrville had come looking for her eyeglasses but could not find them.

"We want our magazine to emphasize the positive and forget about the negative," said Corinda to the editor-in-chief, Bill Collins, who had been hired straight out of Baylor's graduate school and was eager to succeed. "The magazine is going to be one of our most successful projects."

In the second issue, Corinda interviewed Principia, who said: "Sometimes it scares me to stand before all those people because I forget where I am, and then suddenly I wake up, and don't always know what I've done or said."

Applebee read that article twice. "I know what she's talking about," he said to Johnnie Chapman, who was finishing her last shoeshine of the day. "When she stands on stage and lets her mind drift far away, so far until she can't tell what she's thinking, she loses track of where she is and how long she's been standing there. I can do it too. I just drift far away and plug into something else, 'specially when I color. I never thought it was scary, but some people, I guess, think it's insane."

"Ain't nothing insane about that," Johnnie said while making change for her customer. "But you won't find too many who'll allow their minds to run loose that way. Scared they won't never come back to their right senses. And some don't. Them's the ones that goes insane and stays insane for the rest of their lives, but if you're the kind of person who talks to yourself a lot and you think it's all right to talk to yourself a lot, then you'll always be perfectly all right—upstairs anyway."

She tightened the red scarf on her head and then started closing up the shoeshine stand. When she was ready to leave, Applebee walked her two blocks to the bus stop, then headed back to the pawnshop. Along the way he talked to himself about doing the inventory and the monthly paperwork and about whether or not he wanted to move to another section of the city. It was easier for him to exist when he thought about everyday things and kept his mind off Judson, and Principia, so he tried to center his thoughts on ordinary problems. He would get into this routine of thought and his life would go along smoothly perhaps for a whole month, but then, without warning, and when he least expected the past to resurface, he would open the Fort Worth *Star-Telegram* to the very page where her picture appeared. His eyes would quickly scan the article, if there was one, and he would look for any excuse not to read it.

There were days when Principia Martindale rested on the periphery of his mind just waiting for something to hurl her into total consciousness. There were days when he would not turn on the radio for fear of hearing her voice again, and all the time wanting desperately to hear it. Once he saw her on a television set playing all night in a department store window. She was standing on center stage, her arms uplifted, and people were hurrying down the aisle to be touched by her. "If you have come here to be healed, you have come here with the wrong attitude," she was saying. He could barely hear her through the window. "You must come here to worship. If God wants you healed He will heal you, not Principia Martindale."

Applebee watched the program for a few minutes, but after that he refused to walk past the department store again, refused to turn on the television sets in the pawnshop and would not allow one in the back room where he lived.

Often in a newspaper article he would read of people who claimed to have been healed by Principia. And on occasion he would catch the name Rosita López, "a devoted friend to the healer," or Rubendella Hinojosa, who would occasionally take time off from her publicity tours to make an appearance during one of Principia's services. Rubendella was usually mentioned for her singing ability as well as her dramatic monologues done in full costume and make-up. She became especially known for her Sumerian woman, a part Miss Cassy wrote for her, but the monologue that Principia conceived, Deborah sitting under the tree and giving advice to all who sought her, was Rubendella's favorite.

Principia was thought of as a modern-day Deborah. From all walks of life people came to talk to her, touch her or ask for a miracle. Some of her followers arrived on crutches and left them behind as proof that they had been healed; some were in wheelchairs and left them behind. Others left the way they arrived, and many of them came back again and again.

"There's something about her I just can't get enough of," said a woman who was interviewed on her third visit to Judson. "I think it's her smile."

"That's probably part of her appeal," said Applebee, folding the newspaper in half. "She's got a smile that can melt steel. Didn't always use it, but when she did, you felt like you were hit over the head by something." He was sitting down at the Water Gardens and soaking his feet. Johnnie Chapman, leaning against her shopping bags, was sitting beside him. Twice she had tried to take the newspaper away from him, and twice he had insisted that it was the last article he would ever read about Judson, Principia or anything that had to do with Corinda Cassy. When he finished reading, he stared off into space and became silent. Johnnie sensed a dark mood creeping over him. She slipped the newspaper out of his hands and read the last paragraph of the article. The reporter had quoted Corinda Cassy:

"I'm not through yet. I've only just begun. The Lord has now asked me to build a prayer tower. It will be a single shaft of reinforced concrete with an enclosed elevator, and on the very top will be a flying-saucer-shaped structure inside which rows and rows of telephones will ring twenty-four hours a day and be answered by devoted Christians with prayers on their lips. The tower will go into construction immediately and within a year it too will be finished. At first I thought I would call it The Pillar of Prayer, but the Heavenly Father instructed me otherwise. He told me that I was completely off base and then brought me back down to earth again. Now, with both feet firmly planted on the ground, I am sooo happy to announce that we will call it The Prayer Tower and nothing but. Simplicity is always best. I have lived my life with this in mind."

4

With the completion of The Residence, The Tabernacle in the Sky, the parking lots and the plazas with fountains bubbling both day and night; with the completion of The Prayer Tower and a long row of shops, gasoline stations and restaurants that Corinda built along the Avenue of the Redeemed, she said she could not think of a single improvement to make, but Larry Wayne Johnson told her there was much more to be done and if she would make him her business partner, he would help her build a city that would stretch all the way to Mexico.

"I will consider that carefully," said Corinda, kissing him on the cheek. They were standing on the observation deck of The Prayer Tower. The lights from the tabernacle gave Larry Wayne's face an almost translucent glow and Corinda had the feeling she could put her arm right through him. "There are times you seem too good to be real," she said. "There are times when I think I don't know you at all, but I do know that without you by my side I would never have been able to create the city of my dreams."

The next week she invited reporters from all over the country to visit the finished Judson, which she said was the city God led her to create. Newspapers ran series on what was going on out in the Texas brush; magazines picked up the story as well. On the cover of a national magazine the new city was pictured in a panoramic view: spires of glass and steel rose over the flatlands; The Prayer Tower was bathed in purple light and the Avenue of the Redeemed appeared to be a long ribbon of gold. There were fountains everywhere, and prayer gardens, and flocks of white doves that nested in specially designed compartments high up in the tabernacle spires and along the walkway that circled The Prayer Tower.

The tabernacle was equipped with the latest in sound, lighting and video equipment. There was a cafeteria in the basement, a post office next to it, and on the main floor there was a small shop where visitors could buy picture postcards. Directly behind the stage were offices as well as three apartments. Sergio and Rosita occupied one of them, Principia the other and the third was usually empty. Sergio was given the job of guarding Principia's door, and Rosita was hired to be her constant companion, cook for her and offer moments of encouragement. Their apartments were connected from the inside by a sliding door.

Principia's temperature-controlled apartment was designed so she would only be a few steps from her audience. The apartment contained eight rooms and a private garden, but in spite of all the space, Principia stayed in her bed most of the time. From there she read the Bible daily, continued her study of Edgar Young Mullins, dictated inspirational letters to those who had been healed and requested medical reports to prove that a healing had occurred. Larry Wayne, who had worked hard to lose his Alabama accent and to feel comfortable in three-piece suits, hired a secretary to take Principia's dictation, but he never allowed her letters to be mailed without first reading them himself.

During this period of time he was in and out of Principia's apartment, and Rosita saw more of him than she wanted to. "I'll never be able to trust him," she told her husband. "You can't tell if he's looking at you or not. He is like a very rich ghost. Always he wears his white suits, and always he turns up when you don't want to see him. He does not believe in Principia either. You can tell by just looking."

There wasn't much that escaped the watchful eyes of Rosita López. She felt it was her duty to look after Principia's well-being because she could not trust anyone else to do so. "No one here believes in her the way I do," Rosita told Sergio one night when she could not sleep. She sat up in bed and stared at the screen door her father had painted and Principia had repainted. The door was propped up against the wall, and a candle was burning behind it. Sergio was not awake, but Rosita continued talking to him. "Principia has the same kind of power my mother had," she said, adjusting her pillow. "Sometimes my mother was wrong about her predictions, but most of the time she was right—about the big things anyway. It is the same with Principia. Sometimes her energy is low, and she is not able to heal people. Then she gets very sad, and I have to help her remember better days."

During these times Rosita would take Principia walking through the tabernacle and call her attention to the wheelchairs, crutches, braces and eyeglasses that were hanging on the walls. "You have done all this," Rosita would say. "There is no reason for you to be so sad. Now let's think of better things. I want you to remember all the good you have done for everybody."

Between services and bouts of insecurity, Principia occupied herself with a prodigious correspondence to admirers and old friends as well, Billy Ray Poindexter among them. Billy Ray had become a minister of music, but he confessed in one of his letters that he was neither happy with his profession nor was he very successful. "I keep thinking about what you told me a long time ago," he wrote. "You said the Lord was taking me into the ministry of music in order to lead me someplace else, and I still believe that with all my heart."

Principia wrote back: "I am sure you could be instrumental to us here in Judson. Miss Cassy is looking for someone to manage our twenty-four-hour prayer service. People from all over the United States call to request special prayers, and we always have special people who can pray for them."

Billy Ray was hired for the job, and weeks before his arrival Principia started decorating his apartment in the tabernacle. It pleased her to know they would be sharing a common wall. During this time of preparation, her face glowed day and night and her healing services were charged with renewed energy. One day when she was choosing the curtains for Billy Ray's bedroom, she confessed to Rosita that he had been in her heart for years. "He's the only man in the world I would consider marrying," she said. "I think I loved him from the moment we first met. He was sitting at a table. I can't remember where it was, but he was coloring. Billy Ray always loved to color, and he was good at it too."

"I think you're confusing yourself," said Rosita, but Principia insisted that she was not.

That night before Rosita went to bed she told Sergio that

Principia's mind was getting very tired. "All she wants to do is stare into space and think about this man. Whoever he is, I think I wish he wouldn't come here."

A few days after the apartment was ready, Billy Ray arrived in Judson. He was wearing a blue suit that swallowed him whole. He smelled of shoe polish, Old Spice and hair oil. At first Principia didn't recognize him, but after a few words were exchanged, she said, "Oh yes, I remember you now. Somehow I thought you were going to be someone else. I don't know why I thought that."

She sent Billy Ray to live in the guesthouse behind her ranch. "I don't want him near me," she told Rosita. "He's not who he pretended to be, but we'll use him anyway because he's willing to work hard."

After Billy Ray had been director of the telephone prayer and counseling service for a week, Principia appointed him director of the twenty-four-hour prayer vigil as well. She told him it was his responsibility to see that someone was down on his knees and praying for her ministry every minute of the day. A small chapel in The Prayer Tower was used for the vigil, and everyone who worked for The New Heaven/New Earth Inc. was given a schedule for each week's prayer duties. If someone was unable to be in the chapel at his appointed time, the person who was already there was expected to go on praying until relieved. Billy Ray was on call twenty-four hours a day just in case something went wrong with the prayer chain, and often he was awakened late at night or early in the morning and asked to take someone's place before the altar.

"You've given him too much to do," said Corinda Cassy. "You're going to run him off if you're not careful."

"Billy Ray has always been a hard worker," replied Principia. "He won't run off again. He'll stay here and help us this time."

"And how do you know?" asked Corinda.

And Principia answered: "Just the other day when I was sitting in the sunken living room the Lord told me this. He speaks to me all the time, especially in my dreams. Every night He assures me He's a jealous God who wants my total love and devotion. Unlike mortal mind, which is so full of illusions and disappointments, I can always depend on my Heavenly Father to give me comfort, and when I have pleased Him, I can feel His presence charging me with a stronger commitment to perform His will."

Corinda Cassy became worried about Principia's state of mental health. "She's so absorbed in her work that she loses track of who everyone is," she said. "I live in constant fear that her powerful influence over people will one day fail her."

One evening during a healing service Principia told the congregation that she was a fraud. "I don't believe in divine healers," she screamed. The white doves on either side of the stage were so alarmed by the anger in her voice that they tried to break out of their cages. "I believe in divine healing," she continued. "But I cannot believe in any power that is mine, and I don't know what you people are doing here. Go home in the name of God."

The congregation begged her not to leave the stage, but she did anyway, and in the wings she said that her ministry was over.

"You just need a rest, that's all," said Winkie. She and Ravenhill had rushed backstage to give Principia their support.

"All you need to do is take the summer off, and by next fall you'll feel better," advised Brother Ravenhill.

"What do you mean take the summer off," said Larry Wayne, pulling Ravenhill and Winkie over to one side. "We can't afford to take a day off right now. There's no place in this organization for a temperamental little faith healer."

"You ought to be shot for saying such a thing as that," said Winkie. "The world would be a whole lot better if we had less people like you in it."

"Don't listen to him," shouted Corinda. "He's just upset and doesn't know what he's saying. I promise you he doesn't."

"He knows exactly what he's saying," said Winkie, staring hard into Larry Wayne's face. "It's a shame the Lord hasn't given you a clear vision into this man's tormented soul."

"His commitment is neither to you nor to the Lord," said Brother Ravenhill, pointing a finger in Larry Wayne's face.

"May I remind you," said Corinda, "that neither one of you have been right about everything. Now leave us alone with this problem. We'll solve it the best way we can."

"Ma-ha-ya-ma-ha," said Winkie, sitting down on the floor. "I refuse to leave. You'll have to drag me off to get rid of me because my place is with Principia. She needs me."

"I want to be with Winkie tonight," said Principia. "She's the only one who understands what I'm going through."

That night Ravenhill returned to San Antonio with his bus and passengers, but Winkie remained in Judson. She slept on the floor next to Principia's bed, and the next morning, when Rosita opened the curtains at dawn, Winkie leaped to her feet. "Cino-me-oooo-ma-HA, Lord," she whispered.

A cold chill ran up and down Rosita's arms, and she left the room fast. "Sometimes I don't know who is crazy and who is sane anymore," she said, entering her own apartment and closing the door behind her.

"Ma-ha-ya-ma-ha," shouted Winkie. She shook Principia awake. "Oh, let's see what divine messages the Lord has written in the skies today."

Principia sat up in bed and stared into the sunrise. After a few minutes Winkie pointed to a cloud and cried out—Rosita could hear her in the next apartment—"Oh, look! There's John the Baptist. The Lord has put Mr. John the Baptist in the skies today for the purpose of giving us encouragement, and he has done just that a thousand times over."

"I see him too," said Principia.

"Oh, I knew you would," shouted Winkie.

"I think he's coming to baptize us all over again," Principia said. "I've always believed you couldn't ever be baptized too many times."

"He's coming closer closer closer," whispered Winkie. She jumped into bed with Principia and pulled the purple sheets up around both of them. "Ooooh, he just about takes my breath away. I feel so sorry for people who can't see him the way we can."

"So do I," said Principia. "This is only the beginning of many great things to come. Oh, look! There's Deborah."

"I see her as plain as day," said Winkie. "And she looks just like you. She's got your hair, and your eyes, and your hands and your mouth. She's got your smile and your nose and your arms and your legs . . ."

"This woman is crazy!" said Rosita, barging into Corinda Cassy's office. "I've been listening through the door, so I know for sure. All of you are crazy, but this Winkie woman, she is very

very crazy. She makes Principia see things that are not there."

"This has gone on long enough," said Corinda. "Larry Wayne will throw her out today. Just try to act like nothing's going to happen."

Rosita returned to her apartment and started cooking. It always calmed her nerves to be in the kitchen. At twelve noon she served lunch to Winkie and Principia, who were sitting in bed reading the Bible. "We've just seen someone in the air and we think it was Ole Mr. Job himself," said Winkie, motioning for Rosita to sit on the bed with them.

"But we weren't sure who it was," said Principia, "so we're searching the scriptures for clues."

"This food will make you feel better," said Rosita. She was still standing. "I have made chili rellenos, quesadillas, enchiladas, tacos and fresh corn tortillas."

"I'll just have a tortilla right now, thank you," said Winkie. "I never eat very much when I'm feasting on the word of God."

Rosita put a single tortilla on a blue plate and handed it over to Winkie, who studied it for a few seconds and then shouted: "I see Jesus! I see Jesus!" She picked up the warm tortilla with both hands and held it up to the light. "Look!" she screamed. "It's the face of Jesus. The Son of God is made manifest on this morsel of food. Ma-ha-ya-ma-Ha, Cino-me-ooo. Praise his most holy and precious name Jeee-sus."

"I see him too," cried Principia.

"But it's only a burned place," said Rosita. "The grill got too hot, that's all."

"But the Lord is working through you in this way," Principia said. "We never can tell where our Savior will show his face. Oh, Rosita! He has just appeared to us on one of your tortillas."

"And now we're about to eat it," said Winkie reverently. "This is truly the Lord's Supper." She divided the tortilla in thirds. Principia and Winkie ate their portion, but Rosita said: "I'll save mine for later. I want Sergio to have part of it." Then she left the room and didn't return that day.

That night Winkie and Principia feasted on the cold food Rosita had brought for lunch. They read the Book of Revelation twice and discussed it until they both drifted off to sleep. Winkie's hair was in pin curls, and Principia's was braided into one long plait that nearly reached the floor. Neither of them awoke when Larry Wayne slipped into the apartment. He pulled the sheets away from Winkie, scooped her up in his arms and ran for the door.

"Who is it?" asked Winkie, flinging her arms as though she had lost control of them. "Who's got me?"

"Your Heavenly Father," said Larry Wayne.

"Praise you, Lord!" shouted Winkie. But when they were in the bright light of the hallway, she realized who was carrying her. "You are not my Heavenly Father any such of a thing!" she shouted.

"Well, just pretend a little while longer," said Larry Wayne as he ran with her through the tabernacle to a car that was parked out back. "You should be shot between the eyes!" shouted Winkie as she was forced into the car. "'Vengeance is mine saith the Lord.' You better remember this." Larry Wayne slammed the car door, and the driver, who had been instructed to take Winkie back to San Antonio without stopping, sped away.

The next morning Rosita opened the curtains at dawn as usual and then sat on Principia's bed until she opened her eyes. "God called Winkie last night," said Rosita. "He sent her back home to her husband, who is very very sick, so you must pray for him today."

"Lord protect Brother Ravenhill and keep him safe," said Principia, staring out the window and into the sky.

For the next few weeks, Principia, eating enchiladas in bed, studied the cloud formations and refused to get up and conduct a service. During that time Brother Ravenhill and Winkie were not allowed to enter the city, so they composed a letter which stated that Larry Wayne was behaving like another Applebee and that there was nothing ahead but trouble unless the Lord was allowed to have His way.

Principia waited impatiently for Winkie's return. She spent her time eating and sleeping and conversing with her favorite Bible figures. They came to her in her sleep, offered moments of encouragment and advised her to rest until she felt strong enough to hold services again. From time to time, Rosita would open the curtains at dawn and Principia would see Winkie Ravenhill in the clouds, or she would wake up at night and find Winkie sitting with Moses, Elijah, Matthew, Luke or John, and once she was sitting on a rock, a staff was in her hand and a flock of sheep was gathered around her. "Oh, Winkie, you look just like Aunt Wilda," Principia said, sitting up straight in bed. Rosita, up early that morning, rushed into Principia's apartment and found her talking to the empty chairs.

"Rosita," said Principia, her eyes glassy, not yet awake, "I have just spoken to Winkie and she said she took a vote, and no one in the scripture wants me to hold services again until I feel energized from head to toe."

"That is very good advice, I think," Rosita stammered. "Now maybe a cool bath will make you feel better."

But Principia refused to leave her bed.

Larry Wayne believed she was discouraged because she had received too many letters in which the writer stated that a healing had occurred but had only lasted a short time. There had also been many letters from people who asked to have their wheelchairs back, their crutches, their eyeglasses and leg braces. Larry Wayne said that those letters disturbed her most of all, so Corinda gave him the job of writing Principia letters of inspiration and arranging for them to be mailed from all parts of the United States.

"I refuse to be anybody's secretary," said Larry Wayne. "Especially yours. I'll turn the whole thing over to Rubendella."

By then Rubendella was pursuing her own career in California. She had appeared as an extra in a movie of the week, had starred in an X-rated horror film and was singing pop tunes in a night spot along Sunset Strip. Although her work with The New Heaven/New Earth Inc. had diminished her financial worries, she did agree to take on another assignment. She made a commitment to write fifty inspirational letters each week and mail them from Hollywood. "For this," she said, "I can buy a new living room suit." She dashed off the letters in her spare time, between auditions, between shows at the nightclub and when she couldn't sleep. Some of the letters she typed, some she wrote, some she printed. She bought various kinds of stationery and used colored inks to vary the appearance of each letter.

Back in Judson, Larry Wayne would collect all the letters in a basket. He would mix them up and carry them to Principia's bedroom, and together they would examine the postmark, open the envelopes and read aloud all the glorious things Principia had done for others. She especially enjoyed hearing him read to her; his voice was soothing, hypnotic, often put her to sleep, and once, after weeks of encouragement, Larry Wayne moved close to the bedside and while she slept he whispered into her ear: "Principia, you are needed by so many. When you wake up you must continue your good work, for thousands of my people are depending on you." His voice was low and resonant, and on waking up Principia felt as though she had heard the voice of God. "I have conversed with all the major figures of the Bible," she said, "but this is the first time that God himself has visited me in such a powerful way. I feel his energy moving to all parts of my body."

It was then that she, many pounds heavier, got out of bed and resumed her ministry.

"We must never allow her to become discouraged again," said Corinda Cassy to Larry Wayne. "I've worked hard to make this city what it is, and I'm not going to lose it because of Principia Martindale."

Corinda Cassy came to the conclusion that Principia's power was easily destroyed, especially if overexposed to the public, so she kept her hidden away in the spacious apartment in the tabernacle. No disturbing news was allowed to reach her. All of her real mail was censored by a staff of fifteen workers, and she was only allowed to read the letters of encouragement. Her visitors were kept at a minimum as well, and all of them were carefully screened. There was even some doubt in Corinda's mind as to whether or not Principia's parents should be allowed to visit her.

"They can see her on television," said Corinda. "Isn't that good enough. "What if they upset her and we can't get her out of bed again? What if she just stops on us?"

"They are her parents," said Rosita, "and they are getting very old. No matter what you say, if they show up, I will let them in."

By that time, Wilma Lee and Principal were living in a Baptist retirement home on the outskirts of New Bethel. They watched their daughter on television each week, looked forward to her daily letters, and finally they decided they would visit her. They hired a student from Hillister Baptist College to drive them to Judson, and had planned to stay a full week, but Corinda Cassy cut their visit short after two days because Principia wanted to return with them to New Bethel. She longed for the white frame church and the sparrows nesting in the steeple, she longed for her bedroom with the picture window and for her friend Lively Hathaway.

"I'd even like to see those birthday movies you took long ago," she told her father. "I wish I could see them right now." She was sitting up in bed; her purple sheets and comforter were pulled up around her and the curtains covering the east windows were opened so she could keep an eye on the cloud formations.

"I've still got a real nice piece of cotton print," said Wilma Lee. She was sitting at the foot of the bed. "I could make something pretty for you to wear or maybe sleep in."

"I'd like that," said Principia. "But I'm so big now, you'd never get me measured."

It seemed to her that her mother had not changed a day, but her father had suffered numerous strokes; he was shorter, could hardly walk across the room and his shoulders were stooped. Principia administered the laying on of hands and prayed that her father would be healed, but he left her bedroom with slow feeble steps the same way he had entered. Principia cried for hours after they left her apartment, and during the night she dreamed that she had never become an Invincible, that she had never left New Bethel and that she was still a student living at home in order to please her parents. The next morning she woke up believing her dream, and it took Rosita the best part of an hour to convince her of the day and year: October 5, 1962.

"Somehow I thought we were still in the fifties," said Principia, struggling to get out of bed. "I don't know how I got so mixed up."

"Your mind is tired today," said Rosita. "Tomorrow you will feel better."

Her parents visited her again that day, and all she could talk about was how much she wanted to return home. She wanted to see her birthday movies, sit in her father's lap while he read to her and have a good long visit with Lively Hathaway and Dr. Truly. "I'd like to see Aunt Wilda too," she said, "but she would be so disappointed in me because I haven't done a chalk talk in years. I haven't painted a picture for my bedroom window in a long time either. How will my friends in New Bethel be able to forgive me?"

Her parents tried to set her straight. They reminded her that Lively Hathaway and Aunt Wilda were dead, but Principia kept saying there was no such thing as death, and the more they tried to reason with her the more confused she became until all the years of her life seemed to merge together into the present.

"We can't have her carrying on like she's insane," said Corinda Cassy, stomping through the tabernacle in her red cowboy boots. She had been listening to Principia's conversations over the intercom in the executive offices. "This isn't a retirement home and those two are leaving today." Then she entered Principia's apartment unannounced and took her parents out into the hall where they could talk in private. "We're glad you came, but it's time for you to go," she said. "I hate to put it to you this way, but Principia has three very important services this week, and your presence will prove to be too draining on her energy. We have to be very protective of her, you know."

Reluctantly her parents left Judson. Principal was crying and Wilma Lee was struggling to separate the Kleenexes in her purse so she could wipe away her husband's tears.

"I don't want them to ever come back," Corinda Cassy said to Larry Wayne. They were sitting on the terrace of the penthouse she had built for them, the only place where they could be completely alone. "It's possible that they could persuade Principia to give up the ministry altogether, and we can't have that. It's taken Rosita all week to persuade her that she belongs here."

"You have nothing to worry about," said Larry Wayne. "They can't live much longer."

"I can always depend on you to comfort me," said Corinda. "You always say what I want to hear."

Not long after that, word came that Principia's parents had died in their sleep, Principal one night and Wilma Lee the next. Corinda Cassy thought for a long time before she decided it was best to allow Rosita to break the news.

"They died at the very same time, and you should have seen the smiles on their faces," said Rosita as though she had been present at the death bed. "They were all wrapped up in each other's arms, and when the sun came up they looked so happy."

"I always knew they would die together," said Principia with a smile on her face that Rosita found more pleasing than alarming. "They have gone to their heavenly rest. I'm so happy for them because at last they have their reward. The Lord will give them the comfort that I was unable to provide."

She sent more flowers to the funeral than anyone on New Bethel had ever seen, but she refused to attend the service. "Let the dead bury the dead," she said to Rosita. "I have so many other things to do."

That week she had planned additional services in celebration of a Youth for Christ Convention, and she was determined not to cancel them. "There will be many who will not understand why I'm not in mourning," she said to the first gathering of young Christians who had come from all over the States. "I have been accused of ruthlessness toward my mother and father, and for a long time I wondered if those accusations were justified, but now I realize that the Lord's hand was on me, and I acted in accordance to His will. Sometimes the Lord gives us difficult decisions to make. I, like Jesus, had to leave my parents behind and be about my Father's business."

After her parents' burial, Principia's ministry began to flourish again. She gave her total energy to her work, and almost everyone she touched claimed to be healed. But it was then Rosita noticed that Principia's mind began drifting further away than ever before. She started daydreaming more often, and had trouble remembering what year it was, what day it was or who was in the room with her.

Every morning it would take her longer to wake up, and she would usually confront Rosita with many questions.

"Is it nineteen sixty-three or nineteen sixty-five?" she once asked. "And is that a sunrise or a sunset?"

Rosita always answered her questions with patience and with an uneasy heart, but never did she show any outward disturbance over Principia's failing mind. "You have slept too long," she would say playfully. "It is not good for one your age to sleep so much."

"Are we still at war," she asked one morning, "or have our prayers been answered?"

"Did I receive any letters today?"

"Did my parents call?"

"Where is Applebee? Tell him to come see me. I saw his bats last night. They were in my bedroom, and at first I thought they were the Holy Spirit. Maybe they were. I want to talk to him about that."

Every morning Rosita would listen to the questions, try to answer them without alarm and then attempt to help Principia wake up faster. "You must get up and walk around more," she would say. "Here, put this cold cloth on your head and you'll feel better." By midafternoon, she would usually be alert, but by the time her service began she would start drifting away. Some days were easier to get through than others, and occasionally, for long periods of time, several days or several weeks, she would remain completely conscious.

It was during one of those periods of total commitment that Corinda Cassy announced she was marrying her business manager, Larry Wayne Johnson, and that they were going into partnership.

"You should have married him many years ago when you started living together," said Rosita. "And besides that he's too young for you. Long ago someone should have said: 'You cannot ring the bell and be in the procession at the same time.'"

"May I remind you that not everyone knows what you know," said Corinda. "The Christian world is not ready to accept our special kind of love. The Lord sanctified our togetherness many years ago when we met on Highway 90. We have been married by the Spirit all this time, and now Larry Wayne has consented to be married by the law; it's my dream come true. My prayers have at last been answered, and my faith is stronger than ever. The ways of the Lord are often misunderstood, but I trust that in time those who have found reasons to criticize me will also find reasons to love me as well."

The wedding took place on the stage of the tabernacle, which was decorated with white lilies and cages of doves whose voices echoed throughout the cavernous space. The minister of the First Baptist Church of Laredo was called in to officiate. Rosita and Sergio served as witnesses and, Corinda Cassy, staring intensely into Larry Wayne's eyes, read the story of Ruth and Naomi:

"Whither thou goest, I will go; and where thou lodgest, I will lodge: thy people shall be my people, and thy God my God . . ."

Everyone who worked for The New Heaven/New Earth Inc. attended the service except for Billy Ray Poindexter and Principia. "Weddings are too sad for me," Principia said, and moments before the service began she telephoned Billy Ray in The Prayer Tower. He told her he was on his way to the wedding and she promised not to delay him more than a few minutes, but she was in the mood to talk about days gone by, and before long she was asking if he still played the fiddle, if he needed a new coloring book and if Saint George was still roosting over the kitchen door. Billy Ray allowed her to ramble on and on about her first year in Judson, and when they hung up, the wedding was already over and the cake, shaped like The Prayer Tower and decorated with pink roses, was about to be cut.

5

Once, almost ten years after Principia had been chosen to serve as an Invincible, Tawnya Louise came to Judson to visit the healer. Tawnya had finished her degree at Hillister Baptist College, had taken her master's at the University of New Mexico and had taught in American schools in Europe and the Middle East. She had become a successful teacher; she loved her students, was happy with her work and had many offers to go to other schools. She traveled every summer, had been around the world a half-dozen times, and each year her list of favorite places grew a little longer. "If my parents want to see me, they can come to Rio this year," she once said. She had gone to Brazil with a man she had met in Cancún, and in their hotel room in São Paulo she turned on the television set and saw Principia Martindale conducting a service. "Goddamn," was all she could say at first. And then, after the shock had worn off, she said to her friend, "You know, I've got to see this to believe it. I knew she was on radio and television, but I never expected her to put on that kind of show."

The next summer she arrived in Judson in a rented car. She was wearing sandals she had bought in Peru, pants she had bought in Italy and a thin cotton shirt she had bargained for in Calcutta. She wore rings on every finger including her thumbs and had on so many bracelets she couldn't remember where she had gotten them or who had given them to her. The only noticeable difference she could perceive in herself was that she no longer wore make-up, as she had no time for it, and her hair, fashionably cut, was much shorter than it had been at the time she was chosen to be an Invincible.

She arrived at the tabernacle just as a flock of white doves flew down from one of the spires and lighted on the edge of the Fountain of Eternity. Inside the sanctuary there were more doves caged in every corner. As she passed one of the cages, the birds began cooing loudly; their voices echoed throughout the tabernacle and sent chills down Tawnya's spine. "I wonder whose idea this was," she said, looking for a place to sit down.

She drew some stares when she walked down the aisle that night, but she had grown accustomed to that. She walked all the way to the front, took a seat on the fourth row and waited impatiently. She was a little nervous, almost wished she had gone somewhere else that day and wasn't at all sure she wanted to see Principia in action, not so close to the stage anyway. So she got up, faced the stares again and moved to the center of the congregation.

Then the house lights dimmed, the curtain went up and the Cowgirls for Christ pranced their way across the stage singing:

"The Son of God is here today.
Hurray! Hurray!
The Son of God is here today.
To stay! To stay!"

They wore white blouses with blue culottes and matching vests, cowboy hats, boots and lariats at their waists. Miss Cassy had designed the costumes herself, and she was very pleased with her efforts. The Cowgirls for Christ had eighteen different costumes—all of them wash 'n' wear—for twenty-five routines that they alternated, and had been asked to perform during half time at many high school and college football games.

After the cowgirls left the stage, another curtain went up, a one-hundred-voice choir arranged in the shape of a cross broke loose with the "Hallelujah Chorus," and before they had finished Principia came sweeping onto the stage in a long dress of purple cotton with lace around the high neckline, cuffs and hem.

She had been standing in the wings waiting for the Spirit to fill her. There were nights when she had to stand there longer than others, but when the Spirit came upon her she was charged with an energy that everyone around her could feel. "That's why I sometimes run onto the stage," she once said. "I'm so caught up in the Spirit I can't stand still anymore."

She was much heavier than Tawnya Louise remembered and her hair was longer, but there was no mistaking who she was. "Principia Martindale will always be the same," said Tawnya. The man sitting next to her smiled and agreed.

"We've been coming here for eight years," he said. "And if the Lord's willing, we'll come here for eight more. There's nothing wrong with us, but we sure do feel better when we leave."

Tawnya smiled and turned her face toward the stage. The choir was silent, the congregation was silent, and after a long pause Principia, who was standing in the spotlight on center stage and had not yet moved, gradually lifted her arms and began singing what had become her theme song: "It took a miracle to hang the world in space ..." The moment she sang the first line the congregation burst into thunderous applause.

"I just don't believe it," said Tawnya, covering her mouth with her ringed fingers. "I haven't thought of that song in years and years, and I used to sing it almost every Sunday."

After the singing, when the congregation was quiet again and Principia was still standing motionless on center stage, her arms outstretched and her eyes uplifted, Tawnya heard someone say: "She lights up the stage as though she's wired for a million volts." Another voice agreed, and someone else said: "She gives the impression that she's on intimate terms with God." Tawnya Louise sank into her seat and tried to relax even though Principia had not yet moved and her arms seemed to be painfully frozen into place.

Finally she spoke, but still she did not change her position. "Let's get lost in God tonight," she said slowly, quietly. The audience burst into applause and cheers. Then she lowered her arms to her side as Corinda Cassy had instructed her to do.

Miss Cassy had directed Principia's every move on stage; she had coached her on dramatic delivery and gestures, and after a while, Principia's arms instinctively went up on some words and down on others. She was, when Tawnya saw her, approaching the height of her fame, and her dramatic presentation had almost reached its full development.

"We promise to give You, dear Lord, all the praise and all the glory for what is about to transpire," she prayed, her hands locked together under her chin. "Pour out Your precious and most holy power upon us for this we pray in Christ's name. Amen."

Then her voice changed. It was no longer soft, but firm, almost harsh in its tones. "Get your mind off Principia Martindale," she shouted. "Get your mind off your faith. Don't think at all, just let your eyes come to rest on God our Father, and in your self-forgetfulness you will be healed."

The atmosphere in the tabernacle was intense with expectation. Tawnya Louise heard someone say he saw electrical sparks. Someone else said the air was filled with a heavenly iridescence and that love abounded whenever Principia was present.

After preaching a short but fiery sermon, Principia's mood changed abruptly again. Once more her voice was soothing, her mind turned inward, her arms outstretched to include everyone in the congregation. "Someone—has—been—healed—of—a—migraine," she said, pronouncing each word slowly, carefully and with pauses between them. "The healing came instantaneously. I rebuke that migraine. I rebuke it in the name of Jesus."

Once again she was silent. Then, holding the microphone for support, she shouted, "It's on the ground floor. Over in the left-hand section, somewhere in the center, diabetes is being healed. Over there on my right, in the first section, somebody else is being healed at this very moment. You did not come here to be made well, but the Lord has cured you anyway. Don't be afraid; that heat in your body is the power of God."

Then she fell into another long silence and Tawnya Louise wondered if she had the power to single her out. "Has she ever touched you?" asked the man in the next seat.

"I don't think so," answered Tawnya.

"Well, if she ever does you'll know it," said the man. "All her power is in her hands. They're as hot as boiling water."

"But they felt cold to me," said a woman sitting in front of them. "It's her stare that's so intense and hot. I can feel it going straight through me."

"Her power is in her smile," argued an elderly man sitting two rows down. "It's so comforting it almost puts me to sleep."

"She came through Splendora on a bus many years ago," said a lean-faced man sitting across the aisle from Tawnya. "I knew there was something special about her then."

It was Brother Anthony Leggett's first trip to Judson, and he was determined not to pass up the opportunity of speaking to

Principia. His heart was heavy and he was sure she could remove the secret burden he had been carrying for years.

"A-growth-has-disappeared," said Principia, breaking her silence. Her eyes were closed, her arms were by her.side and her voice was calm. "There is a man sitting in the back of the tabernacle. Examine your leg. The growth that was there is no longer. God has healed you while you were sitting there. His power is working tonight. His presence is everywhere at once. Somebody is being touched at this moment, even as I speak. Someone has received the sense of smell. It left you years ago and now it's back. It happened suddenly, just like that." She clapped her hands and extended her arms. "A cataract is melting in the balcony, a tumor is regressing on the main floor, sinuses are being cleared, broken bones are being mended. The lame shall walk, the blind shall see and the deaf shall also be made well, for—Praise God!—there is such power here today. Feel it. Feel it with every inch of your being."

After a brief pause she smiled and a long sigh rippled through the congregation. Hundreds of people had been waiting for that smile and wanting to breathe in the presence of it if only for a few moments. It had been said that Principia's smile alone could heal and that those who came into direct contact with it would never be the same again.

"I'm so happy tonight," she said, still speaking quietly and holding the smile that had helped to make her famous. "I'm so happy because someone is feeling the presence of God for the very first time. You were in the state penitentiary over in Huntsville for many years. This morning you were released on good behavior and tonight you are here accepting Christ as your personal savior, and you're doing it even as I am speaking. Praise be unto the Lord, for this morning you were a convict and this evening you're a convert. Only God can do this!"

Somewhere in the back of the tabernacle a man in his thirties came forward. His complexion was pasty white, his face was drawn and his eyes were burning with the fervor of his commitment. He took Principia by the hand and told her she was a little mixed up. "I was released from the pen two weeks ago," he said. "But you were right about one thing. Tonight I did accept Jesus, and I want the whole world to know it too."

Principia reached out to embrace the man, but before she touched him he fell backward to the floor as though something invisible had struck him. "That's the Lord's hand," said Principia. "I had nothing to do with it. You've been touched by God." She felt the palms of her hands burning. They were so sensitive she could hardly touch them. Then she felt someone tugging at her sleeve. She turned around and there were two women with their arms around each other. Principia touched them both at the same time, and they collapsed instantly. "God is everywhere!" she said. Then others left their seats and came forward to be touched by the woman they had watched on television, had heard over The Radio Church of God and had read about in magazines, newspapers and church bulletins. Some of the people who were touched collapsed at once, some fell with their backs rigid, others doubled over and sank to the floor. The ushers caught them, helped revive them and gave them chairs to sit on.

"Someone is being healed of fallen arches," said Principia, lifting her arms above her head. "I see a tumor the size of a pear dissolving away. Someone is being healed of alcoholism at this very moment. Come forward and claim your miracles. There is someone with spine trouble. Come forward and walk; I know you can, and you know it too. In the name of Jesus Christ of Nazareth, be thou made every whit whole."

People streamed down the aisles, took Principia by the hand and claimed their miracles. Some of them collapsed before she ever touched them, others said they left the stage feeling no different than before and one woman testified that she was healed of a stiff neck on the tabernacle steps one hour before she saw the healer. Tawnya Louise had the urge to go forward and take Principia's hand also. She wanted to know if she too would fall under whatever power might be present, but just as she was about to stand the man across from her got up and stood in the aisle a long time before he made his way slowly to the front. Tawnya watched him squeeze his coattail with both hands while walking toward the stage. "I'd be scared too," she said. "I'm better off sitting right here."

Brother Anthony Leggett took Principia by the hand and spoke to her of their first meeting, but she didn't remember him. "It was a long time ago," he said, trying to remember the speech he had rehearsed. "At the time you promised to pray for me, and now I want you to pray for me again. A beautiful woman is in love with me, but it's impossible for me to return her devotion. My desire . . ." He withdrew his hand and began twisting the class ring around his finger. "My desire runs in the opposite direction. I hope you understand what I'm trying to say. I've always had this problem, and now I want you to heal me."

"Because the spirit is stronger than the flesh, your problem, whatever it is, does not exist," said Principia. "Go home and claim your bride. You're already healed and don't know it. She will convince you of this, not me."

Feeling better about himself, Brother Leggett left the stage and returned to his seat. Then Principia remembered who he was and called after him to come back, but it was already too late. She was surrounded by her admirers and the Spirit was leaving her rapidly. Brother Leggett started down the aisle again, but when he reached the stage, Principia was running into the wings and the curtain was closing.

"All of a sudden I was just standing there on the stage," she said as though it had never happened before. Rosita embraced her. "I hate that part most of all. All of a sudden I was just standing there. I don't think I'll ever get used to that feeling of being so alone and so scared. I can't ever remember getting there. I can't even remember what I've said."

While Principia wept, Tawnya Louise slipped backstage. One of the guards tried to stop her, but she turned to him and said, "You don't understand. My aunt was healed tonight. She's still on stage somewhere and I've got to find her." Sergio and three other men had surrounded Principia and were trying to usher her away when Tawnya caught up with them. "I've got to talk to her," she said. "We used to go to school together. We were chosen to be Invincibles one summer."

Principia, exhausted, leaning on the arms of two men, stopped when she heard the familiar voice, brushed hair and tears from her eyes and looked at the blurry figure standing before her. At first she thought it was Sissy Cisneros. "Oh, I've thought of you so many times," said Principia. "I still have that pink carryall you gave me years ago." Then Tawnya stepped closer and Principia realized she was mistaken. "Tawnya Louise Baker," she said.

"You look so different. I can sense that you are different too."

She invited Tawnya to her apartment, but Corinda Cassy-Johnson refused to allow the visit until Rosita pleaded with her, and then, curious to know what the two would have to say to each other, Corinda agreed to give them thirty minutes together while she sat within hearing range in the next room.

Principia, propped up with pillows, sat in the middle of her bed and stared across her purple comforter at Tawnya, who was sitting in an overstuffed chair next to a table piled high with books. It was hard for Tawnya to believe they were the same age because Principia's face was scarred by deep wrinkles, and her hair, almost covering the pillows, was streaked with golden gray, which seemed to begin at her widow's peak and then fan out in long, thin ribbons.

After a brief summary of her last ten years, Tawnya confessed that she was still not much of a believer. "In fact," she said, "I don't believe at all."

"The mere fact that you find it necessary to look me up and tell me that you are not a believer is a clear sign to me that you do believe but just don't want to admit it right now," said Principia. "As for myself, I still believe deeply, but there are times when I find it hard to believe in what I'm doing because I'm not doing anything at all except surrendering completely and allowing the Holy Spirit to use me for the glory of our Heavenly Father."

"Are you ever frightened by all this?" asked Tawnya Louise. In the next room Corinda Cassy-Johnson sat close to the open door and listened to every word.

"Sometimes," answered Principia. "Just before I go under the power, I feel my hands getting so hot I have to mentally block out the pain. That's when I feel Principia Martindale leaving and the Holy Spirit entering and taking over. Sometimes that's very frightening because it's like going to sleep and knowing all the time that I'm not really going to be sleeping, that I'm going to be doing and saying things that later on I might not be able to remember. Then there have been times when I'm not completely under the power and I begin to feel as though I'm up high somewhere looking on rather than participating in the service. I can see myself and hear myself and I'm shocked by the things I say. That's sometimes frightening too, but my greatest fear is that the

Holy Spirit will leave me for good and I'll be completely lost, the way I am just after a service. There isn't a day that goes by that I don't pray, 'Father, you can have my last dime, but please please, take not Thy Holy Spirit from me.' My only wish is that the Lord will take me before this anointing lifts."

"There were so many people who were not healed," said Tawnya. "If you could have only seen their faces, their disappointment as they tried to walk and couldn't. Has it ever occurred to you that you might be doing more harm than good?"

"At no time is it my responsibility, Tawnya Louise," said Principia. Her voice became firm, and Tawnya could see the anger boiling to the surface, could almost feel it penetrating the room. "It is not at all my responsibility, but"—she regained her composure—"I am human. Every night I watch the congregation leave and you'll never know how I hurt on the inside when I see those who came in wheelchairs being pushed out of the tabernacle. You'll never know the ache, the feeling I feel when someone has come here expecting so much and ends up receiving so little, or the uncertainty that is mine when someone writes and says: 'I was not healed after all. Do you still have my crutches? I need them so badly. Do you still have my wheelchair? Where are my braces; my eyeglasses? Is that prayer I wrote still tacked to the wall? If so rip it down because I stopped believing long ago.'

"One letter like that can almost destroy my belief in all the good that might have occurred here, but I don't receive such letters anymore. They came all at once, and then they stopped. I don't know why, and I don't ask why because the answers I leave with God. I don't have His perfect wisdom and perfect knowledge, but even as the wheelchairs are being pushed out, I often see a happiness that might not have been there before, and if through the lifting up of Jesus, if in telling how good the Lord truly is, I can give hope, then I'd rather not be known as Principia Martindale, the healer, but Principia Martindale, the woman who gives hope, the woman who puts windows where there were no windows, the woman who puts doors where there were no doors, the woman who creates faith where there was no faith."

"You make me want to believe very badly," said Tawnya. "But I want to believe more for you than for me, and I don't think that's the way it should be."

"Just as long as you believe," said Principia. "That's all that counts. Through my studies and meditations I have come to realize that even an atheist is a believer and oftentimes a devout believer who is simply angry with God and therefore refuses to acknowledge His presence in the world."

"You're only fooling yourself," said Tawnya. "But if it makes you happy, I guess that's all that's important."

"I have never been as concerned with happiness as you have," said Principia. She stared directly into Tawnya's face.

Tawnya averted her eyes, staring at a book on the side table next to her chair. It was a first edition of *Faith in the Modern World*. She picked it up and thumbed through it at random, until her eyes fell upon an underlined paragraph. Quickly she read it, but it was not her voice she heard, not the voice of Edgar Young Mullins, the author, but of Principia Martindale: "If Christianity should die, then what? Did you ever consider the dreadful alternative? If Christianity should die, man's intellect would be launched on as endless a sea of speculation as before Christ came . . . Christianity cannot die, for Christ is alive forever. He lives in the hearts of His followers, His reign increases from year to year, His kingdom is spreading from sea to sea."

Tawnya turned through the book and found many paragraphs, underlined, starred, circled as if, she thought, out of some terrible desperation, out of some terrible need to extract every last ounce of meaning from each word. For the first time Tawnya realized how hard Principia had worked to maintain her faith, and she wondered if it was actually faith that was being kept alive. "What is it that keeps Jesus a living, breathing person to you?" she asked. "I had God in my home twenty-four hours a day. I was a preacher's kid, remember, yet I only believed with half a heart."

"But you had social involvements that took you outside the religious community," said Principia. "You had more temptations than I had, and you always fell prey to animal magnetism. You divided your love between God and man, and I did not. Then I started seeing the hand of God at work every day. In my presence I have seen eczema disappear; I have seen cripples get up and walk; I have seen tumors dissolve and broken families healed by the love of God. These things keep Jesus alive for me. I have seen

His miracles and I believe in them all. I have given my life to God, and the miracles that have happened here are the fruit of our union."

Tawnya's mind flashed on a thousand thoughts; some of them came so fast she could not begin to hold them before her, but others lingered for a few moments. "There was a hospital fire in London," she said. "I read about it in *The Times*. The cripples got up and walked to safety, then they collapsed and couldn't move. In Tokyo, I saw a mother lift a car off her trapped child. I asked myself then, where did she get the strength to do that? In Turkey an old man rubbed a cold wet stone on my forehead and my headache vanished. Then there was a sixth-grader in my class in Athens. He could barely read so I went out of my way to make him feel loved and accepted, and before the semester was over he was reading on the same level as his classmates. And what about those patients who are asked to draw a picture of what they think their cancer looks like; with each succeeding picture they draw the cancer smaller and smaller until it goes away. It vanishes. What's the difference between all these things and what you're doing?"

"Nothing at all," said Principia. "The Lord healed those cripples even if it was for only a few moments, and when their faith is stronger it is possible that He will heal them for life. The Lord gave that woman the strength to save her child, and the Lord working through you healed that student. You may not have been aware of it, but it's true. God has His hands in everything good that happens to any of us. The Devil causes all the bad when we are foolish enough to allow him to intervene."

"You've said enough," said Corinda. She swept into the room, announced that their half-hour was over and then stood at the open door while Tawnya, relieved to be saying goodby, shook Principia's hand. The hand was cold, and Tawnya, feeling as though she had touched a living corpse, broke away quickly, left the apartment without another word and made her exit through the back door of the tabernacle. "I won't ever have to come back here again," she said, lighting a cigarette. "Some people come here to get well, but I feel like I'd be sick for the rest of my life if I stayed one more minute."

 6

After Tawnya left the tabernacle Principia fell asleep in the purple gown she had worn to the service that night. She dreamed of New Bethel, Hillister Baptist College and the two semesters she had lived in Blankenship Hall. She dreamed she was living in Tawnya's room and Tawnya was living in hers. It was Tawnya who was calling the roll during a late-night assembly and Lively Hathaway who was climbing in through the second-floor window without snagging her hose.

The next morning Rosita came into Principia's bedroom just before dawn and opened the curtains covering the east windows. "Don't do that," said Principia when she heard the curtains opening. "I don't want that Martindale girl to see me."

"You are dreaming again," said Rosita. "The sun will help you wake up."

"It's still nineteen fifty-seven, isn't it?" said Principia as she watched the sunlight pour into her bedroom.

"No," said Rosita. "We're in nineteen sixty-six now, and you are very famous."

But Principia had trouble waking up that day, and many days thereafter. "She's half awake and half asleep and she talks to herself all the time," Rosita said to Sergio one tired Thursday evening. "She starts out every day like a goose in a new world."

At night Principia would dream long conversations with biblical figures, and on waking she would find them still sitting before her. They never appeared outside her bedroom, but when she needed spiritual companionship, she would retreat to her bed and spend the day or night in deep conversation. Usually she needed to go to sleep and wake up again for them to be there, but there were times when she would say: "Who's here today?" And they would appear before her.

She spent hours discussing the Ten Commandments with Moses and the church at Antioch with Paul. She frequently asked John the Baptist what he thought of Edgar Young Mullins and never got tired of hearing that they were old friends. With Saint John the Divine she discussed the Book of Revelation, and with Deborah she spoke of the similarity of their lives. But her most cherished visits were with the parents of Jesus, and she insisted on seeing them at least three times a week. At length and many times over she sympathized with their loneliness when their son left home to do His Father's work, and on occasions she would attempt to comfort them by inviting the Twelve Apostles into her bedroom to tell, each in his own words, how he met the Son of God and what great miracles He had performed.

There were days when Principia would call Rosita into the bedroom and introduce her to the biblical figures sitting there. Rosita would greet them personally, at times go through the motions of shaking hands with Matthew, Luke, John or Joseph in his coat of many colors, and then she would leave the room quickly and close the door behind her.

"She's going off further and further," Rosita said to Sergio one evening after they were in bed. "Now she's talking to Lazarus and he's telling her what it's like to die."

Principia grew to love and respect the prophet Elijah, who was fed by the ravens in the wilderness; she found the words of Job strangely comforting, but it was Lazarus who became her closest companion. He talked to her at length about death, and she took his words into her miracle services, told her followers that according to her friend Lazarus death was a pure white light inside which all the mysteries of creation were revealed.

It was then that Principia brought a new confidence to the miracle services. She no longer needed to wait in the wings for the Spirit to move her because she lived *within* the Spirit both day and night and was able to surrender more of herself to that power she felt around and inside her. Often she would leave the stage and run into the congregation to pray for someone who could not move, to touch someone on the forehead or to greet old friends who happened to be visiting.

"I don't care if you haven't stood up in a hundred years," she shouted one November evening. "Tonight you will stand. Tonight you will walk, and tonight you will thank God for healing you." Without realizing it, many of her followers forgot their afflictions and sprang to their feet. Some of them were forced to sit back down quickly, but others walked down the aisle and claimed their miracles.

"The Lord is good," said Principia. "There have been thousands of healings in this tabernacle, and there will be many thousands more."

Then she heard a small voice. "We're waiting for you now. We're in your bedroom. We want you to come talk to us." Without a closing prayer, without giving the congregation any warning, she rushed from the stage—to some it was as though she had disappeared—and hurried into her apartment, where she greeted her visitors for the night, among them Saul who became Paul, Gabriel the Archangel with wings of silver and purple and the giant Goliath, whom she had grown to love dearly because he reminded her of an overgrown baby, gentle, clumsy, misunderstood. All he wanted to do was sit behind the door and draw coloring-book pictures, and one day she promised to teach him the art of chalk talk.

"She's happier than she's ever been," said Corinda to her husband. "She's getting better at this miracle business too. She doesn't get so discouraged anymore either, so I think it's high time we stepped up our televising."

"Three programs a week now?" asked Larry Wayne, and Corinda answered: "I think four is more like it, don't you?"

Two months later they had already entered their new programming schedule, and, with the additional television and radio coverage as well as word of mouth and an occasional story in a newspaper or magazine, Principia's fame began spreading the world over. In Mexico they compared her to Teresita Urrea, La Santa de Cabora, who was said to have had incredible healing powers, and in France she was jokingly referred to as a "one-woman Lourdes." A national magazine said she healed by scaring the beJesus out of everybody, and the *Christian Weekly* called her a living saint, the embodiment of the love of God.

A Jungian analyst who visited Judson for a day returned to Switzerland and wrote a paper on the shadow Principia Martindale never found. "If she knew anything about it," he wrote, "she would never be able to heal."

Applebee didn't actually read the articles written about her, but he scanned them quickly, allowing his eyes to fall at random upon words and phrases. He kept telling himself he had no business trying to keep up with the happenings in Judson, yet he skimmed through every article he saw. But it was still impossible for him to watch Principia on television, and it was becoming more and more difficult for him to look at panorama shots of what Judson had become: parking lots, apartments and hotels, prayer gardens and more prayer gardens, shops and office buildings and fountains everywhere you looked.

"I don't think I could ever get used to all that," he said, wondering how Rosita was getting along. Sergio, he knew, could adapt to anything, but he wasn't sure about Rosita. There were days he couldn't get her off his mind.

She would have said, if she had been able to find him, that she had made it the best way she could, only because she did not want to abandon Principia Martindale to God knows what and because she could not go off and leave her parents' graves. For the first time she was beginning to question the proverb she had learned from her mother: "What did not happen in my year did not harm me."

"Somehow I don't think this is true anymore," she said. "There are too many days that are too hard to live through."

There were days when her mind felt as though it were turned wrong-side-out, days when she would work so long her vision would blur, and when gazing over the plaza of glittering bricks she would remember the cottonwood that had once stood where the Fountain of Eternity bubbled both day and night. There were days when she could not control her mind, and once, in August, when she was tired from a hard afternoon of work, she was on her way to her parents' graves when, out of the corner of her eye, she looked across the plaza and there was the cottonwood growing up out of the sand, there was Brother Ravenhill's silver bus and there was Principia Martindale, a child of sixteen, looking bewildered and frightened. God had sent her into the wilderness to preach, and, in spite of her shaking knees and quivering heart, she was determined to obey. Rosita blinked until the plaza returned to the golden bricks and bubbling fountain, but thereafter on bright days, and when she was very very tired, she could gaze through the spray of water, and while the sun threw rainbows at a certain angle, she could see the cottonwood, the church and the fluttering bats, the image of Jesus on the screen door and everything else that Judson had been. Once she gazed into the fountain and thought she saw L. J. Judson himself, but after blinking many times she realized it was only the heat and the reflection of Corinda's husband who, dressed in a pale suit, was staring into the water with a concerned look on his face.

"There is an old saying," said Rosita, speaking through the mist to Larry Wayne. "Even though the monkey wears silk, it is still a monkey."

"What are you trying to say?" he asked.

"That's for you to decide," Rosita replied. Then she walked away making a mental list of all the things she had to do.

While Corinda and Larry Wayne took care of the business end of running a modern-day shrine, Rosita kept Principia's apartment spotlessly clean and supervised the kitchen for the entire tabernacle family, which had grown into a corporation of over two hundred workers and countless volunteers. The cafeteria in the basement of the tabernacle was open seven days a week, three times a day, but according to Rosita the food was not what it could be. She always believed that anything cooked in small portions was better, so every day she continued to prepare special meals for Sergio and Principia. According to Sergio, Rosita made the best tamales, the best enchiladas, refried beans and chili he had ever eaten, and her sopaipillas were the best in the world, according to Principia, who became so overweight that she could hardly walk across the stage.

Three times in one week she fell while walking to the microphone, and each time it took four members of the one-hundred-voice choir to lift her to her feet again. "We can't let this happen every night," said Larry Wayne. "It ruins the mood of the service to see her all sprawled out on the stage." He solved the problem by hiring a carpenter to build a litter and advertising for six strong men to carry Principia into the spotlight.

By then her hair had grown below her knees and her skin had become so sensitive she could only wear pure silk and fine cottons next to her body. Her face, no longer heart-shaped, had become full and round. The wrinkles around her eyes and forehead had disappeared and her complexion had the smoothness of a small child's. There were days when she could hardly do anything for herself, so Rosita was always on hand to feed her, clothe her, bathe her and in the middle of the night when Principia wanted to roll over in her bed Rosita was there to call the strong men to move the healer from one side to the other.

Her apartment was kept at a steady sixty degrees the year round, much too cold for Rosita, but if it was any warmer Principia was prone to smothering attacks and if any colder she was susceptible to pneumonia. Onstage she had three people fanning her at all times, and even then she often carried a small battery-operated fan that she could hold in her hand and cool her face.

From then on her energy was high, her services were more consistent and she looked forward to being with her Earth People during the first part of the evening and her Bible People during the later hours of the night. There for a while Deborah came regularly, and then Ruth and Naomi and then Goliath began visiting her before as well as after the miracle services. He had long red hair, blue eyes and the biggest hands she had ever seen. She spent long hours conversing with him, trying to understand him better, and came to the conclusion that he was a true believer after all. "Oh, if only I had realized this about you years ago," she said. "I don't know why I was so blind. I don't know why I have to realize things too late."

7

For the rest of her life, Principia spent most of her time in bed talking to the array of biblical figures who visited her each day. Winkie Ravenhill continued to make an occasional appearance as well, and whenever she did Principia would always call Rosita in to say hello. "You would not believe what is going on," Rosita said to Sergio early one morning before he had gotten out of bed. "Principia, she is talking to Winkie Ravenhill, Aunt Wilda and Jesus at the same time. She made me speak to them too, so I did. Sometimes I don't know who is real anymore, so all day long I do nothing but pinch myself to see if it hurts. Look, I have so many bruises."

Rosita never knew what to expect next; still she somehow managed to organize her life in a day-to-day routine that she followed with little variation up until Principia's thirtieth birthday, August 27, 1971, when a grand ceremony was planned in her honor. "Now everything will be turned upside-down again," said Rosita. "Why do we have to have such a big party? To tell you the truth, I don't think Principia will know what the fuss is all about."

The celebration was to begin at seven o'clock in the tabernacle. Brother Ravenhill and Winkie had ordered their tickets early and were looking forward to being in the congregation for the first time in years. Since being thrown out of Judson they had established the First Church of Yesterday, Today and Tomorrow in a storefront in downtown San Antonio. They had a membership of fifty-five anointed Christians, and they brought them all to

Principia's birthday celebration. At 6:30 Ravenhill parked the silver bus on the outskirts of Judson. At 6:45 they walked into town.
And at 6:59 they rushed into the tabernacle just as the lights were
dimming. Winkie and Ravenhill, both with binoculars slung
around their necks, sat in the middle of the tenth row and waited
eagerly to catch the first glimpse of the woman who had touched
their hearts more than anyone they had ever known.

After the Cowgirls for Christ performed a marching routine
to "Every Day with Jesus is Sweeter than the Day Before," a fif-
ty-pound cake was rolled out on the stage, and Principia, sitting
on her litter, was carried out behind it.

It was 7:15.

With the help of the strong men Principia was able to sit in a
gilded chair that had been made especially for her, and while the
congregation and the choir, which was shaped like a capital P,
joined in singing "Happy Birthday," Principia gazed over the
crowd of people sitting before her, but she was unable to see any
of them. A blinding spotlight was shining in her eyes, and she
could not see beyond the stage. The light was stronger than usual,
and after the singing she asked to have it dimmed. The techni-
cians dimmed the spotlight, and again she said it was too bright.
Again they dimmed the light, and again Principia said it was
keeping her from seeing her beautiful people. Finally they cut the
light altogether, and to the astonishment of everyone there Principia said it was still far too bright. The house lights came on, the
stage lights were turned off and still she complained that the spotlight was shining in her eyes and becoming stronger by the minute. Someone told her that the lights had been turned completely
off, and it was then she realized that it was no spotlight after all.

"Lord, it's my time, isn't it?" she asked. Then with great effort, she stood up and sang:

> "Jesus paid it all,
> All to him I owe,
> Sin hath left a crimson stain,
> He washed it white as snow . . ."

While she sang, she swayed back and forth and then began to
move with such ease and grace it was as though she were floating
across the stage. Although the spotlights were still off, many peo-

ple in the congregation said that the space around her was so brightly lit that at times—even though she was wearing a scarlet gown—she seemed to disappear into the glaring light. She twirled around gracefully, rejoicing in her newfound happiness and in her freedom of movement, for she had not walked more than twenty steps at any given time over the past year, and everyone who made up the tabernacle family was amazed to see that she could move despite her enormous size and that she appeared to be on the verge of flying away.

"As God is my witness," said Winkie, peering through her binoculars, "Principia's feet aren't even touching the floor."

"I agree with your every word," said her husband, bringing Principia into focus. "She's defying the law of gravity at this moment."

Then Principia stopped singing, stopped dancing as well, and watched her life pass rapidly before her. The people she had known and loved were all there parading across the stage. First she saw her parents and then Lively Hathaway, Aunt Wilda, Dr. Truly, Miss Cassy, Tawnya, Billy Ray, Winkie, Rosita; there were so many she could not name them as they passed, but the image of Applebee lingered longer than the others, and when she saw him she began struggling for a deeper breath. "Don't leave me," she said, but he disappeared into the light. "Come back, Applebee," she pleaded over and over, but she could not speak with clarity and her words bore no meaning for anyone except herself and Winkie Ravenhill.

"She's been blessed with the full anointing of the Holy Spirit at last," shouted Winkie when she heard Principia trying to speak. Winkie stood up in the congregation, threw her head back and shouted to the glory of God: "Cino-me-ooo, Lord Jesus! We thank You, our Savior, for giving our Principia the greatest birthday gift of all, the gift of tongues."

"What's that idiot doing out there," said Corinda. She and Rosita were standing in the wings and peeping through the curtain.

"No one is out there," Rosita joked. "You are just imagining things."

"I most certainly am not," said Corinda. "So stop trying to convince me that I'm losing my reasoning."

"Cino-me-ooo," cried Brother Ravenhill, staring at Principia through his binoculars. "She still looks the same as she did years ago, only she's twice as big."

"Arrest those two fools out there," commanded Corinda. "They're sitting in the middle of the tenth row. And I want them thrown out."

The strong men went into the audience, pulled Winkie and Ravenhill from their seats and tried to peacefully escort them up the aisle. "Don't you lay one hand on me," shouted Winkie, twirling her field glasses around her head. "I hope to Jesus I brain one of you, if not all of you."

"You have no business throwing us out," said Ravenhill. "We are God's chosen."

"Well, God just chose us to choose you to leave," said one of the strong men. He shouldered Winkie and ran with her up the aisle. "Osheee-ma-ha-ya-ma-ha," she cried. "Vengeance is mine, saith the Lord."

"Cino-me-ooo," shouted Ravenhill as he was carried out behind her.

It was 7:41.

When Principia heard Winkie and Ravenhill speaking in tongues, she danced her way to center stage to find her two friends, but all she could see was the blinding light that separated her from everyone else. Lazarus said it would be like this, she wanted to say, but no words would come out. She could feel her legs giving way and her heart trembling. Then, like those she had touched on the forehead, she crumpled up like an empty bag, and while listening to faraway chimes, harps and the voices of angels calling her name, she was taken up in the Spirit for the last time.

She died there, quickly and without pain, and when she closed her eyes for the last time there were members of the tabernacle family as well as the congregation, who knew it instantly because they said the tabernacle was not as brightly lit as it had been and the white doves suddenly sat motionless in their cages and did not make a sound.

It was 7:45.

A few hundred miles away in downtown Fort Worth, Johnnie Chapman, who had worked late that day, came through the back door of the Golden Rule Pawnshop. Applebee was digging for a crayon in his blue plaid book satchel and at first didn't see her standing there. When he looked up a candle moth as big as a sparrow followed Johnnie into the back room. It made one circle around the naked light bulb and left through the back door, which Johnnie held open.

"I hate to see anything like that trapped," she said.

"What was it, a bat?" asked Applebee. "Looked like one."

"Naw," said Johnnie, "just a bug of some kind."

At 8:00 Corinda Cassy was still searching for a heartbeat. "She can't do this to me, not now," she cried. "We're just getting started. There's so much more that I want to do, and without her it's impossible."

Five medical doctors were in the congregation that night, and all five said death had come instantly, but Corinda refused to believe them. "It's no use," her husband said, leading her from the stage and through the crowd that was still in the tabernacle. The white doves began cooing loudly when they passed them. Corinda broke away from Larry Wayne's arm, kicked the nearest cage and the birds escaped, flew in circles throughout the tabernacle and came to rest on the balcony railing. "I hate everything that reminds me of her," she screamed as she looked up at the doves preening themselves.

"Don't worry," said Larry Wayne as he led her into the plaza. "It's not over yet."

"I don't like the way you say that," she said, again almost pulling away from him. "You make me think you know something that I don't."

"I do," answered her husband. "I've had plans for Judson for a long time now, and tonight I've come to many conclusions."

It was 8:14.

In Fort Worth Applebee was painting "Rapture's Heights II" on the back wall of his room, and Johnnie Chapman was catching the bus back to the south side of town. On the outskirts of Judson Winkie and Ravenhill were standing on the silver bus trying to determine what all the commotion was about. The telephone operators were vacating The Prayer Tower and rushing to the tabernacle. The hotel workers were doing the same, but Corinda and Larry Wayne were getting into an elevator that would take them all the way to the observation deck, a small walkway that circled the prayer station. It was enclosed by a four-foot railing of steel and reflective glass. There were three coin-operated telescopes, a candy machine, a water fountain and indoor-outdoor carpet on the floor.

"Oh I just wish these spyglasses were stronger," said Winkie, trying to bring the tower into focus. "The Lord is trying to tell me that something's about to happen, and I just can't get ready fast enough."

"Just keep watching," said Brother Ravenhill, "and if something does happen one of us is bound to see it."

On the tower, Corinda took her husband by the hand and they looked down on the city she claimed to have created: the hotel, the fountains, the prayer gardens, the glistening streets, the tabernacle and the golden avenue leading up to it.

"There are many ways you can use this place without Principia Martindale," he said. "It could be a resort, a convention center, or a model city. With all the trees and gardens you've planted it's already beginning to remind me of a new Eden. All you've got to do now is remove the religion and you've got something entirely different, something that could be more profitable as well. We've got facilities for housing ten thousand people already, and in a few years we can have a city that spreads all the way to the Rio Grande."

"Oh, I've dreamed of such a city," said Corinda, drying her eyes. "I've always believed that the two of us together could do great things."

"We can and already have," said her husband. "Before I met you I was nothing but a poor little farm boy from the sticks of Alabama. I've listened to everything that you've had to say and now you need to listen to me. I'm going to help you forget about Principia Martindale. After tonight you won't give a damn about her. You won't need her. I won't need her, and Judson won't need her anymore either."

"I never really believed in her anyway," said his wife. "But I knew that a lot of people could and would, and that's all that mattered to me. I didn't let myself admit it for a long time, but now I know that it's true. I tried to believe the way she did; I tried to even before I met her because I thought I would be happier and more successful—everyone said I would be—but it didn't work. You'd have to be an idiot to have her kind of faith."

"Either an idiot or a saint, and I'm neither one," he said, smiling tenderly into her eyes.

"Precious," she said, "how I love to hear your words. You're forty-one years old now, and at last you're beginning to talk like a man. I don't know what I'd do without you because you're the only one who's ever understood what I'm all about. I don't want Judson to be another one of my unsuccessful careers, but I'm afraid it's going to be. I'm so confused, you've always been right about that, but it's only because I want so many things at once. I want more than I know I can ever have."

"Have you ever stopped to think that I might want even more?" he asked. "I'm never satisfied either. I got tired of being your chaffeur, your escort, and your manager. I'm going to get tired of being your business partner too."

"Just as long as you never get tired of being my husband," she said.

"I don't think that will happen," he replied in a slow, carefully spoken cadence. Then he lifted her to the railing, sat her down on the ledge, embraced her, kissed her on the lips and said, "Corinda, I always knew this day would come, but I didn't know when."

"So did I, my darling," she said, giving herself to his embrace. "My whole life has been leading up to this."

"You're right for once," he said and kissed her again. She leaned her head on his shoulder, wrapped her arms around him, and when he felt her body relaxing he gave her the slightest push. That was all it took. He stepped backward quickly, and it was over. "Now I can run this damn town the way it ought to be," he said. "I've waited a long time for this." He looked down at her body. She was lying on her back, her face covered with her cowboy hat, one arm twisted behind her, and off to one side, not more than five feet away, a tarantula, crossing the golden plaza, stopped, looked at her and then kept on going as though nothing had happened.

Epilogue

Principia was taken back to New Bethel and buried between her parents. The funeral was held in the church where she had been baptized, and the sermon was delivered by Dr. Norman Truly, her retired Bible professor. The casket, specially made, was lined in purple. Her dress was white, but her hair, billowing over the edge of the coffin, covered the burial garment, Principia's arms and much of her face until the long curls were tamed down with barrettes of white roses.

An estimated eight thousand people crowded around the church, and even more waited in the cemetery, where Billy Ray Poindexter prayed aloud and at great length at the graveside service. The funeral was reported in major newspapers across the United States, but Corinda Cassy's burial was not publicized. In a press conference on the steps of the tabernacle, Larry Wayne told the reporters his wife had been buried according to her wishes, in an unmarked grave. "I put her in a simple pine box," he told the reporters, "and I buried her myself. I am the only one who knows where she's resting."

Rosita, standing over to one side and listening, turned to her husband and said, "If she's not resting in Hell I don't know where she is."

"The earth is fresh over by the rock garden," said Sergio.

"That's too close to my mother and father," replied Rosita. Sergio had never seen his wife's face wrinkle up so quickly.

Late that night, after the reporters had left and after Sergio was sleeping, Rosita sat up in bed and stared at the screen door propped up against the bedroom wall. A candle burning behind the door threw the shadow of Jesus across the room and onto the small cedar chest that had once belonged to Señora Hernandez. "I know what I have to do now," said Rosita in a solemn whisper that made her cold all over.

She slipped out of bed and wandered through the tabernacle to the maintenance rooms where she rummaged around until she found a short-handled shovel. Then she returned to the apartment, emptied the cedar chest of all the blankets and sweaters, put the shovel in it and pushed the chest out of the bedroom, through the front door and down the long white corridor toward the exit sign. Once outside she found a length of water hose on the ground, tied it around the chest and pulled it around the south side of the tabernacle, across the golden plaza and into the shadows of the rock garden.

"Now I will try to think about something else." she said, opening up the chest and taking out the shovel. The ground was very hard, and it took her a long time to break the surface, but she worked diligently through the night, and shortly before dawn, when the sky was streaked with violet rays, she uncovered the remains of her parent's coffins. "I must remove every bone," she said. "They are all precious."

The bones felt warm to Rosita. They felt as though they still had life in them. She could almost feel a heartbeat in her father's skull, and the bones that were her mother's hands were strangely comforting to hold. "I must not linger," she said. "Time is running out."

After she had transferred her parents' skeletons into the cedar chest, she filled in the hole, formed two gravelike mounds of earth, and on them she planted prickly pear. "This way," she said, "no one will be too suspicious."

It was already light when she dragged the cedar chest back across the plaza and into her bedroom, but Sergio was not yet up. By midmorning Rosita had packed and was ready to go. "Wake up," she said, shaking her husband. "Rubendella needs us to be in Los Angeles. It's time we gave her more help. We're going to take some clothes but not many, because we have to have what's inside that old cedar chest, and we have to have the screen door too. I have wrapped it up in two blankets. They had better let us on the bus with it all. If they won't we'll have to carry it on our backs."

Larry Wayne, dressed in a white suit, drove them to the bus station in Carrizo Springs. They had nothing to say along the way, but at the station Larry Wayne offered to wait with them until the bus arrived. "We can wait all by ourselves," said Rosita. And they did.

When the bus arrived Rosita found a good place for the screen door in the baggage compartment. She wrote Rubendella's name and address on the cedar chest, watched it being loaded and then followed Sergio into the bus. "There's no reason to ever come back here again," she said as they left the town. "We will have a new life now."

Larry Wayne left the bus station and drove back to Judson during the heat of the day. The hotel had been closed for a week. The Prayer Tower staff had been dismissed, and the Cowgirls for Christ had been enrolled in a Baptist Academy near Austin. No one was in Judson that day, not a secretary, not a construction worker and not a visitor. Larry Wayne parked his truck on the plaza and walked over to The Tabernacle in the Sky. "I got a lot of plans for this place," he said, looking up at the three spires. While he stood there, he was unaware of the silver bus that had stopped behind him. He heard someone call his name and turned around. It was Winkie Ravenhill. "We've been waiting and waiting for you to come back," she said. She was standing in the door of the bus; her husband was kneeling on the ground in front of her, and his hands were folded over his chest.

"Corinda was a good woman, and the best friend I ever had until she got mixed up with you," said Ravenhill. "We watched the two of you up there on the tower. We know what we saw, and we know what really happened." Then he commenced praying: "O Lord, protect us. Your law is not always the law of the land, and the law of the land is not always Yours."

"Now I've got something to say," said Winkie. "I've been awake for three nights in a row, Mister. And I just got through praying nonstop for eleven hours. I told the good Lord I didn't want to do what he asked me to do, but he just kept on and kept on asking me, so I got no choice, do I." She took a pistol out of her purse. "I never fired one of these things before," she said, "and there's no time to learn. If I hit my target it's the Lord's will and beginner's luck."

She pointed the pistol, closed her eyes and squeezed the trigger six times. Then she opened her eyes again, and Larry Wayne was still standing before her; a smile was on his face. "Missed six times," he said. "I guess that's the Lord's way of telling you something."

"But the Lord's not through yet, son," said Ravenhill. "He's speaking to me right now, and he's telling us to get back in the bus." Ravenhill helped Winkie to the front seat. He started the motor and drove off to the other side of the plaza. Slowly he circled The Prayer Tower and The Residence. Then he headed back toward the Avenue of the Redeemed just as Larry Wayne was crossing the plaza to his truck.

"That's just what you're supposed to do," said Ravenhill.

"Oh, the Lord Jesus is a passenger on this bus," shouted Winkie, bracing herself in the seat. "I can feel him breathing on my face, I swear I can."

Brother Ravenhill pressed the accelerator to the floorboard and steered his bus toward Larry Wayne. "Look at him standing there like he's about to be saved or something," said Ravenhill. "Just standing there and daring the Lord is what he's doing."

When the bus was almost upon him, Larry Wayne tried to escape, but it was already too late. His body was thrown thirty feet straight ahead, but Ravenhill didn't swerve to miss him. "One more time for good measure," he said to Winkie. "Just pretend this is nothing but another bump in the road." When Winkie felt the bus lurch to one side, she leaped to her feet, began singing, clapping her hands and dancing up and down the aisle. Once on the open highway, Ravenhill started tapping on the steering wheel and singing right along with his wife:

> "Oh, the Holy Ghost will set your feet a-dancing,
> The Holy Ghost will thrill you through and through,
> The Holy Ghost will set your feet a-dancing, and
> Tell you what you ought to do . . ."

Larry Wayne's body was not found until the next morning. He was lying on his back. The coat of his white suit was ripped open. A night wind had blown sand over his legs and arms, but his face was uncovered, his eyes open. His murder was never solved, and no one showed much interest in solving it. Ravenhill said he knew it would be that way because it was God's will unfolding. He and Winkie continued their work with the First Church of Yesterday, Today and Tomorrow in downtown San Antonio. They took turns busing their congregation to the services and took turns preaching as well. Over their makeshift altar was a picture of Principia Martindale with her arms outstretched and her eyes closed. When Winkie preached she never failed to mention Principia's name, and Ravenhill often told the congregation as well as his passengers that Principia would be alive today if Corinda Cassy had not allowed herself to fall into the hands of the Devil.

"Once again the town of Judson is up for grabs," wrote a columnist for the Fort Worth *Star-Telegram*. "Who knows who the next owner will be, or even if there will be another owner . . ."

Applebee read the article and threw the paper into the big pool down at the Water Gardens. "Judson belongs to old man Judson and it always will," he shouted. "Nobody, dead or alive, will ever be able to take it away from him either." He stood up and threw his vest and rubber sandals into the water and was about to jump in himself when Johnnie Chapman stopped him. "No use getting so riled up," she said. "Not a bit of use in it. That water'll cool you off for a little while but not for long, not in the kind of shape you're in." She walked him back across town to the pawnshop. She set him down and showed him what was in her shopping bag: all the articles she could find about Principia's death. "You're bound to read 'em sooner or later," she said, "so you better get started while I'm here with you. No use torturing yourself longer than you have to."

She gave him the articles one at a time and held his hand while he read them.

According to the Dallas *Morning News*, Principia Martindale's grave had been trampled flat in less than a day. Her fortune, although it was small, had been left to Rosita López. Hillister Baptist College was already planning to build a new chapel to be named in her honor, and scholarship funds in her name had been made available at various Baptist universities throughout the south. On another page of the same paper, Applebee found a picture of Larry Wayne standing in front of the hotel with the Cowgirls for Christ gathered around him. The caption read: "Mr. L. W. Johnson stated that in time the town of Judson will undergo a few changes."

"He got to looking more and more like Old Man Judson every day," said Applebee. "Whoever ran him down ought to be given a million dollars to get away on, that's what."

"Maybe whoever did it was given something better than money," replied Johnnie Chapman.

She continued to hold Applebee's hand until he had read all the articles. Then she put them back in the shopping bag and dropped it in a trash can. "Well, you read 'em now," she said. Applebee didn't answer. He began sweeping out the pawnshop as though nothing had happened, but every bone in his body seemed to be aching at once. Johnnie Chapman could feel the aches coming right out of him. "You're the kind of person who takes everything to heart," she said. "So what you gotta do is keep on hurting until you can't hurt no more, or until you don't wanna hurt no more. Then you'll be over it, but until that day rolls around just keep on reminding yourself that there's a good side to everything."

Applebee put down the broom and listened.

"Now you can walk past all the department stores you want to. Even if they do have their television sets playing in the windows. Pretty soon you can even turn on the set right here and even if her old shows are still playing up a storm you won't feel the same about watching 'em—glancing at 'em anyway."

For a moment Applebee felt happy again; then a wave of sadness swept over him. He brushed something out of his eye, refused to call it a tear and took Saint George out of the window. The rooster had died of old age, and the taxidermist down the street had stuffed him as a present. "There'll never be another one like you," Applebee said. "And I don't know about you, but I sure hope it's all over with now and we can get some rest." He put Saint George on a shelf behind the cash register and gave the rooster a few licks with a feather duster. "It's just like I always told you," he said, "a little religion never hurt nobody but a whole lot of it has sure as hell done a mess'a harm."

Then he picked up his latest coloring book and went outside to the curb. Johnnie Chapman followed him. "You're gonna be a long time getting over this one, I can see," she said, sitting down beside him. "My pore ole pitiful brain is drawing a blank right now, and I don't know what to do for you, but I'll think of something." She tied the rag on her head a little tighter and stared off into a space where a five-story building had been. Then she came to her senses and patted Applebee on the back. "If you don't like what's happening to you right now," she said, "just think about all the things you don't want to happen to you right now that ain't happening to you right now. Then you'll be a little bit better for a little while and pretty soon you'll be a whole lot better for good, 'specially with Johnnie Chapman here; she ain't never got up and left nobody yet."